Advance Praise for
The Alehouse at the End of the World

"This island of the dead is more active than a lot of retirement communities. Richly conceived, enjoyable, and a treat for readers of myths and legends."

—*Kirkus Reviews*

"The talented and erudite Stevan Allred is a natural storyteller, weaving together in *The Alehouse at the End of the World* various threads of Eastern and Western myth, fable, and legend, into an inviting, raucous romp through the lands of the dead, where a lonely fisherman, accompanied by an entertaining cast of avian co-conspirators, wanders in search of his long-lost beloved. You will frequently gasp, occasionally wring your hands, and always delight at Mr. Allred's sharp ear for dialogue, unerring instinct for suspense, and magisterial command of the fanciful world that may await us all in our next life."

—Michael Shou-Yung Shum, author of *Queen of Spades*

"*The Alehouse at the End of the World* will take you on a fast-moving ride through sixteenth-century farce with a present-tense echo effect. Bard-like in its constellation of bird-gods and rough hewn characters tossed around like breadcrumbs, the epic voyage catches you between laughter and a tear forming at the edge of your eye. Like life does."

—Lidia Yuknavitch, author of *The Book of Joan*

"Like the best ales, *The Alehouse at the End of the World* grows more flavorful and complex with each page as Allred pours you a well-balanced, fantastical story of love, adventure, and deceit. This brewer enjoyed it to the last drop!"

—Lisa Allen, Head Brewer at Heater Allen Brewing

"A book rich in love and life and death and language and magic. You wonder where a tale of a crow and a blue-skinned fisherman could lead, and it turns out to be a wild journey of masterly storytelling, sneaky humor, bracing sensuality, and deliciously tricksy words."

—Shawn Levy, author of *Dolce Vita Confidential*
and *Paul Newman: A Life*

"*The Alehouse at the End of the World* will swallow you whole. You'll land on the Isle of the Dead and walk with the fisherman who longs for his beloved. The crow will repel you with his solipsistic drama, and the goddess will seduce you as part of her plan. Stevan Allred's luscious language drives the novel, and his playful remix of lyrics and religious systems satisfies deep questions about the afterlife and the soul, which he describes as "a vibration so quiet it can scarcely be heard . . . the thing that gives self-awareness." Reading this novel delights like a fine ale."

—Kate Gray, author of *Carry the Sky*

"Stevan Allred, armed with an abiding love of narrative, and an arsenal of sentence-by-sentence wit and tumble, draws us into an epic battle for the soul of the afterworld, and we are led ever on by language dangerously funny. The creatures that illuminate this journey with their eternal ponderings and arguments are not necessarily human except in their search for reason and love, driven as they are by power, sex, and the beautiful mystery of death."

—Joanna Rose, author of *Little Miss Strange*

"Crows and fishermen, gods and goddesses, love and deceit, boats full of the dead, clams that are much more than clams, an island inside the belly of the beast, and batches and batches of ale. *The Alehouse at the End of the World* is a comic epic that made me feel like us messy mortals can actually make a difference."

—Yuvi Zalkow, author of *A Brilliant Novel in the Works*

"Stevan Allred has spun an original myth with its own vocabulary and weather system. The imagery alone has impressed new memories upon my psyche. Peculiar and inventive yet true to the human condition, *The Alehouse at the End of the World* holds familiar tyrants and temptations, confronted in the most unexpected ways by an unforgettable cast. The experience I found in these pages is the reason I read—to reach inconceivable places, to be touched, to be changed. By canoe, winged goddess, or whale, I would follow Allred anywhere."

—Renee Macalino Rutledge, author of *The Hour of Daydreams*

"Drawing on European, Asian, and North American traditions, Stevan Allred stitches a remarkable tapestry of love, death, and talking birds. Turns out that a modern version of ancient myth is exactly what we need in these trying modern times."

—James Crossley, bookseller, Island Books

"A fable, an adventure, a story filled with treats for us lovers of words and culture and the world. This is one of the rare books that I never wanted to end. Completely satisfying, dramatic, hilarious, a wonderful world. I'll buy a lot of copies of this book for my holiday gift list."

—Doug Chase, bookseller, Powell's Books

"The Alehouse at the End of the World mines our primal desire to go through the looking glass or the back of the wardrobe. Stevan Allred is an ingenius guide. His Isle of the Dead is a dark place that crackles with life, full of shapeshifting, bed-switching heroes fighting for the fate of the living world. An epic tale from a master storyteller."

—Scott Sparling, author of *Wire to Wire*

"Alehouse echoes ancient myths of creation and undoings in the practice of love with a blend of Shakespearean comedy and Melvillian language on a classic odyssey to the end of the world and beyond. Trust me, people. This is the wildly inventive and lovingly hilarious work of a master craftsman."

—Robin Cody, author of *Ricochet River*

"Allred's imagination staggers the imagination."

—Jan Baross, author of *José Builds a Woman*

"This is why adults still need fairy tales: there are some archetypes more familiar than our own faces, and they help us survive, they teach us to live, they compel us to grow. Allred has the sly and quixotic writing chops to pull off this charming story, which is both wickedly funny and achingly poignant. He manages his characters as well as a puppeteer, and imbues them with such heartfelt passion and pathos, it's mesmerizing. Do not miss this delightful tale."

—Dianah Hughley, bookseller, Powell's City of Books

Praise for *A Simplified Map of the Real World* (Forest Ave, 2013)

"Funny, sensual, piercing, honest, witty, and a braided woven webbed stitch of stories and people unlike anything I ever read. It catches something deep and true about the brave and nutty shaggy defiant grace of this place. Fun to read and funner to recommend."

—Brian Doyle, author of *Mink River*

"Beautifully crafted and marked by incisive wit."

—Kristine Morris, reviewer, *Foreword Reviews*

"Stevan Allred's stunner of a debut novel is a complex portrait of small-town life."

—Maria Anderson, reviewer, *Necessary Fiction*

"*A Simplified Map of the Real World* is a highly-skilled collection of interwoven stories, surprising in its various styles and voices. But the real surprise is how close Stevan Allred gets to the beating heart of what it means to be human. Petty, profane, sacred, scared, hilarious. We're all in this book. And that's quite a triumph."

—Tom Spanbauer, author of *The Man Who Fell in Love with the Moon*

"Stevan Allred's characters are delightfully wrong-headed. They make questionable choices—sometimes terrible ones—and get themselves into all kinds of trouble. But the worse their mistakes, the more I care for them, because beyond their difficulties what Allred gives them is the essential dignity of longing. No matter how misguided, all strive toward some ideal, and no matter what mess they make of their circumstances, they end up more alive for having given themselves over to desire. To read their stories is to journey through passions that transcend the confinements of small town life—and it's a journey that's by turns funny, surprising, and heartbreaking."

—Scott Nadelson, author of *The Next Scott Nadelson*

The
Alehouse
at the
End
of the
World

The Alehouse at the End of the World

Stevan Allred

FOREST AVENUE PRESS
Portland, Oregon

© 2018 by Stevan Allred
Illustrations © 2018 by Reid Psaltis

ISBN: 9781942436379

Cataloging-in-Publication Data is on file with the Library of Congress.

1 2 3 4 5 6 7 8 9

Distributed by Publishers Group West

Printed in the United States of America

Forest Avenue Press LLC
P.O. Box 80134
Portland, OR 97280
forestavenuepress.com

for Nikki
who is my beloved

This is an old story, a story of a tyrant and a rebellion, of monsters and humans, of love and death. Know this: there are creatures who travel back and forth from the spirit world to the land of the living. There are moments when things both sacred and mundane slip the bounds of time and pass through from one side of the mortal veil to the other—a breath of song, an ancient incantation, a blade, a bucket, a silver chain. Fate demands that it be so and plays an endless game of gods and goddesses, of regents and rebels, of lovers and fools. The coin is tossed, spinning life and death through the air, and here, as the fire burns low and the hour grows late, the telling begins.

Book One
THE RISE OF KING CROW

THE FISHERMAN LIVED ALONE AT the edge of the sea, in a shack beneath the shade of the tallest shore pine for leagues, on a bluff above a shallow cove. All his days he had worked the sea, as a sailor, and a carpenter, on ships both great and small, and as a fisherman, gillnetting for the fishmongers in the portside markets, or trailing a line from his skiff to feed only himself. He had sailed all the seven seas, and sailed seven more seas beyond those, and he had seen many things. Tattooed on his arms were the names of ships he had sailed, and of sailors with whom he had weathered storms, and escaped from monsters of the deep. On his chest he bore the likeness of his beloved, her face covered over now with curls of gray hair.

He stood watching the waves. In his hands were a letter and a silver chain. The sea was calm that day, and light glanced in swift patches as the waves rose and broke. A thing of beauty indeed, but the fisherman had no eyes for beauty just then. The sea in front of him was thick with fish, and for that he should be thankful, but the letter in his hands had taken from him all sense of what was good about his simple life.

The letter had appeared on the sand in front of his shack that morning, with no footprints leading to it, nor from it, as if it had fallen from the sky. The words were the words of his beloved, as told to her eldest son from her deathbed, and before she died, she had taken the silver chain from round her neck. *Send it to him,* she'd said, *and tell him I waited. Tell him he is my one true love. Tell him I forgave him long ago, and that I will wait for him on the Isle of the Dead.*

He had been marooned here on this empty stretch of beach some several years, and he had given up all hope of making the arduous journey back to his beloved. It was here he would live out his meager life. Or so had he thought.

He put the silver chain round his neck. Fate was calling to him, telling him to find his way back to the woman he loved. He spread his arms, and he trembled in the whole of his body as tears fell from his eyes, and he turned his face to the heavens.

"I surrender," he shouted. "Do with me as you will."

In answer the waves kept breaking, lapping one over the other on the wet sand at his feet. The gulls cried their shrill cries as they rode the sea breezes above him, scouting for fish. The wind blew across his bare chest and ruffled the wisps of hair on his head. To be a fisherman was to be patient, and if he had learned one thing in his years on the earth, it was to know how to wait for the answer without any irritable reaching after fact and reason. He felt the rise and fall of his chest. He hoped to hear the voice of his beloved call to him from out of the wind, but he heard only the shush of the waves breaking on the sand. Tiny crabs scuttled back and forth with the lap of the waves. The wind died down.

A squadron of pelicans gathered down the beach from him, milling about, clucking and croaking to one another, gradually working their way closer, until some were less than an oar length away. The one closest regarded him with its yellow eye, tilting its head from side to side. It bore a pine twig in its bill, freshly torn from one of the shore pines. A drop of pitch glistened on the torn end of the twig.

Ah. Thus came the message. If he were to go to the Isle of the Dead, he would need something to light his way. He must prepare himself.

One by one the pelicans turned to face the waves, until the whole squadron stood together, pointing at the sea with their bills striped red and blue. He heard the sound of human speech in their avian voices.

"This way," they croaked. "This way."

THE FRIGATE BIRD HAD WATCHED from his perch in the shore pine since before dawn, and when the fisherman went to weed the meager patch of maize behind his shack, the frigate bird swooped down low and dropped the letter, with the silver chain folded within it, in front of the fisherman's door. Then he flew back to his perch to bide his time while events played themselves out, for he did not wish to be seen. Not just yet. A great deal, he suspected, depended on what the fisherman did next.

If the fisherman took the bait, he had only to oversee the beginning of the fisherman's voyage, and for this, he had prepared well. The loom was dressed, as it were, the warp in place, and ready to receive the weft. When he was done he would return to the shore and find a celebratory mug of ale. There was a chicheria in Chancay, some sixty leagues north, where a passable ale was served alongside the local chicha, but if memory served, there was a true alehouse in the port city of Chimbote, some seventy leagues farther on. He'd fallen in with a pirate there once who'd bought him several mugs of ale and then tried to slit his throat so he could gut him for dinner. Men were always thinking that a bird of his size would make a tasty roast. He'd left the man clawed and bloodied, his cheek marked for life with a four-toed scrawl, and he'd stolen his purse of doubloons for good measure.

He was, as he freely admitted to himself, a piratical bird. As he had brought the letter from the Spice Islands to the fisherman, nothing had given him more pleasure than the several times he'd stopped a thief bent on robbing him. Beings such as himself still walked the earth, but they were rare, and a six-foot-tall frigate bird who strode into an alehouse with a spyglass and a pistola stuck into his belt, and who said "Avast there, ye blackguards, best not snatch that letter tucked into me belt or I'll put a ball from me pistola right between your beady little eyes"—well, that was a bird who put a fright into a whoreson's heart the likes of which he had never felt before.

The Turropsi* had given the frigate bird a long life, and during it he'd killed men when he had to, though mostly in his own defense. He had stolen what he needed when he needed it, and while he preferred to steal from those who were themselves greedy and had too much, this was no hard and fast rule, and he was not above doing whatever his own survival required. He had cheated fools, for there were many who could be cheated upon in the land of the living, with no one ever the wiser until it was too late.

But he had never cheated the Turropsi. He was their servant, and always had been. He did what was asked of him, for the Turropsi had mothered him into being, and they had given him special license to be the brigand he was. Ages went by when they asked nothing of him, and when they did ask for his services, he was given his tasks only one or two at a time, lest his own foreknowledge interfere with the weaving of their pattern.

Now the fisherman came back from weeding his maize, and found the letter. He searched the sand for footprints, which made the frigate bird chuckle, as there were none. Then the fisherman opened the letter, and out poured the silver chain, so finely made that it flowed like water into his hand. He put the chain round his neck, and the frigate bird's eyes were keen enough that he could see the fisherman's tears welling up. The fisherman looked up at the sky, his arms spread, and then out to sea.

Ha! thought the frigate bird, *the letter has done its work.* He waited the rest of the day on his perch, enjoying a well-earned rest from all the flying he had done to get there. The fisherman made preparations for a sea voyage, honing his knife, checking the sail and the oars for his skiff, and gathering pitch to make pitch balls, which he then threaded on the silver chain. The frigate bird watched the sunset, which ended with a green flash of light as the

---

* The Turropsi, dear reader, who are called also the Spinners, the Morai, the mokosh, the Norns, the dísir, and many other names, are the weavers of fate. They are a kind of immortal jellyfish, their number uncountable, their origins so ancient as to be unknown, and they sort all that is out of all that might be. They are unknown in the land of the living, except by their many contradictory legends, but you may trust this account of them to be accurate in every detail.

last bit of the sun set below the horizon. *A sign,* he thought, *of good fortune ahead.*

The fisherman went into his shack to sleep.

Best enjoy this respite, the frigate bird thought, *while it lasts.*

THE FISHERMAN WOKE WELL BEFORE first light. He hung the leather pouch that held his flint and steel off his belt. He took the letter from his beloved and folded it smaller and smaller until it fit into the leather pouch. The pitch bundles were threaded on the silver chain round his neck. He put on his broad-brimmed hat, and he walked down the path to the cove. The sail was rigged but he left it furled. The sea was calm. He pushed the skiff into the cove and settled himself between the oars. He put the oars in the water and pulled, and he felt the strength of the muscles in his shoulders, and it was good.

Now he was on the open sea, well past the break of the waves on the reef, rowing from swell to swell. The moon was already set, and the stars were bright in the sky. The wind was out of the southeast, and the fisherman shipped his oars. He raised the sail, and his spirit rose as it always did when the wind filled the sail, and his faithful skiff pulled forward. There was phosphorescence in his wake.

He rowed until the sun came up, and he kept on rowing until his shoulders and arms felt like lead. The wind was shifting. He rested himself, drank water from his goatskin, and he chewed down some dried fish. The cove where he lived was behind him, and well below the horizon now. The sun was high enough in the sky that he could see down into the water a fathom or two. Jellyfish floated by in silvery outline against the dark water, their undulant bodies cupping and swelling.

If he were fishing he would let out the sheet line and turn the skiff northward, taking advantage of the current. But he was not fishing, and he kept the sail steady, and he rowed with the wind behind him, cutting across the current. His only course was to sail west until he could sail no longer. To reach the Isle of the Dead, he reasoned, he must be ready to die.

Above him a frigate bird rode the wind. He had seen them, as all sailors had seen them, a week's sail from land, and he knew them to be stouthearted voyagers. They were riding the wind together, the fisherman on his skiff and the frigate bird, its long narrow wings spread wide, gliding on the winds aloft. Together the wings and the slender black body made the sign of a cross against the sky. It seemed uncommonly large.

Ahead of them, the sky slowly darkened to a gray the color of a shark's back. A storm was coming, and soon he would take down the sail, lest it be torn from his mast. He kept on rowing, straight ahead, into the wind.

WHEN THE STORM BROKE OVER him rough swells sloshed water into the skiff. The waves grew taller and taller, and the wind ripped white foam from their tops. He pulled on the oars with all his strength. If the storm was bringing death to him, so be it. It was what he was here for. Death would come for him and carry him to his beloved. There was no use in thinking of anything more than that. He rowed.

The sky was as black as a pirate's heart. Raindrops the size of hummingbird eggs pelted him, and he opened his mouth and drank them in. Thunder shook the air so close and so hard his ribs rumbled. Bolts of lightning forked, and forked again. The rain now a torrent, his skiff filling with it, the water soon over his feet. He shipped the oars, and he bailed water with the bucket he kept stowed in the stern. The wind ripped his hat off, breaking the leather cord that held it on his head. The skiff was sideways now, and it rose up the face of the next wave only to tip back on itself, heaving the fisherman into the storm.

He hit the water face-first. An oar plunged into the sea next to him, and he grabbed for it but missed. When his head broke the surface again, his skiff was already out of sight. He rode the next swell, and in a flash of lightning he saw it, his skiff upside down, and already too far away to reach. He was doomed, but he would die a sailor's death. The swell broke over his head, and he swam downward. He would slip this skin off his rack of bones and let loose his soul that it might fly to the Isle of the Dead.

He was fathoms beneath the surface when a great dark shape came at him. It was moving fast. A predatory eye as big as a barrel-head looked him over and blinked once. Then the whale was upon him. The cavernous mouth opened, and a mighty inhalation of water sucked him in. The jaws shut, and he was squashed against the roof of the mouth by a great slab of tongue. He was pulled farther in, down the throat, the passageway narrowing and slimy.

His arms were pinned to his sides. A flap of flesh as big as a devil ray opened, and he was forced headfirst through a tight slit. He coughed, his lungs wild for air. He opened his mouth expecting only to suffocate, but there was air to breathe. It smelled of cuttlefish and kelp.

He was in the belly of the beast. When he pushed against the walls of the gut they stretched. He lay his head against the wall, and he heard a sound like a huge bellows filling with air. His skin prickled. He'd been swallowed alive. His knife was gone, he knew not when nor where. He touched the silver chain round his neck. If only the whale had bitten him in two instead of swallowing him whole.

He could breathe, but the heat was terrible. It seemed to open his pores and draw out all his vitality, and the fisherman's body sank slowly down the sloping wall of flesh. He was overcome by a weariness he could not resist, and so he slept.

THE FISHERMAN THOUGHT IT SHOULD be dark inside the belly of the whale, but the light was red. Tiny bits of phosphorescence glowed around him on the walls of the gut. Above him he heard the steady throb of the whale's great heart, beating.

There was a story old sailors told about a monstrous whale who swallowed men whole. It was a story he'd never believed, until now.

THE BURNING ON HIS SKIN and the terrible heat made the passage of time tediously slow, but the fisherman had no way to mark it into watch hours, even less so into night or day. There was little to do, but the gut had crevices along its length, and his hands found fish bones and cuttlebones in those folds of flesh. And something more. In one crevice, beneath a small pile of cuttlebones, he felt something round and leathery, and he worked it out of the crevice. It was a leather pouch, and the something round inside it had a handle. He drew it out of the pouch and held it up in front of his eyes. It was a magician's glass, a device for making the very small appear larger than it was. A rare find, although not of much use to him now. The leather pouch was worn but intact, and he hung the glass in its pouch off his belt, next to his flint and steel.

HIS TONGUE WAS SWOLLEN IN his mouth. He was growing weaker, he could feel that, and his thirst was a patch of desert scree that started with his chapped lips and ran all the way down his throat. He tried sucking some moisture out of the slime all around him, but that only made his tongue swell more. When he slept he lacked the strength to even dream. His mind was wandering away from its moorings.

He was in the belly of the whale, that much he still knew. How many times he had passed back and forth through the curtain of sleep he could not tell. At times he heard a keening sound through the wall of gut around him, a high-pitched, unworldly song that was beautiful nonetheless.

As he fell from wakefulness one last time he knew, dimly, that this was no longer sleep, that he was passing into the dark dementia that would lead to his own demise.

WHEN THE FISHERMAN WOKE NEXT he was on his back. His swollen tongue protruded from his lips. He was crazed with thirst, and in his delirium, he saw a pelican's bill above his face, with a drop of blood hanging from the tip. The pelican looked at him with one yellow eye, taking him in with all the intelligence of an apothecary. The drop of blood let go, and it fell and fell and fell while the pelican regarded him, his yellow eye inhumanly round but somehow compassionate. *I am crazed,* the fisherman thought, *I am washed ashore at the gate to*

Bedlam. The drop of blood fell onto his tongue. It lay sweetly there.
A musty scent like myrrh teased through him, and a tiny pulsation
spread across his tongue. The pelican's yellow eye winked from side
to side.

More of the world's bewitchery. It was enough to make him pass
out again.

WHEN HE WOKE NEXT THE fisherman squinted into a bright but
overcast sky above him. The sun was directly overhead. He was on
a beach, and waves were lapping over his legs. A cuttlefish beak was
in his hand. He was enormously tired, but his tongue was back to its
normal size, and he was no longer thirsty. He lay there a long time,
listening to the cluck and clatter of birds he could not see. They were
behind him somewhere, having a long conversation. At long last he
felt enough strength to roll himself over on his side, and then to sit up.
The bird sounds behind him stopped for a moment, and then resumed,
louder and more upset than before. The sea was green. He was on an
inlet, long and narrow, with rocky cliffs topped by fir trees. Giant fir
trees, the like of which he had never seen before, not even in the fjords
of the northern seas.

His legs, below his knee breeches, were as white as an orca's belly,
as were his forearms, his hands, his belly, his feet. He had lived every
day of his life outdoors, and his skin had long since been tanned to the
color of almonds. Yet here he was, an albino, washed up on a beach.
He rubbed his eyes, which changed nothing, and then he closed them
for a dozen slow breaths, but when he looked again, he was still
bleached white. Had his eyes been magicked? He could not tell. He
had been swallowed whole by a whale, had he not, and lived in the
belly for days. Explanation enough for any number of strange things,
he supposed, although it did not answer the question of how he had
come to be here. He was on no coastline he knew. He had no memory
of leaving the whale's belly.

The bird sounds were getting closer. The fisherman turned over
onto his knees and stood his weary body upright. There were three
birds walking across a sandy beach toward him. He blinked several

times, trying to get his eyes to see them properly. He looked at the beak in his hand. It was proof that he really had been in the belly of a whale, that this was not all some strange and terrible enchantment. But what about his tongue? He had been dying of thirst, and now his tongue was back to its normal size.

Perchance he was dreaming. Because the birds coming his way were very large. They cleared the jumble of driftwood at the high tide line, and they had to be six feet tall. He dug the sharp point of the cuttlefish beak into the palm of his hand to wake himself up. But he did not wake. He only felt the pain he was causing himself.

Worse, he realized that all along the birds had been speaking as humans speak. They had the throaty voices of birds, but they formed words, the way a parrot does. But these were not parrots. And they were not simply repeating a human phrase over and over, they were talking.

They were a cormorant, a pelican, and a crow. The cormorant wore a pair of spectacles, pinched onto his bill in the manner of a scholar or a scribe. The pelican was perhaps the very one who had fed him a drop of blood.

The crow stepped up to him and looked him up and down with one black eye. He leaned in with his beak so close that the fisherman saw the flat feathers lift up over the crow's nostrils when he sniffed at him.

The crow stepped back and looked at him with his other eye. He puffed out his chest feathers. He opened his beak to speak, and the rank smell of carrion filled the fisherman's nose.

"You featherless piece of shite," the crow said. "What brings you here?"

Insults from a talking bird—what manner of varlet was this? *Ye gods,* the fisherman thought, *I must have sailed off the edge of the world. Or been swum there by the great whale.*

The pelican cooed soothingly, as if to tell the fisherman that he was not entirely in agreement with the crow's phrasing. The cormorant stretched his neck, making himself taller than the crow, and looked down on the black bird. His spectacles gave him the superior air of a barrister who has secretly bribed a judge. The crow paid him no mind.

"Where am I?" the fisherman said.

"You stink," the crow said. "I thought you humans took baths now and again."

All the birds were circling him, looking him up and down, first with one eye, then the other, the cormorant regarding him over the top of his spectacles. The pelican stopped in front of him. "Are you lost?" His long bill lay against his chest, and his yellow eye was not so unfriendly as the crow's. "How do you come to be here?"

"We know how he got here," the crow said, but before he could continue, the pelican turned and spread his wings, shielding the man from the crow. He shook his wide wings, rattling his feathers. "However he arrived here," the pelican said, "this man is our guest."

The crow scratched at the sand and uttered several harsh caws. "Guest, you say? Not my guest. He's trouble, anybody can see that. Look at the mischief he's already caused."

"Mischief?" the fisherman said. "What mischief? I've only just got here." He didn't like these birds, especially the crow, whose black eyes regarded him as if he were nothing more than flotsam, and maybe worth a peck to test his flavor. The cormorant and the pelican had bills long enough to grab the fisherman by the throat and strangle him. His knife was gone, lost when he was swallowed by the whale. All he had to defend himself with was the cuttlefish beak, and they would rip him to pieces before he could do them much damage.

Perhaps he could distract them with flattery. "Friend crow, are you one of the gods of this place?"

"I'm no crow, you fool," the crow said. "I am Raven, and I am the King of the Dead."

"Imposter," the cormorant said, "you are no raven." The cormorant opened wide his hooked bill, ready to wring the crow's neck, and the crow pulled away. "Swallow your pride," the cormorant said to the crow. "It is not poison, you will not perish."

"Oh, and I suppose you think you can be king here?" the crow said. He stalked around in a belligerent circle, muttering to himself, "All I ask is a little respect."

Ye gods, what a tiresome bird, the fisherman thought. "Please," he said, "I am a simple fisherman. Tell me where I am."

The pelican turned back to the fisherman, his wingspan taking in the whole of the inlet as he swung from side to side. "This," he said, "is the Isle of the Dead."

At this the fisherman sank to his knees and bowed his head. The gods be praised, he had arrived at his destination. "At last," he said. "I am here."

The cormorant stretched his neck down, his head now below the fisherman's, and tilted so the bird was looking up at him. "We don't get many of your kind who are so happy to arrive." His eye was a blue that put the fisherman in mind of his beloved's eyes. But the cormorant's eye was perfectly round, and his rapt gaze was unnerving. Staring into it made the fisherman feel queasy.

He stood again, and faced the three birds. "I have come for my beloved," he said, "who has preceded me."

"Aw," they all said, their chuttering voices more birdlike than ever. "Aw, aw, aw." They clucked and cooed and cawed at one another at some length in the lingua franca of birds, very like a flock of chickens who have discovered a wayward chick. From time to time they looked at the fisherman—the cormorant with curiosity, the pelican with pity, the crow with scorn. The crow ended their discussion with a series of caws, louder and louder, until the cormorant and the pelican were silent.

"This is an old story," said the crow. "I suppose you want to take her back with you?"

Back? The fisherman had never considered the possibility. "All I want," said he, "is to be with her for the rest of my days."

The crow began clawing at the sand. "Naw, naw, naw," the crow said. "We don't allow that sort of thing here. You have no more days, you walking pile of whale scat. You're dead."

"He is not dead," the pelican said. "I saved him from death."

"Kiaww," the crow said, "that was your mistake, not mine."

"*Prima facie*, he did not come on the canoe with the others," the cormorant said. "Ergo he is not dead."

"Canoe?" the fisherman said. "What canoe?"

The cormorant and the pelican began to cluck each to the other, the pelican saying such things as "He lives, he lives," and the cormorant, for his part, muttering *"Habeas corpus, autem non est mortuorum, et non sequitur, non habemus potestatem,"* and other such barristical phrases.

The crow puffed up his chest feathers and spread his oily black wings. "Knock it off, aw aw aw aw!" he said. "Quiet!" The other two birds puffed up their chest feathers and spread their wings, and they were anything but quiet. They all three chanted and flapped in ripe cacophony, with the pelican, who was the shortest of the three, sometimes hopping from one foot to the other. All of them with their necks stretched up for added height, although this was of most benefit to the cormorant. They kept this fracas going for some time, and then, as if on some signal that only birds could see, they all stopped at once and turned to face the fisherman.

"Not an easy thing to do, finding your beloved," said the crow. "There are so many here."

Was that an overture to a bribe? The fisherman responded in kind. "I've come a long way to find her," he said. "Surely there is a way?"

The crow went back to clawing in the sand, and he uncovered a clam. He flipped it over, and then he covered it back up. The pelican and the cormorant clucked in alarm at this, but the crow spoke, as if to cut them off. "Just how much is your beloved worth to you?" he said. The crow leaned in, the sharp tip of his beak a finger's width away from the fisherman's nose. "Your right eye?" the crow said. "Your left eye?" The fisherman wrinkled up his nose in disgust at the crow's carrion breath. The crow gave him a hard look. "How about both eyes?" The fisherman stared right back at him. He was not going to let this foul-mouthed maggot-pie of a bird have the better of him.

He thrust his chin forward, and he was about to speak his mind when the crow pecked at the fisherman's eye, plucking one out and swallowing it. The fisherman screamed, and he fell to the ground, half blind and moaning. Blood ran down his face. He clapped his hand over his empty eye socket.

"You puttock," the cormorant cried. "You filthy mouldywarp." He pointed a wingtip at the crow's gullet. "Give it back." The crow spread his wings and flapped them at the cormorant. The two birds faced off, puffing up their chest feathers, circling each other like pugilists, though the cormorant looked frightened—and overmatched. Their heads bobbed, but before they started jabbing at each other with their nebs, the pelican opened his wide wings and stepped in between them. All the while the fisherman writhed in pain, his blood staining the sand.

"Must you?" the pelican said to the cormorant. "The last thing we need here is scuffling and name-calling while this man lies here half-blind. And you," the pelican said to the crow, "please, give back the man's eye. It is ignoble of you to treat a guest this way. What would Raven say?"

The crow, at the mention of Raven, cocked his head to the side. "Aw aw aw aw aw," he laughed. "Not here to tell us, is he, now?"

The pelican regarded the crow steadily, his yellow eyes opened wide. "Then we must all rise to our best selves in his absence," he said. His bird voice was calm, though his tail feathers trembled. The crow gazed back at the pelican, obstinate until the cormorant stepped up with his wings spread, the two birds together crowding the crow with their wingspans.

"You are better than this," the pelican said. "Please, give it back."

Thus was the crow persuaded to yield.

The crow folded his wings and stepped back. "Bullies," he muttered, but they paid him no mind. He hurked the fisherman's eye up from his craw, and he opened his beak wide. The fisherman screamed again, horrified, and dug his fingers into the sand.

The cormorant's long bill reached in and took the eye from the crow's mouth with the careful touch of an alchemist's pincers. He tilted his head, and he looked a question at the pelican.

The pelican bobbed assent, and brushed a gentle wing across the fisherman's brow. "Be still," he soothed, "be still, still, still." The fisherman's mouth gaped, he was sweaty with pain, and his remaining eye, looking up at the birds, was wide with terror, but he nevertheless fell still.

"Pull your hand back from your face," the pelican cooed, and the fisherman did so. Blood flowed down his cheek from his empty eye socket. The cormorant stood over him with his plucked eye at the ready. All his years as a sailor he had avoided the surgeon's gruesome kit, and now he was in a surgery of birds.

The cormorant put the fisherman's eye back in its bloody socket and regarded him for a moment. The fisherman began to grimace and to twist his head about, as if he were trying to see upward and backward and side to side all at once. The pelican clucked, and shook his head, and the cormorant nodded. "My apologies," the cormorant said, "It's upside down."

"Be still," the pelican cooed again, and again the fisherman was momentarily soothed and fell still. The cormorant righted the wronged eye, and stood back to admire his work. The pelican dug into his feathers as if he were rooting around for a particularly vicious feather mite, and then pierced his own breast with the sharp tip of his neb. When he drew forth his bill, a drop of blood glistened on the tip. He let the blood drip onto the fisherman's wounded eye. The pain the fisherman had felt was now something tiny and far away. And so the fisherman was healed.

"You've won that round," the crow said, "but this is no guest." He pointed at the fisherman with his beak. "This is the troublemaker who put out the sacred fire."

The fisherman was standing again. "What fire?" he said. "I see no fire."

"You pig-widgeon, of course you don't," the crow said. "You put it out."

The fisherman looked all around, up and down the beach, across the inlet, and into the trees beyond the high-tide line. "Where?" he said.

"Ah," the cormorant said, "you're an empiricist. Let me show you what this place looks like at night. Cousin Pelican, will you assist me?"

The pelican removed the spectacles from the cormorant's neb with his bill, and he gave them to the fisherman. "Put them on," the cormorant said, "and they will translate from the unknown to the known."

The fisherman did as the cormorant bade him, perching the spectacles on his nose. The sun disappeared, and the sky with it. In their place was an enormous cavern, so vast that the fisherman only sensed the walls and the ceiling. It was dark, yet he could see, as if he had been given the night vision of a civet cat. Phosphorescent waves lapped the beach. A low throb sounded in his ears like the beat of his own heart. There was a faint glow to the sky, as if the shine of the moon had been scattered all across it, but there was no moon. The three birds stood next to him, just as they had before.

"That was the sacred fire, which has burned since the beginning of time," said the crow. He pointed with his wing at a blackened mound some distance closer to the forest from where they stood. "Then that clotpole of a whale showed up and shat you out onto the beach. And then he turned around and swam away, but before he left, he slapped his fat flukes on the water and sent the biggest wave we've ever seen up here."

"There are always complications," the pelican cooed, "when someone from the material world finds their way here."

"Why do you blame me," the fisherman said, "if the whale did it?"

The pelican plucked the spectacles from the fisherman's face, put them back on the cormorant, and it was daylight again.

"Do you see a whale here?" the crow demanded. "If you can't be with the one you blame, then blame the one you're with, that's what I always say."

"Calm yourself," the cormorant said. "In difficult times, always seek a solution that is new."

"Kiaw," the crow said, "spare me the platitudes. I say we skin this one alive, and cut out his fat to start a new fire. That's my idea for a new solution."

"What we have here," the pelican said, "is an exception to the rules."

The three birds began arguing amongst themselves. *It was the whale's fault,* said the cormorant, *naw, naw, naw, it was the man's,* said the crow, the whale's, the man's, around and around, their necks stretched up, each trying to be the tallest, the pelican imploring the other two to please stop bickering. The fisherman stepped back a pace, and they paid him no mind. *The rules are the rules are the rules,* said the crow, *oh shut up, who made you the King of the Dead, you're nothing but a crow,* said the cormorant, *friends, friends, let us make peace amongst ourselves,* said the pelican. *We'll see who's nothing but a crow after the sun goes down, you little chickadees,* said the crow, stretching his neck taller so that the cormorant stretched his neck taller. They circled each other like that, the both of them with their wings spread wide, the pelican with them, cooing and clucking and suing for peace, and then the crow bobbed his head down low and pecked a vicious peck at the cormorant's wingpit.

"Auk!" cried the cormorant, a bare patch of red skin showing blood beneath his outstretched wing. The pelican tried to step between them, but the crow gave him a savage peck as well. The crow seemed to have the better of them both now, as if he had somehow grown more powerful since the last time they fought.

The fisherman stepped back another pace, and then another, until he was far enough away to turn and walk off. If these birds were truly the gods of this place, then the gods must be crazed.

HIGH IN A TREE, AS light gathered on the far horizon, just outside the lanai where slept Dewi Sri, Goddess of Rice, the first crow of the day called out, *caw, caw, caw.* Dewi Sri awoke, a cold feeling of dread beneath her breastbone brought on by the remnants of a dream. For a hundred times a hundred years there had been peace in all of her realm, and all was well. But of late her sleep had been vexious, and though she went about her duties with serenity, and found joy in the fecundity of the rice paddies, and peace in the multitudes of fireflies who gathered over them after the sun set, she felt something coming her way. Something dark, and inescapable.

In the dream she stood before the stone statue of her long dead brother, Sedana, and there was a warning in his gaze. Her brother's lips moved, and she wept because she could not hear him. Now her tears fell on a copper dowsing rod she held in her hands. She knew her brother wanted her to find something with it, but she knew not what. She walked into the forest, dowsing as she went, hoping her rod would pull on her arms and reveal her purpose. A shadow passed over her as if a great bird flew above, and then she heard her brother's voice, speaking quietly, telling her to clear her mind. She stood still and banished all thoughts, and as she did so, the dowsing rod turned in her hands, and pointed at her face.

Thus it was that she awoke with such a chill inside her. She was the last of her line, and nearer the end of her days than the beginning. Her family had many things for which to answer, and it was her fate to pay those debts.

Again the crow called out, *caw, caw, caw.* Dewi Sri formed the abhaya mudra with her right hand, banishing the little-death of fear from her mind. Her hand was upright, and palm out. Her fate was her fate, and nothing more. Where fear had passed through her, there was nothing now.

She opened her eyes, and rose to face the day. The great festival of the rice harvest was coming, and she had much to do.

THE FISHERMAN HEADED DOWN THE beach toward the sea. Let the birds argue. He must get far enough away from them that he could clear his thoughts.

To begin with, where was he really? Was he dreaming, or bewitched? It was the pelican who'd said this was the Isle of the Dead, but could he trust a talking pelican? The crow claimed to rule the dead, but the others said he was an imposter. And where were the dead? When they had shown him the great cavern (what manner of sorcery was that?) there was nothing but a pile of smoking bones. If that was all there was to the afterlife, he might have found all that was left of his beloved in her grave.

The crow had said there were so many here, and that it would be difficult to find her, but that made no sense. There was no one here but himself, and the three birds. They might be gods, or they might be monsters, but in either case, they were tricksy varlets, and not to be trusted. And what about himself? Was he alive, as the pelican said, or was he a dead man still walking? He felt alive enough, his heart beating as always, his lungs drawing breath as ever. Had he simply gone moon-barking mad, and all of this was phantasmagoria? His mind had slipped its moorings when he was in the belly of the whale and left him floating in an awful confusion. But here he walked the sand on sturdy legs, and his mind was sharp enough. What he lacked was not sanity, it was facts.

And what was this about a canoe? They hadn't answered his question—it was possible they were hiding something from him. The more he thought about it, the more it seemed like these monstrous birds were scoundrels and liars. Even the cormorant, who had put his eye back after the crow plucked it out, was a scoundrel, if only by his association with the crow.

He was nearly out to the point where the inlet met the sea. By the look of the wet sand the tide must be going out. The breeze off the ocean had the smell of salt air and sea life. There were small holes opening in the sand, clam holes if he knew anything about clams, which he did. The three birds were too far away to pay him any mind, and he knelt and dug around one of the holes. It was only a moment before he felt the hard shell of a clam. He scooped it out of the sand, a buff-colored, oblong shell the length of his hand from heel to fingertip. His stomach growled. He had no idea how long he had been in the belly of the whale, but it was enough time to nearly die of thirst, so it was no surprise that he was hungry. His growling belly gave him proof that he was yet alive.

The clams were plentiful, and easy to dig. He gathered an armful of them, and then he made his way to the high-tide line, looking for a place to build a fire. He found a spot behind a large driftwood log that was sheltered from the wind. He gathered the driest of the wood around him, and he laid a careful fire made of twigs and wood shavings he made with the cuttlefish beak. But before he lit it, a series of loud squawks came to him on the shore breeze, and so he walked down to the water, where he could see around the curve of the beach to the spot where the birds were.

They were still there, still circling each other, still arguing. The crow appeared to have gained the upper hand, or beak, as it were, for the other two bowed their heads even as they kept on squabbling. The crow passed a wing in front of his face, and it seemed to the fisherman that he grew taller then. The other birds fell back, and the crow flapped his wings, and cawed an especially screechy caw, and he shooed the pelican and the cormorant down the beach.

Well and good, the fisherman thought, for he was in no hurry to speak to them again. He went back to the fire he was building, and knelt. He took from round his neck his beloved's silver chain, and held it for a moment with his eyes closed, feeling the weight of it in his hand. The sun, having burned through the overcast, made the silver glow, and he brought the chain to his lips and kissed it. On it were the several pitch balls he had made for this very purpose before he left his shack by the sea. He took one of the pitch balls from the chain. It was still sticky inside its kelp wrapping, and it would catch fire easily. He reached for his flint and steel, hanging in their pouch off his belt, and there was the magician's glass. He had forgotten about it, but now he drew it forth.

Once, in Shedet, a large port town on the coast of the Nubian Sea, he had chanced upon a magician who had such a glass as the one he now held in his hand. For a small price the magician, who called himself Melquiades, allowed anyone, the credulous and the incredulous alike, to peer through the glass into the windows of a tiny castle. Inside the windows there was room after room of tapestries and paintings, of banquets and armories, of bedchambers and dungeons. A great horned beetle in royal attire held court with lesser beetles in lesser attire, and all of them were served by ants in matching livery. Truly a wonder of the world, but what the fisherman remembered now was how the magician, again for a small price, made Archimedes's fire burst forth from the invisible rays of the sun.

Now the fisherman held the glass so that it shone a bright white light on the pitch ball. A dragonfly hovered in the air, watching him, its body shining iridescent blue, the gaze of its black eyes unreadable. The insect plunged in the air, hovered again near where the focused beam of light hit the pitch ball, backed away some inches, and then rose and hovered by the fisherman's ear, as if it had a secret to tell.

It took some patience, but patience was one thing the fisherman possessed in abundance, and after sufficient time had passed, the pitch ball began to bubble, and then caught flame. He blew ever so gently, transferring the flame from the pitch ball to the wood shavings and twigs, until he had a small fire. He might have done the whole task more quickly with his faithful and familiar flint and steel, but the magician's glass held the delight of novelty, and of a skill newly acquired. The dragonfly, having witnessed the miracle of fire drawn right out of the air, flew away, driven off, perhaps, by the smoke.

Gradually the fisherman added larger and larger pieces of driftwood to the fire, and he found himself cheered by the whole enterprise. The ordinary crackle of it was a reminder of home. He lay his head back against a driftwood log, and he let the sun soak into his skin. While he waited for the coals to burn down enough to put on the clams, he thought of his beloved, and he pondered when he might see her. Difficult, the crow had said, but he'd not said impossible. There was hope, and there was the pleasure of imagining the look, when she first beheld him, of joy on her face.

Or would it be horror? His skin was a deathly white. He touched his arm, which had the dry texture of parchment. The hair was gone entirely from his head, his arms, his legs. His face felt smoother than his beloved's breasts. Even his eyebrows were gone. He looked around, and seeing no one, he lowered the fall front to his breeches to examine his nether parts, and they too were smooth and hairless as a young boy's. All this made his tattoos the brighter, as if they were freshly inked rather than older than the gray in his hair. The hair he no longer had.

A shadow passed over him as he marveled at this, and in the next moment, he saw an enormous frigate bird perched on the limb of a dead tree, above his fire.

"Ahoy there," the frigate bird said. "Caught you with your pants down." The frigate bird puffed up his bright red throat pouch, and he laughed a rattling laugh. He wore a belt with a pirate's pistola stuck into it on one side, and a brass spyglass on the other.

"Ye gods," the fisherman muttered, "what now?" He pulled up his breeches and buttoned them. "Ahoy there, great bird," he said. "What brings you here?"

"Why, the smoke from your fire," the frigate bird said. "Only fire around here is the sacred fire, but that seems to have gone out."

"So I am told," the fisherman said.

"Bad business that," said the frigate bird. "Don't know what the crow will do when the next canoe full of the dead shows up." Again the frigate bird puffed up his throat pouch, and again he laughed his rattling laugh.

"How's that?" the fisherman said. "What's this about a canoe full of the dead?"

"You're new around here, aren't you?" the frigate bird said. "The dead arrive from the far shore every night at midnight. The crow harvests their souls, and he throws their bodies onto the sacred fire to keep the Kiamah beast warm."

"The Kiamah beast?"

"Yes, the Kiamah beast," the frigate bird said, "who is monstrous large, and in whose belly lie the lands of the dead, and the realms of dreams and visions, and any number of other fens and hollows too numerous to mention here. Have you never heard it said that in the belly of the beast lie many mansions? Did your elders teach you nothing at all?"

The fisherman had heard many tales about the afterlife, but none that he held certain. Some said the afterlife was a paradise, and some said there was a court of the gods that passed judgment on the lives of mortals. Some said there was no afterlife, and others said that the life we knew was merely a dream from which death awakened us. He had heard tales of a hole in the sky that led to the land of the dead, or the kingdom of the dead, and the letter from his beloved had called it the Isle of the Dead, as had the pelican. But in all his travels he had never heard any mention of the Kiamah beast.

"And where is this beast?" the fisherman asked.

"Why, all around us," the frigate bird said, spreading his wings. "He is invisible during the day, but at night, you will see we are inside him. Up there, where you see the sun, his great heart beats all night long."

Either this frigate bird was a part of the bewitchment, or his words were proof that what the fisherman had seen through the cormorant's spectacles was real. But the fisherman was a stranger in a strange land, and far from having his bearings.

"You are uncommonly large for a frigate bird," the fisherman said. "Do you know the other birds here?"

"Oh yes," said the frigate bird. "We are old friends."

"Tell me, what manner of beings are you?" said the fisherman. "Are you gods?"

The frigate bird cocked his head to the side, as if to consider how best to answer. "Demigods might be closer to the truth," said he.

Gods, demigods, or monsters, they were trouble, or so thought the fisherman. Still, this one was a likeable fellow, and he seemed honest enough, even if he had the bearing of a pirate.

"And where," the fisherman asked, "are we at this moment? Is this really the Isle of the Dead?"

"Of course it is, pilgrim. Of course it is."

"If this is the Isle of the Dead," the fisherman asked, "where are the dead? I seek my beloved, who has preceded me here."

Before the frigate bird could answer, the crow came walking up to the fisherman's fire, trailed by the pelican and the cormorant, who walked with their heads down and bobbing, as if in obeisance to the crow. They circled the fisherman's fire once, the crow looking at it first with one eye and then the other, and then they stopped.

"Ahoy, Cousin Cormorant," the frigate bird said. "Ahoy, Cousin Pelican, and Cousin Crow."

"Greetings and salutations, my peripatetic friend," the cormorant said, "or perhaps I should say volapatetic."

"Halloo, Cousin," the pelican said, shuffling his broad webbed feet and hopping with pleasure at the frigate bird's arrival.

But the crow merely cawed, *kiaww-aw-aw-aw*, his tone peevish, as if the frigate bird's friendly greeting were unwelcome. "Quite the fire you've got going here," the crow said.

The cormorant and the pelican preened, stroking their feathers with their bills, all the while keeping a close eye on the crow. Both of them had bare patches of bloodied skin at their necks and on their breasts.

The fisherman kept his distance and said nothing. A dangerous bird, this one, and a quick one to strike the first blow. The fisherman had an urge to cover his eyes with his hands, but he resisted, not wanting to show the crow any weakness.

The crow stopped on the other side of the fire. "Would you mind telling us, O great keeper of the flame," the crow said, his voice now artful and flattering, "how you got it started?"

The fisherman considered this wheedling request. So now he was a keeper of the flame rather than a foul pile of whale ordure. Perhaps there was some leverage in that.

"I have my ways," the fisherman said. He poked at his fire with a stick, arranging the burning embers for cooking.

"A lovely thing, a fire," the crow said. He eyed the pile of clams at the fisherman's feet. "Getting ready for a meal, are we?"

The fisherman squatted and felt the heat coming off the coals with his hands. He looked at the crow and nodded. The crow was hinting that he was hungry. Here was the way to open negotiations.

"May I offer you a clam?"

The pelican and the cormorant stopped preening themselves, and looked at each other as if they were about to speak. The crow spread his wings and flapped them once. "Kiaw!" the crow cawed. "Quiet!" He began scratching in the sand on the other side of the fire.

"Going to cook those clams?" he said. "I prefer mine raw. Toss me one, will you?"

The fisherman did so. The crow snatched the clam out of the air with his beak. Behind the crow the cormorant and the pelican clucked amongst themselves, but as they were speaking in the lingua franca of birds, the fisherman couldn't make out what they were saying. In the tree above him the frigate bird spread his wings wide and flapped them in agitation, as if he wanted to swoop down and steal the clam from the crow. They called this crow an imposter, and spoke ill of him to his face, but still, he held some sway over them. He'd pecked them into submission, by the look of it.

The crow dropped his clam to the sand, and he bent down and prised it open with the tip of his beak. *Clever bird*, the fisherman thought. His stomach growled again. It was time to put his clams on the fire. He gathered up a few of them, but before he could drop them on the coals, the crow scooped the clam out of his clamshell, and he came round the fire with it in his beak. The fisherman stepped back, but the crow came right up to him. He turned his head from side to side, showing the clam to the fisherman. The pelican and the cormorant chuttered in alarm behind him.

This was no common clam. This was a clam with two arms, and two legs, and the body of a woman, and she stretched her arms and yawned as if she were waking from a very long sleep. She was unclothed and shapely, her skin was a pale gray like an oyster, and wet and shiny in the sunlight. She opened her eyes, her face as delicate as a porcelain doll's, and for a moment she looked right at the fisherman, her lips parted as if she were about to speak. And then the crow swallowed her whole.

"Soul of the dead," the crow said, and he laughed, "aw aw aw aw aw. Tasty little morsels. Was it anybody you knew?"

Souls of the dead? Had he just glimpsed his beloved's soul? The fisherman screamed. The clams fell from his hands. Something wretched rose in his gorge, and his stomach heaved. Only bile came up. He leaned over and let it spill forth from his lips, only to see it land on the clams at his feet. Unspeakable desecration, yet he had not meant it so. A chill wracked his body, and his shoulders shook. He was in the company of monsters, and they had made him behave monstrously.

"Awww," the crow said, "poor fellow. Was it something I ate?" Again that cruel laugh—*aw aw aw aw aw*—the crow's beak wide and his open gorge red and slick. "Fiend," the cormorant said. "Barbarian." And he came round the fire with his wings spread, beating at the crow, who fell back, still laughing. Tears fell from the pelican's eyes. "How could you?" he said. "That soul will never be reborn again."

The crow turned his back to them and hopped away, and then he snatched another clam from the pile and flew off.

The fisherman fell to his knees. He picked up a clam and wiped it clean on his breeches. He gazed at it. Tears ran down his cheeks. "Have I come all this way," said he, "only to see my beloved devoured by that hellish bird?"

The pelican cooed soothingly. "No, I think not. The chances are slim."

The fisherman picked up another clam, and he held one in each hand, and he looked from one to the other. "Is this my beloved?" he said. "Or this?"

"Only the crow knows for sure," the cormorant said. He dug his bill into his chest feathers, preening them with quick, practiced strokes.

"Did he just eat her?" the fisherman shrieked. "Did he just fly off with her?"

"How has your luck been running lately?" the cormorant said. The pelican stepped forward and spread his wings, showing the backside of one of them to the cormorant. "What my friend means to say," the pelican cooed, "is that there are as many clams on this beach as there are grains of sand. So there's no point in worrying yourself. We're sure she's here, and we'll help you find her."

"Is that the royal—?" Before the cormorant could finish, the pelican shoved his wing into the cormorant's open mouth, and gave the bird a look to silence him. The cormorant screeched, and he flapped his wings and flew off.

"How?" the fisherman said. He sat on the sand, looking carefully at each clam in his pile. He might as well have been trying to guess the sex of a chicken by looking at an egg. One by one he put the clams down, arranging them in rows on the sand. "How the devil do we find her?"

The pelican, his wings folded now, stretched his neck out and bent down to look at the clams, regarding them with first one yellow eye and then the other. "I wish I could tell you," he said, "and yet I have no answer for you." He cooed, perhaps as much to soothe himself as to calm the fisherman.

The frigate bird spoke from his perch above them. "Remember, you have something the crow needs," he said. "If the crow fails to light the sacred fire again, the Kiamah beast will be angry with him."

The fisherman looked up at the sky, where the crow circled far above them. "Crow," he called out, "come down here. Perhaps we can help each other."

The crow flew lower and lower, spiraling down through the air. He still had the clam he'd snatched, gripped in his claws. "A bargain?" the crow called down. "You wish to offer me a bargain?" He flew at treetop level, still circling, and then, as he flew over some rocks, he let go of the clam. The fisherman sprang to his feet, but there was no way he could catch the clam before it hit the rocks and broke open. When he reached it the tiny creature inside was gasping for air, a shard of clamshell protruding from his belly. This one was an old man, who rolled onto his side and drew his knees up to his chest. And then he breathed no more, and was still.

The crow landed next to the fisherman, and he began to strut back and forth like a sea captain on the deck of a ship. "You see how it is," the crow said. "I'm the only one who can find her for you. You'd best give me what I want."

"And what is that?" the fisherman said.

"Why, your fire of course." The crow hopped up on a driftwood log, and now loomed over the fisherman. His crow feet edged sideways until he stood in the smoke from the fire. "Awww," the crow said. "Love that smell."

"Show me my beloved," the fisherman said, "and I'll give you my fire."

"Perhaps," the crow said. "Or perhaps I'll just steal your fire and be done with you."

The cormorant dropped out of the sky and landed between the crow and the fire. "Fair's fair," the cormorant said, "and thievery is the work of a knave. Steal the fire, and you will only prove yourself a scoundrel. Would the true King of the Dead stoop so low?"

The crow puffed up his shiny chest feathers, and fixed one haughty eye on the cormorant. "You've no right to judge me," the crow said, "but as to the matter at hand, if Señor Stercutius† here gives me his fire, I'll dig up his beloved's clam."

"She is alive then?" said the fisherman. "You haven't eaten her?"

"You're on the Isle of the Dead, fool," the crow said, "your beloved is most certainly deceased. As you will be too, soon enough." The crow hopped down from the driftwood log, muttering to himself that a live human on this shore was blasphemy, and an affront to the King of the Dead. He paced back and forth, cawing in a most ugly and threatening manner. They all watched him, the fisherman feeling his patience spooling out like a fishing line, the pelican embarrassed by this treatment of a guest, and the cormorant affronted by the crow's ignoble behavior. *Kiaww*, the crow muttered on, why should the King of the Dead have to barter for fire with a mere human? It was an insult on top of the blasphemy.

"Oh, shut up," the frigate bird said. "He means is her soul still alive, you barnacle brain."

"Her soul?" the crow said. "That slimy little morsel? Of course it's still alive. Although why you attach such significance to it is beyond me."

"You know why," the pelican said. "The clams are part of the cycle. And to eat a soul"—and here, the pelican shuddered—"why, that's the real blasphemy here."

"Just so," the cormorant said, "our charge here is to serve the transmigration of souls from one life to the next. Ergo, no souls, no canoe coming at midnight, and no canoe leaving at dawn. And no reason for us to be here."

Ah, the fisherman thought. This business of souls and clams was all new to him, but the comings and goings of boats were always a good thing to know.

† Stercutius, dear reader, is the Roman god of dung.

"So my beloved's soul is still alive," the fisherman said, "and you can produce it."

The crow stopped his pacing, and with one black eye he regarded the fisherman as if he were an insect. "Yes, dung beetle, I said I would dig it up."

"Do you swear on the Kiamah's snout?" said the cormorant.

"I so swear," said the crow.

"So be it," said the fisherman. This was no time to take offense at yet another insult from this insufferable bird. "The fire is yours."

And so the deal was struck. The fisherman was required to keep his fire going while the crow searched for the soul of his beloved, and the crow was made to promise that he would return by sunset with the right clam. The crow flew off, leaving the pelican, the cormorant, and the frigate bird with the fisherman.

"That crow," the frigate bird said, "is a picaroon if ever I saw one."

"A picaroon, and a poxy pignut," the cormorant said, "but he is bound by his oath."

"I heard him say he was the King of the Dead," said the frigate bird. "What truth is there to that?"

The cormorant spread his wings and rattled his flight feathers with an air of exasperation. "With Raven gone missing, the crow has it in mind that he shall rule in his stead. We have opposed him in this, but he has a beak quick to do us injury, and he grows ever more belligerent. And more than this, his powers grow mysteriously stronger, as if he has made a pact with the Kiamah beast."

A change in rulers, thought the fisherman, *is a time of turbulence. A time of both risk and opportunity.* He'd best keep his ears open and his wits sharp. But there were more immediate matters pressing on him. He threw more wood on the fire. His belly growled again. He looked at the clams he'd laid out in rows, and he felt queasy. He was hungry, sure enough, but he was no cannibal of souls. He gathered them up and went back to the wet sand of the inlet, where he buried them, one by one, just above the lapping waves. The memory of that woman's bright little eyes looking right into his plagued him. One minute she was there, and the next she was a squirmy lump in the crow's throat. Ye gods, what a fate.

To rid himself of the upset in his belly he sat on the sand and

thought of the crow plucked and roasted, sitting on a large silver plat-
ter. There was an alehouse in Hav where they held a celebratory feast
for the winner of the annual roof race, a race the fisherman himself
had nearly won when he was a young man, failing only because one
of his stilts snapped three rooves from the finish line. At the feast an
elephant-bird was served, the meat savory and succulent, and now he
remembered sitting at that great table with all the other roof-runners,
only this time he had won the race, and he was given the honor of
carving the crow, and he cut off one great drumstick, a piece of meat
the size of a small ham, and he took a great bite from it, and everyone
cheered. The crow was delicious, the most satisfying fowl he had ever
eaten, and the fisherman was no longer queasy.

He waded out into the inlet until he was waist deep, and then he
stood and peered into the water. Farther out he saw the dark shapes
of fish swimming along the sandy bottom. If only he had a net to cast,
or a hook to bait and a line to throw. He looked down the inlet toward
the shallows at the far end. Perhaps he could herd a fish there, and
snatch it right out of the water with his bare hands. All his life the
sea had fed him, but now he lacked so small a thing as a dip net, or
even a line and a hook.

A shadow passed over him, and a moment later the cormorant
landed on the water nearby. The fish scattered, and the cormorant
paddled over to him.

"Nice day for a swim," the cormorant said.

Sunlight glanced off the cormorant's spectacles in a way that
suggested someone possessed of superior knowledge. "I suppose," the
fisherman said, "that you fellows eat a lot of fish."

"Why yes," the cormorant said, "I suppose we do."

"As do I," the fisherman said. "I'm actually a fisherman by trade."

"Do tell," the cormorant said. "And do you find that a satisfying
line of work?"

"I do," the fisherman said. "Not so much as a line of work, but as a
means of feeding myself when I am hungry."

The cormorant peered over the tops of his spectacles at the fisherman. "Yes," he said, "I know what you mean."

"How do you catch them?" the fisherman said.

"Like this," the cormorant said. He rose up in the water and arched his neck and dove with his body following his neck all in one sinuous motion, and the water closed over the bird without a sound. He moved swiftly through the water until the fisherman could barely see him, and then he surfaced. The tail of a fish stuck out of his bill, and the cormorant stretched out his neck, and he swallowed it whole. It made the fisherman shudder to see that live thing struggling inside the cormorant's throat, and now he was queasy again. And angry at himself, for he was growing hungrier with every passing moment, and yet his belly twisted itself in knots at the mere sight of this creature feeding. In life, hunger made a killer of all beings great and small, such were the circumstances of all who lived, and it was foolish to allow one's feelings to hinder what was only natural. But, having survived the belly of the whale, to be swallowed alive was a fate he would no longer wish on anyone. Better the sharp rap to the head.

The cormorant swam over to him again. "How do you catch them?" he said.

"I use a hook and a line," the fisherman said, "or sometimes a net."

"Ah, yes," the cormorant said. "I've read of such things." Sunlight was once again glancing off his spectacles, and the fisherman noticed a curious thing. Not only were the spectacles still perched on the bird's bill, but they appeared to be dry. The bewitchery of this place revealed itself in the smallest details. Sorcerers all, these birds.

"I don't suppose you've seen a net or a hook around here."

"I fear not," the cormorant said. He paddled toward shore, and the fisherman followed. "Perhaps you might fashion one yourself?"

The fisherman nodded. "I might, given a supply of strong cord." It would take him the better part of a day, even if he had the material. "There are no tradesmen here, though, no chandlery, no store of such goods?"

"None whatsoever," the cormorant said. He stood on the wet sand and spread his wings to the sun, drying them.

"As I thought," the fisherman said. "Might you be able to conjure such a thing?"

"Conjure, sir?" the cormorant said. His turquoise eyes grew larger and rounder. "You mistake me for someone I am not, for I am no conjurer, nor ever have been. I am a scholar, and a barrister, and lately, the crow wishes me to know, an advisor to the king." He rattled his wings, turning this way and that, his feathers shiny in the sun. "What you might do is strip some bark off one of the cedar trees. The bark of the cedar tree is woven into many useful things, many useful things indeed."

The pelican waddled down from the driftwood fire and joined them. "Hallo, good fellows," he cooed, "what say ye to a swim?"

The cormorant folded his wings, and turned to face his companions. "I was about to tell our guest here about all the useful things one can make from cedar bark. Baskets, of course, and hats, and all manner of clothing, and mats, to name but a few. And cord, which may be of particular interest to our guest, since he would like to go fishing."

"Ahh, fishing," the pelican said. "A pleasant way to pass the time."

"As to hooks," the cormorant said, "One can be fashioned from hemlock, which can be found in the forest, or better yet, there are yew trees here, *Taxus brefifolia*. The wood is hard to work but worth the effort, or so have I read."

"Perhaps you could show me the proper tree," the fisherman said. He was only being polite, for he knew well what a yew tree looked like. He was growing ever more hungry, and the thought of spending a day fashioning the tools of his trade made his stomach growl again.

"Oh my," said the pelican. "Such a noise." He lay his bill against his chest, and his yellow eyes blinked their curious sideways blink. "Are you hungry?" he said to the fisherman.

"Famished," the fisherman said.

"Why are you wasting time speaking of nets and hooks?" the pelican said. "Catch the poor fellow a fish, for pity's sake."

The cormorant looked askance at the pelican. *"Dat homini pisces ciba illum diem. Docet piscibus in ciba illum diebus,"* said he.

"Good heavens," said the pelican, "must you show off by speaking Latin at a time like this?"

"Give a man a fish, and you feed him for a day," the cormorant said, his spectacles shining in the sunlight. "Teach him how to fish, and you feed him for a lifetime."

"I know how to fish," the fisherman said.

"He's hungry, you big dodo," the pelican said. "The man can't weave himself a net when he's dying of hunger."

The fisherman fixed a hungry eye on the cormorant. He let his face become pitiable, and he pulled his belly in slowly until it became a hollow. The cormorant might be a deity, and a sorcerer, but the pelican was trying to shame him, and he thought it best to follow the pelican's lead. But the cormorant turned away, spreading his wings again in the sun.

"It's no good insulting me," he said. "I'm merely taking the scholarly approach, offering my knowledge, and asking for nothing in return."

"Oh, for crying out loud," the pelican said. "I'll do it myself."

The pelican flew out over the inlet, skimming along a few feet above the water, until, quick as a shot from a pistola, he turned sideways in the air and dove straight down into the water. When he came back up a fish could be seen struggling inside his ample bill. He flew back to the fisherman, and he opened up his bill to reveal a fine fish.

"Take this," he said. The fisherman reached in and pulled out the fish, still alive, and he waded back to shore, where he gave the fish a quick and merciful rap on the head against a rock. Perhaps the pelican was one of those rare deities who were helpful, and therefore worthy of a man's prayers.

"I am once again in your debt," the fisherman said. He took the fish back to his fire, and he found that with the cuttlefish beak he could gut the thing. It was a clumsy operation that made him long for his knife, but the beak was better than nothing. The birds watched him as he built himself a cooking rack out of green alder branches lashed together with sea grass. He spitted the fish and hung it above the fire to cook.

"Tell me something," the fisherman said. "What is this business about the canoe?"

"Ahh," the pelican said. "It is this way. The canoe arrives at midnight, filled with the just dead. They are led ashore, and the crow harvests their souls. The souls burrow into the sand, where they become clams."

"And what do they do inside their clamshells?" the fisherman asked.

"They dream," the pelican said. "They dream whatever heaven they desire, and they are happy."

"Forever?" the fisherman asked.

"Oh no," the pelican said. "No, they slowly make their way to the other side of the inlet, crawling along through the sand. Takes quite a long time, I'm told. They're not in a hurry, and their sense of direction is poor. But eventually, they turn up on the other side. And there they are dug up, and the canoe takes them back to the material world, where they are reborn."

"Dug up?" the fisherman said. "By whom?"

"The canoe is paddled by two fish eagles, a he and a she. They dig up the clams, and they paddle away with them in the dawn."

"And what course do they follow?" the fisherman said. "Out to sea?"

"Yes," the pelican said, "to the far shore, where they release the souls within the clams for rebirth, and gather the newly dead."

"The dead come there from the land of the living?"

"They do."

So there it was, a way back home. He must cross the sea, and follow the trail of the dead back to the living. He would collect the soul of his beloved at sunset, and they would see what fate held for them, but the fisherman was beginning to think they might do well to get as far away from this place as they possibly could.

His coals were hot, and well banked, but the fish was going to take some time to cook, so the fisherman lay back and closed his eyes. He had a sailor's habit of falling asleep quickly, and he was gone in a few breaths.

The cormorant sidled over to the pelican. "I know he's our guest, and deserving of our hospitality," the cormorant said, "but he can't stay here. The crow will never allow it."

"It's not the crow I'm worried about," the pelican said. "The Kiamah beast will wake up at sunset, and he will be angry. We'd best watch each other's backs, or we'll end up like Raven."

Both birds shuddered, their feathers rattling with fear. The frigate bird called out to them. "Cousins," he said, "do not despair. This fisherman may be exactly who we need to restore this land to its proper order."

The cormorant and the pelican flew up to treetop perches next to the frigate bird.

"What do you mean?" the cormorant said.

"It is no accident that he has arrived now," the frigate bird said, "so soon after Raven's disappearance. The threads of fate are weaving themselves into a new pattern. We must buck up, and be a part of the change that is afoot."

"I miss Raven," the pelican said. "The crow is a savage, and cruel. He frightens me. He ate a soul today, and that is a crime for which we may all be punished."

"Do not be ruled by your fears," said the frigate bird. "You must stand up to the crow when the opportunity arises."

"Though I am but a scholar, I shall do so," said the cormorant.

"You're braver than I," said the pelican.

The cormorant stretched out his long neck at this praise from the pelican, and jabbed his bill at the sky. "Where is Raven?" he said. "The crow said Raven was banished, but to whence?"

"I don't believe that tale of banishment," said the frigate bird. "I think the crow killed him."

"Then *ubi est corpus*?" said the cormorant. "Where is the body?"

"Methinks the crow fed him to the Kiamah," said the frigate bird.

"Shhhh," the pelican said. "Don't say that. The beast might hear us."

"The Kiamah?" the frigate bird said. "He's asleep."

"He may have spies," the pelican said.

"Spies?" the frigate bird said. "There's nobody here but us."

They all looked at one another, their eyes gimlets boring in like surgeons trepanning each other's skulls.

"I am no spy," said the cormorant.

"Nor am I," said the pelican.

"Nor I, neither," said the frigate bird.

"Suspicion clouds the mind," the cormorant said.

"Trust me," the pelican said, "you can't trust anyone anymore."

"If we don't hang together," the frigate bird said, "we shall surely hang separately."

The three birds, on a cue that only birds can see, began swiveling their heads, looking in all directions. Even the frigate bird was wary, despite his brave talk, and the pelican, frightened by their conversation, let loose a large gobbet of guano, and, thus lightened, flew off.

"Scared shite-less, that one is," the frigate bird said.

The cormorant clucked in agreement. "Things were better here before Raven disappeared."

"Amen to that," the frigate bird said.

DEWI SRI, DIVINE REGENT OF Bali Dwipa, the land of peace, sat in meditation in the temple of her ancestors. It was here she came for guidance when she was in the midst of tribulation. For many nights her sleep had been troubled by ominous dreams, and though she went about her duties with her usual calm, her spirit was troubled.

She spent her days sending her spirit to the rice rituals, which were constant, and varied, and far too numerous for her to attend all of them in person. Though no one in the land of the living knew this, she kept herself informed of all that mattered by listening to the whispers of the fireflies that lit up the rice paddies each evening. It was from this knowledge that she chose when to manifest herself in person, rewarding those tempeks and those subaks who were exceptionally devoted to her, and who did the most careful work on their irrigation ditches and in the paddies themselves. Thus did everyone in the land of the living hope to earn the blessing of a personal visit from the Rice Mother.

On many an evening Dewi Sri hosted feasts in her palace, with music from the gamelan players, and costumed dancers reenacting the legends of her ancestors, the gods. She sat at the head of these festivities, clothed in silk and songket, her smile serene. But within her there was another nature, a nature that craved the touch of others. She was the Rice Mother, true enough, but she was also a fertility goddess, and she loved to couple. She had her choice of lovers, male and female alike, and made full use of that choice. And there were other evenings when she was alone, and it was on these evenings that she sat in solitude, seeking the center point of all that was, and all that should be.

Now, before her, the statues of her ancestors stood with nothing but serenity on their stone faces. Dewi Sri sat in full lotus, with her hands clasped in the ushra mudra, her fingers interlaced, her left thumb encircled by her right thumb and forefinger. Before she could hear the voices of her ancestors, she must find the balance point within, at the center of the eleven directions. In the land of peace, she must find her own peace. But peace eluded her, and the longer she sat, the further away it was. She could not stop herself from feeling the mudra as the coupling of her left thumb with the fleshly circle of her right thumb and forefinger.

She had been too long at the work of being the Rice Mother, for the rice paddies proliferated, and her people grew more numerous, and she returned their devotion with her devotion. But it was time to balance her second chakra with the thrust of a hard q'hram into her quiver. Or with the oft-practiced touch of one of her courtesans, who knew her quiver well.

So much for meditation. She stood and spread her wings, flapping them gently as she walked out of the temple. She took flight, returning to her quarters in the highest part of her palace, and there she retired to the canopied bed in her lanai. She struck a clear urgent note on the gamelan gong that summoned her handmaiden.

"Bring me rose oil and ylang-ylang and lavender," she told her handmaiden. "Then summon Ni Tut Sulastri and I Tjok Putra."

"Both of them, my lady?"

Again she slid her left thumb through the fleshly circle of her right thumb and forefinger. A smile tugged at the corners of her mouth.

"Yes, both. The elder shall instruct the younger in the arts of love."

Thus would she find the balance point within, by releasing the pent-up need. She was, after all, a fertility goddess.

THE FISHERMAN WOKE FROM HIS catnap and checked his fish, which was not quite ready. He turned the spit, and he shaded his eyes with his hand. The frigate bird flew off his perch, his long narrow wings spread wide, and swooped out over the inlet. There he caught an updraft, and spiraled upward, his forked tail marking a black V in the sky. They were all glide, the frigate birds, rarely flapping their wings, as graceful as a ship under full sail. They flew many leagues from shore, father out than any other sea bird, and they were a sailor's first sign that land lay beyond the horizon. All his days as a sailor he had held them in high regard, despite their reputations as brigands who harassed boobies and other birds, stealing their food.

The sun was bright, the sand at his feet hot, and the sun was making its daily traverse across the sky. That gave him his bearings—the inlet opened to the sea eastward, and the mountains were to the west. His camp was on the south shore of the inlet. All good things to know.

He walked down to the water, where the cormorant stood in the shallows, gazing at the fish swimming by. "It's a fair wind," he said, by way of making conversation with the bird.

"Hmmm?" said the cormorant. "A fair wind? I suppose so. Fair enough for Cousin Pelican to hover above us." The pelican was indeed above them, holding his place with his spread wings.

"But aloft the tree tops sway," said the fisherman, pointing. "The wind is aloft, and from the west."

"Hmmm?" the cormorant said, looking up now. "The west? No, no, you mean the east," he said, pointing a wing at the treetops.

"But the sun is moving westward," said the fisherman, "toward the mountains."

"I beg to differ," the cormorant said. "You're quite mistaken. The sun rises in the west, and sets in the east. Always has."

"That's right," the pelican said. "Where you come from it's all backward, rising in the east, setting in the west. It would make me giddy as a maple seed, I should think."

Giddy was precisely how the fisherman felt. East was west, and west was east, and if these bird-gods were to be believed, when the sun went down he would see that outside was inside, and the sun was the great beating heart of the Kiamah beast. His head buzzed like a beehive, and felt as if it might spin right off his neck. He put his hands on his head, and was startled to feel no hair there. His naked scalp was as smooth as an apple, and his face was without stubble. Surely he had been here long enough for his whiskers to grow. He held his hands out in front of himself, and his arms had the faintest tinge of blue to them.

Strange and stranger were the changes worked upon him by his sojourn in the whale's belly. Still, some things never changed, and hunger was one of them. He walked back to his fire, where his fish was finally cooked. He laid the fish down on a flat rock, peeled back the skin, and put the first juicy tidbit in his mouth. He had nothing for seasoning, and no way to eat except with his hands, but here was another truth about hunger, something his beloved had told him once: hunger makes a banquet of the simplest meal.

Each toothsome bite restored the fisherman's spirits. His belly filled at last, he built his fire up until the flames were waist high, the crackling yellow flames a comfort to him as he waited for the crow to return. He sat on a driftwood log and kept himself still, unwilling to show his companions how his heart flapped like a loose sail, his blood running hot and cold by turns. The sun's transit across the sky pained him with its slow pace, as if it were a ship becalmed on slack seas. There were clouds scattered across the sky, lit from below by the sun setting in the east, and that eastward motion, wrong as it was, only added to the icy upset coursing through the nerves in his belly. It was a strange brew of feelings, and it put him in mind of several things: the nardly thrill he felt when he stepped on shore knowing he would have a woman for the first time after months at sea, the tight-chested last moments before a pirate ship closed the gap on its merchant prey, the flat-eyed sorrow of a man just dead. The crow would come, bearing the soul of his beloved, and would honor their bargain, or by the gods he would throttle that cursèd bird, even if it meant his own life was forfeit.

The cormorant and the pelican perched on a log across the fire from the fisherman, silent, waiting, their heads down, their bills resting on their breasts. The frigate bird had returned to his branch above. The bottom edge of the sun's disc reached the tops of the mountains and began to disappear behind them. The pink bottoms of the clouds turned orange as if lit from within, and as the color changed, the fisherman found within himself some measure of calm. It was a calm he borrowed in part from his unruffled companions. He was swordless, and knifeless, with only the cuttlefish beak to defend himself, but he had his hands and his wits, and he had not reached the age he was by relying solely on the brute force of weaponry. He had the strength of a man who worked hard every day to survive, though he had thickened in the middle, as many an old stud does, long before he loses his desire to service the herd. He had seen many things in his sailor's life, and tricksy though this crow might be, the fisherman had taken his measure, and would not be fooled again. Above all else, as in any battle of wits or strength, his best advantage was his willingness to die.

Against the fiery display of clouds came the crow, a black silhouette high above. "Ko, ko, ko," the crow thundered, his voice shaking the very air. "Ko, ko, ko." The crow word made the fisherman swivel his head like a vole looking for a bolt hole. There was danger here, and he'd best escape.

"What sorcery is this?" the fisherman said, his ears ringing.

"Stand fast," the frigate bird said. "He is as unsure of the outcome here as we are."

The cormorant, though but a scholar, puffed out his breast and stood fast. Only the tremble of his tail feathers betrayed his fear.

The fisherman stood, the crow dropping closer. He thought of asking the frigate bird for his pistola, but something within him said no, let fate unspool its thread. Now just above their heads, the crow beat his wings against the air to slow himself, the feathers on the trailing edge spread like so many fingers. His crow's feet touched down on the sand, and without pause he began to strut back and forth. He had a long narrow basket on his back, held there by a woven strap across his breast.

"Ko, ko, ko," the crow thundered again. "Behold the King of the Dead."

"Oh, shut up," the frigate bird said. "Nobody likes a show-off."

The crow stopped in mid-strut to look up at the frigate bird, surprised, it seemed, that anyone dared to resist him. "Mind yourself," he said, "I'm not here to be liked." But he spoke without his magical thunder, already taken down a peg because the frigate bird refused to be bullied. This was a game the fisherman had played before, and the best tactic was to engage. He stood so the fire was between himself and the crow, and he spread his arms wide.

"Where is my beloved?" he said, his voice seeming to come from the fire itself, "for as you see, I have kept my end of the bargain."

"Do not trouble yourself," the crow said, "I have found her. Not an easy task," he said, his voice oily and slick. "So many just like her, they're thick as maggots on a beached whale."

The fisherman threw a piece of wood on the fire, and sparks exploded upward. "Where is she?" he said.

The crow stepped round the fire toward the fisherman, who circled the same way, to keep the fire between them.

"Afraid I'll pluck your eye out again?" the crow said. "You needn't be, I've already dined this evening," and the crow laughed, "aw aw aw aw aw."

"By the gods," the fisherman said, "if you've eaten my beloved's soul, I swear it will be the last meal you ever take."

"Oh no," the crow said. "She's right here, in my basket, safe as a mother's embrace. Once I've made a bargain, I'm quite strict about keeping my word."

"Then hand her over," the fisherman said. "The fire is yours."

"Yes, well, you're right about that," the crow said. At this the frigate bird, the pelican, and the cormorant all leaned in. The fisherman too, for they all felt it coming. "Yes," the crow said, "the fire's mine, for I have done what I promised."

"Speak plainly," the fisherman said. "Hand over my beloved, that was your promise."

"No," the crow said, "I promised to dig her up, and I have done so. I never promised to hand her over, and as I've said, I am a stickler about keeping my word. It would dishonor me to do otherwise."

"Auk! You brigand!" the cormorant said. "You scurrilous scoundrel." The cormorant hopped off his log, spread his wings wide, and stretched his neck up as tall as it would go. He opened his capacious bill, curled his wet tongue gluttonously, and said, "I'll swallow you whole."

The crow puffed up his chest feathers and cawed at the orange sky. "You'll choke to death long before you get past my feet," the crow said. He turned his back on the cormorant in a show of contempt, and he raised his tail and let a gobbet of guano fall on the sand. The cormorant flapped his wings murderously at the crow, ready to leap on him.

"Steady," the pelican said. "Let's not get carried away here."

"Shite bird," the cormorant said. He gawped his bill rudely at the crow's back, scooped up some hot coals from the fire, and tossed them at the crow, but they fell to the ground, harmless. The crow turned round to face him again, raised his foot to his beak, and brushed away a speck of ash.

"Sorry," the crow said. "Were you speaking to me?" The cormorant flapped his wide wings, his bill opening and closing as if he were ready to eat this crow, but he did not attack.

The frigate bird drew forth his pistola with his bill, and tucked it into his wingpit, aimed at the crow. Then he cocked it, again with his bill, and he said, "What is it you want, crow?"

The crow gave the pistola a sharp-eyed glance, but he showed no fear. "Oh, nothing," the crow said. "I'll just take my fire and go."

The fisherman studied the crow through the flames. The frigate bird was right, the crow wanted something more, or else why was he standing there? Although how he could take the fire anywhere was a bit of a mystery. Still, he was a god, and he must have his ways.

"So soon?" the fisherman said. He raised what would have been an eyebrow, if he still had eyebrows, at the cormorant, and pointed at the log behind him with a sideways nod of his head. The cormorant folded his wings and returned to his perch, next to the pelican. He seemed content, for the moment at least, to let the fisherman handle his own affairs, although he continued to open his bill from time to time, as if to remind the crow how good he was at swallowing things whole.

"It is my mistake," the fisherman said. "I thought we had a clear bargain. But I see that the words of the bargain are important to you, as they should be. Is there not some way to arrange this so we both get what we want?"

The crow busied himself for a moment, rooting through the feathers on his chest in search of feather mites, the very picture of nonchalance.

"I see you're quite a reasonable man," he said. "My compliments to the mother who bore you. A lovely woman, I'm sure. She's here, by the way. I ran across her when I was looking for your beloved."

Aha, thought the fisherman. The crow didn't know everything, for if he did, he would have known that the fisherman's mother had been a courtesan who sold him to a gang of thieves when he was old enough to pick a pocket. From that misdeed the fisherman held a lifelong hatred of slavers and slavery, and he had long since lost all desire to ever see his mother again.

"We were speaking of my beloved," the fisherman said, "and what I might offer you to complete our bargain."

"An offer, you say? How th-aw-aw-oughtful of you. Let me think for a moment," the crow said. He made a show of it, pacing back and forth on his stiff legs, his head bowed as if lost in thought.

He was a greedy knave, this crow, always after more for himself. The fisherman had encountered his type before. Customs officials looking for a bribe, toll keepers at the gate to a city, procurers standing at the doorway to the temple where the sacred whores lay waiting, they all wanted two things—money, and the feeling that they had bested their adversary. A man had two choices. Kill them, or give them what they wanted, and a clever man did not rush them through their moment of glory. It was best to reserve combat for only the most obstreperous cases. One never knew how many relatives a bribist had, but they were likely to come after the man who slew their meal ticket.

"There's a rumor," the crow said, his voice as well oiled as the flesh of a salmon's cheek, "that you have in your possession some sort of magical glass with which to start a fire. Is that true?"

Hmm. So the crow knew about his magician's glass. There must be spies about. He'd been alone when he started the fire, but the frigate bird had a spyglass, and he'd shown up soon after. Now that was a thing to consider when he had the time.

"You are remarkably well informed," the fisherman said. "I have it right here," he said, putting his hand on the pouch that held it.

"Might I see it?" the crow said.

"Why, of course," the fisherman said. "But I think it wise to speak of our bargain before I bring it out."

"Aren't you the clever one?" the crow said. "All right, let us be plain about the matter. I take the fire, because it is mine already. You give me the magic glass, and if I'm satisfied with it, I'll give you the clam that contains your beloved's soul."

The pelican and the cormorant both clucked at this, but the fisherman needed no warning. "You'll give me the clam with my beloved's soul whether you like the glass or not," the fisherman said. "I believe you already know that you'll be satisfied with the glass."

The crow regarded him through the smoke from the fire. This fisherman was a worthy adversary, someone who gave as good as he got. A worthy adversary, and a man who would keep things from getting dull around here, as they were wont to do. A good thing to know, for of all the things the crow detested, boredom was very near the top of the list.

By now the last of the sun was just disappearing behind the mountains, and the glorious display of color in the sky was fading. The crow raised his wings, and he passed one of them in front of himself, and now he had the body of a man, with arms and legs and hands, though he still had the head of a crow. The fisherman was astonished, as he was meant to be, but he kept his astonishment from his face. Best to stare this shapeshifter down.

The crow wore a breechclout woven from strips of cedar bark. The basket was still on his back. He took it off, and he pulled a clam out of it.

"Your beloved," the crow said.

A great upwelling of feeling overtook the fisherman. He struggled to conceal this, too, and was grateful for the smoke and flames he stood behind, but the pelican knew what he was feeling, and cooed in sympathy. The fisherman took the pouch with the magician's glass off his belt. "Your glass," he said.

The crow and the fisherman met at the edge of the fire, and in a gesture as old as ransom, they handed clam and pouch to each other at the same moment. The fisherman held the clam tenderly in both hands, and he put it against his chest. The crow took the magician's glass out of the pouch and looked through it, which made his black eye very large, and then he held it up to the fisherman's face. "My, what an ugly nose," he said, "it's enormous."

They stepped back from each other, and the crow said, "I believe that concludes our business together." The crow held the open mouth of his basket over the fire, and with a gesture from his other hand, the fire flew into the basket, leaving behind only the blackened fire pit. The crow shouldered his basket and walked off toward the woods. He stopped for a moment when he had a little distance between them.

"Let me know," he said, "if you want your dear mother's soul. I'm sure we can come to some arrangement."

"I shall," the fisherman said. *Not bloody likely,* he thought, but this was no time to declare himself unnecessarily.

It was dark without the fire, but, just as had happened on the beach earlier that day, the fisherman found he could see well enough in the dark. He cupped his beloved's clamshell in his hands, admiring the curve of the shell. He had traveled so far, and now she was so close.

The crow now gone, the cormorant hopped off his perch on the driftwood log and opened his bill over the fire pit. A hot coal fell out, glowing all the more brightly for the darkness into which it fell.

"Oh my," said the pelican. "That must have been torturous. How did you manage to keep your mouth shut?"

"There is an old adage," said the cormorant, his bill spreading in a grin. "Better to keep one's mouth shut and be thought a fool, than to open one's mouth and remove all doubt."

"Good fellow," the fisherman said. "This will save me some considerable bother." He set his beloved down on the sand beneath the driftwood log, tucking her carefully out of harm's way, and he set about rebuilding his fire. "That was clever of you to steal an ember."

"An accident," the cormorant said, "but a happy one. If the truth be known, that ember got caught in the back of my mouth, and I was too embarrassed to cough it up."

The fire crackled and grew, giving off a comforting orange glow. The fisherman retrieved his beloved's clamshell, and the pelican and the cormorant stood on either side of him, examining it as if it were a newborn babe.

"'Tis a beautiful clam," the pelican said. "Nicely shaped."

"Indeed," the cormorant said, "Very, uhmmm, clammy, shall we say?" He pointed a wingtip at the grooves that ran lengthwise along the clamshell. "Those striations have an organic rhythm to them that is very fetching. And you handled the crow with great aplomb."

They all nodded at one another, clucking and cooing and murmuring the sorts of things one did after a successful negotiation. Things had gone pretty well, all things considered. Only the frigate bird on his perch above was quiet.

The fisherman held his clam in the palm of one hand and gently stroked it, imagining his beloved sleeping inside, dreaming of him, her lovely eyelids softly closed, a beauteous smile on her lips.

"What do I do now?" the fisherman said.

"Do?" the pelican said. "What do you mean?"

The fisherman pointed at the clam. "I want more than her soul locked up in a clamshell. I want to make her whole again."

The cormorant and the pelican looked at each other, and they looked at the fisherman. They both shrugged. All three of them looked at the frigate bird on his branch.

"Don't look at me," the frigate bird said.

At this, the fisherman rolled his eyes at the frigate bird. "Are you not gods?" he sputtered. "Can you not tell me what I must do?"

"Perhaps I can look it up," said the cormorant. He produced a book from under his wing, *Mortimer's Compleat Atlas of the Afterlife,* and he began flipping through the pages with his bill. "Canoe of the dead, cultural perspectives, fish eagles, local deities, hm, hm, hm, nautical deaths, ah. Here's an overview of the whole process." The cormorant began to read aloud in a low voice as he skimmed the article. "After dying in the material world, the newly dead awaken at the edge of the Sea of Bones, on the far shore of the spirit world. They are often confused, and many do not accept the fact of their own death, for most of what they think they know about the afterlife is wrong," and here the frigate bird interrupted to say, "Ain't that the bloody truth." The cormorant turned a page and murmured on. "Their spirit bodies are whole, and they function much as their material bodies functioned, hence their confusion. Their hearts have quit beating, yet they walk and talk, they hunger, they thirst, they feel pain. They are clothed as they were at the moment of their deaths, and often carry an object that was close at hand. Mm-hmm, mm-hmm, the great canoe appears, the fish eagles sing them aboard, they cross the Sea of Bones in the canoe, they sing the sacred songs, their souls become clams, eventually they are reborn, so on and so forth, but no mention of extra-clamical restoration of the soul to the body," the cormorant said, as he leafed through the rest of the atlas, and then let it fall shut. "Nor intra-clamical restoration either, for that matter. Nothing here of any use, I'm afraid."

"So much for 'compleat,'" said the frigate bird. "Is that the best you can do?"

The cormorant, who thought of himself as the most scholarly being in the room, if only they'd had a room to be in, considered, the firelight glinting off his spectacles. "Hm, hm, hm. I shall have to study the matter further," he said, and at this, the frigate bird, as vexed as the fisherman, rolled his eyes.

"Try kissing her," the pelican said, "it often works in fairy tales."

The fisherman, dubious, furrowed his forehead, although really, he had nothing to lose by trying, and he looked the clam all around, considering the proper place to apply his lips. The clamshell, he decided, was not very kissable, but he kissed it anyway, a bird-like peck with his lips. Nothing happened.

"That's no kiss," the frigate bird said. "Kiss her like you mean it."

The fisherman closed his eyes, remembering the soft kisses of his beloved, how she nibbled at his lips, how she moaned when he returned the favor along the sweet skin of her neck. He put his lips to the clamshell, kissing it up one side and down the other. But the clamshell remained a clamshell, rough to the touch, and not at all a thing that kissed him back. Exasperated, he held the shell out to his companions.

"None of you know what I'm to do with this?" the fisherman said. "I thought there would be some way to make her a woman again."

"I'm sure there is," the pelican cooed. "We just don't know what it is."

The fisherman sat down on his driftwood log. He set the clam on the log next to him, and he put his head in his hands. This was simply too much to bear.

"I don't suppose there's an alehouse on the Isle of the Dead?"

No, no, no, they all clucked, no such a thing here. "But," the frigate bird said, "I have some hashish. Care to join me?"

Hashish? Not since he had sailed with a crew of Moors had he had the pleasure. "Perfect," the fisherman said. "Come on down."

"Sorry, pilgrim," the frigate bird said. "It's easier for me to fly off a perch. Would you mind coming up here?"

Well, less than perfect. But after all he'd been through, if he had to shinny up a dead tree to smoke the frigate bird's hashish, he was more than willing.

"Bring one of those embers up here," the frigate bird said. "We'll need it for the pipe."

Ever the helpful one, the pelican plucked an ember from the fire and flew up to the frigate bird's perch. The fisherman tucked his beloved's clamshell into the front of his breeches and shinnied up the tree. The cormorant joined them.

"I didn't know you indulged," said the frigate bird to the cormorant.

"Ordinarily I do not," the cormorant said. "But this is a singular occasion."

The frigate bird drew forth his pistola. "Here," he said to the fisherman. "This is a lot easier if you have hands." He told the fisherman how to break the pistola in half, and how to open the secret compartment in the handle. There the fisherman found the bird's hashish, and the bowl to the pipe, which fit cleverly into the pistola's breech. He began loading the pipe with a generous amount of hashish.

"How would you do this if I weren't here?" the fisherman asked.

"Show him," the frigate bird said to the pelican. The pelican waved his wing in front of his body, and now he was an old woman with sagging breasts and a pelican's head. Her belly was plump and round, her skin wrinkled and ridged. A sarong hugged her fleshy hips.

"Zounds!" the fisherman said. "I thought you were a man."

The pelican shrugged. "Would you like me better as a man?" she said. "It's easy enough to do." She tilted her head and laid her bill between her breasts, ready to do the sailor's bidding.

The fisherman considered. He had, he realized, no knowledge of how to tell a male pelican from a female. He nodded at the pelican, who passed her hand in front of her old woman's body, and now she had only one breast. "Sorry," she said, looking down at herself, "I'm a bit out of practice."

Whether the pelican had a man's body or a woman's, thought the fisherman, there was still the undeniable fact of the pelican's head, with its long, striped bill, and those round, yellow eyes. The pelican, for her part, passed her hand in front of herself again, and restored her absent breast.

It was no matter to him, he decided, whether the pelican be male or female. Her eyes, though, were strangely beautiful.

"Stay as you are," said he.

"As you wish," she said. She opened her bill just a bit, and the fisherman realized she was smiling at him. He smiled back.

"And what about you?" the fisherman asked of the frigate bird. "Are you also a shapeshifter?"

"I have other gifts," the frigate bird said. He puffed up his throat pouch for a moment, showing off the bright red skin there, and let loose a rattling sound, as if his throat pouch held a tiny drummer with a tiny drum. "For example," he said, his throat pouch deflating, "I have the hashish, and if you'll pass me the pipe, we can all partake."

Full of surprises, these birds. He handed the pipe to the frigate bird, who put the barrel of the pistola into his bill as if he were going to shoot himself. The pelican dropped the hot coal she'd kept tucked in her bill into the bowl of the pipe, and the frigate bird puffed, sipping air through the barrel until he produced a wisp of fragrant smoke. Then he pulled on the pipe, filling his lungs, and he passed it on to the pelican. "Excellent," the frigate bird said, letting a stream of smoke rise from the corner of his bill. "From Mazar-i-Sharif," he said, "the very best they have to offer."

They passed the pipe around, the frigate bird and the cormorant handling it carefully with their feet, the smoke drifting lazily around their heads, and the fisherman's thoughts drifting lazily with the smoke.

"And you?" the fisherman said to the cormorant. "Are you a shapeshifter as well?"

In answer the cormorant, whose eyes were closed, passed a lazy wing in front of himself, but nothing happened.

"Open your eyes," said the pelican. "You know we cannot shapeshift unless our eyes see hand or wing in front of us." The cormorant raised his languid eyelids and passed his wing in front of his face, and now he appeared as a great horned owl, the curve of his beak like a scimitar.

"Go on, show him how scary you are," said the frigate bird.

Now, as if he'd awoken from a dream, the owl's amber eyes grew fierce, his eyebrows menacing, and he regarded the fisherman hungrily, as if calculating whether he could carry him off in his talons. The fisherman was so alarmed he nearly fell off his branch.

"Stop that!" the pelican said, "you're scaring our guest." The frigate bird cackled a laugh, the owl passed a wing in front of himself, and the cormorant reappeared. The fisherman let loose a sigh of relief.

He looked at all three of them, the hashish lifting his squelched spirits, and he considered the twist and turn of recent events. Mere days lay between him and the calm of his solitary life on the beach. Yesterday he was trapped in the belly of a whale, all but dead, and now here he was, up a tree with companions of dubious quality, any one of whom might be a spy. He had recovered his beloved's soul, his belly was full, and he was smoking a premium grade of hashish.

Zounds, it was good to be alive!

THE CROW WALKED SWIFTLY THROUGH the forest to the pyre of scorched bones. The wave that had put the fire out had knocked the pyre catawampus, and that necrotic, disjointed stack—scapulas and skulls, sacrums and illiums, ulnas and radii, carpals, clavicles, phalanges and vertebrae, tibias, fibulas, sternums and humeri, ischiums, mandibles, tarsals, and patellae—what lovely, important-sounding words the cormorant had told him when he asked—the pyre was all collapsed in on itself, and reeked a redolent stench of seared tendons, sizzled ligaments, and charred calcium. The crow drew in that sacred stench, and asked himself again, as he had countless times before, whether he loved the roasted pig fragrance of the early fire, when the flesh was burned right off the bones and spiced with the piquance of singed hair, more than this smell, with its lingering notes of thickened marrow, scorched iron, and the faintest hint of mesquite.

Already the beast was stirring, and there was little time to lose. If the monster awoke before the fire was lit, his wrath would know no bounds. The crow plunged into the collapsed pyre, tossing bones this way and that, clearing a bare spot in the center of the fire pit. There the crow made a loose mound of knuckles and toes, and he encircled it with a cone of ribs and thigh bones, laid loosely together. While he worked, the crow sang an ancient song, a song the Old Gods once used to call forth all the creatures and all the plants from the time before time, only now the crow sang the song with the Kiamah beast's name, forsaking the Old Gods, who were dead gods devoured by the beast, for the crow served the living evil that was the Kiamah. He circled the pyre of bones four times, and each time he stopped to offer the glow of the embers in his basket to each of the four directions.

Then he emptied the basket into the center of the fire pit, and he drew a breath of air as big as a whale's lungs, and he blew on the embers. They glowed hotly in the dark night of the Kiamah's belly, and flames grew tall out of that hot glow, and now the cone of ribs and thighs was fully ablaze. Clouds of smoke belched upward, and the crow threw on more bones from the jumble around him, building the pyre taller and wider, and as the fire grew larger the crow passed a wing in front of his face, and grew himself a cubit taller, and now every bone was in the flames. "Kiamah, Kiamah, kiaw aw aw," sang the crow, his power strong and growing stronger, "I give you thanks." And the Kiamah answered with a great smoky belch that shook the whole cavernous belly. The sacred fire was once again lit.

THE HASHISH SMOKERS WERE WELL lit, all four of them, the fisherman so thoroughly 'shish-faced that his head was an anthill, and his thoughts were ants, waving their feelers at one another as they crawled along the tunnels of his mind. The frigate bird puffed up his chest feathers, fixed a haughty eye on the cormorant, and mimicked the crow—"You've no right to judge me"—his voice dripping with self-importance, and then he uttered from his nether end the mother of all farts. That set all of them to laughing, and saying over and over, "You've no right to judge me. You've no right to judge me," until they had a chorus going, the fisherman having found a melody for the words, and they sang the refrain into the dark night. The pelican stood and shimmied on her branch, shaking her ample breasts and the jelly of her belly in time with the words, and when her sarong slipped off, she let it fall to the ground. They stared at her open-mouthed and openbilled, as it were, until the pelican looked down at herself and giggled, and they all laughed and laughed as she danced naked before them. Their hilarity finally spent, they grew quiet for a moment, but as soon as the pelican looked at the fisherman, they both started giggling, not knowing, as one does not always know when under the influence of hashish, exactly why they were giggling, and soon they were all four giggling again.

Their laughter was cut short by a thunderous belch rumbling

through the air, shaking the dead tree on which they all perched. The fisherman clung to the trunk with both arms, and the birds wrapped their claws more tightly round their branches and flapped their wings to keep balanced.

"What was that?" the fisherman said.

"The Kiamah," the frigate bird said. He pointed at the orange glow from down the beach. "The crow has lit the sacred fire again, and the beast, though he dozes perpetually, is hungry."

There came then a silence while the hashish smokers looked around in the darkness, remembering that they were inside the belly of the beast. Above them was a sound so deep and rhythmic that only now did the fisherman realize that he had been hearing it for longer than he knew.

"The beating of the Kiamah's heart," he said.

Yes, mm-hmm, so it is, the birds muttered. The fisherman looked at them all, his strange companions, their eyes heavy-lidded slits. The frigate bird was on a branch above, and his legs were a startling blue. His long narrow bill was cruelly hooked, not unlike the cuttlefish beak. He had been most helpful earlier, but was that not the way with a spy, to be friendly and ingratiating? And what of the cormorant, who had so swiftly shifted himself into an owl earlier, or was it the other way around? How was he to know which was the creature's true nature, owl or cormorant? And the pelican, whose woman's body was so unnaturally topped, her shoulders sloping up to meet that feathered head. A gentle creature by all she had done. Yet the way she sat with her head bent and her pelican bill tucked into her human armpit was somehow the most disturbing thing of all.

"I think," the fisherman said to her, his voice drowsy with hashish, "I'd feel better if you changed yourself back into a bird."

"Oh, mm-hmm," the pelican said, and she waved her hand lazily in front of herself, with the result that her round pelican body returned, and she was feathered down to her waist, but with her human legs beneath her, and her bare human buttocks sticking out behind.

The fisherman sighed and closed his eyes. The birds seemed to be drifting off to sleep, accustomed, no doubt, to sleeping on their perches. He, on the other hand, was stuck where he was for the moment, waiting for his arms and legs to remember how to shinny down a tree.

That was the way with hashish. If one climbed up the rigging to get a fine view while one smoked, it might be a while before one quite remembered how to climb back down. Best to let his mind wander, and so he kept his eyes closed, and he caressed the clamshell tucked in the waist of his breeches.

He was going to have to care for her until he discovered the means to render her whole again. So there was a puzzle, for what did a clam require? Sand and sea was their natural home, but he could not bury her in the sand for fear of losing her. He would have to keep her close. Did she thirst or feel hunger? He had no idea what she might need in the way of food and water. The pelican had told him that the souls slept happily in their shells, dreaming of heaven, but with all the commotion of being dug up by the crow, and flown through the air in a basket, was she awake now? Was she desperate to get out, or had she fallen asleep again, content to wait out eternity? Might she hear him, and know his voice? As he pondered all this he let his arms and legs do what they knew how to do, and he shinnied down the tree.

Smoke from the pyre of bones drifted his way, the smell meaty and rather pleasant, although he shuddered when he thought of what was burning there. The beating of the Kiamah's heart filled his ears with a funereal rhythm, but he was alone on a beach with his beloved, and that was a blessing not to be ignored. Perhaps he would bathe his beloved in the waters of the inlet before they turned in for the night. Yes, and sing to her the sailor's song she had so loved when she was alive. His own fire was banked low, giving off little in the way of light, and as he walked by the fire pit his foot came down squarely in the gobbet of guano the crow had left earlier.

"*Merde*," the fisherman said. That filthy crow. He looked down the beach at the orange glow from the crow's pyre of bones, and he cursed the crow—*may he dine on nothing but turds for the rest of his unnatural life*—for his word was as slippery as bilge slime.

The crow's guano was sticky, and it gathered sand with each step the fisherman took. He snatched up the pelican's sarong, and he walked down to the beach and waded in. He lowered his beloved's clam into the water, rinsing her clean, and he held her next to his heart, where her shell touched the silver chain round his neck. In a low voice he sang to her the sailor's song that had always been her delight.

Believe not what the landsmen say,
Who tempt with doubts thy constant mind,
They tell thee, sailors, when away,
In every port a mistress find.
Yet yes, believe them when they tell thee so
For thou art present wheresoever I go.

When he finished, he held the clamshell up to his ear, listening for any sign that she had heard him, but the clam was silent, as clams are wont to be. So he kissed her, not with the hope that something magical would happen, but simply because he wanted to, and he wrapped his beloved in the sarong. He tied the sarong tightly round his waist with the clamshell secure against his belly, and he dove beneath the surface and swam out to the middle of the inlet. There he lay on his back, the gentle waves rocking him, and he found that with his ears filled with water, he could no longer hear the beat of the Kiamah's heart.

When he returned to his fire pit he undid the sarong from round his waist. He'd had no time to prepare himself a bed, but he was so tired he lay down on the sand next to the fire pit, with nothing but his arm for a pillow, and he held his beloved close. As he drifted off, he heard, from the mouth of the inlet, a song sung by a chorus, and led by two reedy voices, growing closer as the canoe of the dead made its way into the inlet from the sea. The rhythmic sound of paddles stroking the water soothed him as it passed by, and he was far too tired to even raise his head to look. Tomorrow he would look, tomorrow he would find the way to release his beloved's soul, tomorrow all things were possible.

THE CROW STARED INTO THE flames of the sacred fire, seeing all manner of visions in the shifting shapes. It was a good bargain he had struck with the Kiamah. Raven had been a fool to trust him, a god made gullible by his own arrogance, and by the dimming of his wits as he grew old and gray. The crow had played the part of loyal retainer: unctuous, servile, and too timid not to be trustworthy.

"Crow," Raven had said to him, "I grow weary of my nightly trips to feed the Kiamah, and it is my wish that you go in my place."

"Yes, my lord," said the crow. "I am at your disposal."

"Fetch me a basket of eyeballs, and take them to the Kiamah's snout as an offering," said Raven. "Make sure you tell the Kiamah they are from me." Raven never dreamt that the lowly crow would take the opportunity to speak to the Kiamah on his own behalf. "And be sure to include a goodly number of conaria, lest the beast get too lively."

"Yes, my lord," the crow said.

The feathers on Raven's head were white with age, and his rheumy eyes no longer held the steady sagacity that had been the hallmark of his rule on the Isle of the Dead. Save for his nightly trips to feed the beast, he seldom flew anywhere on his tired old wings these days. For a thousand times a thousand years he had ruled the Isle of the Dead with an even-wingedness that was admirable, but now he grew forgetful, and relied ever and ever more on his companions. Once he had been all-seeing, and he had known that his own fate was to be usurped by this very crow, and so he had kept the crow close at hand so as to never let him gain an advantage. But now, in his dotage, with his mind dimmed, he had forgotten the danger that once kept him vigilant, and so it was that the Turropsi had had their way with him, as they do with all beings who walk or fly or slither or swim.

Now was the crow's time to rise up. He had flown from the Isle of the Dead to the far corner of the sky, and there he had entered the throat of the beast, careful not to tickle him with his wings. Onward he flew, the basket of eyeballs strapped to his back, the Kiamah's throat scarred in places from swallowing such huge chunks of the spirit world, until he emerged into the mouth of the Kiamah, where he landed on a tooth.

The Kiamah drowsed, his belly full of all he had swallowed, and his capacity for wakefulness held in check by the conaria he was being fed. The crow shed his crow form and spread his arms, as if he were addressing the greatest of the gods. "O Kiamah, swallower of the spirit world," the crow called out, "it is I, the crow, who brings you a tasty morsel."

The Kiamah grunted, and then he yawned, and the crow held on to the tooth with all the strength of his human arms so as not to be inhaled into the Kiamah's lungs, and held on again so as not to be exhaled into the outer darkness beyond the beast's lips. The Kiamah's mouth snapped shut, almost crushing the crow, who escaped by letting go of the tooth and sliding between cheek and gum.

"What have you brought me, crow?"

"A fine delicacy," the crow shouted, crawling through the gaps between the Kiamah's teeth. He emptied the basket of eyeballs and conaria onto the Kiamah's tongue, and he sang a magical song of the crow to make the treats grow large enough to satisfy the beast. Then he slipped between cheek and gum again, while the Kiamah chewed and swallowed.

"Delicious," the Kiamah said. "Bring me more."

This the crow was happy to do, for he relished the chance to sneak a few morsels for himself, and he would take full advantage.

"You are the devourer of all things," the crow said to the Kiamah. "You are the strongest of the strong. I will bring you more tomorrow."

And so it began. Each night, while the pyre of bones burned, the crow flew to the Kiamah's snout with a basket of eyeballs, or a basket of nipples, or a basket of nether parts, always with a goodly number of conaria thrown in, and each night, the Kiamah demanded more. The crow told Raven that the Kiamah was well pleased with his nightly offerings, but he never mentioned Raven to the Kiamah, until one night, the Kiamah said, "Where is Raven? Is he too lazy to fly here himself?"

"Oh no," the crow said. "Raven is not lazy. Far from it, he is ever so busy with his duties as the King of the Dead."

"Does he not speak of me?" the Kiamah said. "Does he not remember that I am the Kiamah, who is above all kings? Is Raven too proud to fly here himself?"

"Well," the crow said, whispering now, "you didn't hear this from me, but Raven is quite proud of himself. He boasts often about being King of the Dead."

"Is that so?" said the Kiamah, and then the Kiamah harrumphed a great harrumph. "Yet he says nothing about his master, which is to say me?"

"Yes," the crow whispered, "it is so. Well, to be honest, he does speak of you on occasion."

"And what does he say?"

"I am afraid to tell you," the crow said. "You must promise not to devour me in your anger."

"Do not bargain with me, Crow. Tell me what you have heard."

The crow flew to the back of the Kiamah's tongue, ready to flee. "He says, O greatest of all beings, that you are nothing but a bloated lizard, too sluggish to even think."

The Kiamah gnashed his teeth together, grinding them with the fearsome sound of the earth itself shaking and quaking. The crow flew back down the Kiamah's throat a short way, and returned to the Kiamah's mouth only when the beast quit grinding his teeth.

"Bring me Raven," the Kiamah thundered, "and he will know full well my displeasure."

"Yes, your magnificence, I shall do so." The crow turned as if to leave, and then turned back. "Have you considered, O king of kings, that you will need someone to rule the Isle of the Dead in his place? Someone to keep the sacred fire burning, and to carry out your wishes?"

"Mmm-hmmmfh," the Kiamah grunted. "Yes, I suppose so."

"Indeed, your sagaciousness," said the crow. "Might I offer you my services?"

"Good idea," said the Kiamah, "Let it be so."

All of this was as the crow had foreseen. He had only to return to Raven and tell him that the Kiamah had so enjoyed his nightly treats of late that he wanted to thank Raven in person. Raven, flattered by the prospect of the Kiamah's gratitude, suspected nothing, for to him, in this, the winter of his life, the crow was nothing but an errand boy. And his last errand for Raven was to lead him to his own demise.

The crow had helped Raven to limber his tired wings by leading him through a series of exercises, the two of them lifting first one wing and then the other, and then flapping both wings together until Raven's creaky old joints were loosened up enough to fly. Raven was ready for a nap after this, but the crow reminded him of his audience with the Kiamah, and said that the beast was eager to show his respect to Raven, and that he most likely had a gift for him. They flew off together to the far corner of the sky, and then up the throat of the beast, the crow urging Raven onward when he tired, and letting him rest for a good long while just at the top of the Kiamah's throat before they entered the cavern of the beast's mouth.

As soon as the crow announced the presence of Raven the Kiamah made quick work of him, gnashing the last of the Old Gods to pulp between his teeth. The crow, once again sliding himself between cheek and gum, watched from his vantage point, so close that he would himself be gnashed to mush if he moved forward the slightest bit. And when he saw Raven's syrinx appear midst the gore, he gobbled it down, so that now, with Raven's voice box in his gullet, he would possess the power to sing forth the souls of the dead.

Aw aw aw aw aw, thought the crow. *What a clever fellow am I, for I have brought about the murder of Raven, and no one's the wiser.*

Only a fortnight had passed, and the pelican and the cormorant were already in his power. Oh, they put on a show of being independent, but he knew how much they feared him. As well they should, for he could make them disappear just as cleverly as he had Raven. He was lord and master of the Isle of the Dead, and no one, not even the frigate bird nor that newly arrived hairless rogue, could stop him now.

"Interlopers," the crow muttered. "Friggin' frigate bird." And that walking pile of putrid whale muck, so fixated on his beloved. How pathetic was that? Well, they were complications, to be sure, but they were nothing he couldn't handle. And soon, he would have more allies in the belly of the beast. He would summon his congress of crows, and together they would rule the Isle of the Dead.

THE SUN ROSE A JAUNDICED orange, sick from the crow's nightly bacchanal. The fisherman awoke early. The dead tree where he had left his companions the night before was empty. He unwrapped his beloved's clamshell and he saw that the striations of her shell, which the evening before had been shades of gray, were now as brightly colored as a rainbow.

"Praise the gods," he cried out, "she lives!" For surely this was proof that what he held in his hands was no ordinary clam. She had spent the night in his breeches, and she was the better for it. He held her against his heart. Perhaps she could hear it beating, and she would know he had come for her. Her clamshell fit perfectly between his palms. He gazed again at the striations of color, red and orange, yellow and green, blue and violet, and he held the shell up to his ear. She was so close it made his heart ache. In the quiet of the dawn he felt the faint throb of her being, resting inside that shell, as one hears the whisper of a ghost in a dream. It was a wisp of a feeling, not yet quite a sound, but it gave him comfort.

He wrapped her in the damp sarong and laid her down again. He was stiff from sleeping on the sand, but as he moved around, gathering a supply of firewood for the day, his limbs loosened. His fire had gone out while he slept. He shaved a pile of wood shavings with the cuttlefish beak, and he brought out his flint and steel. He took a pitch ball from the silver chain round his neck, unwrapped it, and laid it in a bed of shavings. The pitch ball smelled of his home on the cove, and he wondered if he would ever find his way back. With the practiced strokes of a lifetime, he struck the spark that kindled his fire, and blew on it to make it grow. More wood made the fire crackle, cheering the fisherman further.

He ate the rest of the fish from the evening before, and now, warmed and fed, the fisherman picked up his beloved. He had some questions for the crow, and it was time to get some answers. He walked down the beach to the pyre, a veritable hillock of glowing red embers covered in ash. There were marks in the wet sand where the canoe of the dead had been beached, and many footprints. Next to the pyre was a tall wooden statue of the three birds, carved from a single log and painted in shades of green, yellow, and red. They sat one on top of the other, with the pelican on the bottom, the cormorant on her shoulders, and the crow atop the cormorant, with his wings spread for flight, and a look of mischief in the narrowing of his eyes. The pelican's bill was opened wide, and within it could be seen a wise old woman's face. She was either sleeping, or she was in a trance.

Something in the pyre burned through, and the embers settled, making a sound as dry as grasshopper wings scraping against themselves. The wise old woman opened her eyes, which were round and yellow, and she looked at the fisherman and winked at him. The pelican closed her bill, and the figures of the statue slowly woke up, stretching their wings and yawning. The fisherman gaped at them, astonished, as the figures he'd taken for carved wood came to life, their bright colors changing chameleon-like to the blacks and browns of their daytime plumage. The crow flapped his wings and hopped down from his perch on the cormorant's shoulders.

"Good morning, whale patty," the crow said. "Happy as a clam, We trust?" And at this, the crow laughed his awful laugh—*aw aw aw aw aw*. Behind him the cormorant remained sitting on the pelican's shoulders, both of them with their wings folded, but their eyes open.

The fisherman considered his reply. His first impulse was to drop the front of his breeches and piss on the crow's feet, but he thought better of it. Instead, he bowed his head, both to hide his anger and to fool the crow into thinking that the fisherman accepted him as a superior being. The royal "we" was an invitation to flattery, and flattering words he would offer, but not from a position of weakness. He unwrapped the sarong enough to reveal the clamshell inside, and he held it up to show the crow. Then he raised his head and looked the crow straight in the eyes, and he spoke.

"O wise and benevolent crow," he began, "I thank you for honoring the terms of our bargain—"

But the crow interrupted him. "What was that you said? Speak louder, featherless one, and let everyone hear what you say."

The cormorant rolled an eye at this, and the pelican, squatting beneath him, shuffled her feet in embarrassment. The fisherman sighed. Why, oh why, must this bumptious bird be so difficult, and when, oh when, would he suffer the comeuppance he so richly deserved? The answer to the first question was obvious—because it was his nature to be so, while the answer to the second was known only to gods greater than those here assembled. Still, this was no time to raise a ruckus, so the fisherman began again, more loudly this time.

"O wise and benevolent crow, in whose grace we all wish to abide, let me be the first to congratulate you on your clever restoration of the sacred fire, which I, in the depths of my ignorance, unwittingly caused to be put out. And let me say further that only a crow such as yourself, which is to say a crow of great power, could have done so with such ease. You are truly a virtuoso amongst builders of sacred fires, and a dazzling example of crowish magnificence, before whom I am ever humbled." As he spoke, the fisherman imagined a steaming pile of fresh manure growing ever taller in front of the crow.

In reply, the crow belched. "Livers," he said, "so earthy and tender, though chewy if undercooked. But they give us gas." Then he raised his tail, and from his dungbie he let loose a foul petard. "Awww," he said, "such sweet relief," and then his attention returned to the fisherman. "Well said, O inept drencher of eternal flames. Pray continue, for We sense a request from you in the offing, and We are breathless with antici"—and here, while the crow paused, the cormorant and the pelican waved their wings to clear the air of his odious vapors—"pation."

"Yes, your crow-ness," the fisherman said. The crow looked down his neb at this form of address, but the fisherman pretended not to notice. "May I draw your attention to this clam, which you so benevolently gave to me last evening? I am wondering if you, in your capacity as King of the Dead, have within your power the ability to restore my beloved's soul to her human body?" The cormorant was shaking his head, no, no, no, this was not a good idea to ask the crow for anything, while the pelican looked on sadly, ready to draw forth a healing drop of blood from within her breast, but with no precise notion of where she might drop it.

"Naw aw aw aw aw," the crow laughed. "I've been waiting for this," he said, so entertained that he forgot the royal "We." "This is, as I said when you first arrived, an old story. You come here looking for your beloved, and when you find her, you want her to be just the way you remember her." The crow again looked down his beak at the fisherman, his two black eyes as heartless as lumps of coal. "Well, cookie, it doesn't work that way. Dead is dead, and your beloved's body burned in the pyre the night she arrived. So there's no going back to what was."

The fisherman pursed his lips, unwilling to take no for an answer.

"What you say is true," the pelican said, "but we have, on rare occasions, seen exceptions made to the usual course of events."

The crow turned his head and glared an eye at the pelican. "No one asked you to speak," he said.

"Have you no mercy?" the pelican said. She was trembling beneath the cormorant, but she looked right back at the crow, convinced, as always, that there was a spark of decency in anyone, and that she could nurture that spark into a flame. "Look at what the man has done to get here," she said. "Has he not proved himself worthy? He has her soul, you've shown him that much favor, can you not tell him what he needs to do?"

"Kiaww," the crow said. "Do I look like someone who stands around answering questions just because someone asks?"

"Well, sir," the fisherman said, "you are the captain of this ship, as it were. If not you, then to whom shall I turn?"

The crow gave the fisherman a hard look, but he could not see any lack of sincerity in him. The fisherman stood with his eyes cast down, cradling the clamshell in his hands.

"All right," the crow said. He began to pace, crow-hopping back and forth. "Let's see now," he said, "can you sing? Or play an instrument? There was a fellow who turned up here once who was a powerful good singer, and he got his beloved back. Although his efforts came to naught in the end, as I recall."

The fisherman shook his head. "I can sing, but not so's anybody would be impressed."

"Do you know any sacred songs?" the crow said, still pacing. "Anything handed down from an immortal ancestor?"

"No," the fisherman said. "I know the usual drinking songs and bawdy ballads, but nothing of a religious nature."

"I thought not," the crow said. "Highly entertaining, those bawdy ballads, I'm sure, but not the sort of thing to raise the dead. Do you have anything to barter with? I'm partial to shiny metal objects, although it would have to be something really special."

The fisherman kept his hands at his sides, keenly aware of the silver chain round his neck. Must he barter it away to bring his beloved to life? His pride rose within him, for he was loath to part with it, even though it appeared it was the only thing he had that might satisfy the crow's greed. He put a finger between the necklace and his neck, raising the silver chain.

"Might this be of interest, your crow-ness?" said the fisherman.

The crow stopped pacing, but he barely glanced at the necklace. It was a pretty thing, but he could steal it whenever he wanted.

"Hardly sufficient," he said. His beak opened into an enormous yawn, and he stretched his wings and flapped them a few times before folding them back up. "Well," he said, "I guess that about covers it. I had quite a night last night, so if you'll excuse me, I'll ask you to go back to your end of the beach now."

"Wait," the cormorant said. He hopped down off the pelican's shoulders, his spectacles perched on his bill, and a thick book under his wing. He made his way to the crow, waved his wing in front of himself, and now he wore the cap and gown of a scholar. "We are your advisors—

"Royal advisors," the crow said.

"Yes, royal advisors," the cormorant agreed, although he took a moment to look over the tops of his spectacles at the crow and sigh. "And, as such, I feel compelled to remind you that there is another way." The cormorant opened *Constantine Hermanopoulos's Compendium of Barristical Terms and Legal Precedents for Mortals and Gods*, and flipped pages with his bill, muttering *habeus corpus* and *non compos mentis*, and other such barristical terms to himself. "Ah, here 'tis," he said, "the relevant passage." He held a wing up and whispered to the crow from behind it. The crow listened, and then dismissed the cormorant with a toss of his head.

"So," the crow said, making a great show of how royally bored he was with all this, "Our cousin the cormorant—"

"Distant cousin, to be accurate," the cormorant said, taking a step back from the crow.

The crow, royally exasperated, let loose his own sigh, and continued. "Our distant cousin," he said, looking down his beak at the cormorant, "reminds Us that if the soul within the clamshell were to suckle some breast milk, a new body might possibly be persuaded to grow. Having had no direct experience with this procedure, We make no guarantees."

"And," the cormorant said, "go on, *corpus delicti, quid pro quo*. Tell him the rest."

The crow sighed another royally bored sigh, and then spoke in a rapid, almost singsong voice, as if he were now the barrister, reading aloud the fine print of a particularly boring will. "Should you chance upon some breast milk here, and find a woman willing to suckle your beloved's soul, you will be allowed to live here together for a year and a day. After that, she goes back to her shell, period, end of story, blah-di-blah-aw-aw."

The crow puffed up his chest, his feathers shiny in the morning light, and he fixed one of his black eyes on the fisherman, and spoke now as a judge who took pleasure in passing a harsh sentence on a miscreant. "However," he said, "under no circumstances will you be allowed to leave here with her. And if you stay, you too will die. We will take great personal satisfaction in piercing your belly with Our beak, and pulling out your entrails while you watch. We shall pluck out your tongue, and pluck off your nose, and your ears, and gobble them down. And We shall eat your very soul, and neither you nor it will ever return to the material world. *Capisce?*"

"Understood." The fisherman bowed deeply in front of the crow, the crow's threats rolling off his back like storm water off an oilskin. "Thank you, Lord Crow," he said. "I am in your debt."

The fisherman backed away on the soft, dry sand, his head lowered, the very picture of an obsequious courtier, save for the fact that he was dressed in nothing but his breeches. Like most petty officials, the crow could be flattered, and the result was better than he had hoped. Surely he could find a young mother amongst the newly dead who arrived on the midnight tide. Surely a young mother, just separated from her suckling babe, would be willing, perhaps even eager, to offer her breast to his beloved's soul, wouldn't she? And, in spite of what the crow had said, surely he could find a way to escape this dreadful place with his beloved. The frigate bird had told him there were many places within the Kiamah's belly. Perhaps they could escape the crow's influence and live out their lives in peace.

BREAST MILK INDEED, THOUGHT THE crow. *Now there's a good chuckle.* He might as well send that sailor fellow off to hunt for a wing-backed ziphius, the oft-rumored but never-seen flying whale, or the fabled two-pronged unicorn, with two heads and no tail. Still, he was perturbed by the cormorant's intrusion into matters of state.

"Cousin Cormorant," said the crow, "We'd like to have a word with you."

"Must it be now?" said the cormorant. He was busy with his bill, rooting around in his feathers for feather mites.

The crow leaned in and plucked a tail feather from the cormorant's arse.

"Auk!" said the cormorant.

"Thank you," said the crow. "We are pleased to have your attention. We should like to remind you that We will solicit your advice when We need it, and that you should not offer advice for which We have not asked."

"Must you use the royal we now that he's gone?" said the cormorant. "There's no one here but us, and this charade you play grows tiresome."

"Tiresome?" said the crow. "We shall show you what tiresome is." The crow passed a wing in front of his face, and grew himself taller by a cubit, and he seized the cormorant by the neck, his cruel beak nearly strangling his hapless royal advisor. He lifted the cormorant up until his feet dangled, the cormorant gasping for air.

The pelican flapped her wings and squawked. "Stop that," she said, "you're hurting him."

The crow let go of the cormorant, who flopped to the sand and lay there panting. "Listen, you pribbling, prabbling pair of flap-billed scuts. This is no charade. We are the King of the Dead, and We shall have your obedience, or We shall have your lives."

He brought his beak to the pelican's ear hole, and he snapped his beak shut. The noise made the pelican startle. "You're next," said the crow, "should you choose to oppose me."

The pelican cowered, her shoulders up and her head down to protect as much of her long neck as she could. "I am your humble servant, Lord Crow," said she.

"Excellent," said the crow. He put his wing round the pelican's shoulders, and drew her aside. "We are most gratified to hear you say so. And We have a task for you to perform, so that you might prove your usefulness to Us."

"Yes, Lord Crow?"

"Indeed," said the crow. "We grow weary of feeding treats to the Kiamah. From this moment hence, it shall be your task to gather such morsels and take them to the beast."

"Yes, Lord Crow."

"He favors crunchy bits. Ears, nipples, noses, that sort of thing. Also he is fond of tender bits, lips, both nether and upper, zibiks, scrotums, and so on. Also eyeballs. You must gather them from the newly dead after We have sung their souls free."

"Yes, Lord Crow."

"And one more thing," said the crow, "you must always include a goodly number of conaria, for it is the conaria that keep the Kiamah beast drowsy."

The pelican, who had kept her head down and her eyes averted, now dared in her desperation to obey the crow, to look up at him.

"I fear, Lord Crow, that I do not know where to find the conaria."

Now the cormorant gathered himself together, and regained his feet. "The conarium is an organ," said he, "located in the brain. Some call it the pineal gland, and some the third eye."

"Oh," said the pelican. "How does one get at it?"

"We use Our beak," said the crow. "It's a puny thing, but not so hard to harvest once you've cracked the skull open."

"Ohhhh," said the pelican. "Is there no other way?"

"There is not," said the crow. "You must do this every night, without fail, for trust Us, We do not want the beast to aw-aw-awake."

And so it was that the pelican was given the ghastly task of keeping the Kiamah beast sedated. Cracking open skulls and rooting around inside the brains of the dead made her bilious, and she did so only because she feared the wrath of the crow, and because it was her nature to keep the peace. But each time she filled her basket with handfuls of ears and eyeballs, navels and nipples, and always a goodly number of conaria, she felt, deep within her, a recoil, as if her very soul cringed.

THE FRIGATE BIRD CROUCHED ONE-FOOTED on a perch in the roof of the world, his position precarious, his spyglass to his eye, held there by his other foot. This was the curse of having no hands, but his foot was his only means of holding the spyglass, and the spyglass his only means of watching the Turropsi. They had summoned him from a brothel in Qali, where he had struck up a friendship with a madam, a tickle-tail who was broad minded enough to play at rantum-scantum with a feathered brigand such as himself. She was adept at her arts, and good company besides.

It was his custom to spy out what he could before he entered the dominion of the Turropsi. They lived just beyond the edge of the story of all that is, in a realm of swirling mists, the great standing wave of the present at their backs. The bottom of the wave pulled the mists of all that was possible toward itself, and the Turropsi, a vast swarm of them, formed a net through which their many hands deftly sorted, out of all that might be, what they wanted for their intricate design. Ahead of that net, farther into the mists, were more of them, who used their paddled arms to hold back what was not wanted, and to let through what was. The frigate bird was sometimes allowed to fly into those mists, and it was there that he acquired the knowledge of thoughts as yet unthought, and heard songs as yet unwritten, and saw visions of stories as yet untold.

Far out in the mists, in that region called the Fetch, he saw a line, as if there were a break in the usual ebb and flow. He trained his spyglass on it, and saw that the mists there were funneled through a single point, and beyond that point the mists were heavy and dark. There was a knot of the Turropsi around that point, as numerous as bees in a hive, and they were troubled. Some swam back toward the great standing wave, no doubt carrying with them some new knowledge of this disturbing singularity, while others held back, and it came to him that the Turropsi knew that single point as something monstrous, and fearsome, and that they wished to contain it before it reached the great standing wave.

He felt a hand on his shoulder, and was so startled he dropped his spyglass and nearly fell off his perch. Several things then happened all at once, the frigate bird turning to see one of the Turropsi, that Turropsi reaching an arm to snatch the spyglass before it fell out of reach, the frigate bird himself falling sideways and flapping his wings, the Turropsi pulling him back with several more of its many arms.

The Turropsi were beings like a soft sea creature, part jellyfish, and part octopus. Their movements rippled with an undulance that made him queasy if he stared at it too long. They had clear, dome-shaped, faceless heads, within which could be seen a glowing red organ, and it was from here that their speech seemed to emanate.

Where their heads joined their bodies, they wore a necklace from which depended an abacus of golden beads.

Below the head was a silvery, cup-shaped body, and from that body hung tentacles too numerous to count, with which they could touch the many possibilities floating in the mists. Amongst the tentacles there hung as well some several arms, thicker and more muscular than the tentacles. One arm ended in an eye, with which they gazed into either the uncertainties of the future, or the certainties of the past, and another arm ended in a wide paddle, for shaping the flow of possibilities before they reached the great standing wave, and the remainder of their arms ended in many-fingered hands. This one now handed back to him, with one arm, his spyglass, while with another arm the creature steadied him on his perch. The creature's tentacles fluttered beneath the body, the Turropsi hovering in place.

Never before, to the frigate bird's knowledge, had any of the Turropsi come to the roof of the world. They must have a great need to send one of their own this far into the time-bound cosmos to summon him, for their lives were never-ending as long as they stayed outside the bounds of what already was. This Turropsi risked its own death by coming here.

The Turropsi never spoke aloud to him, but rather their words formed in his mind, and there he heard the creature say, "This way." Several arms beckoned him onward, and together they flew from the roof of the world and into the mists of the Fetch, where this Turropsi led him to a vision of a winged goddess, who lived in a palace high up on the slopes of Mount Agung, in the southern reaches of the great sea. To find her he must start in the land of the living, on Bali Dwipa, a beautiful isle with many rice paddies, and he was to fly upward through the mists that hugged Mount Agung until he passed through the roof of the world. Now the many voices of all the Turropsi were in his head, like a chorus that spoke with one voice, for they were, the frigate bird knew, like a hive of bees, who acted with one purpose, and who all together formed one great mind. "Her name is Dewi Sri," the voices said. "Go to her, and when you have found her, we shall instruct you further."

This the frigate bird was more than willing to do, for Dewi Sri was a great beauty, with a saucy curl to the smile on her full red lips, and the sway of her hips was full of promise. He bade the Turropsi farewell and left the Fetch then, and flew back to the roof of the world. On his way he set aside his plans to return to the delights of that tickle-tail in Qali.

Onward, thought he, for his services were needed elsewhere.

THE CROW, AFTER HE HELD court, decided to drowse away the morning perched on a favorite branch, high up a cedar tree. He'd made quite a night of it, gorging himself until his belly was so full he stuck his wingtip down his throat, so that he might start in again. Three times he'd hurked up his feast of delicacies. Or was it four? Aw-aw-aw-offal, so rich and earthy, heart meat and sweetbreads and liver. Liver was salty, like braised blood, with a hint of wild plums. And tongues, a new favorite. The meat was firm and flavorful, and boneless. What a binge he'd gone on after the first time he tore out a tongue. So many tongues, so little time.

All those bodies coming out of the canoe, milling around, wondering were they really dead, and if they were, where on earth had they gotten to? *Nowhere on earth, my little chickadees. You have left the earth behind.* It must be confusing, this dying, this letting go of who they had been, and what they had done. They all seemed to think they were special, and that their questions deserved to be answered. They wanted an explanation, they wanted sympathy, they wanted to go back home. But there was no return passage for them on the canoe, and explanations, let alone sympathy, were beneath his station as King of the Dead. Sympathy was the pelican's bailiwick. He had his own duties to perform. Getting the dead to line up and be still long enough to cough up their souls was no easy task. *Listen to the song, chickadees, you'll feel so much better if you just listen to the song.*

All those wriggly little balls of slime, dropping to the sand and burrowing in. Though now that he'd eaten a soul straight from the shell, and knew how tasty those were, he ought to try one of the little slimeballs. They might be even better. There was no more Raven, no one to tell him not to, least of all that busybody, the pelican. And what a pleasure it had been to scandalize her. She took the whole business of clams and souls far too seriously. Anybody could see that there were plenty of them, and really, once his plot with the Kiamah had come to full fruition, none of this would matter.

From his perch he could see most of the inlet without being seen himself. The pelican was busy rebuilding her nest, which had been inundated by the wave the great whale had made with his flukes. The cormorant sat on a log, reading *Early Empiricists in the Lands of Araby*, the title in gold leaf on the cover. They'd tottered in when the night was mostly gone, clucking and giggling, obviously impaired, and it took the cormorant three tries to settle himself in his customary perch atop the pelican's shoulders. Even then they looked a bit unsteady, and the crow had considered, before he landed on the cormorant's shoulders, whether or not he might be better off sleeping in a tree. But after half of eternity with that cursèd Raven sitting atop the cormorant who sat atop the pelican who sat atop his shoulders, he was reluctant to give up the privilege of being the top bird.

Heat shimmered the air above the pyre of bones, still burning down from the night before. What a useful thing it was to hold court in the morning, for it shored up his legitimacy as the new king. How many times had he sat with his head bowed before Raven, speaking only when spoken to? Too, too many.

"Kiaw aw aw aw aw," the crow said. "'Tis good to be the king."

He sang his crow song, the sweetest, most mellifluous, most melodic, most utterly expressive, most divinely regal song there ever was, although he knew the other birds, tasteless bumpkins that they were, found it grating and repetitive. But that was their loss, wasn't it, and if they didn't like his singing, they could fly upside down and be-shit themselves for all he cared.

The last of his song echoed off the cliffs, and in the quiet that followed the crow flew from his perch and rose high above the inlet, searching for that meddling scoundrel, the frigate bird. Never before had that blackguard taken such an interest in the Isle of the Dead. He was up to something, and no doubt about it. The crow looked north, and the crow looked south, and the crow looked out to sea, his sharp crow eyes piercing the mists, but the frigate bird was not to be found.

Now the crow flew lower, the better to spy out that rube of a sailor, who was wading out into the water. He had his fire burning again, that walking, talking dunghill, and the crow's blood grew hot with his anger. Had he not bartered the clam for the fire, and wasn't this new fire a trespass on their agreement? Of course it was, and for that there must be a reckoning. The sailor was engrossed in his clam, holding it up to his ear as if it possessed the power of speech, and so the crow flew low over the sailor's fire and let fall a nice fat gobbet of guano. He missed the fire by a yard, but still he left a foul surprise for the sailor, and there was plenty more guano where that came from. He would improve his aim with practice.

The cormorant and the pelican were paying him no mind, the one busy reading and the other busy nesting. *Excellent,* the crow thought, *now is the perfect time to visit my diggings.* And so he flew into the canyon at the back of the inlet from whence flowed a stream. His wingtips brushed the rock walls at the narrowest spots, so great was his wingspan, a proof that his stature was regal and imposing. He flew into the bowl at the head of the canyon, and into the mist from the waterfall there, which bathed him with cool droplets of water that clung to his feathers. Swiftly he circled the bowl, banking his turn, the rock walls flashing by mere inches from his belly. He spread his wings and slowed himself to land in the cave behind the waterfall. The cave was shallow, but the crow had been busy, digging away at the back. He passed a wing in front of himself, and now he was one of the mole people, squat and paddle-footed, yet with a stature befitting a god. This was a shape he had practiced often of late, and he knew it well. What a sly fellow he was, a trickster beyond all others, full of guile. He crawled into the hole he'd started at the back of the cave, and he began to dig. Ahh, the smell of the earth, the feel of it giving way to his claws, the velvety darkness wrapped around him, it was all so delicious. And the silence. A deity never had a better chance to be alone with his thoughts.

Deeper and deeper he dug his burrow, packing the earth to the sides with his paws. How far he had to dig, he did not know, but he kept at it, smelling his way forward, delighting in the thousand different scents of the earth, here loamy and damp, there rusty and dry. He dug until he was thirsty, and then he made his way back to the beginning of the burrow. He passed a paw in front of his face, and made himself a crow again, and he flew to the pool at the bottom of the waterfall, where he quenched his thirst. Soon he would dig his way through to the material world, and once through, he would wreak havoc upon all that was.

"Aw aw aw aw aw," the crow laughed. "What a bad, bad, bad bird am I!"

THE FISHERMAN CHECKED HIS FIRE, and then he walked out to the point where the inlet gave way to the sea. Here the waves broke off shore, a sure sign that there was a sandbar beneath the surface. Twin pinnacles of rock framed the mouth of the inlet, the distance between them the broadside of a ship. He stood with his back to the cloistered kingdom of the crow, the salt air fresh in his nostrils. He would bathe his beloved in the waters of the open sea.

Beyond the pinnacles was a narrow beach. The beach was cliff bound, with dark rubble at the base, and then sand. He rounded the point and walked northward along the base of the cliff, picking his way through the rubble. When he turned back to look it was as if the inlet did not exist, for he could no longer see the gap in the cliff walls that was its mouth. The empty sand was dotted here and there with whitish rocks. The waves rolled in and broke, their rhythm a comfort to him, and a reminder that he had always been a man of the sea. They spent their force in foam and flux on the rising slope of the beach, the waters of each wave pulled back to shape the next, and in that constant motion sometimes rolling the strewn rocks closer, and sometimes dragging them seaward.

There was something strangely familiar about those rocks. He saw, in the rising curl of the next wave, a rounded one, and he marveled at the way it floated in on the surface of the water after the wave broke, shiny and white in the foam. It rolled up the beach and came to a rest on the wet sand. He walked down to it, and when he picked it up and turned it, a pair of empty eye sockets stared back at him.

A skull. Human. He dropped it. The skull lay on its side, and seawater from a spent wave half filled the empty brainpan. The rounded end of a leg bone poked through the sand a few feet away. All along the beach he saw bones, some on the surface, some half buried, some barely there. He saw jawbones, kneecaps, teeth. Here a ribcage lay buried, the sand striped with ribs. A pelvis appeared in the curl of the next wave, and it washed up on the beach as if it held no more significance than a jellyfish.

He headed back toward the mouth of the inlet unnerved, and he hurried along the sandy beach to put some distance between himself and all those bones. He went back to his fire, and he lay his beloved down in the shade of a log. He took wood from his pile and added it to the coals, and the ritual of keeping the fire going restored to him some small sense of ordinary life.

He squatted by the fire for a time, poking at it now and again to soothe himself, but he could not idle the day away. The problems of shelter and sustenance remained, and he busied himself with the task of gathering the next day's firewood, thankful that it was so plentiful here. He laid the last armful of wood on his pile, and then he unwrapped the sarong, and he saw that the clamshell was dry. He had not even bathed his beloved in the open sea. He held her up to his ear, but he heard nothing this time. The hellish Sea of Bones had made him lose sight of his purpose, and now her soul was at risk.

He carried her down to the waters of the inlet, where he waded in until he was waist deep. He dipped her in the cool water, and held her there, her shell secure between the palms of his hands. A shadow passed over him, and when he looked up, he saw that cursèd crow high above, a dark silhouette against the blue sky, and he remembered seeing that sky through the cormorant's magic spectacles. Whether the things these birds conjured were real, or if they simply beguiled him into seeing things that were not there, mattered little. They were sorcerers, that was plain enough. Best to be humble, and patient, and to plot an escape.

But he did offer a prayer to the pelican, who he thought was likely a goddess of renewal, for she had healed him. It was always best to pray to the local gods, even if one did not believe in them. When he looked up again, the crow was gone.

Ah, the freedom of birds. In his youth, on a voyage that took him to Xcalak, in the Kingdom of the Mayans, he had seen the sages of Uxmal flying on their wondrous planks. If he could fly like them, held aloft by wood and incantation, he would simply spread his arms and be gone, leaving the hellion crow and all his carrion-grubbing ways behind.

He held the clamshell up to his ear again, and the faint throb of her being had returned. The fisherman allowed himself a sigh of relief. He headed back to his fire to fetch the sarong, but before his feet cleared the waters of the inlet, the crow swooped low over his head and dropped a large splotch of guano at the edge of the fire pit, and his relief was overtaken by anger. He ran to his fire, and he kicked sand over the guano, cursing as only a sailor can curse. "Shite!" he yelled. *"¡Mierda! Cac! Skita! Dr'q!"* and with each word he stomped his foot and shook his fist at the sky. "I'm sick of this dung heap of a place! I want to go home!"

His anger eased, he took the sarong and soaked it in the waters of the inlet. The gentle waves of the inlet calmed him, and his breathing slowly returned to normal. He tied the sarong round his waist again as a kind of belt, with his beloved tucked securely against the small of his back.

It was time to explore inland. He walked along the beach, past the great pyre, still hot from the night before. Although he kept an eye out for the crow, that scurvy lurch of a bird was not to be seen. The pelican cooed a greeting as he walked by but stayed busy, scraping a nest for herself in the sand. The cormorant once again wore the cap and gown of a scholar, but he looked up from the book he was reading and called out a greeting.

"Ho," said the cormorant. "How are you on this fair morning?"

"Thirsty," said the fisherman. "Is there fresh water at that end of the inlet?"

"Oh yes," said the cormorant. "A freshet flows from a canyon there."

The fisherman nodded, and, eager for a drink of water, he bade the cormorant farewell. A furlong or two beyond them the inlet gave way to a salt marsh. There were reeds and grasses growing in hummocks, and farther on, cattails and water lilies and lotus flowers. Enormous trees grew almost to the edge of the marsh, and he entered the cool shade of the forest, where the ground was firm and the walking easier. Here and there a maple or an oak was mixed in with the conifers. Deeper in was a jumble of fallen limbs and undergrowth, but he found he could pick his way along just inside the border without much trouble. The oaks had the girth of ancient giants, and the firs and cedars grew straight and very tall, like masts. What boards he could mill from those oaks! The fisherman marveled at the ships that might be built from them, with masts the height of the walls of the great cities.

Rock cliffs walled in the back of the marsh. There were mountains beyond those cliffs, hazy and blue in the distance. No birds called, no insects whirred, no squirrels chirped, as if this were a place before places, in a time before time. In the silence he heard the soft shush of water flowing, growing louder as he neared the cliff. The wetlands narrowed and gave way to dry land along the base of the rock wall. He came to the freshet, which flowed from a narrow canyon, the water so clear as to be invisible where it was still, and the streambed a mosaic of stones, of rusty red and malachite green, of silky brown and azurite blue, all of them rounded and smoothed. He knelt to drink from the stream, the water soft and sweet in his mouth, and he drank his fill, though it made his teeth ache with the chill.

He returned to his camp, his thirst quenched. Fresh water he had in abundance, though he would have given a great deal for a thing so simple as a bucket. Or better yet, some carpenter's tools, with which he could fashion a bucket, and a simple hut for shelter. But having none, he looked about, and took note of the dry sea grass in the strip of land where the beach gave way to the forest. And so he spent the middle of the day gathering a mound of dried grass and making himself a sort of nest from it. When he was done he had a softer bed than the sand he'd slept on the night before. He had to laugh when he stood back and looked at it, for there was something undeniably bird-like about his efforts.

Now he took his beloved's clamshell down to the water for a swim. Swimming together had been one of their great pleasures when they lived in her hut on Ambon. Often they had swum out past where the swells broke and floated on their backs, holding hands, their worldly cares left behind. They spoke little, the sky vast and blue above them, and they loved each other much. When it was time to return to the shore, they swam in to the shallows together, and his beloved wrapped her arms round his neck and he carried her through the surf. The weight of her was sweet in his arms.

He waded out until he was waist deep, and he lowered the sarong

into the water, and he unwrapped his beloved's clam, clasping it
between his palms. His grip was firm, for he feared that if she fell
from his hands she would burrow into the sandy bottom and disappear. She was, he reasoned, a clam, and so she would do as clams do.

He brought her shell back out of the water, and he saw that the striations of color were now indigos and deep greens, and not so vibrant
as they had been the day before, but still beautiful. How strange and
marvelous was this vessel in which she lived. There was a tiny opening at one end, a gap where the lips of the clamshell did not quite
meet. Perhaps she could hear him. "Cariña,"‡ he said, speaking aloud
his love name for her for the first time in many a year, "I have come
for you at your request." He took the silver chain from his neck and
draped it across her shell. "You see," he said, "we are meant to be here
together, for your chain found its way to me, and its arrival was the
first in a chain of miracles that have brought us together. Fate has
been kind to us."

He listened, but the clam made no reply. He kissed the tiny opening at the end of her shell. "To be expected," he said, "given your
current abode." And so he sang to her a sailor's song.

> *she sat down right beside me*
> *and took me by the hand*
> *she kissed me till my lips did bleed*
> *she loved me on the strand*
>
> *O she's the girl I left behind me*
> *she's the girl I left behind*
> *she's the girl I left behind me*
> *the girl I've come back here to find*

The sound of his own voice soothed him, and he was in great
need of soothing, although his outward appearance was calm. But
there was little that was not extraordinary about his circumstances,

---

‡ *Cariña*, dear reader, is not proper Spanish, which would be *cariño*, but when it comes to
love and the terms of endearment, let us not quibble over spelling. The fisherman's Spanish
is a sailor's Spanish, and all he cares about is giving his beloved the love name that best suits
his heart.

and the uncertainties regarding his beloved's future weighed on him. He had only the crow's word for the notion that he could produce his beloved in her corporeal form, and the crow was a tricksy varlet, and not to be trusted. Still, the cormorant had produced a book of laws for the Isle of the Dead, and the crow had, however begrudgingly, acceded to the cormorant's advice.

The sun was now three quarters of the way across the sky, heading for the eastern horizon. The fisherman walked back to his fire and his bed, and he lay himself down to sleep. He would be on watch tonight at midnight, ready to greet the canoe when it arrived. Best to rest himself until then. Everything hinged on whether or not he could find a woman willing and able to suckle his beloved's soul.

THE GREAT CAVERN OF THE belly of the beast was lit with brightest moonglow, which waxed and waned even though the moon was no more, just as the tides yet rose and fell, as if the sea itself honored the vanished moon. Now came the sound of the fish eagles singing their song, high and keening, as the canoe of the dead entered the inlet from the sea. Their canoe was elaborately carved, the prow rising to a head with the fierce eyes, eye mask, and hooked beak of their kind, the stern with the fish eagle's fan of tail feathers. They stood one in the prow and one at the stern, their wings spread, beating the air together in time. Between them sat a row of paddlers down each side of the canoe, the strokes of their paddles matching the beat of the fish eagles' wings, the canoe gliding through the water with the silky strength of an orca.

The paddlers were the dead, their paddles worn smooth by the innumerable hands of those who had come this way before, and as their canoe sliced through the waters of the inlet they added their own voices to the fish eagles' song. They sang the high lonesome sound of lives left behind, of love lost, of all that was once possible fading into what would now never be. Onward they came, and the song made one fantastical creature of them, a cedar-bodied chimera with paddling arms and flapping wings and a fish eagle for a head. Carved along both sides of the canoe were the Old Gods: Cedar Man,

Bear, Sasquatch, Clam, Eagle, Coyote, Orca, Raven, and many more. All of them gone now, devoured by the beast, for that was the way of things after the Kiamah came, and the Old Gods gave way to the new.

THE CROW PERCHED IN HIS favorite perch, and the canoe, full of fresh fuel for the pyre, turned its prow to the beach. The nightly arrival of the dead was proof that all men came to their just end. Although really, justice had nothing to do with it. All that mattered was that their bodies be burned to warm the beast.

Justice, it struck him, and not for the first time, was sentimental, a luxury for the living. It had no place here, and he was just the bird to show the dead how things really are.

The pelican was on the beach in her usual spot, ready to greet the new arrivals, the cormorant and that sailor fellow with her. Their conversation fell silent as the fish eagles' song filled their ears. Though the crow would have liked to eavesdrop on them, he was not overly concerned. No doubt the sailor was going to look for someone to suckle his clam.

"Aw aw aw aw aw," the crow laughed. This was likely to be a night like no other.

With a last mighty pull on their paddles, the dead beached their canoe. Their song finished, the fish eagles held their wings spread, and directed the dead to climb down. Those in front went first, and were followed by the rest of the paddlers. They kept coming, more and more of them, a man holding a pot-metal funnel, a woman with an awl in her hand, the tools they had been using the moment death overtook them. They gathered on the beach in a huddled mass, and it seemed to the fisherman that the number of the dead on the beach far exceeded the number of paddlers in the canoe. Without the fish eagles' song to bind them together, they fell into confusion. The pelican moved amongst them, greeting them with kind words, assuring them that they were where they were supposed to be.

They were men, women, and children, and they were full of questions. "Is my husband here?" a woman asked. "Yes," the pelican told her, "but you must be patient." "Is this a dream?" a man asked. "Oh no," the pelican said, "but something wonderful will soon happen." "What will happen?" a child asked, and the pelican said, "You will find out what comes after life, and you will be content." "Are you a pelican?" another child said, and the pelican said, "Why yes I am. Aren't you the clever fellow?"

The fisherman entered the crowd, looking for women of childbearing age. His beloved was wrapped in her sarong at his waist, freshly bathed. "Where am I?" an old woman asked him. "Is this heaven?" a girl with the face of an acolyte asked. "I'm hungry," said a boy, "Is there any food?"

"I don't know," the fisherman said. "I think not," he said. "I'm hungry too," he said, pushing his way past their questions and their reaching hands. "Care for a bite of my apple?" said a woman, with a wide grin and a gap between her front teeth. She put her hand on the front of the fisherman's breeches, and whispered into his ear. "For a ducat I'll give you a ride you'll never forget." The fisherman pushed her hand aside, and kept moving. He had neither the inclination nor the ducat for a common gill-flurt. Through the crowd he saw a woman holding her arms across her belly the way one might cradle a newborn pup, and he made his way to her.

"Pardon me," he said. "Are you a mother?"

"Aren't we a bit cheeky," the woman said. "What business is that of yourn?"

"It's a long story, ma'am, and I mean no disrespect, but I have an urgent need for a nursing mother."

"Ahh," the woman said. She looked him straight in his face, understanding softening the glare she'd greeted him with at first. "You've a young babe, and no mother to feed the wee one."

"Yes," the fisherman said. Best not to go into too much detail at the outset. "Are you, by chance, in a position to be a wet nurse?"

"That I am," the woman said. "But I'd as soon nurse my own babe as someone else's. He died of the pox, not three days ago, and here am I, dead meself, I suppose. Do you know where I might find him?"

"Alas, no," the fisherman said. "You'd have to speak to the crow about that."

"Crow?" the woman said. "What crow? And what sort of place is this, where I have to speak to a crow to find me babe?" She rose up on her toes, and began looking about, and she cupped her hands on her breasts as she did so. "I don't mind telling you, sir, that me tits is full till me nipples ache. I tell you what, you help me talk to this crow, and he finds me babe for me, and I'll be happy to share what I've got here with yourn."

"Mmmm," the fisherman said. "The crow is, well, not exactly a very helpful fellow. But I could certainly relieve some of the pressure you're feeling at present. Perhaps we could speak to the crow afterward."

"You could relieve the pressure?" she said. "Just what have you got in mind? Where's that babe of yourn?" She looked around him on one side and then the other, as if he might have behind him a servant holding his babe.

"She's right here," he said, patting the sarong tied round his waist.

"There?" she said. "She must be a little bit of a thing."

There was nothing for it but to produce his beloved's clamshell and hope for the best. He drew it out, and held it cupped in his open palms.

"Things are a bit different here," the fisherman said. "If you'll allow me to explain—"

"Are you mad?" she said. "That's nothing but a clam." She took a step back from him, and bumped into a woman behind her. "Get a load of this," she said. "Straight from Bedlam, this one is, thinks that clam there is a newborn babe."

"No, not exactly a babe," the fisherman said. "It's a clam, true enough, but inside is the soul of my beloved, and if you let her suckle, she will become a woman again."

"A woman from a clam?" the second woman said. "What a nutter." She turned to another woman and said, "Did you hear that?" as did the first woman, and word began to spread, the murmur spreading through the crowd, and people pointing at the fisherman.

"That blue fellow."

"Wants to suckle a clam?"

"Why is he blue?"

"Who knows? This whole business is more than a bit strange, don't you think?"

The fisherman pressed forward, trying to reach anyone before the rumor did, working his way to the canoe, where people were still disembarking. But they were men and boys, they were women too old to be of use to him and girls too young, and as he watched, he realized he really did not know how a wet nurse came to be a wet nurse. Was it necessary for the wet nurse to be nursing her own child? Or was it the suckling itself that brought forth the milk, never mind whose babe did the suckling? He thought it was the suckling, but would his beloved's clam be able to suckle?

He could only hope so. Desperate as he was, when the last man clambered down from the canoe, and turned back to help a comely young maiden, the fisherman seized the only opportunity left to him. She was of marriageable age, and the bodice of her dress was stretched taut with her bosoms. Could a maiden be a wet nurse? He did not know, but well endowed as she was, she looked a likely prospect.

"There you go, daughter," the man said. "Let us find someone in charge here, and we'll get this travesty sorted out."

He was a man of some means, judging by his cloak and breeches, and his boots with bright buckles. Not the sort to take much notice of a humble fisherman, but there was no helping that.

"Pardon me, sir," the fisherman said. "I'm sorry to be so forward, but I must ask you if your daughter could assist me in a matter of great urgency."

"Excuse me?" the man said. "What is it you want?"

The fisherman hesitated, unsure of quite where to begin.

"Come on then," the man said, "Be quick about it. I've urgent matters of my own to attend."

"Well, sir," the fisherman said, "This is going to sound a bit daft, but here on the Isle of the Dead, it happens that the souls of the dead are found in the shells of clams. Like this one," he said, holding forth his beloved's shell. The man took his daughter's hand and drew her close.

"Say again?" he said.

"It so happens," the fisherman said, speaking more quickly now, "that this particular clamshell contains the soul of my beloved, and if your daughter here, who is such a virtuous exemplar of womanhood, would be willing to let my beloved's soul suckle on her breast, then my beloved will be restored to her own womanly body, and I would be eternally in your debt."

"Suckle, you say?" the man said. "Like some common beast of the barnyard? You insult me, sir, and you insult my daughter. Be gone with you, before I run you through with my blade." The man reached for his boot, from which he drew a knife, the handle of such a size that it promised a formidable blade to follow.

The fisherman backed away. He was unarmed, and, even if he somehow won a fight with the father, the fight would gain him nothing with the buxom daughter. The man swept his daughter into the cover of his cloak, and headed into the crowd. "I shall report him to the authorities," he said, "and we shall see him in the stocks."

Ye gods, the fisherman thought, *this was going to be difficult.* He tucked the clamshell back into the sarong at his waist, and he waited by the canoe, hoping that somehow an opportunity would arise.

While all this was going on, the three birds worked at getting the crowd lined up in rows, which required that the cormorant and the pelican explain over and over again that everyone must line up and be still so that further explanations could be offered. The crow, for his part, did little, other than to let his patience wear thin, and to occasionally squawk rudely in someone's ear. "Line up, you big rube," he said, "awwww, right over there." And he would point with a wing to where a ragged line of the newly dead was beginning to form on the beach.

When at last everyone was in line, the crow uttered a very loud "Kiaaaw!" He strutted back and forth in front of them as he spoke. "First things first," he said. "You are all dead." And at this, he laughed—*aw aw aw aw aw.* "Second," he said, "I'm going to sing you all a song, the most beautiful song you've ever heard, and you will all remain silent and listen. After I've finished singing, I will take a few of your questions, with preference given to those who aw-aw-offer me anything bright, shiny, and metal that you might have on your person."

The man of means stepped forward from his place in the line, with his daughter still held close under his cloak.

"Just a moment, sir," he said. "Before we proceed, I have a matter of some urgency to report, regarding an insult to my daughter's honor."

"Really?" the crow said. "Your daughter's honor, you say?"

"Yes, sir," the man said. He hooked his thumbs into the sides of a vest he wore, as if he were a barrister before the high court. "May I proceed?"

"Oh, please do," the crow said. "I can scarcely wait to hear what you have to say."

"May it please you," the man said. "I have been approached by a man wearing the clothes of a pauper, who has insinuated that my daughter would be willing to perform an unnatural act involving a clam."

"A clam, you say?" The crow looked down to where the fisherman stood at the prow of the canoe. *This is too, too rich,* the crow thought, *and just the sort of mischief to keep things from getting dull.* "Please, go on. Of what nature is this unnatural act?"

"Well, sir," the man said, "if I may, I should like to speak it out in a more private circumstance. Is there somewhere we may retire?"

"Look about you," the crow said. "What you see here is what there is, and as you can see, there is no place to which we might retire."

"May I approach?" the man said.

"Oh, yes," the crow said. "Please do."

The man took his cloak off, wrapping it round his daughter's shoulders, and he left her to step up to the crow. With his voice lowered in discretion, he said, "I do not wish to injure my daughter's delicate sensibilities by saying this for all to hear, but that man down there"—and here he pointed at the fisherman—"asked my daughter to suckle some foul clam he's carrying around. He's got some cockamamie story about a soul trapped inside."

"Cockamamie, you say? I see nothing cockamamie about such a story. Sounds right enough to me. But your daughter, does she have any milk in her breast to aw-aw-offer?"

"Certainly not, sir!" the man exclaimed. "She is virtuous, and betrothed to a man of considerable fortune, an earl, no less, whom she would never dishonor. You insult me sir, with your insinuation."

"Do I?" the crow said. "Well, good. You strike me as a man who has borne far too little insult in his life. Insults build character, a quality you clearly lack."

"This is outrageous," the man said. "Do you know to whom you speak?"

"I do not," the crow said. "Pray enlighten me."

"I am Samuel Chowder, Esquire. I am the Viscount of Sark, and I daresay I am your superior in every way, and most especially in character. I demand satisfaction."

"And you shall have it, as soon as you listen to my song."

"I will not be put off one moment. Not for you, not for your song, and not for any cause on this earth."

"Well, that's a good point, because the earth you are familiar with is quite a long way from here," the crow said. "And here, we do things my way."

"Where I come from, sir," the man said, "we eat your kind." He was flushed with anger, and fairly trembling with the urge to strike this crow.

"Do you now?" the crow said. "Well, cookie, here, I eat your kind. Isn't that ironic?"

The man reached down and drew forth the knife from his boot, which he brandished at the crow. "Now we'll see who's to dine and who's to be dinner," the man said.

"Samuel Chowder, Esquire," the crow said, "Viscount of Sark. Do I have that correct?"

"Yes," the man said, "not that it's any of your business." He circled to the right, light on his feet, shifting the knife from one hand to the other, a man who knew how to handle himself and his blade. The dead gathered, making a ring around the crow and his adversary.

The crow raised a wing and brought it down in front of himself, shifting into human form, though he still had his crow's head. A collective gasp came from the crowd, and Samuel Chowder, shocked by the sudden transformation of his foe, stopped moving. The crow grabbed him by the shoulders, and he plunged his beak into the man's chest. Ribs cracked, the man's eyes bulged, and the tip of the crow's beak pierced right through the man's back. Samuel Chowder's knife fell to the ground. The crowd shuddered, many of them looking away, while the eyes of others showed rank terror as they watched. Though his daughter, showing her mettle, spat at the crow, and had to be held back by those around her. The crow pulled back and plunged his open beak at Chowder's heart. With a wet, sucking sound, he worked his beak wider and deeper into the man's chest. More ribs cracked. Grown men, shaking with fear, pissed themselves. The crow lifted Chowder right off the ground, and shook him, and then tore his heart right out of his chest. Chowder slid off the beak and fell to the ground. He stared at the blood-rimmed hole in his chest. Something slimy and pale lay there, his very soul, naked and exposed. The crow took Chowder's heart in his hand and held it up for all to see, thick dark blood dripping down his wrist, and Chowder shrieked when he saw it. And then he fainted.

The crow turned himself round inside the ring of the dead, showing off his grisly prize. He sat Chowder up and slapped him until his eyes opened. "Samuel Chowder," he said. "Esquire. Viscount of Sark. I always like to say the name before I eat the heart." He opened his beak wide and put the man's heart in, and he swallowed it whole.

The crowd, as one, uttered a cry of horror. A man in a red cap fell to his knees, heaving up his last meal, and others followed suit. Men moaned, women wailed, children cowered, and a great amount of weeping swept through the crowd. Chowder's daughter dropped to the sand, her senses dark.

Chowder gazed dully at the crow, his jaw slack. The crow uttered a loud belch before he spoke. "By the way," he said, "in my capacity as King of the Dead, I hereby decree that your daughter's betrothal has been, shall we say, annulled." At this, Chowder's face took on the aspect of a tragic mask, and Chowder uttered a howl of despair. Tears ran down his ruddy cheeks, and the crow opened his bloody beak wide and laughed, "Aw aw aw aw aw."

The crow stood tall, and grew himself taller by a cubit, so that he towered over everyone. "Get back in line," he thundered to the crowd. "Line up behind this tasty morsel of meat."

When they were all in line the crow said, "Listen to my song. You have something inside you that wants out. Let it go, for it's of no use to you now." His song began as a series of twitterings and clicks, of rasping moans and rattles from deep down his throat, growing louder and louder, until it became a harsh chant—*kaw, kaw, kaw, kaw*—that went racketing on and on and on. They listened, their chests juddering—*kaw, kaw, kaw, kaw*—and though the sound curdled the very marrow in their bones, and made them want to run to escape it, they found they could not turn away. Something within them responded to the crow's insistent chant, something that rose up from deep within their bodies, something that had been wrapped round their hearts their entire lives and had never been separate. Now this something must leave them, called out by the song of the crow, and there was naught they could do to stop it. One by one, several by several, and many by many, they coughed up their souls. Slimy with mucous, pale as pearls, squishy as squids, their souls fell out of their mouths and landed on the sand. And as the dead watched, their souls burrowed into the sand and disappeared.

"Any questions?" the crow bellowed. But the newly dead were left dazed and even further confused by the loss of their souls. Dozy and stupid, they stared at the crow, who again laughed his terrible laugh, "Naw aw aw aw aw." At the crow's command, they marched up to the pyre of bones, blank-eyed and ashen of face, and they climbed onto the fire. From time to time, the crow spied a pendant or a scarfpin he fancied for its gleam of metal, or a pennywhistle or a pair of tongs, and he plucked them away, and tossed them onto a small pile of such things near his feet. When all the dead had heaped themselves onto the pyre, the crow blew on the embers to make them grow, and in no great amount of time the sacred fire blazed high again.

The fisherman had stayed at the canoe, but as soon as the dead marched away, the fish eagles beat their wings and ran the canoe to the other side of the inlet. He was left entirely alone, save for his beloved clam. "I've failed you, my darling." He was close to tears, but rather than surrender himself to weeping, he began to hum an old Portuguee song, as much to himself as to the soul he held in his hands. It was the song of a man whose life is on the sea, and who longs for the woman he left behind. Or maybe it was the other way around, for his command of the Portuguee tongue was slight, and perhaps it was the song of the woman left on shore, searching the horizon for the ship that will bring back her man.

At the pyre he saw the crow tearing at the bodies there with his savage beak. His skin was shiny with sweat, and glowed a deep red in the firelight, but he was as impervious to the heat and flames as the phoenix. The fisherman lowered his eyes from the sight, and he walked up the beach to where Samuel Chowder, Esquire, had tried to defend his daughter's honor. Ye gods, that horrific scene would never have happened had he not approached them. He was cursed no matter what he did, and not one step closer to the restoration of his beloved's body.

There was, however, one small thing to be gained from this otherwise dreadful evening. The fisherman picked up the knife of Samuel Chowder, Esquire, and it was a fine blade indeed, forged by a master, and honed exceedingly well. There was a lot a man could do with a blade like that.

"Come, beloved," he said to the clam, "let us take a swim together, and then we shall retire for the night."

The fisherman slept poorly after his swim. In his dreams he was troubled by a deep cough, as if his lungs were trying to turn themselves inside out.

THE PELICAN, TOO, SCARCELY SLEPT that night, troubled as she was by the violence of the crow. The cormorant had climbed on her shoulders as always, and he promptly fell asleep. But she felt him tucking his head as far into his wingpit as he could, and she knew he was afraid. Low bird on the totem pole, she listened to the crow snore, his belly fat with his grisly treats. The comfort of the heat from the pyre felt undeserved. Her bill was wide open, and within it, tears fell quietly down her old-woman face.

She sorely missed Raven, who was aloof and regal and a friend to no one, but who nevertheless conducted his affairs in an orderly manner. Raven had ruled here for a thousand times a thousand years, and a thousand days more than that, since long before the Kiamah. Before the Kiamah, the fish eagles had brought only the souls of the dead on the canoe, nestled together in baskets like so many shelled oysters. In those times, the sacred fire was a beacon to guide the canoe. The birds had simply taken the baskets up and down the beach, tipping them over gently so the souls could burrow into the sand and form their clamshells. Afterward the birds gathered at the beached canoe and talked amongst themselves, drinking lotus blossom tea they warmed on the sacred fire, and listening to whatever gossip the fish eagles brought from the material world.

All this and more the pelican remembered while the cormorant and the crow slept. The Kiamah had come from the bottom of the sea, where he birthed himself from all the evil in the souls of the dead who were killed in the War of the Gods. Those warriors were so consumed by battle lust that they beheaded their captives, and did not tarry to give their own fallen so much as a prayer before they threw them all overboard. This evil sank to the bottom of the sea, and gathered there like quicksilver, festering for a hundred times a hundred days, until it formed a serpentine line of oily muck, and became the Kiamah. On a black night when the moon was no more than a sliver of silver, the Kiamah rose up to the surface, his long, sinuous body leaping into the night sky, and he swallowed the moon first thing. The pelican saw the moon disappear into the mouth of the beast, and she was so frightened she dove to the bottom of the inlet without warning anyone. This was her shame, which she carried always.

The moon was salty, and in his thirst the Kiamah swallowed all the lakes and rivers, and with them he swallowed the Old Gods, Otter and Turtle, Frog and Dragonfly, Goose and his lesser cousin mallard, and all those who kept their lodges on the banks and in the water. The Kiamah gnashed the Old Gods between his teeth, grinding them with his molars, and killing them once and for all. The pelican and the cormorant escaped by making themselves small, and hiding in Bear's navel, who was asleep for the winter. Next the Kiamah swallowed the mountains and the forests, and with them he swallowed the Old Gods, Bear and Sasquatch, Cedar Man and Coyote, Wapiti and his lesser cousin deer, Rattlesnake and Ant, and all the rest, grinding them to blood and pulp with his molars, devouring their spirits, and growing ever larger and more powerful. This time the pelican and the cormorant escaped by hiding in Orca's blowhole. Next the Kiamah swallowed the sea, and with the sea he swallowed the Old Gods, Salmon and Orca, Shark and Squid, Crab and Starfish, Mussel and his lesser cousin oyster, and all the other gods who swam or scuttled or clung, and these too he gnashed into blood and pulp, until they were no more, and their spirits were devoured. This time the pelican and the cormorant escaped by hiding in the clouds, from whence they watched the Kiamah grow ever larger with all he swallowed.

Last the Kiamah swallowed the air, and with the air he swallowed the Old Gods, Eagle and Owl, Heron and Hawk, Swallow and Flicker, Hummingbird and his lesser cousin flycatcher, and all the rest, gnashing them, grinding them, and devouring their spirits. Only the frigate bird escaped entirely, for only he of all creatures who flew could fly far enough and high enough to leave the spirit world behind. The Kiamah devoured all else, save for a few of the birds, who flew into his mouth and hid between his teeth. These few, the pelican and the cormorant, and Raven's lesser cousin the crow, they also survived, and with them Raven, who was the only one of the Old Gods left alive. The Kiamah agreed to let these few live if they would do his bidding. He let Raven go on ruling the Isle of the Dead as he always had, with the pelican, the cormorant, and the crow as his servants, as they had always been. So to them fell the task of harvesting the souls of the dead, who arrived now on the Isle of the Dead with their bodies intact, as the Kiamah decreed.

This also did the Kiamah decree, that the bodies of the newly dead should be burnt upon the sacred fire, so that the heat of that fire might sustain him, and the smoke of that fire might cleanse him. He sent Raven and the pelican and the cormorant back to the Isle of the Dead, but the crow he drew aside, and to the crow he boasted that he was greater than any god, old or new, and he told the crow to be his eyes and ears on the Isle of the Dead, for he did not trust Raven, who might well seek to avenge the deaths of the Old Gods.[§]

So it was Raven who tended as ever the sacred fire, and Raven who enlisted the frigate bird as his envoy to the material world, and it was Raven who told the fish eagles that they must now build a bigger canoe, so that they might gather the bodies of the newly dead on the far shore and bring them to the isle. The pelican continued to be kind and compassionate to all, and the cormorant continued the duties of a scholar-philosopher, and of a barrister when one was needed. It was the cormorant who discovered, through his scholarly perusal of the *Minutes of the Mediterranean Society of Mind-Altering Potions*, that feeding conaria to the Kiamah would keep him drowsy.

---

§ 'Twas at this meeting that the Kiamah, dear reader, speaking almost as if he were looking over the shoulder of the author of this very chronicle, decreed that when the tale of the Kiamah was written, that only his name should be capitalized, and that the rest of them should all remain lowercase beings, raven not Raven, crow not Crow, cormorant not Cormorant, and pelican not Pelican. Then the cormorant spoke on Raven's behalf, saying Raven was the last of the Old Gods, and that his name should also be capitalized, and the cormorant produced a copy of *The Shikaakwa Manual of Style (Pre-Gutenberg Edition),* and read out the relevant passage, so that the Kiamah was persuaded. Thus was Raven granted the privilege of having his name remain capitalized, as ever it had been.

And when Raven grew into his dotage, he gave to the crow the grisly duty of harvesting the conaria, and taking them to the Kiamah, and by doing so he made clear to all that the crow was still the lowliest amongst them.

And so the bodies came, and were burned in the sacred fire every night, so that the heat of the burning bodies would feed the Kiamah, and Raven ruled over the new order for a hundred times a hundred years, and a hundred days more than that. And in all that time the sacred fire had never gone out, nor had there been so much as a ripple of change in the nightly routine. The dead had obeyed Raven without question, his bearing being one of nobility. He spoke to the dead in reasonable tones, never raising his voice, and the three of them, pelican, cormorant, and crow, had ushered the dead from canoe to pyre without much fuss. A line of torches showed the dead the way, and when it was time for them to cough up their souls, they were told first that someday soon they would be reborn again, and that their souls would sleep happily and in comfort until that day came. Then Raven sang softly to them, cooing and cawing as if he were soothing his own chicks in a nest. If someone objected in any way, the pelican gave them a soothing cup of blue lotus tea. Most succumbed to its soporific effect, and anyone who still resisted was brought to Raven, who opened his neb and breathed a calmative breath into their faces, transporting them from agitation to acceptance.

Now the old traditions had changed. The crow's song was harsh, as if he were berating forth the souls of the dead rather than coaxing them. The torches were gone and the soothing tea as well. The dead were arriving in ever greater numbers, and the crow wanted them moved swiftly to the pyre. He had always taken shiny bits of metal from the ashes, but now he took anything he fancied from the dead before their bodies were burnt. Raven had lived an austere life, never indulging himself by feeding on the dead, but not so the crow, who had been sneaking tasty morsels from the pyre for a long time before he usurped Raven.

Eternity was not supposed to be this hard—so thought the pelican. The savagery of the crow last night sickened her, and made her pluck at her feathers with worry. The only hopeful thing was the fisherman, who she hoped had been sent from the material world to restore the natural order of things. She should find a way to help him, that much was clear. Old crone that she was, she had no breast milk to offer, but there must be something she could do.

AT DAWN, HIGH ATOP MOUNT Agung, Dewi Sri lay on her side, her eyes closed, the forest outside her palace awake with the buzzing and whirring of cicadas beyond counting, and the song and chutter of birds beyond number. She listened, as she often did when first she awoke, and felt both the familiar comfort of this, her home, and the nearly endless longueur of her life here. She had lived a hundred times a hundred years in this most beautiful of all places, and yet there were times when the beauty of it was tedious. She wondered if she were nearing the end of her long life.

When she opened her eyes, the frigate bird was beside her, sitting as he would sit to sleep in a nest. There was mischief in the way his head was cocked to one side, and she read the frigate bird's desire for her in the ruffling of the red feathers of his throat pouch. Poor fellow, he could not help but reveal himself, for he wore his heart on his throat.

She had allowed him into her bed for her own pleasure, and he was a most welcome change from her usual paramours, this buccaneer, who took charge of the coupling, and showed her not one whit of deference, treating her instead like a bit of pirate's booty he had captured for his own amusement. And yet he had also shown her how to ride his bill with her nether lips to the very heights of pleasure. He was a brigand, but he was generous in the arts of love.

When he caressed her bare bosom with his wingtip, looking to arouse her into continuing the frolic of the night before, she brushed it aside and sat up. The time for him to take liberties with her had passed, however welcome those liberties had been. She gave him her most serene smile, the smile of someone beyond desire, and the pleasures of the flesh.

He looked properly abashed for a moment, and at that she was pleased, though she gave no sign of it, for she was well-practiced at the theater of being a queen.

"I am at your service," he said. His throat pouch collapsed, and she knew she had the better of him now.

"Are you?" said the goddess. "It might be prudent for me to count my treasures before you leave, for you are widely known as a thief."

"You wound me, dear lady," said the frigate bird. "You are yourself the only treasure I desire."

She kept her gaze steady, for she knew full well which of them needed the other more. "You spoke last night," said she, "of a favor I might do you, beyond the favors I've already shown you." And here she let show, in the saucier curve of her lips, some of the lust she'd shared with him, and then, just as swiftly, returned her face to serenity.

"I am sent by the Turropsi," said he, "to fetch you to their domain."

"The Turropsi?" said she. "Who might they be?"

"They are the weavers of fate, my queen."

"Ah. The Nasib, we call them here. And what do they want of me?"

"I am not privy to the whole of their design," said the frigate bird, "but one ignores them at one's own peril."

"So have I heard," said Dewi Sri. She rose from the bed and found her sarong, tossed aside the night before after she had made a delicious slow torture of unwrapping it from her shapely hips. Now she wrapped it round herself again, leaving her breasts bare as was her custom, and she thought of her ancestors. This was the call of her destiny, foretold by her dreams, and she must either answer it, or disgrace her family.

DAWN CAME WITH A QUALMISH light over the inlet, cast by a bilious green sun rising in the west, and in that light the fisherman's skin was a bluer blue. As the sun rose the green faded from its light, and the blue tinge on his arms, which had started out as almost the same color as the cormorant's eyes, became a pale hue, yet did not lose entirely its blueness.

The fisherman sat in the sand next to his fire, turning his new knife over and over, feeling the balance of it. It was a far better knife than the one he had lost when he was swallowed by the whale. The blade was larger, the steel well forged and hammered, and the keenness of its edge sufficient to split hairs, not that he had any hairs to split. Sharp enough that he might have shaved with it, but he had no need of shaving. Two days he had been here, and yet he had no stubble on his face, nor on his head, nor in his nether parts. Blue skinned and hairless, and would his beloved love him more or less for that?

He gave the knife an upward toss, and it turned once before it fell handle first into his hand. A well-balanced tool that would lend itself to many purposes. He would make a spear of it with a stout pole, and use it to spear fish. He would cut down branches and build himself a lean-to. And if it came to murder, this blade would make short work of slitting the crow's throat.

He was rooting around in the forest, his beloved wrapped in the damp sarong at his waist, when he found a stout stick, of a length suitable for making himself a short spear. He came out of the forest, headed for his fire, and there the pelican was. She opened her bill and smiled her skew-whiff smile at him, and he smiled back. She was a strange friend to have, but he was grateful for her presence nonetheless.

"Ho, fisherman," the pelican said. "How does the morning find you?"

"Ho, pelican," the fisherman said. "I am well enough, and you?"

The pelican squatted on her flat gray feet on the driftwood log by the fisherman's fire, and the fisherman sat beside her. The pelican produced a fish from her pouch, a gift for the fisherman, and with his fine new blade he cleaned it with a few swift sure strokes, and spitted it over the flames to cook. He gathered the entrails on the blade of his knife, and he was about to toss them into the fire when the pelican said, "Oh, I'll take those." She opened her bill, and the fisherman dropped them in.

"To each his own," the fisherman said. The pelican stretched out her neck and swallowed.

"How is your beloved?" the pelican asked.

In reply the fisherman produced his beloved's clamshell from the sarong. The striations of blue and green had darkened to the blues and violets of twilight, colors that were the last to surrender to the black of night.

"Lovely colors," the pelican said. "I've always been partial to deep shades of purple."

"They keep changing," the fisherman said. "Is that the usual way?"

The pelican considered for a moment, and then she hopped down off the log, and lay her bill alongside the clam and closed her eyes to listen. "Yes, I believe so," she said. "Your beloved is dreaming of the night sky, just after sunset."

The fisherman nodded. "She loved to watch the sun go down. We lived on a beach, where the sunsets were glorious." The pelican's striped bill lay in his lap, a thing of beauty. He stroked the neck feathers of his friend idly with a finger.

The pelican cooed. "How romantic," she said. "She was the love of your life, was she not?"

"She was," the fisherman said. "She came to me late, when my beard was already gray of whisker, and my pate thin of hair. I had long since decided that love was a young man's game, and a foolish illusion."

"Was she young herself?" the pelican asked.

"Oh no," the fisherman said. "She was midway through her fourth decade, and I had begun my sixth."

For a thousand times a thousand years the pelican had watched the dead arrive on the canoe, but she had not always understood what she saw in those brief interludes before their souls were harvested. This much she knew, that in death, love was often lost, and seldom found. She had never been paired with anyone in all her days, but the idea of romance excited her now as it never had, and here, in the fisherman, she had someone who could tell her how it all worked.

"You two had much in common?" the pelican said.

The fisherman nodded. "We were well matched in temperament, and in our love for a life lived close on to the sea."

"How did you meet her?" the pelican said.

"I met her on the island of Ambon," he began, "one of the spice islands, in an alehouse known as the Firefly. What started as a sailor's dalliance with a comely barmaid grew straightaway into something greater, for we were quickly besotted with each other, and though we were not young, we were as eager as any pair of young lovers the world has ever seen.

"To prove my love, I spent the last coin in my purse to buy a silver chain from a sea captain, who claimed it was once an adornment of the Raha of Siam. I did not believe the sea captain's story, but I gave the chain to my beloved, and there was delight in her eyes when first she saw it, and it was so finely made it lay like a silk cord against her skin. Every morning when she woke she touched it before she opened her eyes, and every evening she brought it to her lips before she gave herself to sleep."

"This is that same chain?" the pelican said. She brought an eye close to the chain, and studied it well. "It must feel divine," said she, "to have a lover who gives such a gift." She lay her head back down in the fisherman's lap and looked up at him. He ruffled her neck feathers, and then stroked them smooth again. "Do go on," she said.

The fisherman shook his head ruefully at the foolishness of the next part of his tale. "For all the heat of my passion," he said, "for all the adoration in her eyes, the sea still called to me. Not so much for the voyage itself, but because I wanted to live out my days with some hard coin to show for my years as a sailor. And there was coin to be had working the ships of the spice trade. I told my beloved I wanted to build her a proper house, to show her that she was my queen, and for this I needed some hard coin, for brass hinges. The rest I could make, but I wanted only the best for her, and brass hinges I could not make.

"She looked at me strangely then, as if I were some creature she had never met before. She told me she needed no house other than the house of our love. She was happy enough in her hut between the sea and her garden. Her voice grew louder with each thing she said. 'For brass hinges you would leave me?' she shouted, 'for brass hinges?' Only then did I know my own foolishness. I begged her forgiveness, and by evening we were back in each other's arms.

"That night I lay next to her on a sleeping mat on the hard-packed ground, listening to the quiet rise and fall of her breath, and I thought I had laid my foolishness to rest. But my dream of sailing one more time, and of returning home with a purse fat with silver so that I might live out my days in a proper house, with a proper bed, that dream crept back into my thoughts like a thief and stole away my resolve. And so, a few weeks later, I sailed on a dhow carrying nutmeg, mace, and cloves to Malacca, a journey that took me away for a fortnight or two. She let me go, for she could see that my need was great, and we renewed our love when I returned."

"I have seen the dead quarrel over money," said the pelican. "It is a strange thing," she said, "given that they have no more need of it once they arrive here."

"There is much blood spilled over it where I come from," said the fisherman. "And much heartache made for the lack of it."

"As we see in your story. Please, do go on."

The fisherman nodded his agreement. "I made several voyages on the dhow, earning a little coin each time, and each time, upon returning to my beloved, our love was the more fierce for my having gone away. She forgave me my absences, and I came to take her indulgence for granted.

"Some two years later a sailing ship arrived in the harbor of Ambon to take on cargo. The ship was bound for a great city on the North Sea, halfway around the world, where spices fetched a price to ransom a king. Those who signed on to sail her were promised a rich reward. I worked for days loading her with fresh water and spices, dried fruit and dried fish, and I made some coin. But it was not enough coin to satisfy my pride, and so I came to my beloved the night before the ship sailed, and I asked her to let me go.

"'Two years,' I told her, 'and I will return, and we will live out our days in comfort.'"

The fisherman drew a spiral in the sand with the tip of his stick, circling inward. The striations in his beloved's clamshell were turning to blues and jaundiced yellows, the colors of a bruise.

"And so began the quarrel that broke us," the fisherman said.

"A quarrel?" the pelican said. She raised her bill from the fisherman's lap and stood, flapping her wings before she settled herself again on the driftwood log next to him. "Surely a love so great would have survived a mere quarrel?"

The fisherman raised his eyes to the heavens and shook his head no. "That night we had a great row, and she told me that if I left I should never come back. I would not let her order me about so, for though she was the queen of my heart, she was not the captain of my actions. Or so thought I at the time. I turned my back on her and walked away. She came after me, I thought to wrap her arms round me and beg me to stay, but instead she clawed my back from shoulders to waist, and spat upon me, and cursed me as a sailor, who are the worst of all men. I walked away bleeding, and full of pride, and unrepentant for the wrong I had done her."

"And so you set sail?" the pelican said. The fisherman nodded.

"I did, and I was well paid when we sold our cargo. My purse was heavy with silver, and I kept it behind a hollowed-out plank above my bunk. And out of devotion to my beloved, I kept the fall front of my breeches closed, and stayed away from the bordellos and the temple whores. But on the return journey we sailed into a never-ending gale that forced us west by southwest for forty days and forty nights. The ship was pummeled, the sails stretched, our every effort to outrun the high seas useless. We were blown a thousand leagues off course into the southern sea, and we were on the wrong side of the world.

"In the end we were shipwrecked off the coast of a barren land. The last of the sails ripped from the mast, and the ship wallowed. The gales blew our ship onto uncharted rocks where it was battered apart. Most of the crew took to the boats, and they were promptly capsized and swept from sight. I watched the last jack sailor of them rise up the side of a great wave, cursing all the gods of the sea as only a sailor can curse. And then he was gone.

"I stayed on board the wreckage until the last, clinging to the remnants of the stern. What saved me was the lessening of the storm. The winds weakened, the rain let up, the seas grew less fierce. Pieces of the ship floated all around me on the waves. I made out a beach in the distance, and beyond it a line of trees. A large block of beeswax floated up from the hold, and I slipped into the water. I wrapped my arms round the beeswax and kicked my way shoreward."

The fisherman shook his head as if he scarcely believed that he had survived. The pelican cooed at him, her bill by his ear, and he felt the soothing note of her voice where the soft skin of her pouch touched his shoulder.

"I was marooned on that barren shore. My purse, fat with silver, went down with the ship. I built myself a shack from the wreckage that washed up on the beach, and a sturdy little skiff with which I fished the local waters. I resigned myself to living out my days there, with nothing but my memories of her to keep me company.

"Or so I thought, until the letter arrived. It was written by her brother after she died, and it told me that her last words were that she still loved me, and that she would wait for me on the Isle of the Dead." The fisherman fingered the silver chain round his neck. "The chain was folded within the letter, so I knew it was from her. And so I set out in my skiff, and was swallowed by the whale, and the rest you know."

The pelican cooed and clucked. "'Tis a story of a great romance," said she, "and it is not yet over."

"I let pride be my undoing," the fisherman said, "and it shipwrecked my heart."

"Pride," the pelican said, "is at the bottom of all great mistakes."

They sat quietly and gazed into the fire. The fish on its spit dropped the occasional bit of fat to sizzle on the coals. The fisherman rose to turn the fish, and when he sat back down he placed the clam-shell on his knee. She was so close, his beloved, and yet he could not hold her in his arms.

A shadow passed over them, and when they looked up, they saw the crow, who flew on a bit and then circled back. He came in low over the fire, and he let loose a gobbet of guano that landed on the fisher-man's head. The fisherman shrieked as guano ran down his cheeks, and his eyes burned with the sharp reek of ammonia. He jumped up and ran to the inlet, where he plunged into the water. He swam a few strokes underwater, and when he surfaced, water ran off his head and carried sticky guano into his eyes.

"Swive me!" he cried. He sank his head underwater again, shaking it and then swiping at his eyes with his fingers. The burning slowly lessened. He used his hands to clean his pate, and then he came up for air. The pelican was flying straight at him, coming in for a water landing. Her speed took her past him as she hit the water.

"Are you all right?" she called.

"My beloved," he yelled. "She must have fallen from my knee." The crow might have taken a second pass and stolen her. He took a stride toward shore, and another, and another, the pelican paddling to keep up with him.

"Wait," she said, but the fisherman was too worried to wait. The pelican flapped her wings and paddled her feet, half swimming, not quite flying, until she was in front of him.

"Stop!" the pelican said, and the fisherman stopped. The pelican opened her bill, and there, in the bottom of her pouch, lay the clam, like a baby in the womb. "I brought her along. I thought you might want to bathe her."

"All I want," the fisherman said, "is to slit that crow's throat and be done with him. Can you give me one reason why I shouldn't?"

The pelican's yellow eyes were steady, save for one sideways blink of her inner eyelids. She dipped her bill into the water, filling it with the sea, and then raising it up and letting the water spill out.

"Take her," the pelican said, opening her bill wide. The fisherman did so, and he tucked the clam into the sarong still tied round his waist.

"Violence only begets more violence," the pelican said.

"So I've noticed," the fisherman said. "But a dead tyrant commits no more evil acts."

"You are no match for the crow," the pelican said. "Only a god can kill a god."

"So kill him," the fisherman said. "Surely this would be a better place if he no longer were king here. Surely you, or the cormorant, or the frigate bird could kill him."

"We cannot," the pelican said. "He is too powerful. Once we might have, but now that he rules in place of Raven, he is our master in more ways than one."

The fisherman shook his head, his anger subsiding. He waded toward shore, and the pelican swam along beside him.

"There may be a way," the pelican said, "but we shall have to be clever."

"And what way is that?"

"Patience," the pelican said. "We do not yet know."

THREE DAYS AND THREE NIGHTS then passed on the Isle of the Dead. The fisherman spent these days caring for his beloved, and establishing his camp. He moved his nest of grasses under a cedar tree at the edge of the forest, and built himself a lean-to of branches, sharpening the ends with his new knife so that he could drive them into the ground. He cut smaller branches from live cedars, and wove these limber boughs crosswise across the top of his lean-to, and that night he fell asleep with the piquant resin of fresh-cut cedar reminding him of the sweet-and-sour fragrance of his beloved's loins. It rained while he slept, and although the raddled structure kept him from being soaked, he awoke damp and shivering.

And so he scouted the cliffs for better shelter. He wanted a cave, where he could have a fire pit at the mouth, and a bed beneath an overhang of sheltering rock. He found no such place along the cliffs that enclosed the inlet, and so he turned his attention to the forest, where he sought the darkest places, where the canopy overhead was thickest, and would provide the most shelter from the rain.

There were no paths in the forest, only a hodgepodge of fallen limbs draped in moss, and a riot of ferns, nettles, and sowberries. Here and there a yew tree grew in the shadow of the forest giants. It was slow going, clambering over dead branches, weaving his way through the undergrowth. The canopy was high above him, and through it the sun sent arrows of light from an ever-replete quiver. A gleam of metal in the forest duff caught his eye, and he bent down to find a gold brooch, with a large ruby set in the metal, and a girandole of pearls hanging below. It was finely made, the sort of reward his courtesan mother was given by her princely patrons, and worth a small fortune. He put it in his pouch with his flint and steel, and he offered a prayer to Sadr, god of navigators, in hopes that he might find his way back home, where a jewel such as this might buy some ease for his beloved and himself.

He was well into the forest, and when he raised his eyes he saw a curious mound a little farther on, beneath a cedar tree as big around as a large coracle. The dull gleam of tarnished metal broke through the surface of the mound, which was very nearly as tall as he was, and wider than the tree it stood beneath. It was a mound of shiny metal objects, rather like the treasure hoard of a dragon. There was a good deal of jewelry—brooches and pins, earbobs and rings, bracelets and beads—all of it in a jumble of silver and gold, copper and brass, nickel and bronze. The mound of bijoux was layered with dried guano, and topped with generous dollops of fresh crow mess. When the fisherman looked up, he saw a stout branch a good ways above the pile, a branch suitable for the perching of the crow, and so he understood this mound to be the crow's own collection of pretty things. The crow must sit on that branch, examining his treasures until he grew bored with them, and let them fall to the ground.

From the inlet he heard the raucous, grating laughter of the crow—*aw aw aw aw aw*—and he immediately felt like a thief about to be caught out in the very act of thievery. He put back the silver torsade he was holding, which had been, perhaps, the crowning glory of a lady's hat, and he looked all around for the crow, or one of his spies. He stepped back from the mound, and it was then he saw, almost buried at the base of it, the head of a felling axe.

The fisherman walked slowly all the way round the cedar tree, his head swiveling in all directions, up and down and before him and behind him and to the sides, and he saw that other bits of jewelry lay scattered on the forest floor. When he came back around to the mound, he knelt and carefully pulled the felling axe out of the pile. The handle was gone, rotted away, but the head was intact, and still had an edge of sorts, although it was covered in rust. There was a clanking of metal as the mound settled on itself, filling in the space where the axe had lain, but the fisherman reassured himself that he was alone, and unobserved, and then he pulled from the pile a wedge, and a second wedge, and a forming chisel.

Praise the gods, he was a carpenter again. With these few tools and his knife he would need no cave for shelter. He lacked a saw, and a hammer, and a beetle, and various other tools of his trade, but this was treasure enough to change his life here, and he dropped to his knees, and said a quick prayer to Ebisu, the lucky god of fishermen and merchants, and another prayer to Dayea, goddess of secrets. He carried his new tools back to his lean-to, taking care to stay in the forest and avoid the open sky lest he be seen from above. He covered the tools with the forest duff under the cedar tree that was his shelter, and then he laid himself down in his nest, where the light through the cedar's boughs and the raddled roof of his lean-to was soft on his eyes, and he allowed himself a moment of hope.

IT WAS DURING THOSE THREE days that the colors of his beloved's clamshell dimmed, and the striations lost all sense of the sky, let alone a rainbow. On the morning of the third day he brought his beloved's clamshell out into the light, and the striations were colored in shades of umber. The pelican came by his fire that morning, and when he showed her his beloved, she clucked deep in her throat.

"Of what does she dream now?" the fisherman asked.

Again the pelican lay her bill alongside the clam, and closed her eyes to listen. "She dreams now of her dead body being laid out, and then buried beneath the earth."

The fisherman said, "And is she happy? You told me the souls dreamt of whatever heaven they desired, not of being dead and buried."

"This is troubling," the pelican said. "First she dreams of twilight, and then of burial. I fear that we are losing her."

At this the fisherman's spirits fell, for he knew not what to do. Two nights had he stayed away from the nightly landings of the canoe of the dead, afraid that his presence there would provoke more violence from the crow. Staying away troubled him, for there was no other chance to find a woman to suckle his beloved's soul, but his dreams were vexed by the eyes of the dead, his sleep poisoned with the crow plunging his beak into the chest of Samuel Chowder, Esquire. He had only seen it from afar, over the backs and heads of the crowd, but in his dreams he heard the terrible crack of those ribs breaking, and he saw the man's daughter faint dead away. He had bolstered himself with the illusion that his beloved prospered in her clamshell, even as he avoided finding her a wet nurse. Now it seemed he had no choice but to return to the pyre to seek her salvation.

"I have a notion," the pelican said, "a way that I might bring forth your beloved from her shell."

"Yes?" the fisherman said. "Do tell."

The pelican hopped down off the log, and examined the clamshell. "Yes," she said, "you see the opening there, where her clam foot can come out? Hold her so the opening is straight up."

The fisherman did so. The pelican lay her bill against her breast and vulned herself, piercing through her flesh with the hooked tip. She drew forth a drop of her own blood, which hung from the tip of her bill, red and rich with life, and she let it fall into the opening in the clam's shell. The striations of umber deepened and reddened, and the fisherman felt a trembling from within the shell that matched the trembling of his own heart.

"Something's happening," he said. He gazed at the shell, willing it to open. The pelican brought one yellow eye close, but the trembling stopped, and the shades of umber faded, and the shell did not open. The pelican lay her bill against the clamshell, and she listened with her eyes closed, and then she raised her head. A tear fell from one of her yellow eyes.

"She dreams that she is a grain of sand, falling through an hourglass."

The fisherman held his beloved to his heart, and he wept.

AND SO ON THE THIRD night he returned to the beach to again meet the canoe of the dead, and he stood shoulder to shoulder with the cormorant and the pelican. His beloved was tucked into the front of his breeches, and although the night was cool, sweat trickled down his sides from his armpits.

"I am a peaceable man," the fisherman said.

"Mm-hmm," said the pelican and the cormorant.

"I do not wish to cause any harm," the fisherman said.

"Mm-hmm," said the pelican and the cormorant.

"That crow is going to feck with me, isn't he," the fisherman said.

"Mm-hmm," said the pelican and the cormorant.

The pelican, overcome with worry, plucked at her feathers with her bill. She pulled one out from her belly, and let it drop to the sand, where it joined a few of its fellows.

"Stop that," the cormorant said. "Restrain yourself, you're a god."

At this censure from the cormorant, the pelican seized a few more feathers with her bill and pulled them out, revealing a small patch of bare skin.

"I can't help myself," the pelican said.

The fisherman put his hand gently on the pelican's neck and stroked her there. "Calm yourself," he said. "We've a job to do here."

Now the canoe of the dead entered the inlet from the sea, the singing sad and particularly beautiful that night, for it so happened that there was in the canoe an entire choir of castrati who had fallen to their deaths when a high balcony collapsed at their patron's castle. The dabbling wet sound of their paddles dipping into the water gave time and tempo to their song, and the canoe of the dead came out of the darkness and into the red glow from the pyre of bones.

The crow flew down from his perch, and the canoe turned to beach itself, the paddlers putting their backs into it to drive their vessel up on to the sand. The crow landed behind the fisherman, and he leaned forward to whisper in his ear.

"Good evening, your feculence," said the crow. "Back for another clambake, eh?" And the crow laughed, "Aw aw aw aw aw. Well, this should be a lot of fun."

The crow hopped up to the prow of the canoe, shoving the fish eagle aside. "Welcome, one and all, to the Isle of the Dead," he said. "Please, step down and warm your bones on our lovely fire."

A rough-looking bunch of brigands were the first to disembark, the manly crew of some marauding pirate ship, a scarred and battle-worn lot who were missing an eye here and a hand there. They were followed by the dead from a battlefield on the steppes of Khazaria, fierce-looking horsemen all, and not a woman amongst them. Then a long line of boys climbed down, each one more seraphic than the last.

"Where are the biscotti?" said one. "We were promised biscotti." "Sì," said another, "e espressi, per favore, ci hanno promesso espressi."

The fisherman's spirits drooped as boy after boy came out of the canoe and began milling about.

"Is there a café about?" they asked. "We're all famished, all that paddling has simply worn us out."

No, sorry, uh-uh, no such a thing here, said the birds, please line up over there. The crow watched the fisherman as each of the newly dead stepped down, his black eyes delighting in the man's growing despair. There came a few women after the castrati but these were old women long past their childbearing years, and though some of them hoped to find their long-lost babes, their infant children who had died years and years before, they were in no shape to suckle them.

"You should have been here last night," the crow cawed. "We had a caw-aw-adre of royal wet nurses come through, their udders bursting, poor dears."

"You didn't fetch me?" the fisherman said to the pelican.

"I was going to," the pelican said. She plucked at her belly, worrying the feathers there, and when she looked up again, her yellow eyes were filled with tears. The cormorant held up a wing, and from behind it he whispered into the fisherman's ear.

"More savagery," he said. "The crow ate their nipples as soon as they set foot on the beach."

"I see how it is," the fisherman said. Fate had brought him all this way, and put his beloved's soul in his very hands, only to beleaguer him. The last of the dead climbed down from the canoe, an old man with a cane, and a giant of a Cossack with the face of an executioner, who made a great show of cracking his knuckles and glaring at the fisherman, as if he were choosing his next victim.

"I think I shall go hang myself," the fisherman said. He could make a noose out of the sarong. Or he could jump off a cliff. No one was listening to him now, the gods too busy herding the dead to pay him any more mind. He headed back up the beach toward his fire.

He was not, in truth, feeling much like killing himself, which seemed a messy proposition, and an indulgence that would satisfy the crow far too much. But it was time to face the ugly truth. His quest was over. In the morning, he would take his beloved down to the wet sand and bury her, so that she might recover her clammish health, and someday be reborn again. And then he simply had to find the way back to his home on the cove.

"GOOD LORD, THAT WAS BORING," said the cormorant. He was walking up the beach with the pelican in the light of morning. Once again the crow had held court, strutting back and forth in front of them, spouting off about what a great king he was, the size of the pyre last night, the night air warmed with the dulcet scent of castrati roasting on an open fire. He'd complained about their lack of testicles, but he'd more than made up for it by eating their tongues. "And making us sing that awful song," the cormorant said. "My throat hurts just thinking about it."

"'Tis a catchy tune though," the pelican said, and she began to sing, *"We all live on the Isle of the Dead, Isle of the Dead, Isle of the Dead—"*

"Stop that," the cormorant said. "I'll have that silly ditty stuck in my head for a week."

The pelican ceased, a little forlorn at giving up the comfort of her new favorite song, yet unwilling to inflict any discomfort on her fellow deity. The fisherman was ahead of them. He was on his knees in the wet sand, digging a hole with his hands. A dragonfly flew in off the waters of the inlet and hovered above him, its wings whirring, but the fisherman paid him no mind.

"Greetings and salutations," the cormorant called out. The fisherman kept on digging. Tears ran down his cheeks and fell to the ground. The sarong with his beloved's soul inside lay next to him. The hole he was digging was the size of a bucket from a well. He was shaping the inside of the hole to a perfect roundness, and so intent on his purpose that the birds stayed silent while they watched.

"Where I come from," the fisherman said, "digging a proper hole is the last good thing a man can do for someone he loves." The birds clucked and cooed in agreement, and the fisherman scraped and patted smooth the inside of the hole. Satisfied finally that it was as round as he could make it, the fisherman leaned back. He brushed the sand from his hands, and he picked up the sarong, and he unwrapped his beloved from the folds of the cloth.

"I fear I am too late," he said. "I meant to bury her alive." The clamshell lay in the palms of his hands, leached to the same shade of white as the bones that littered the beach beyond the mouth of the inlet. "Is this not the color of death?" he said.

Now gathered around the hole, the pelican, and the cormorant too, shed funereal tears. With great care the fisherman lowered his beloved's clamshell into the hole, laying it to rest on the bottom. "I am sorry," he said. "I meant well, but I have done you harm."

A great sob unleashed itself from within his chest, and with it all the grief he had been carrying inside came rushing out. His breath caught again and again in his throat, was squeezed tight there, and then let go. His voice keened beyond words. The pelican laid a wing across the fisherman's shoulders. A small clot of sand fell into the hole,

and scattered a few grains onto the clamshell. He plunged his fingers
into the sand and smashed a handful to each eye. He leaned back on
his heels and raised his face, and he wailed out his grief.

The sand fell from his face, and he opened his eyes. Seaward, high
above him, two figures flew in tandem. One was the frigate bird. The
second was unknown to him, but as it came closer the creature appeared
to be part bird and part woman. Gold flashed off her wing feathers.
They circled the inlet and then soared in and landed on the beach, and
immediately the frigate bird turned to his companion and puffed up
his red throat pouch. She gave him a slow, regal nod, barely deigning
to acknowledge his display of ardor, and then she turned her gaze to
the fisherman, and to the pelican and the cormorant, taking them in
with a serene benevolence on her features. She was a great beauty, her
lips full and red, and her eyes large and a very deep brown. Her hair
was obsidian dark and shiny, and coiled on top of her head. She wore
a gold hibiscus flower on the front of that coil. She was bare-breasted,
with a sarong snugged to her hips, and her skin was the color of freshly
ground nutmeg. Her arms were connected to her wings as far down as
her elbows, and she had long willowy wrists and slender hands, and
tapered fingers. She brought her wings down and closed them across
herself, and now she was clothed in feathers, her chest and shoulders in
greens and yellows, here and there flecked with gold, and her belly and
legs with her flight feathers, in brightest red, and every shade of pink.

"May I present to you," said the frigate bird, "Dewi Sri, Goddess
of Rice, Supreme Matron of Motherhood, and Divine Regent of Bali
Dwipa, the Isle of Ritual."

The pelican and the cormorant bowed, and the fisherman blinked
the last grains of sand from his eyes. "Your holiness," the birds said,
"we are honored by your presence."

"As am I by yours," said the goddess. She put her hands together in
prayer, and bowed her forehead to meet the tips of her fingers.

"It has come to my ears," Dewi said, "that you are in need of a wet
nurse."

Taken aback, the fisherman stammered for a moment, and then
managed to say "Yes, Your Grace."

The goddess stood with her back to the sun, radiant with the
heavenly light behind her, and the dragonfly floated in the air above

her head, its wings buzzing, as if it were her familiar. Dewi spread her wings, and with her hands curved gracefully back toward herself, she gestured at her breasts. "Will these do?" she said.

Her lush breasts curved upward from her chest to nipples a deeper shade of brown. The fisherman gawped at them, overwhelmed by his sudden good fortune, and unable to speak.

"Close your mouth," the frigate bird said, "and stop looking at her like you've never seen a woman before."

The fisherman lowered his eyes. "Forgive me," he said. "I mean no disrespect." He took a handful of sand and squeezed it, just to feel the reassuring grit of it against his skin. "It's only that," and here he stifled a sob, "I fear you are too late."

"Bring her to me," the goddess said.

The fisherman reached into the hole in the sand and retrieved his beloved's clamshell. With his head bowed he approached the goddess, the perfection of her toes, the curving grace of her ankles, the slant hem of her sarong draped above them. He knelt before her, and raising his arms in front of his bowed head, he offered his beloved up to her care.

"Look at me," the goddess said, and when he did so, a single note in his ears chimed, and the chime spread to his chest, the gaze of the goddess tuning him from the inside out, his whole being trembling with the clear ringing tone of a gamelan gong. All that was wrong with the world fell away, and inside that sound the fisherman hovered like a hummingbird, drinking nectar from the goddess's lips. She opened her hands to him and took the clamshell, holding it between her palms. She closed her eyes and felt along the seam where the two halves of the shell joined, and then she brought the shell to her lips and hummed into the tiny opening at one end. She hummed a lullaby, low and sweet, and the fisherman, the sound shimmering within him, saw his beloved's clamshell begin to open. Slowly, slowly, the gap between the two halves of the shell widened, and there she was, lying on her side with her knees drawn to her chest, shiny and wet and still. Dewi Sri blew a gentle breath into her face. The fisherman could scarcely watch, so fearful was he that his beloved's soul was beyond revival. But they all leaned in and waited, gods and human alike, their breath held, like so many relatives awaiting the birth of a child, and at long last the delicate creature trembled, and then stirred. Her legs straightened, and she sat up, a veritable Venus on the half shell, and stretched her arms and yawned.

"She lives," said the frigate bird. The pelican and the cormorant murmured their assent, and the fisherman wept.

Dewi Sri slid her slender fingers beneath the soul and lifted her out of the shell. She brought her, tender as a newborn babe, to her breast, and swaddled her in her folded wings.

"This will take some time," said Dewi Sri. "Is there some place I might sit?"

The fisherman, with the frigate bird, the pelican, and the cormorant trailing behind, led the goddess to his fire, and he offered her the best seat on the driftwood log.

"My humble home," the fisherman said, "is entirely at your service."

The goddess sat, no longer accompanied by the dragonfly, who had flown away when they left the edge of the water. She resumed her humming, crooning a song beyond words to the soul at her breast, while the others watched, waiting for the miracle to bloom.

"Please," she said, "talk amongst yourselves. Or go about your business, whatever that might be. We're going to be here a while."

And so the fisherman gathered firewood, and tended his fire, and the frigate bird told his companions of his flight to the eastern reaches of the Sea of Bones, a distance of many farsakhs,¶ to the island where Dewi reigned.

"The winds were against me," the frigate bird said. "There are storms out there where there never were before."

"What are we to make of that?" said the cormorant.

"The belly of the beast grows ever larger," said the frigate bird. "It is swollen with the foul humor of the monster's bellyache."

¶ Leagues, miles, parsecs, or farsakhs, dear reader, it's all about the distance from here to there. A farsakh is an ancient Persian measure of distance slightly longer than a league, and a league is the distance a person can walk in an hour. (Bear in mind that in ancient times an hour was defined as one twelfth of the time from sunrise to sunset, so the length of an hour varied according to the season.) The fisherman, being a sailor, thinks of a league as three nautical miles, but he's not really sure how long a mile is, because in ancient times all measures of distance were locally defined. The Zoroastrians defined a farsakh as the distance at which a man with good eyesight could tell if a beast of burden was black or white—go figure. To the pelagic frigate bird a farsakh is half the distance he can fly in half a sailor's watch, or about six miles.

"Ah yes," the cormorant said. He now wore the cap and gown of a scholar, and he produced a thick book from beneath his wing. "I believe these papyri from the Middle Kingdom cover the subject." The book, *A Treasury of the Medical Scrolls of the Pharaohs*, fell open, and the cormorant began flipping through the pages with his bill, pausing only to push his spectacles down more firmly, so that they would not fly off. "Abscesses, dropsy, dysentery," he murmured, "hair—stimulating growth thereof, leprosy, limbs—feebleness thereof, rheumatism, wait a minute, I've gone past it," and now he flipped pages back the other way, "polyuria, liver disease, gangrene, fainting spells, ah, here 'tis: dyspepsia." The cormorant peered at the relevant entry over the top of his spectacles. "Dyspepsia—aggravated, dyspepsia—caused by worms, dyspepsia—common, ah, here we are, *dyspepsia gargantua*: 'A disease peculiar to certain gods, goddesses, demigods, daemons, and chimeras, especially those of outlandish stature, in which the belly becomes so distended from gluttony that it develops its own weather.'"

"I believe I just said that," said the frigate bird. "So what's the cure?"

"Cure? Cure. Hmmm, cure, cure, cure, ah. *Hic est*," said the cormorant. "There are several preventives and remedies, depending on the severity of the case. Chamomile tea, tea tree oil, oil of liverwort, orc's liver, sliced thin and served raw. Essential oils, to be rubbed on the belly while colored light is reflected into the nostrils. Change of diet."

"If only we could go back to the way things used to be," said the pelican, "when Raven was here, before the Kiamah swallowed us."

"Too late for that," said the frigate bird. "And I doubt that there's enough chamomile tea in all of eternity to treat the Kiamah."

"'In extreme cases,'" the cormorant read, "'similar to bovine bloat, the belly may be pierced with a wide-bore trochar above the pyloric valve to give the foul humor an exit point. Care should be taken as to the strapping down of loose objects, such as trees, horses, and the rooves of houses, as the force of the body's wind in such cases may be very great.' Do any of you have a notion as to where the Kiamah's pyloric valve is?"

"None whatsoever," said the frigate bird, "but it's a comfort to know that the physicians of the Middle Kingdom had some experience with this."

"Actually," the cormorant said, "a lot of what's in these scrolls is copied from other, more ancient scrolls, some of them of dubious origin."

"Dubious origin? What are you saying?" the frigate bird said. He looked over the cormorant's shoulder and said, "You can read these ancient hieroglyphics? They are nothing but gobbled gook to me."

"You mean gobbledygook," the cormorant said.

"Pedant!" the frigate bird said. "Of course I do—have you no sense of word play?"

The cormorant, momentarily abashed, covered his face with his wing before he resumed speaking. "Be that as it may, I am saying you can't rely on everything you read," he said. "And I can read these ancient writings because my spectacles were made from the magical Urim and Thummim, and through them the wearer can read all languages."

"What a marvel those spectacles are," said the fisherman. "But let us return to the matter at hand."

"What care is it of ours," said the frigate bird, "if the Kiamah has a bad case of gas? If we treat his bloat, then he survives, and we all remain trapped in his belly. If we do nothing, and the gas gets worse, eventually the beast will explode and die, and we shall die with him. We'd do better to find a way to slay the beast than to worry about his digestive malady."

"Worse yet, we might get caught up in the Kiamah's belly storm," said the pelican. "He could fart us all into the Outer Darkness with such force that we'd all be killed."

"The beast would survive, and we would not," said the fisherman.

"There, there," cooed Dewi Sri to the bundle in her arms, "our little girl here has some gas of her own." And with this she brought the bundle in her arms up to her shoulder, and patted her back, and they all saw that the beloved's soul had grown a newborn's body, and was now the size of a weaned kitten. The fisherman fell to his knees, and touched his forehead to the sand. "Praise the gods," he said, "it's a miracle."

"Yes," Dewi Sri said, "a kitling baby is always a miracle." The baby in question uttered a baby-sized belch, and everyone crowded around to see her face. Her eyes were scrunched shut, and her wet mouth opened up in a baby-sized yawn. Her face had the overcooked flush of a newborn, and her hair was dark, wispy, and tight against her scalp. Dewi Sri guided her mouth back to her breast. "Give us some air, please, gentle sirs," she said. She gave the pelican a nod and said, "And lady." The pelican offered Dewi Sri her skew-whiff smile in return, and everyone backed away.

"So this is how it goes?" the fisherman said. "She returns to us an infant?"

"Yes," said Dewi Sri, "but by nightfall she will be a child, and by the light of dawn, she will be the woman she was when she died."

Again the fisherman knelt at her feet, and he took one of them in his hands, and he kissed it, and then he rubbed her foot with both hands.

"Good man," said Dewi Sri. "The goddess approves."

The fisherman smiled. His beloved was close at hand, and the goddess was pleased with him. Far, far back in his memory was a scene such as this. His mother reclined on a lectus, with the scroll with which she had been teaching him to read—Plutarch's account of the death of Cleopatra—fallen from her hands. He was rubbing her feet with olive oil scented with elderflowers, and his mother, her eyes closed, murmured instructions to him. "You're good at this, boy," she said. "Remember what you do now when it comes time to court a woman." It was a rare moment when they had been happy together, a moment that had not crossed his thoughts in more years than he could count. He pressed his thumbs into the arch of Dewi Sri's foot, and she rewarded him with a happy hum of approval.

And so the day passed. They all hovered around Dewi Sri like so many aunties, and she kept shooing them back like so many flies. The fisherman tended his fire, and cooked a fish the pelican brought, and his beloved suckled and slept by turns. At midday his beloved's fingers were reaching for the goddess's lips, and as the sun began to set in the east her legs stuck out from the cradle of the goddess's arms like the ungainly gams of a newborn colt.

By nightfall the fisherman was giving the goddess the latest of several long foot rubs. The birds were gathered by the light of the fire, preening themselves and keeping watch on the body growing in Dewi Sri's arms.

"She must be getting heavier," the frigate bird said. "Is there anything I can do to help?"

The goddess, consumed with the twin pleasures of nursing and having her feet rubbed, could barely murmur a reply. "My shoulders," she said, "you could rub my shoulders."

The frigate bird, bereft as he was of a pair of hands, could only stare at his feet. But the pelican waved a wing in front of herself, and she stood behind the goddess in her old woman form, and she did as the goddess bade her to do. The frigate bird shot her a jealous glare, and his throat pouch flared red. It was at this moment that the crow stepped out of the night, and into the light of the fire.

"Kiaw-aw-aw," said the crow, "what have We here?" His skin was oiled, his breechcloth bore the head—his head—of the crow clan, and his beak was shiny black and sharp. He stood with his arms spread, inviting their admiration, his black eyes lit with the flames of the fire.

The fisherman stood, his hand resting on the hilt of his knife, which was tucked into the top of his breeches at his hip, and the cormorant and the frigate bird closed ranks with him, the three of them ready now to defend the goddess.

"You're not welcome here, crow," said the frigate bird.

"Not welcome? The King of the Dead, not welcome in His own kingdom? Who are you, you red-necked stint, to make such a demand on Us? And who, pray tell, is that fair maiden behind you?"

"Stand aside, gentlemen," said Dewi Sri. "Let the crow see who has come to visit his kingdom."

"And what a tawdry kingdom it is," muttered the frigate bird.

"What's this?" said the crow. "Tawdry? I see nothing gaudy or gimcrack about this place." He threw his shoulders back and broadened his chest, his arms spread to encompass all that was his. He glared at the frigate bird, his black eyes full of ire and outrage. The frigate bird glared back, and he puffed up his feathers, and stood ready to draw his pistola from his belt. Dewi Sri raised a hand, her fingers shaped in the mudra for peace, her face serene.

"Good sirs," she said, "I have a newborn soul at my breast, and for her sake, indeed for all of our sakes, I ask that you set aside all your old enmities." The goddess hummed a soothing hum, and the crow and the frigate bird were soothed enough to take a step back from each other.

"Cousin Crow," the goddess said, "we have a history together. Do you not know who I am?"

The crow took a long slow breath while he looked the goddess up and down. "We are pleased to make your acquaintance, O beauteous one, but We are sure that if we had met before We would remember such a beguiling goddess as yourself."

Dewi Sri stroked the face of the babe growing in her arms, who smiled back at her from within the blissful slumber of a well-fed tot. Satisfied that her charge had everything she required, the goddess raised her eyes. The slightest of smiles was on her lips, but there was laughter in her gaze, as if she thought the crow a court jester, here for her amusement.

"Let me tell you the story," said the goddess. "In the time before time, long before the world snake, Ananta Boga, made Bedwang, the world turtle," said she, "Batara Guru, the highest of the high gods, decreed that all the gods should build him a new palace. But Ananta Boga is a Naga, a serpent-god, and has no arms and legs, and so could not work on the new palace, and for this he was sorely troubled. He wept in despair, and three of his tears fell to the ground. It was then that the miracle occurred, as each of these three tears became a shining beautiful egg when it touched the ground, and each of these eggs shone with the luster of a pearl of the greatest price. Ananta Boga the world snake put the three eggs in his mouth, and he set off to offer them to Batara Guru, in lieu of working on the new palace."

"A charming story, your ravishment," the crow said, "but We fail to see what it has to do with Us."

"Patience, Crow, for you are about to hear what this story has to do with you. Ananta Boga was on his way to the palace when he met you, Cousin Crow, and you asked him where he was going, but he could not answer because he held the eggs in his mouth. And for failing to answer you thought him to be arrogant, and lacking in the proper respect, and you attacked him furiously. One egg fell from his mouth and broke, and Ananta Boga slithered off into the tall grass to hide, but you followed him, and again you attacked him in your fury, and again an egg fell to the ground and broke. And while you devoured the succulent contents of the broken egg, Ananta Boga escaped. He slithered off to the new palace with his last egg, which he gave to

Batara Guru, who accepted the offer of this egg like a pearl of the greatest price, and Batara Guru decreed that Ananta Boga should nest this egg until it hatched. And Ananta Boga did so, and when the egg hatched, inside was a beautiful baby girl, and Ananta Boga gave this girl to Batara Guru to raise as his own. And this girl grew up to be the most beautiful of the goddesses, and that is who stands before you now, for I am the hatchling of that egg like a pearl."

The goddess put her palms together in front of her forehead, and she bowed ever so slightly to the crow, and all who beheld her saw that her skin was radiant in the firelight.

"And now you have come here to accuse me of this aw-aw-alleged crime?" said the crow.

The goddess smiled serenely at the crow. "Speak not of accusation," she said, "for I have come merely to thank you, crow, for you were a midwife to me."

At this, the cormorant and the pelican clucked and chuckled, and the fisherman and the frigate bird joined in, all of them clucking and chuckling at the thought of the crow as a midwife, midwifery being that most joyous of the helping occupations, and the crow being the least helpful creature they knew.

"We are no midwife," said the crow, "but We accept your compliment, dear goddess, though We must confess, We do not recollect this serpent of whom you speak, nor anything about devouring an egg. Be that as it may, We can't help but notice that you have a child at your breast. Are We to understand that you have brought forth our friend's beloved from her clamshell?"

"She has, Lord Crow," said the fisherman. He bowed his head, for he felt it best to flatter the man-bird before him, but he kept his hand on the hilt of his knife. "As you have instructed. Friend."

The crow kept his eyes on the goddess, not bothering to acknowledge that the fisherman had spoken. "A charming sight," said the crow. "So maternal, so lactitious, so mammalian. You've come a long, long way to perform this act of mammary mercy. May We invite you to share our hospitality later? To grace us with your comely presence? We have a nightly bonfire, with singing and dancing and tasty morsels on which to dine. 'Tis what all the travelers come here to see."

"So have I heard," said the goddess. "But I fear I must decline this evening." She wrapped the child at her breast more tightly within her winged arms. "For as you see, duty calls." She offered the crow the serenity of her smile, and then, as if a mask had fallen from her face, her smile broadened, and her eyes sparked with a lust that was most unmotherly, and directed straight at the crow. The crow's tongue licked the rim of his beak, and then just as swiftly, the mask of maternity was back on Dewi Sri's face.

The crow gave her a lascivious wink. "Another time then," he said.

"May it be so," said the goddess. She returned his wink with one of her own, languid and knowing, and then she cooed at the baby at her breast.

The frigate bird puffed up his throat pouch and rattled melodiously from within it, but neither goddess nor crow paid him any mind. The crow backed away from the fire until the darkness hid him, and then he waved his arm in front of himself, and he flew off into the night.

ALL NIGHT LONG THE GODDESS Dewi Sri nursed her charge, who grew and grew and grew, her legs lengthening and filling out, her hair sprouting and growing until it hung nearly to the ground. The tot became a child, and the child a maiden, and the maiden a woman, and the woman a matron. She nursed, and she slept, the goddess singing her lullabies to keep her settled and content. The fisherman slept only fitfully that night, anxious as he was to hold his beloved in his arms again, but whenever he awoke the goddess put a finger to her lips, and bade him not to stir. At first light he rose to feed his fire, and to stretch his limbs, and the goddess crooked her finger to bring him close. His beloved was sleeping, her lips edged with milk, her face older than when he had last seen her, but still the face he loved.

"Let her sleep," the goddess whispered, "she's worked hard all night. She'll awaken soon."

The fisherman nodded. He trembled, light-headed and giddy as a youth beneath the balcony of his first love. To distract himself he found a stout stick, and he began to whittle a handle for the felling axe he'd found in the crow's hoard. He was soon to be with his woman, and they would need a proper way to shelter the night.

The cormorant and the pelican had long since wandered off to meet the incoming canoe, but the frigate bird was perched on a driftwood log, sleeping. In the blue light before the sunrise began he opened his eyes, spread his wings, which were a fathom and a half in length each, and shook the dew off them.

"Good morning to all," he said. He stretched out his neck, and he gazed at Dewi Sri with what looked to the fisherman to be the light of love in his eyes. *Completely smitten*, thought the fisherman. *Love makes fools of us all.* The frigate bird's throat pouch puffed up for a moment at the sight of the goddess, a flash of brightest red in the light of the dawn, and he uttered a rattling sound.

"Good morning," the fisherman murmured. Dewi Sri offered the frigate bird a serene smile, and then placed a finger to her lips, and pointed with her lovely brown eyes at the woman sleeping in her arms. The fisherman set aside his whittling, and he headed down to the beach with the frigate bird at his side.

"The moment is almost come," he said.

"For me too," said the frigate bird. "She is the most beautiful woman I have ever seen."

"The goddess, you mean," said the fisherman. "Yes, she is a great beauty."

"Huzzah to that," said the frigate bird. The waters of the inlet were calm and flat, with gentle waves lapping the shore. They stood side by side, man and bird, both of them with hearts quivering. The frigate bird began to preen his wing feathers, lifting them one by one and straightening them.

"There was a temple for the rice goddess near where we lived on Ambon," said the fisherman, "with a stone figure inside. But she is far more beautiful in the flesh."

"Oh yes," said the frigate bird. He puffed up his throat pouch until it was the size of a wineskin, and from within it, again he produced his hollow, rattling sound, as if a cat were purring inside an empty barrel. "I have reason to believe," he said, "that she finds me in her favor."

The fisherman nodded, unwilling to venture a guess as to what the goddess might feel for the frigate bird. The frigate bird let the wind out of his throat pouch, offering a sigh full of longing as he did so. He reached down with his beak and pulled on the grip of his pistola, loosening it from his belt.

"I shall have to kill the crow," he said, "if he tries to seduce her."

The fisherman, who had nothing but murder in his heart for the crow, nodded in assent. "You'll get no argument from me," he said. "But that weapon, is it more than merely a hashish pipe in the guise of a pistola?"

"The handle is weighted with lead," the frigate bird said, "and with it I shall bash in his brains if the occasion arises."

They stared into the water, side by side, enjoying together the thought of the crow's violent death. A breeze from the sea rippled across the frigate bird's feathers, and he lifted his wings away from his body as if to air them.

"I've been meaning to ask," the fisherman said.

"Yes?"

"You're on the ground. I thought you had to fly from a perch. How will you get back in the air?"

"Oh," said the frigate bird. A tremor of delight rose up his neck, and his head shook. "The goddess will carry me aloft on her back."

"Oh," said the fisherman. "She can do that?" He looked the frigate bird up and down. The creature was taller than he, with a body the size of a yearling lamb. "You're not too heavy?"

"She's done it before." There was something dreamy in the frigate bird's voice, the sound of a memory that clearly had him twitterpated. "Just yesterday when we left her palace she let me climb on her back, and together we rose into the sky above glorious Mount Agung."

"She must be very strong," said the fisherman.

"Well yes, I suppose. She is, after all, a goddess. But I'm not the burden you might think me to be. I'm mostly feathers, and my bones are hollow. In fact, my feathers weigh more than all of my bones put together."

"Really?" said the fisherman.

"So I am told," said the frigate bird. "Here, let me show you. Kneel down, and I'll hop up on your shoulders."

The fisherman knelt, and at a word from the frigate bird, dropped onto his hands and knees. The frigate bird flapped his great wings and hopped onto the fisherman's back. The curved claws on his toes pricked his skin as the bird made his way to the fisherman's shoulders.

"Go ahead," the frigate bird said, "stand up."

The fisherman did so, surprised at how little effort it took. The bird on his shoulders weighed no more than the feather-filled pillow of a lady-in-waiting.

"Now watch," said the frigate bird. Again he flapped his great wings, letting go of the fisherman's shoulders, and then he sailed out over the water, rising on a lift of air, spiraling upward with only the slightest toil. Higher and higher he rose, skimming invisible currents of air, his wings long and narrow, his body slender. He was a black silhouette with a forked tail, and there was something devilishly elegant about the figure he cut against the morning sky.

All his life the fisherman had watched the birds of the sea. When he was a boy, diving for the coins sailors threw from the decks of their ships, he watched the gulls wheel and soar and envied them their flight. What a fine thing it would be to fly as the frigate bird flew, soaring with scarcely any need to beat his wings against the air. To fly above all boundaries, and over any obstacle, he and his beloved together, to escape all that held them from going home.

The frigate bird circled the inlet, showing no sign of returning to the beach, and so the fisherman walked back to the fire. There he found his beloved awake. She sat on the driftwood log next to the goddess, who held her close with one arm. Her eyes were open, and she stared into the middle distance. She was wrapped in a sarong that matched Dewi Sri's, though she wore hers over her breasts. The goddess's wing feathers covered her shoulders in the cool of the morning. She took no notice of the fisherman, who stood before her, quivering.

"Cariña," he said, his love-name for her soft on his tongue.

"Yes?" she said. She looked at him as if he were a stranger. "Is that how I am called?"

The fisherman nodded. The voice was hers, and the face was hers, the curve of her lovely high cheekbones as dear as ever to him.

"I have come," said he, "as you have asked."

She offered him a smile full of politesse, but no warmth, and then a tremble passed through her, and the smile faded. "I fear, good sir, that I do not know you."

The fisherman stood still as a heron waiting for a minnow to swim by. Blink, blink, blink went his eyelids. He pressed the tips of his fingers into his forehead, wanting to alter this moment with the sheer force of his will.

"You wrote to me," he said. "A letter. You bade me come to the Isle of the Dead to find you."

"Did I?" she said.

She studied his face. Her eyes were the blue of the sea in the calm of a clear morning, and steady as a navigator's hand holding the ballastella as he sighted the lodestar. The goddess withdrew her arm from the woman's shoulder.

The fisherman pointed at the tattoo on his chest. "This is you," he said.

His beloved took in the face inked on the fisherman's chest, with its hibiscus flower tucked behind one ear, and she slowly shook her head. "That face is no more familiar to me than yours," she said.

The fisherman shut his eyes for a moment as he held in a gasp of frustration. His hands went to the chain round his neck. "We lived together in your hut," he said. "I gave you this silver chain." He lifted the chain off his neck, and held it out to her.

She looked at the chain, which was still threaded through a pair of pitch balls, but she did not reach out her hand to take it.

"Forgive me," she said. "I remember nothing of my life before I awoke on the shore of this strange land."

He stepped forward, and he put the chain round her neck. He was close enough to put his hands on her shoulders. They were cold, and he offered her the warmth of his hands, but the look in her eyes bade him step back. The fisherman looked at the goddess, who pressed her lips together and shook her head ever so slightly, as if to say she had done all she could. He fell back a pace or two, and he dropped himself heavily onto the sand, where he sat cross-legged with his head between his knees. Had he looked up he would have seen his beloved's furrowed brow, and the consternation of the goddess, and the shrugs the two women exchanged as they looked at each other, neither of them with the faintest idea of what properly should come next.

The goddess stood, and she put her palms together and touched the tips of her fingers to her forehead. "Perhaps you two would like some time alone," she said. "With your kind permission, I shall take my leave." The fisherman and his beloved murmured their consent, and with this the goddess left them, and walked down to the edge of the water.

The fisherman scooped a handful of sand and held it in his fist, letting it trickle down like an hourglass. He felt himself to be the empty carapace of his own life, a brittle husk drained of meaning, and bereft of purpose. His lips were dry and chapped.

"Dewi tells me you rescued me," his beloved said. "She tells me that I've died, and now you've brought me back to life."

"Yes," said the fisherman. "It is so." The cruelty of his fate was beyond belief. He drew a finger through the sand, making an aimless furrow zigging first this way and then zagging that.

"Then I owe you my thanks," said she.

The fisherman nodded, his head still between his knees. He was nothing more than an entertainment for the gods, who treated him as a shadow puppet, fit only for their brutish amusement.

"This is a strange place," his beloved said. "I thought the afterlife would be swathed in mist, and we would sip the nectar of the gods from golden cups."

"It's not what I expected either," said the fisherman. "Nothing has turned out the way I thought it would. There's nothing to drink here but water, and nothing to eat but fish."

There was the softest of breezes coming off the shore. The sun rose high enough in the west to clear the cliffs, and a ray of light as yellow as the center of a forget-me-not fell on the two of them. The fisherman looked up, and as he did so, his beloved's belly growled long and low, the borborygmus of someone who has not eaten in a very long time. She looked at her belly as if it were an entirely new thing to her.

"You're hungry," he said.

A smile of understanding spread across her lips. "A bite of fresh fish," said she, "would do me a world of good."

"All right," said the fisherman. "I know a thing or two about fishing."

The fisherman took up his knife, and he went into the woods and cut long strips of bark from a cedar tree. He returned to the fire, where his beloved was contemplating the silver chain she held in her hand.

"This is a fine chain," she said.

"The finest I could find for you," the fisherman said.

She raised her eyes to his, her lower lip caught between her teeth, and in her gaze the fisherman saw sorrow and consternation, and not one whit of recognition. He sat next to her on the driftwood log and busied himself with lashing his knife to the stick he had been whittling for an axe handle. When it came time to tie off the ends of the cedar strips, his beloved put the silver chain round her neck again, and she reached for the spear he was fashioning.

"I know how to do this," she said. He offered her the spear, and watched as she tied a strangle knot, her fingers nimble and sure of themselves. When she finished, she handed the spear back to him, and she stared at her hands as if she had never seen them before.

"I know how," she said, "but I don't know how I know."

"Your father was a ship chandler," the fisherman said. "And his father before him, and his before that. The work of sailors and the ways of the sea were familiar to you."

Cariña turned this thought over in her mind, looking beneath it, behind it, and beyond it, for thoughts were new to her, and there was much to consider.

"Did you know my father?" she asked.

"I had not the pleasure," the fisherman said. "When we met, your father had already passed on, and it was your brother who ran the family chandlery."

"Ah," she said. *My mind is a dark place,* she thought. *Memories are what light it, and I have none.* "Where was this?"

"In the Spice Islands," he said. "On the isle of Ambon. On the far side of the world from where your father was born."

"Ah," she said. She had a family, even though she felt as if she had sprung from nothing. She had words, her mind was full of words. "And my father, and his father, and his father before that, are they all here?"

"Perhaps," said the fisherman. "Only the crow would know for sure."

"The crow?" she said.

"The crow," said the fisherman, "is the local satrap, and a foul tyrant, and he means neither one of us any good."

She took this in with the unflappable calm of a seasoned sailor who discovers that his sinking ship has caught fire. It was a quality that the fisherman had always admired in her.

"We are in danger then?" she said.

The fisherman considered. "I have been promised by the crow that we might live together here for a year and a day. The crow is a creature of violence, and foul cunning, and not to be trusted. Even so, he is bound by certain laws, and I believe he will allow us the time we have been promised."

The fisherman stood and held his hand out to his beloved. She took his hand in hers and stood, and together they walked to the beach, although she let go his hand after only a few steps. The loss of her touch made the fisherman want to wrap his arms round her and hold her close, but instead he simply walked with her, spear in hand, and kept his eyes on the sand beneath his feet. Patience, he counseled himself. He had waited this long. He could wait a little longer.

When they reached the wet sand at the water's edge, the fisherman saw that there were clam holes scattered everywhere. This was how it had begun, this adventure of the clam, and he began to tell his beloved the story of how he had come to be here. He was not a boastful man, but he was not above casting himself as the hero of his tale in order to win back her favors. He had earned the right, had he not, by setting out in his skiff and sailing into the storm? His skiff had been split to splinters, he had been swallowed by a whale and shat out on the Isle of the Dead, and as he told her all this, he watched for any sign that she still loved him. They waded together in the shallows, and while she listened politely to his story, she seemed distant, as if she had other, more weighty matters on her mind. She asked again about her father, would she find him here, and her mother, and he explained about the clams burrowing their way across the inlet, and the canoe of the dead, and the rebirth of the souls in the land of the living.

"My parents," she said, "could tell me who I am."

The creases across her brow and the furrows between her eyebrows were deep with worry. The fisherman stabbed his spear into the sand beneath the waters of the inlet and put both his hands on her shoulders. "I will do anything in my power," he said, "to make you happy here."

The steadiness that had been in her eyes before was gone. She trembled beneath his hands. "I know I should be grateful," she said. "But I have no notion as to why my happiness should matter to you."

She pulled back from his touch, and said, "I should like to go back to the fire. Come find me when you've something to eat."

The warmth of his fire and food for her belly were all she would take from him. *Of course she rejects me,* he thought, *for I am hairless and blue.* He bent and pulled his spear out of the sand so she would not see the tears forming in his eyes. "How can you not know me?" he said. He spoke to the air between them, to the unseen power of fate that surrounded them, his voice tight and shrill.

"I don't even know who I am," she said. "Try to fathom what that feels like."

DEWI SRI SAT IN A shallow cave just below the peak of the highest mountain on the Isle of the Dead. Even a goddess needed a moment of respite on occasion, and the others would not find her here. Below her were the fisherman and his beloved, tiny figures sitting beside their fire. Above them the frigate bird circled on a column of rising air. What passion they had shared, but she banished from her thoughts the memory of their night together, for she had matters of much greater import to consider.

The morning after their liaison he had led her to the roof of the world, and from there to the realm of the Turropsi, where she was given an audience. The Turropsi were like no other creature she had ever encountered, tentacled like a creature of the sea, yet borne upon currents of air like herself. Their tentacles hung beneath their pellucid bodies, which were like shimmering cups turned upside down. She was surrounded by a covey of them, hovering in the mists of all that might be, with the great standing wave of the present at her back.

Out in the Fetch, they told her, something approached that would destroy them all, ending the weaving that balanced destiny and free will, good and evil, the mutable and the immutable. A great change was coming, the most perilous they had ever seen, and beyond it, if the Kiamah beast swallowed the material world, lay a thousand times a thousand years of dark stagnation, in which evil was fully ascendant.

They would not have it so, they told her. Great change, they said, meant great opportunity, and a great change required a great sacrifice. The few must defeat the many, and a hero must slay the beast. You are the hope of the future. Bind together your allies, and find your hero. Or be that hero yourself.

"I am no hero," she said. "I am a fertility goddess. It is not in my nature to slay anyone."

Listen to us, they said, and do not argue. What was needed, they said, were lovers who were willing to die for love.

"Lovers?" Dewi had asked. "Why?"

That is the way of things, they told her. It was not for her to question why. Understand this: that to save the material world and the spirit world they needed a lover from each realm. The frigate bird had brought such a person from the material world to the Isle of the Dead. He must be reunited with his beloved, and together they must die. Out of this sacrifice, out of the smoke of their bodies burning on the pyre, would come the renewal of all that was.

"What has all of this to do with me?" Dewi had asked.

You are chosen, they told her, for your skill at weaving the pleasures of the flesh together with the needs of the people.

"How am I to fulfill this task?" Dewi asked.

That is a pattern not yet woven, they told her. This much we can tell you—the new ruler of the spirit world must be the offspring of the crow. His daughter is the one favored by us. Go to the Isle of the Dead, and revive the beloved one. Go there, and seduce the crow. Return for further instruction once you have done this much.

The chorus of their voices, it seemed to Dewi, had beneath it a counterpoint of contrary mutterings at this point, though she could not make out what they were saying. But round their necks they each and all wore a gold abacus, and many of them now clicked their beads this way and that, and their mutterings rose in pitch and volume until the voice of the chorus silenced them, as if they were disobedient children.

One more thing, they told her now. The first rule of the Turropsi is that you do not speak of the Turropsi. You must speak of us to no one save the frigate bird. To do otherwise would be to risk undoing our intricate design.

She was unaccustomed to being ordered about. She was the Rice Mother, and a goddess, and it was she who gave the orders. If she was to do their bidding, they must tell her more. But before she could give voice to these thoughts, they silenced her with a vision of a dark mass out ahead of them in the Fetch, a mass so immense they could not go around it, nor under it nor over it, nor move it aside. When that dark mass reached the great standing wave of the present, it would overtake all that was. They showed her Mount Agung, her palace dark and desolate, the rice paddies in all their fecundity reduced to stagnant ponds, the villages of her people empty. She would risk this? They showed her the Kiamah beast swallowing the material world, her beloved Bali Dwipa obliterated. They showed her the beast swallowing their own realm. The Turropsi themselves would be obliterated.

No more questions, they told her. You are meant to help us.

She had formed the abhaya mudra with her right hand then, to banish the little-death of fear from her mind, but her hand trembled still. A calming breath kept the tremble from her voice.

"One more question," she said. "How much time do I have?"

There is time enough, they told her, for love to work its magic, but not so much time that you should dally. Go now, they told her, for the sooner you begin, the sooner this catastrophe will end.

THE FISHERMAN RETURNED TO HIS camp with a pair of fine fish for their morning meal. His beloved had the coals banked for cooking, and her hands were busy lashing the legs of the spit together with cedar strips. She smiled at the fisherman, but it was the practiced smile of a woman who knows her place in an uncertain world, not the smile of love. She watched as the fisherman gutted the first fish. He laid the mess of guts on the far end of the driftwood log for the pelican to eat, should she happen by. His beloved reached for the second fish, and the spear.

"I know how to do this," she said.

Strange, the fisherman thought, *how the soul was a dull creature with no more sense than a clam when it came to remembering the past. Yet she remembered how to gut a fish, how to bank a fire, and how to tie a lashing or a knot. But not me.*

"Have you any seasoning?" she asked.

"None," he said. "Had I a kettle we could boil salt water and make salt."

"A kettle," she said, "would be a fine thing."

She tossed the fish guts on the pile, spitted the two fish, and laid the spit in its place above the fire. Her lips knew how to speak, yet the life she had lived with him was cast adrift on the flat sea of her empty memory. He was marooned, and for company he had the constant torture of the face that he loved.

"Cariña," he said, and he held out his hands to her. Perhaps her lips remembered more than mere speech. She came to him, her eyes lowered, modest, coy, and she took his hands and raised her face, ready to play the part of the princess in the fairy tale. Their lips met, hers soft and yielding, his shy and tentative, and they lingered in osculation, the fisherman waiting for some heat to warm them both, but nothing came. His beloved pulled away, and she opened her eyes into his, and she shook her head no.

"That's not the story we're in," she said.

So it isn't, thought the fisherman. His love for her was constant, he had always thought so, yet it needed to be fed with her love for him, and so was perhaps a lesser love than he had always believed. They let go their hands and turned away from each other and stared into the hot coals beneath the spitted fish.

"What story is this?" the fisherman said. "I thought I knew, but I've lost my way."

His beloved considered, and her lips parted several times as if she were about to speak. "I do not know," she said at last. "It's as if I am filled with half-remembered dreams. I see their shape, but the people in them have no names."

The fisherman nodded his assent. If they knew the story they were in, they would know what to do next.

He sat on the driftwood log and picked up his spear. He felt the blade with his thumb, and wished for a whetstone, for although the blade was not yet dulled, he knew it would need sharpening before the day was out. There was a faint smell on the breeze that told him rain was coming. He had a shelter that needed to be enlarged if it were to hold the two of them this evening.

Now here was a story he knew well. All his life, harsh weather had been his mistress. She would be obeyed, or he must suffer. It was time to get to work.

THE CROW SAT ON HIS favored perch, drowsy in the morning light, as was his custom. The cedar tree was fragrant with pitch, but not nearly so fragrant as his musings about Dewi Sri. Gone from his thoughts was his usual morning reverie about the tasty morsels he had torn from the flesh of the dead the night before. His head was filled with the black shine of her coif, gleaming in the light of the sun, like feathers preened to perfection. Her wings were more beauteous than a doubled rainbow. Such colors! Such iridescence! Such divinely angled barbs!

Contrary to his usual practice, the crow sat on his perch in his man form, his legs dangling, his skin oiled, his chest broad with pride. He was the undisputed King of the Dead, he was the master of all he surveyed, and now fate had sent him a woman—a goddess, no less, worthy of being his consort. Yesterday all he had cared about was fortifying his hold on power, and enjoying the privileges of a divine ruler. He'd had no thought of a companion, no intimation of the heat simmering in his loins, no desire for the touch of another. Today he could think of nothing else. He held his hands in front of himself, and saw for the first time that they were meant for no other purpose than to touch the skin of a woman, that his fingers had life only to trace the curve of her lips. He would give his kingdom and more to touch her bounteous breasts. How he longed to nuzzle his beak between them! Such uplift! Such heft! Such perky little nipples!

So what if that flaming dingleberry of a fisherman, against all odds, had found a way to revive his beloved clam—let him. His quest for breast milk, after all, had led the goddess to the Isle of the Dead, and soon she would be his. She wanted him, did she not? Was that not the meaning of that look she had given him? He had no experience of the fairer sex to guide him, but his breast was filled with desire for her, and that was all that mattered.

It was a fair day on the inlet, the sun warm, the breeze off the sea fresh, and the sky above a fervid blue. And there she was, Dewi Sri, in all her glory, circling the inlet, her wings spread wide and flecked with gold. His heart soared at the sight of her, for she had stolen it with a single glance, a heart he did not even know he had until he had lost it to her.

But she was not alone up there. The unmistakably sinister shape of the frigate bird joined her, and they flew lazy circles in tandem. He had never liked that meddling frigate bird, but now he despised him. That son of a fart was not fit to clean up her guano, let alone fly with her. She was more beguiling than the Bride of Babylon, more enticing than the glitter and gleam of ten thousand gold and silver goblets, and the frigate bird was a foul, lowborn thief, known to steal the eggs of other birds for his breakfast.

The crow passed his arm in front of himself and took on his crow form. His lady was clearly in need of companionship of a better quality than that vile, shite-eating vulture, that sluggardly scalawag, that pompous, piratical poltroon. It was time to show this awkward Autolycus** of a rival what he was up against: the awfully handsome, audaciously autocratic, aw-aw-awe-inspiringly clever regent of the Isle of the Dead, King Crow.

"Aw aw aw aw aw," said the crow, and he let loose a gobbet of guano to lighten his load before he sailed off his perch,

The crow flapped his wings and lifted himself higher and higher, until he was well above Dewi Sri and that miserable miscreant. How dare he annoy her with his pathetic and hopeless infatuation. The crow let the wind aloft carry him over the top of the circling pair, and he dropped his shoulders and glided down into formation with them, on the other side of Dewi Sri from the frigate bird.

"Hallo, Goddess," he said, "'Tis a fine fair day for a flight of fancy, wouldn't you say?"

"Good day, Crow," said the goddess. "And yes, it is. A fine day indeed."

**It is from that autodidact the cormorant, dear reader, that the auto-aggrandizing crow has heard the tale of Autolycus, son of Hermes and Chione, and grandfather to that autonomous voyager Odysseus. Autolycus was well-known in ancient times for his onslaught of assaults on the pr-aw-aw-operty of others, though, if truth be told, the crow remembers his name almost entirely for its authoritative sound.

"No one invited you up here, you poxy pip," said the frigate bird. "Your mother's tits are on a pole for all to see in the center of the souk."

"Lick my hairy onions," said the crow. "Your grandmother was a barboog, your mother is a barboog, and you are the son of a barboog."

"Your mother was a maggot," said the frigate bird, "and you are nothing more than a pimple on the arse end of a low-flying duck."

"Boys," said Dewi Sri. "Behave yourselves. I insist on some decorum from my suitors." She turned to the frigate bird and said, "Perhaps you should go on about your business. We shall renew our acquaintance anon."

The frigate bird nodded and hid his disappointment with a fierce glare at the crow. "May a thousand infections afflict your zibik," he said, and to the goddess he said, "I shall take my leave now. I look forward to continuing our conversation in more suitable circumstances." And then he flew off westward, across the Sea of Bones.

"Your mother's rooster is covered in gummas," the crow called after him. The goddess put a finger to her lips and bade him be quiet.

"My apologies, dear lady," said the crow. "He is not worthy of you, and to see you together is maddening."

"The lover who is worthy of me has mastery over their own feelings," said the goddess. She gave him the serenity of her smile, and he felt himself calmed. In return he opened his beak in a broad grin, although to anyone watching, he would have appeared to be a fledgling simp begging his mother for food.

"May I show you my kingdom?" said the crow.

"I should be enchanted," said the goddess.

Together they flew higher, so that the whole of the Isle of the Dead was below them. The inlet was but a small portion, but when asked by the goddess to what use the rest of the isle was put, the crow was slightly flummoxed.

"There's nothing much out there," he said. "Empty land, a forest full of quiet, and not a creature stirring. A dull place, with nothing bright and shiny to delight the eye, and no other crow for company."

Dewi Sri allowed a gentle wingtip to brush his with the lightest of touches, and she said, "You've lived here a long, lonely time, haven't you?" The crow nodded, afraid to speak lest the tremble that would surely afflict his voice become a sob, and the sob become a shriek. He had never felt his loneliness so keenly before. In fact, he had never felt it at all, fixated as he had always been on his own lowly position in the spirit world, and how he might rise to power. "You shall never be lonely again," said the goddess, "for now, you have me." And at this, the crow wept.

THEY FLEW OUT OVER THE Sea of Bones, chatting about this and that, the way they both loved long walks on the beach, and the glow of an open fire, and a dinner by candlelight. The crow was so besotted with her that he easily imagined himself as an entirely new being, wise and forgiving and untroubled by the vicissitudes of regency. Yet the whole time they flew together, the gold hibiscus flower at the front of her coil of hair and the flashes of gold from her feathers snatched at his attention, and he stole sidelong glances at her breasts, and dreamt of fondling them with his hands.

"We have so much in common," said the crow. "Where have you been all my life?"

"I have been asking myself the same thing about you," said the goddess. They were headed back to the inlet, and the beach along the edge of the Sea of Bones lay before them. "Shall we tarry down there a moment, and indulge ourselves in a long walk along the shore?"

"It would be my pleasure," said the crow. They coasted down together, wingtip to wingtip. The moment the crow's feet were on the ground, he passed his hand in front of himself and his body took on its man shape, although his head remained, as ever, a crow's head. He took the hand of the goddess in his, the thrill of touching her running like . . . like . . . like lightning in his veins! They walked along the sand, paying no mind to all the bones scattered about by the surf.

"The sunrise must be beautiful here," said Dewi Sri.

"Oh, yes," said the crow, who was struck by how sagacious her observation was. Of course the sunrise would be beautiful here. He had lived on the inlet for a thousand times a thousand years, and yet he had never watched the sun rise over the Sea of Bones. This woman, with her wisdom and her keen sense of beauty, would make a new crow of him, a kinder, gentler crow. A compassionate crow. Not only would he see the suffering of his subjects, but he would regret, ever so deeply, that it had to be so.

"I can well imagine," said Dewi Sri, "coming here after a night of passion, and watching the sun's orb rise over the waves with you."

The goddess turned to the crow, and the perfect bow of her lips widened, and the tip of her tongue licked her upper lip. She closed her eyes and offered him a kiss. The crow leaned in, but his beak got in the way, and he had to settle for rubbing it along the side of her neck. His breath was rank, but she would bring him some cloves to chew when next she saw him.

She caressed the back of his head and whispered to him that she would like nothing better than to watch the light of dawn break from the shelter of his arms. "My dear one," she said, "there is an old saying where I come from. We must harvest the rice before we can cook it."

"Rice?" said the crow. "Not something I've eaten much, but I like mine raw."

"Such a funny fellow"—the goddess laughed, pulling back to look him in the eye—"such a rapscallion, such a wit. We shall spend many a happy hour amusing each other, of that I am sure. But darling," she said, and at this word, the crow's loins grew hot, "I am a goddess, and it would be unseemly if we consorted together in the wild. I shall need a proper bed in which to receive you."

"A bed?" said the crow. He was used to sleeping on a perch in a tree, or on the cormorant's shoulders. Long ago he'd built himself a nest far up a cedar tree, but he scarcely spent any time there, and in any case, he had a feeling that the goddess wanted something a bit more elaborate. Dewi looked up at him, and she stroked the length of his beak, and let the promise of her fancy for him shine forth from her eyes.

"Yes darling, a bed. A four-poster, with a canopy of finest silk, and thick bedding, of the softest goose down, and pillows scented with orchids. Our love must have a home fit for gods such as you and me." She stroked his arms, tracing the curve of his muscles, and cooed her approval. "You're so strong," she said, "prove your love for me by granting me this wish."

"Yes of course," said the crow. He was dizzied with desire, and his hand rose with a mind of its own to touch her breast, but she caught it in hers and brought his palm to her lips for a kiss.

"All in good time," she said. Her smile made his heart melt. She stepped back from him a few paces and raised her arms above her head, bringing her palms together. She began to hum a low melody, and the crow felt his chest glow, as if a crimson flame were burning beneath his breastbone. Her wings were spread in all their glory, and she danced for him, her hips swaying from side to side, her head moving back and forth in the space between her arms, the bounty of her breasts mesmerizing. His eyes were half closed, his eyelids heavy with the ardor he felt for her. The front of his breechcloth bulged with his zibik, and he was completely besotted with her pulchritude.

"Your wish," he said, "is my command."

"Under my thumb," the goddess hummed, "Mm-hmm, mm-hmm, mm-mm-hmm."

By the end of the day the fisherman had more than doubled the size of his lean-to. His beloved had gathered a mound of dried grass and laid it out for her bed. Together they wove branch after branch into the raddled roof, until only the smallest of raindrops would find their way through. They spoke little, and let the rhythm of the work render pleasant the passing of the hours. When the roof was finished, his beloved lay herself down in her bed and closed her eyes.

"Cariña," the fisherman said, his pet name for her spilling forth from his lips as naturally as breath itself, "I must go into the forest. I shall return soon."

"Mm-hmm," said his beloved, her voice drowsy and languid. *She has every reason to be tired*, the fisherman thought, having come from clamshell to full stature in a day's time. But did she know how alluring she sounded, and did she have any idea how he struggled not to crawl in and lay his amorous body next to hers? She could be a tease, he knew this, the better to arouse his interest, but this torture she worked on him unwittingly was almost more than he could bear.

In the shade of the forest the moss on the tree trunks was thick and lush. He peeled great swaths of it, fragrant with the earthy smell of the bark beneath, until he had gathered an armload so huge he could barely see around it to walk. He brought the moss back to the lean-to, where his beloved lay sleeping, and he lined his own bed with it, and he covered her with a blanket of green. She murmured her thanks, and then sleep took her from him.

The fisherman backed out of the lean-to. He fed his fire, and he took note of the darkening rain clouds offshore. He walked down to the inlet, and he stripped off his breeches, and he went for a swim.

He swam the length of the inlet and then returned to his starting point, where he could see the glow of his fire. He turned on his back, and was soon joined by the pelican, who floated next to him.

"Ho, fisherman," said the pelican. "How does the evening find you?"

"Ho, pelican," said the fisherman. "Let us return to the shore, and I shall tell you."

The fisherman swam shoreward a few strokes, the pelican paddling along beside him, until his feet found the bottom of the inlet, and he waded onto the sand, and then on to his fire. The pelican joined him, squatting by his side on the driftwood log. The fisherman fed the fire, and then said, "Let us keep our voices low, for my beloved sleeps just there, and she is weary."

"It must be vexious," his friend said, "to have your beloved so close, and yet she does not know you."

"It is," said the fisherman. "It burdens my heart. She is exactly as I remember her. Her voice is the same. The bronze of her skin and the blue of her eyes, the same. The way she guts a fish, the same."

"Just when you've found her again," the pelican said, "you lose her. Tell me, what was she like when first you met?"

"Aye, what a beauty she was. And still is." His tone became that of a teller of tales, of one who knows his story well because he has oft told it before, if only to himself. "That first night, in the Firefly, she served me a flagon of ale, and she was shapely in her sarong, the sway of her hips as she walked away a fine thing to behold. Her manner was saucy and brash, as if she knew exactly what she wanted from me, and that it was her choice whether or not I was worthy of her favors. Her blouse was of cotton, a finely woven buckram that lay softly and quite fetchingly on her bosom. She took a coquette's pleasure in the game she played with me, leaning in closer than needed to set my ale on the table, her cleavage but inches from my hopeful hands. I watched her as she flirted with every sailor in the alehouse, from callow youth to seasoned jack tar like myself, gauging my chances. There was a bagnio down the way, a bath house in the oriental style, with women ready to sell me their affections, but I held myself aloof from those pleasures, preferring to think the barmaid fancied me, and that she might claim me as her own."

The pelican's striped bill lay in the fisherman's lap, and her yellow eye gazed up at him, rapt. "This is the way of it in the material world?" said the pelican. "Tell me more."

The fisherman's fingers were drawn to the fine feathers along her neck, and he stroked them as he went on with his tale.

"I spent the next evening in the Firefly, having bunked alone the night before. Each time she brought me my ale she stopped to talk. Was I sailing on the morning tide? No? And why not? Was there something keeping me in port? 'I am not ready to sail,' I told her. 'I've had enough of the sea, and this isle of spices is as fair a land as ever I have seen. Perhaps I'll settle here.' 'I've heard that before,' she told me, 'but I've never known a sailor who could settle anywhere for very long. You've all got a woman in the next port,' said she, but her smile was friendly, as if having a woman in the next port were not so great a sin. 'Once I was that sailor,' I told her. 'But now you're not?' she said, with a saucy curve to the rise in her eyebrow.

"Late on the third night she sat herself down on my lap and gave me a nuzzle. 'Come to my hut,' she told me, her lips to my ear, 'and let us see what kind of love we might build together.'"

The pelican considered this. She had no experience of love, nor lust, save what she had observed in the newly dead after they came off the canoe. They often looked around for their mates, who were seldom there, and they lamented their absence. But there were others who were pleased to be free of those they left behind, and still others who took the opportunity to couple with a stranger, once they understood where they were, as if death gave them license to do something they had always wanted to do, but had not done.

"Were you true to her always?" she asked. "Or did lust lead you astray?"

The fisherman considered a moment before he answered. "My love for her is as constant as the stars by which all sailors navigate," he said, "but it was not always true. Once, I sailed from Ambon, where we lived, to Qali, where the great ships came from the north to fill their holds with ivory and spices and tea. I was gone some several months, chasing the silver coin I wanted to build us a better home. In Qali I crept down Cock Alley when my loneliness was too much to bear, dipping my wick in the punch houses and bagnios. In my absence, my beloved took some solace in the arms of a freebooter who arrived on a privateer. But the freebooter was gone by the time I returned, and forgotten as soon as my lips kissed hers.

"We did not hold these dalliances against each other, neither did we speak of them overmuch when we were together. But my beloved wanted me to stay home. Not to keep me in her bed, but to keep me in her heart, as she told me, for she missed me sorely when I was gone, and faulted me my need for the adventure of the sea, and for silver, just as she faulted herself for falling in love with a sailor. Still, our love was as fierce as ever, and we reveled in each other's company night and day."

"So that is the way of it in the material world?" the pelican said. "One grows lonely, and then wanders?"

"Many wander," the fisherman said, "and many do not. For my beloved and me what mattered is that we always returned."

"As you have come here, to find her again," said the pelican. The pelican spread her wings, airing them in the cool evening air. She looked the fisherman up with one yellow eye and down with the other, thinking what a strapping good man he was. Cariña was lucky to have him, and yet, she had him not.

"For such a fine tale, I will bring you a fish," she said, and flew off over the inlet.

With all this remembering of his days with Cariña, the fisherman's loins were heavy with blood, and his lonely heart rattled in his chest. There was but one cure for what he felt. He must have her love again.

Patience, he told himself. She must come to him of her own free will.

FAR ABOVE THE INLET, AT the top of a column of rising air that spiraled perpetually upward in the warmth of the day, Dewi Sri circled, alone. 'Twas one of the pleasures of having wings, to rise on this air current, entering at the bottom and gliding to the top, as she had watched, the day before, the frigate bird rise. Though he was lighter than she, his form more slender, and so he rode the current without ever flapping his wings. He was, in the air, both elegant and nefarious, as he had been in her bed.

Now the frigate bird entered the column of rising air at the bottom, and rose up to meet the goddess. His heart was full of ardor, and his mind was full of courtly phrases he might use to woo her. For he would have her as his own, if he could, whatever that might take, and he let the spiral current of air take him to her.

They flew side by side and wingtip to wingtip, the frigate bird stealing glances at the goddess, and the goddess herself serenely facing the wind. She settled her breath, and thus calmed, found the balance point within.

"Where is that scoundrel crow?" the frigate bird asked.

"He is sleeping on his perch," the goddess said, a well-chuffed smile on her lips, "having been up all night, vexed because he knows not how to build a bed."

Excellent, thought the frigate bird. *I shall seize the moment.*

"Look at them," she said, pointing with her eyes at the fisherman and his beloved, wading in the inlet below. "He is full of desire, his heart is ruptured with it, and it is all for naught. That which is eternal in humans is without memory, and his beloved does not know him. Therefore he suffers."

"As does she," said the frigate bird, "for the lack of desire for a man who has declared himself to her. If her memory were restored, would she not love him as before?"

"Perhaps," said the goddess. "But when love's moment is lost, it is seldom recovered."

"Is that our tragedy as well?" said the frigate bird. His heart aflutter, he took the liberty of brushing his feathery wingtip on the wingtip of the goddess. "What of the night of passion we spent in your palace? We are lovers, are we not?"

They flew on in silence, the goddess directing her steady gaze at the far circle of the horizon, the wind molding her sarong to the fair form of her legs.

"We are all of us but parts of a pattern not of our own making," said the goddess, "and will always be so. You know this. Let the moments fold themselves, like the beautiful origami they are. And do not cling—it will only cause you pain."

Dewi's words, so diplomatically phrased, were nonetheless a dagger piercing his heart. He was being spurned, however gently. He let out a long sigh, and his throat pouch collapsed.

"So this is not our time?" said he.

"This is not our day," said the goddess, and she gave the frigate bird the boon of her serene smile. "How can you not know this?" said she, "You, who travel outside the bounds of time, do you not know your own destiny?"

"Even a traveler such as I has many blind spots," the frigate bird said. "I see the threads of fate, but not always my own place in them."

"The Turropsi themselves have blind spots," said Dewi Sri, "for they did not foresee that this woman would have no memory of the fisherman."

"They told you she would know him?" said the frigate bird.

"Not in so many words," said the goddess, "but 'twas clear they expected her to."

The frigate bird considered, and said, "If not even the Turropsi know the way forward, we are in greater peril than we knew."

"So it would seem," said she. "It shifts the burden of planning onto us." The wind fell off just then, the two of them dropping precipitously for a moment until the air held them aloft again.

"The way forward leads through stormy weather," said the frigate bird.

Dewi again pointed at the fisherman and his beloved below. "He needs a diversion," the goddess said. *As do you*, she thought. "A man in the throes of love spurned needs something to take his mind off his woe."

He nodded, his spirits buoyed by the hope that if he helped Dewi Sri she might bestow her favors on him again. "I have just the thing," said the frigate bird. "Grant me but a few days, and we shall have the beginnings of a new enterprise."

"Let it be so," said the goddess.

They flew on together, circling the inlet, and the world around them spun, as indifferent to the tumult of feelings within the frigate bird as it was to the serenity of the goddess.

THE CORMORANT CAME UPON THE fisherman as he sat alone by his fire, the remains of a roasted fish beside him.

"Ho," said the cormorant, "might I join you?"

The fisherman barely looked up, but he offered, with the palm of his hand, the remainder of the driftwood log. His beloved had wandered off and was now swimming in the inlet. She had turned down his offer to accompany her. The cormorant hopped up on the log and spread his wings to dry them.

"Forgive me," he said, "but this cooking of the fish before one eats it seems like a lot of bother, and surely it ruins the delicious wriggle of a live fish sliding down one's throat, does it not?"

"I suppose it does," said the fisherman, "but the thought of a live fish in my belly makes me bilious. I've eaten fish raw, in the islands of Nippon, and fish salted and stored in barrels on long sea voyages, but I prefer mine cooked over an open fire. The smoke gives it a meaty flavor that I quite like."

"Perhaps I'll try it sometime," said the cormorant, though he was certain he would not care for it. The fisherman stirred his coals with a stick, not, it seemed, because the fire needed it, but rather to pass the time. He was deep in some rumination, his brow troubled, his mouth turned down at the corners. The cormorant was not one to intrude, so he sat quietly for a while, until the fisherman finally spoke.

"I cannot fathom," he said, "how it is that my beloved can have a soul, and yet have no memories of her past life."

"An excellent question," the cormorant said. There was nothing he liked better than to ponder such things, and he hoped that the fisherman would be a worthy interlocutor. "It takes us straight to the metaphysical, which, as it happens, is a particular interest of mine."

"Is it?" said the fisherman. "Then perhaps you can tell me, what exactly is the soul?"

"Opinions vary," said the cormorant, "but most of the scholars in the material world are entirely too speculative for my taste. To be sure, they haven't had the advantage of coming here and seeing how the afterlife truly works. In a physical sense, the soul is a humming thing, a vibration so quiet it can scarcely be heard, but at the moment of death it congeals into that gob of mucous wrapped around your heart, the thing that the crow gets you humans to cough up with that cacophonous song of his. But in a metaphysical sense, the soul is something eternal. Only humans truly have one, and it is the part of them that precedes their individual lives and exists outside of those lives. It is the thing that gives self-awareness to a newborn babe, however rudimentary that self-awareness might be."

"I've heard such talk from scholars before," said the fisherman. "But why does Cariña have no memory of herself?"

"Hmm," said the cormorant. "Yes, that is the heart of the matter, pardon my pun. Well, what happens here is that the soul is separated from the body and given a chance to renew itself before returning to the material world. There's no need of individual memories for that to happen."

"Yet she remembers how to tie a knot, and how to skin a fish, and how to tend a fire. How is that possible?"

"Another excellent question," said the cormorant, who was delighted to be able to show off his scholarship. "Please understand, most of what I'm about to say is speculative on my part, but my theory is this: the memory of events resides in the mind, but the memory of skills resides in the body. It is her hands that remember how to tie a knot, not her mind. Her lips remember how to speak."

"And to kiss," said the fisherman.

"Just so. But once her soul had been removed from her, and her body thrown on the pyre, her mind was boiled away, and everything she once knew of her own history, everything she had experienced in the material world, boiled away with it. She no longer knows the story of her own life, and so she is reborn as a tabula rasa."

"A blank slate." The fisherman looked at the cormorant then with great sadness in his eyes. "She will never again be the woman I once knew, will she?"

The cormorant offered the fisherman what he hoped was his most sympathetic cluck. *"Sic transit gloria mundi,"* he said. "So passes away earthly glory. You cannot resist it."

The fisherman looked up at him, his suffering writ across his sorrowful face. But something else came into his eyes, a fierceness, a passion, a refusal to submit quietly to his fate.

How he suffers, thought the cormorant. And, *amantes sunt amentes*—lovers are lunatics. They set such store by these feelings, which were all too fickle if the ancient scrolls were to be believed. Yet there was something ennobling about the way the fisherman suffered, as if longing sharpened his humanity.

Perhaps, thought the cormorant, *the fisherman's service to a lost cause is the best part of him.*

Book Two
THE CONGRESS OF CROWS

AND SO IT CAME TO pass that romance bloomed on the Isle of the Dead even as, out in the Fetch, death and destruction grew ever closer. Both the fisherman and the crow were in the throes of love, and the frigate bird, too, was drunk with infatuation, though he had lost his place on the goddess's dance card. But like the others, he kept his wounded heart soothed with the balm of toil.

The fisherman, for his part, felled a cedar tree, and began the task of turning the fragrant wood into boards, loving them into shape with his hands. The frigate bird traveled from the spirit world to the material and back again, marshaling the implements the fisherman needed to build a home. Tools arrived in the hands of the dead, saws and planes, chisels and gouges, whetstones and files. Slowly a square room began to take shape, the proper house that the fisherman had long ago promised his beloved.

Their days fell into a rhythm, with the fisherman spearing a fish or two in the mornings, and his beloved fetching water from the stream with a wooden bucket that had been in the hands of a laundress at the moment her heart gave out. His beloved took over the cooking and the tending of the fire, and the fisherman sharpened his tools while she readied the day's first meal. He soon had a fine double-sided whetstone from the famed coticule quarry in the Ardennes, a better stone than any he'd held in all his years as a ship's carpenter. His belly full and his tools finely edged, he set about the day's work, and for her part, Cariña began a garden. She, too, was aided by the frigate bird, who caused seeds to be brought over, and by the pelican, who took a keen interest in her efforts to produce vegetables and grains. They discovered that a gobbet of the crow's guano and a drop of the pelican's blood mixed in a bucket of water made vegetables grow at a stupendous rate, and in short order they had potatoes and carrots, lettuces and maize, and wheat for bread.

They were spent in mind and body by the end of the day, but they had the satisfaction of surveying the results of their labor before the sun set each evening. They slept apart, but so close together in the lean-to that neither of them could roll over without consideration of the other, for they were cautious about touching each other. In that region of his thoughts where words held sway, the fisherman was careful not to think of himself as having any special claim on her favors. But in his heart his yearning for her was fierce, and though he held his feelings in check with the forbearance of a deep-water sailor, his desire for her was as much a part of him as his ribs, or his hands, or the way he knew how to shape a plank to fit tight against the next plank.

THE FISHERMAN AWOKE TO SOMETHING nuzzling at his ear, as if his beloved were nipping gently at his earlobe, and tracing the curve of the auricle with a fingernail.

"Cariña," he murmured, scarcely daring to believe that his beloved was finally warming up to him enough to touch him. He brought his hand to his ear to caress her hand, but what he felt there was bony, and too thick to be a finger, yet too thin to be her hand.

"Am I dreaming?" he said.

"It's me," came the whispered reply.

The fisherman opened his eyes to the visage of the frigate bird, who was leaning over him, the curved hook at the end of his bill scarcely an inch from his face. For a brief, nightmarish moment the fisherman felt as if he were about to have his eyes pecked out, but the frigate bird pulled away, and backed out of the lean-to. His beloved lay next to him, still sleeping. It was dark out, the middle of the night, and in the seaward distance the song of the paddlers on the canoe of the dead was approaching.

"Come with me," said the frigate bird. "We have need of your hands."

They walked together, man and bird, along the hard, wet sand, the canoe overtaking them as it made its way into the inlet. No matter how many times he saw it, the sight of the canoe, with the fish eagles flapping their wings in time with the paddlers paddling, and the sound of it, with the high-pitched keening of the fish eagles soaring over the massed voices of the newly dead, these sights and sounds filled the fisherman with awe. Beneath all that glorious sound, the Kiamah beast's heart kept its own time, deeply thumping, deeply thumping, in a rhythm as old as blood.

The canoe was beached, and its passengers were disgorging themselves from within it by the time the fisherman and the frigate bird joined the pelican and the cormorant. These two were greeting the dead, reassuring them that all was as it was supposed to be. The crow stood some distance away, waiting, the silhouette of his body sinister against the glow of the burned-down pyre.

An old farmer jumped down from the canoe, and he turned and reached his arms up. Someone dropped a full grain sack into his hands, and another, and another, and then a smaller and lighter sack, fragrant with a smell reminiscent of the hemp fields of Circassia, but with a hint of citrus on top.

"Give him a hand," said the frigate bird. "This cargo is ours." He plucked a coin that was tucked into his belt and dropped it into the outstretched hand of the old farmer.

A wheelbarrow was handed over the side, and the fisherman helped the farmer set it on the sand. Next came a cask, which was empty by the heft of it, but a well-made example of the cooper's art.

Then several more cloth sacks, very heavy, and a spade of good steel, with a thick tang embedded in an ironwood handle. Lastly, at the bidding of someone within the canoe, a stevedore by the look of him, the fisherman came aboard to help with a mortar and pestle. The mortar was as big around as a cart wheel, and the stevedore, with no more than a nod of his chin and a grunt, directed the fisherman to lift it with him. They brought it to the edge of the canoe, and the frigate bird yelled, "Stand back," and they dropped the stone on the sand. The fisherman took note of the space beneath a thwart in the prow of the canoe wherein all this cargo had been stored. A space big enough for a man or two to stow away in, and in the darkness, if they were covered by a blanket or a tarp, they would likely not be seen.

The stevedore dropped the pestle, the size of a small amphora, off the other side of the prow, and the fisherman jumped down and rejoined the frigate bird.

"What is all this?" said the fisherman.

"Barley," said the frigate bird, pointing with a wing at the grain sacks, "and hops. You remember you once asked if there were an alehouse on the Isle of the Dead?"

A broad grin grew slowly across the fisherman's face. "I do."

"And would it please you to know that this scroll here"—the frigate bird indicated a roll of parchment tucked into his belt—"contains the recipe for making ale?"

"It would," said the fisherman. He picked up the sack of hops and smelled it. His grin stretched even wider, and he closed his eyes, overcome by the memory of the alehouse he had once frequented in Hav, where they hung their hops to dry from the rafters.

And so they loaded up the wheelbarrow, and carried their goods back to the fisherman's home.

"These heavy cloth sacks," said the fisherman, "these are not grain?"

"No indeedy," said the frigate bird. "That's cement, the very best, made according to the ancient Roman formula."

Curious, thought the fisherman. He was a woodworker, and had never had much to do with masonry, but he had been to Rome, and seen the Colosseum, and the Senate, and the temples of the gods. Those buildings had stood for centuries, untouched by the ravages of time.

"And what, pray tell, are we going to build with cement?"

The frigate bird put a wing across his shoulders, and walked companionably beside the fisherman. "Something," he said, "the likes of which the spirit world has never seen."

THE WOMAN, FOR HER PART, saw each thing in the world in delicate detail. Her own hands were a newborn source of wonder, the way her fingers grew out of her knuckles, the flow of the lines across her palms, the one hand a mirror for the other. She was struck joyful by the play of light on the waves of the inlet, by the subtle shift in the shades of green in the boughs of trees as the sun made its transit across the sky. The rich, euphoric brown of the long tubes of kelp stranded along the beach made her smile, and she had no need to know why. To have dirt from her garden under her fingernails, to have smoke from a cooking fire scenting the air, to have the company of the pelican as they swam together in the inlet, this was all she needed of jubilation.

Beyond the garden, the house the fisherman was building took shape, rising plank by plank from the ground, the boards covering the frame like skin on bones. The fisherman's clever hands, his fingers covered with calluses and cuts from his tools, were a marvel to her, although she was careful not to let him see her staring at them. She liked the sound of him hammering away, or drawing a saw to cut through a piece of wood. She gathered the curled shavings from his auger and threw them on the embers in the morning for the simple joy of watching them take flame. He was a good man, she thought. There was no guile in his face, bereft as it was of eyebrows, and that, along with his blue skin, gave his countenance an innocence she found sweet. *Perhaps it is true what he says, that we loved each other once, for surely he loves me still.* She should go to him, and let him take her in his arms, the way he clearly longed to do.

The light shifted as a cloud passed before the sun. Her garden was weeded, and it was not yet time to begin the evening's meal. They had a year and a day to be together, so had he said. *Time enough*, she thought, *for me to take my time.* The moment might yet come when she felt drawn to him as he was to her. And he had assured her that she owed him nothing beyond the pleasure of her company at dinner each night, and that much she gave him.

With a last look at the fisherman she let her feet take her where they would, and that was down to the water, away from him. The inlet was calm, and she took off her sarong and dove beneath the surface.

THE CROW, FOR ALL THE thousands of years he had occupied his perch on the Isle of the Dead, was naught but an eager squab when it came to love. He believed, as all first-time lovers do, that no one's heart had ever boiled over with such ardor as did his. He was the very avatar of romance, and there was no one to rival the goddess, with her scent as delicate as jasmine, and her skin as soft as the downy lining of a nest. He loved the colorful sarong she wore and the way the sunlight played upon her hair.

"Oh, my darling," she soothed, "such a fine bed you'll build us. In it we shall scale the heights of passion, and I will make such a lover of you as this world has never seen."

The crow sighed. He had yet to begin the building of this bed she wanted, for he had not the slightest idea of how a bed was built.

Dewi began to hum, and the crow's head was filled with the clear ringing tones of gamelan. "I am exceedingly fond," said she, "of carved bedposts."

Carved bedposts? To learn to carve something fit for a goddess would take a good deal of time. The thought of so much delay made his zibik wither. "Darling," said he, "I fear I am no carver."

"Look at me," the goddess said, and when he did so, a single note in his ears chimed, and the chime spread to his hands, the gaze of the goddess tuning him from the inside out. She brought his hands to her lips, and kissed the palms, and stroked each of his fingers with hers, and all the while his hands buzzed with the good, good excitations of the melody she hummed.

"You are a carver now, my sweet," said she, "for I have given you this boon."

The crow looked at his hands as if he had never seen them before. To be in love was to lose himself, only to find a better self in the eyes of his darling. "Kiaw!" he cried, "kiaw aw aw aw aw!" All he lacked now was a carving knife.

The goddess reached for his breechcloth, and the crow's zibik, ever ready, gave a quick throb and began to grow. At long last, the moment was come! But her hand drew forth not his meat whistle, but a carving knife that she had magicked into a belt of tools that hung from his hips.

"You have everything you need," said she, "now go forth and carve." And she spun him round by the shoulders, and gave him a gentle shove in the middle of his back.

My zibik is hard enough, thought he, *that if I were to put an edge on it, I could carve this entire forest into toothpicks.*

THE PELICAN PLUCKED WEEDS WITH her bill, and tossed them aside. She liked this new thing in the world, this gardening, and if she shifted into her old woman shape, she liked the crunch and the flavor of what grew here. Cucumbers she liked most especially, and raw potatoes, still in their skins, with the smell of the dirt fresh on them. And the flatbread that the woman baked on flat stones banked around the fire. Her feathers, nourished by all this good new food, were growing back in the bald spot on her belly where she'd worried them away with her nervous bill. But more than gardening and eating, she liked having someone new to talk with, someone womanly like herself. And with the scandalous doings of Dewi Sri and the crow, there was plenty to talk about.

"Did you see them yesterday?" the woman said, "staring into each other's eyes? She's got him turning backward somersaults at the flick of an eyelash." The silver chain the fisherman had given her shone against her skin in the sunlight, and she felt the fine texture of its links. She had removed the last of the pitch balls so that it would lie flat. The fisherman, she knew, kept hoping that she would remember something of her past life, but there was no such longing within her, although the chain drew her fingers to it like no other object in the world.

"Too true," said the pelican, "and now he's carving those bedposts for her, day and night. When the canoe of the dead arrives, he rushes them off without all that strutting and savagery he usually does. He doesn't even bother to line them up, he just sings that awful song of his, and they cough up their souls, and then off they go in a big rabble to the pyre. He leaves the tending of the fire to the cormorant and me, and he goes back to his carving."

"Are they sleeping together?" the woman asked. The bedroom arrangements of one's betters were eternally amusing, she thought, although she did not know how she knew this.

"Oh no," the pelican said. "She's much too clever for that. She's got him convinced that they can only consummate in a bed fit for a goddess. And he barely sleeps anyway since she arrived. He's too busy carving, and rubbing her feet every time she sits down."

"Do you think they'll have a wedding?" the woman asked.

"They shall have," said the pelican, "whatever Dewi wants."

WHILE THE CROW CARVED BEDPOSTS, Dewi Sri explored the Isle of the Dead. She flew over the forest, skimming the treetops and breathing in the tang of cedar and fir boughs. This forest was so different from the one where she lived, with its tumult of flowering trees, looping jungle vines, brightly colored snakes, and chattering, screeching monkeys. Here was only quiet, and the soft shush of tree branches moving with the wind. Moss grew everywhere, and hung from the trees like living shrouds.

She invited the cormorant to accompany her on one of these flights, and together they circumnavigated the isle. They landed then on the peak of the highest mountain, at the center of the isle, and stood together on that rocky promontory. The sun was bright, and the cormorant's spectacles seemed magically to have lenses of smoked glass in them.

"I've never thought to come up here," said the cormorant. "The view is phenomenal."

"'Tis strange," the goddess said, "to see a forest so green and yet so empty of life."

"Strange?" said the cormorant. "I should think that it is only natural that the Isle of the Dead be full of lifelessness."

The goddess stood with her wings spread, the wind at the top of the mountain wafting through her feathers. "Where I come from," said she, "there are rice paddies everywhere, and the land is teeming with creatures, and never silent. At night the fireflies gather above the paddies by the thousands, and the night is lit by their tiny lanterns."

"Of course," said the cormorant. "For you are a goddess of life, while we here serve life's antipode."

Far below, the waters of the inlet were a deep green, and a rainbow hung in the mists above the waterfall.

"That canyon," the goddess said, pointing with one of her elegant fingers at the cleft in the land beneath the rainbow, "have you been there?"

"No," said the cormorant, "I have not. Only the crow goes there."

"Oh?" said the goddess. "How interesting. I suppose you've known the crow a long time?"

"Oh my, yes," said the cormorant. "For eons."

"He's a complicated fellow," said the goddess.

Blink, blink, blink went the cormorant's eyes. "I suppose," he said. "Things are different around here now. Not so long ago his elder cousin Raven was in charge. Back then the crow's job was to make sure the sacred fire never went out. He was a lowly fellow, a humble scavenger who picked at the scorched bones as he banked the coals in the morning light. Nobody paid him much mind."

"He is strapping and sinewy, and not without a certain charm," said the goddess, "and yet you ignored him."

The cormorant looked over the tops of his spectacles at the goddess, first with one eye, then the other. "In his man shape he is well-built," said the cormorant. "But charming? He is a trickster and a scoundrel, and he is drunk with his newfound power."

"He has been making up for lost time, has he not?" the goddess said.

"Hmmm," said the cormorant, stroking the place where he would have a chin if he had a chin. "I suppose you're right."

Dewi Sri folded her wings and leaned back against a boulder, sunning herself, her wing feathers softly nacreous in the bright light. "There is another side to him," she said. "The crow in love is a crow you've not seen before. And as to being a scoundrel, surely a scholar such as yourself knows that women love a scoundrel, both for the way he excites them, and for the thrill of taming him."

"I am a scholar of many things," said the cormorant, "but love is not amongst them."

"Then begin your scholarship of love by studying the story unfolding all around you," she said. "The fisherman loves his beloved, who knows him not, so therein lies the tale of love unrequited. And both the crow and the frigate bird love me, and I shall play one off against the other, and therein lies the eternal triangle of love."

"It is an old story, I know," said the cormorant, "yet not one we've seen in these parts." He shifted his weight from foot to foot, and then spread his wings as if he might fly off. "Forgive me for making so bold as to say this, but it would seem that you are brewing trouble."

"Change can be troublesome," said the goddess, "but this place is ripe for it. Be not afraid. Things other than trouble shall be brewed here."

The cormorant rattled his flight feathers to shake off the sense of impending doom he felt. The goddess meant to use her feminine wiles against the crow, that much was clear, and how could that mean anything but trouble once the crow realized her plot? And what of the Kiamah beast, kept drowsy with conaria for now, who would swallow the material world if he awoke? The goddess made no mention of that flagitious monstrosity, and instead advised him to study love, which seemed unwise, given the circumstances. Better he should study the arts of war.

"There is an old curse," said the cormorant, "that says 'May you live in interesting times.'"

"So there is," said the goddess. "But there is an older wisdom that says each moment is the only moment you have. Take courage, friend. It is no accident that I am here, and you shall have a part to play in what comes."

The goddess stood and offered the cormorant her beatific smile. Then she spread her wings and flew off the edge of the precipice. The cormorant watched her grow smaller as her wings carried her aloft.

"Auk," said the cormorant. "That is precisely what I fear."

THE GODDESS LOOKED CLOSELY AT the bedpost she held in her hands. It was one of four that the crow had carved according to her most detailed instructions. Its foot was a turtle, and from the back of the turtle two snakes rose, entwined around each other. The crow produced, from the tool belt he wore round his waist, the magician's glass he had schemed away from the fisherman, and she held it to her eye, the better to see his workmanship.

"Marvelous," she said, "so intricate." She stroked his shiny beak, and kissed the flat feathers that covered his nostrils, and whispered her dulcet demand into his ear. "Although I wonder, O dearest one, why the snakes have no scales?"

The crow's heart fell at the hint of disappointment in Dewi's words. The bedposts were taller than he was. It would take him days upon days to carve so many scales. But one look into her eyes was all it took for him to accede to her request, for here was yet another way to please her. Pleasing the goddess made the blood run hot to his zibik, and while the stiffening made him want to put his hands beneath his breechcloth, he was determined to save himself for her, and only her.

"Only because, my angel," he said, "I have not yet carved them."

THE GODDESS, HAVING SURVEYED THE canyon on the wing, announced that she would take the woman and the pelican there for an afternoon of womanly pleasures, and so she led her female companions to the waterfall. They brought with them baskets full of lettuces and snap peas, jicamas and spinach, romanescos and zucchinis, and smoked fish flavored with sage. They brought combs and soaps and blankets, they brought perfumes and unguents and kohl, things the frigate bird, ever eager to please the goddess, had ushered to the Isle of the Dead in the canoe. Out of deference to the woman's lack of wings they walked through the narrow canyon to the waterfall, the pelican in her old woman shape, the goddess with her wings raised like a great parasol, to keep them from trailing in the stream, and the woman behind them, wading in water up to her thighs where the canyon walls fell too close to afford them a dry path.

When they reached the rocky, steep-sided bowl at the end of the canyon, the goddess, arrested by beauty, flittered her wings and hovered in the mist from the waterfall, turning slowly to take it all in. Maidenhair ferns growing from rocky niches bobbed a greeting to her, and lichens brightened their colors in her presence. The woman and the pelican were rendered openmouthed and mute by the wanton beauty of the place. Sunlight glanced off the water and danced on the canyon walls, and the air was edged with salt from the sea and tinged with the sweet and sour redolence of cedar sap.

Dewi, for her part, found herself drawn to the waterfall, which, for all its misty cascade, bright in the sunlight, seemed to hide a dark presence. There was more here than met the eye, thought she, though she could not say what that might be. She was well out of her familiar surroundings back on Bali Dwipa, and she found the quiet of this place, its lack of animal sounds, unnerving.

Perhaps that was all it was. She turned away from the waterfall, rejoining her companions, and they set down their baskets and spread their things on the sandy beach. Off came their sarongs, and the three women waded into the pool at the base of the waterfall, splashing one another and laughing. The sun was warm and the water cool, and the cascade from the lip of the rock bowl gathered rainbows of prismed light in honor of their arrival. The women swam for a time and then gathered on the shore to dry themselves, and to partake of their repast, and to talk.

They sat together and ate, taking turns feeding one another, and Dewi Sri entertained them with the tale of how the War of the Gods began. She sat in lotus position atop a flat boulder with her back to the sun, drying her wing feathers. "I lived in the palace of Batara Guru, my foster father, he of the four arms and the ophidian neck, and I grew from a little hatchling doted on by all to a young woman who was desired by all. Even Batara Guru desired me, forgetting in his lust that I was his daughter, and he wooed me with lavish gifts. He ordered the other gods to build for me a palace, which is my home to this day, and he bestowed upon me these wings with which I fly." Here the goddess stood and spread her wings, turning so that her audience might see their beauty.

"At first I thought he was acting out of a father's devotion," the goddess went on, once again seated. "But he lured me to his bedchamber

with the promise of a gift beyond all others, and there he showed me
his great q'hram, and asked me to touch it, to prove my love for all
he had done for me. I refused him, and fled to my brother Sedana's
palace. Sedana gathered many of the gods to a great council, and
it was decided that Batara Guru must be killed for his attempt to
corrupt me. But some of the gods did not believe my story, and they
sided with Batara Guru, who told them it was I who had tried to
seduce him, so that I might take his q'hram in my mouth and devour
it, and thereby gain all his power for my own." There was a furrow
between Dewi Sri's eyebrows, the only sign on her serene face that her
tale troubled her in any way.

"This was a foul lie, and further proof of Batara Guru's corruption,
for it is ever the case that power lies heavy on the soul of anyone who
bears it. I wept for my father, who had lost his way, and I refused to
fight against him and begged for a truce, that we might avoid the
war. But Batara Guru, in his pride and in his shame, would have
nothing to do with peace, and so the war began." Here the goddess
paused to take a sip of water from her teacup, and thus refreshed,
she went on.

"Now it so happened that at the same time there was also a great
war in the material world, and the dead arrived on the shore by the
thousands, waiting for the canoe to take their souls across. Sedana
and Batara Guru made great speeches to persuade the dead to join
one side or the other, and the hot breath they exhaled filled the dead
with battle lust, so that even women and children became warriors.
Fate decreed that the battles be fought at sea, and the two armies,
Sedana's and Batara Guru's, they each built many warships, and
they forged many swords, and they sailed their armadas out to where
the water was deep. There they flung fireballs at one another's ships
with trebuchets, sinking some of the ships outright, and destroying
the sails of others. They boarded these floating hulks and had at one
another with their swords and their knives and their cudgels, bash-
ing in skulls and beheading the bodies. They fought for forty days
and forty nights, first one gaining the advantage and then the other.
The killing never stopped until the sea was red with blood, until the
bodies filled the sea and covered the waves, and one could walk from
one shore to the other upon them." The goddess stared off into the

middle distance for a moment, and brought her palms together, and touched her fingertips to her forehead in remembrance of the dead.

"The bloodlust that had consumed these fallen warriors sank to the bottom and gathered there like quicksilver," said the goddess, "their twice-dead souls putrefying for a hundred times a hundred days, and it was from this evil, oily muck that the Kiamah birthed itself." The pelican shivered at this, and murmured a prayer that they all might be delivered from evil, while the woman sat with her arms wrapped tightly round her body, chilled from within by visions of war. The goddess too was still for a moment, for the birth of the Kiamah was part of her family's shame, and she was the heir to that shame even now.

"The gods fought until they were exhausted," the goddess went on, "until on the final day of the war, Sedana and Batara Guru met face to face, in the middle of the sea, where they stood on the bodies of the dead. They drew their terrible swords and laid into each other, and the sky turned black, and lightning flashed and thunder stormed each time their swords clanged. So caught up in their struggle were they that they did not realize that they were both slowly sinking into the sea, the bodies beneath them bursting and then collapsing after so many days in the water. When both gods were up to their necks they each thrust their swords into the other, and they slew each other, my brother Sedana and my father Batara, and it was only then that the war ended."

The pelican was weeping as Dewi Sri's story came to a close, and the woman, too, had tears in her eyes. They sat in silence, the dark tale of the War of the Gods made darker by the brightness of the day, and the beauty of the waterfall.

"Your beauty," said the woman, "has been the cause of a great deal of woe."

"It is a kind of power," said the goddess, "and like all power, when it is put to an ill use, it takes its toll. It is my saving grace that it was not I who misused this gift."

The pelican lay her head next to the goddess's, and stroked her arm. "You must be so sad," said she, "to have lost your family this way."

The goddess considered for a moment. "Once, I was," said she, "but that was a long time ago, and in my grief I learned a great lesson, which is to let go the past, and savor the moment. And something else was gained, for now, in my kingdom, a woman rules instead of a man, and we are all the better for it."

"It's an old story you tell," said the woman. "I feel the shape of it when I close my eyes and watch the shadows within me. Men are forever playing with their knives, are they not, and speechifying about all the injustices they think they must remedy?"

The women nodded in agreement, and they left off speaking of war, and they began to take turns with their unguents and perfumes, applying them to one another. The goddess produced a fine brush made of hair from the belly of a mongoose, and she brushed kohl round the woman's eyes, black above, and green below. The pelican opened her bill and let show her woman face within, and round her eyes too the goddess brushed on kohl, and then pelican and woman took turns with the brush, each of them brushing kohl round an eye of the goddess. They found a still spot in the stream, where the light of the sun reflected back at them like a mirror, and they admired their handiwork, and they were well pleased. A dragonfly hovered over them, the iridescent blue of its body bright in the sunlight. It flew from one to another of the women as each of them spoke, pausing in the air as if to underline their words with the thrum of its wings.

"So," said the woman to Dewi Sri, "what will you do with your swain, the crow?"

The goddess laughed. "The crow is but a child when it comes to romance, as eager as the rawest youth to prove his devotion to me." She held out her hand, and the dragonfly hovered there, within her grasp, although she did not close her fingers round it. "What a beautiful creature," she said. "How did you get here?"

"It must have come across on the canoe," said the pelican. "We have no such animals here."

"Then it is a rare creature indeed," said the goddess, and she offered it the vaya mudra, the mudra of air. The dragonfly hovered closer, as if to kiss her fingertips.

"The crow is dangerous," said the pelican. "You have no idea of his savagery."

"I am well aware of his bad habits," said Dewi Sri, "but he is not without his charms, for he is well-formed, and clever, although he is no match for me."

"Do tell," said the woman. "And to what extent have you sampled those charms?" She cast a glance at the pelican, whom she could tell had not the nerve to ask the goddess what they both wanted to know. "Just how well-formed is he?"

Dewi Sri raised an eyebrow and grinned at the woman. The dragonfly hovered a few inches from her mouth, marking her words with the buzz of its wings. "Well-formed indeed, if I may judge from the lump his q'hram makes in his breechcloth. He shall have to be schooled in the art of love, of course, for a man with a large q'hram so quickly thinks he already has all the answers to a woman's needs."

"Is it so grand, this pleasure of coupling?" said the pelican. "The opportunity has never come my way."

"Oh, yes," said the goddess. "So long as one's lover knows the way of it. I shall lead the crow to his best self," said she. "And along the way, I shall have the pleasure of mastering him in body and soul, and of bending him to my will. I shall hold his whirligigs in my hand, stroking his tenderest parts as he begs me to take his q'hram in my mouth, and I shall do so, but first, I'll have him kneel before my southern face, and I shall take a randy ride on that beak of his, which has a purpose he has not yet dreamt of." Here the dragonfly zoomed away, taking a turn around the inside of the rocky bowl before returning to the circle of women.

"You speak like a common gill-flurt," the pelican said.

"A woman who understands the power and the pleasure is no gill-flurt, but a queen," said the goddess. "And a man who will be both master and mastered in the act of love is no lecher, but a king. And should we not rule our own lives together, as king and queen, and thereby share the pleasure that our bodies are made to give one another?"

"Really?" said the woman. "You would give yourself to him?"

"I will not deny myself the pleasure," said the goddess, "if the proper moment arrives. To school such a god, with his rare apparatus, in the art of love, is not a chance to be missed. You might want to try him out yourself, once he's had the benefit of my tutelage." *What better way*, thought the goddess, *to keep the crow distracted.*

"Surely not," said the woman, "for you would be jealous, and I would not risk that offense."

The goddess waved away the woman's words with a flick of her wrist. "The jealous poison their own banquet, and then eat it," said the goddess. The dragonfly hovered in front of her lips, its insect eyes black and gleaming. "No offense would be taken, so long as you wait your turn."

"The fisherman may not be so forgiving," said Cariña.

The goddess considered for a moment. At home, in her palace, she kept no secrets from her paramours, and required the same of them. But here, where she served the Turropsi, perhaps a different approach was needed, for the crow was sly, and capable of subterfuge. She would do well to meet his cunning with cunning of her own.

"Then you should take care that you are not found out," said the goddess. "He will not miss a slice from a cut loaf, unless you tell him."

"He's had no slice from my loaf since I've arrived here," said the woman. She laughed, to think of her quim as a loaf, and wondered, smiling, if in this afterlife she was now a virgin.

Ah, thought Dewi, *they were not yet coupling. Here, perhaps, was a way to recover love's lost moment.*

"Take pity on him then," said the goddess, "and give him the first slice. For your sake, as much as his, for a woman needs pleasure even more than a man."

"Oh," said the woman, her lips pushed into a bow. She thought for a moment, and felt, for the first time since she had awoken here, a stirring in her loins. Her flesh remembered things that her mind did not, and what the goddess proposed sent a thrill through her. She met the gaze of the goddess, and she nodded her head.

"So be it, then," said the goddess, her smile broad. *'Twas ever the case that a good coupling was just what the plot needed.*

"And what of me?" said the pelican. "Am I to have a turn?" There was a sad downturn to the curve of her bill, for she had come to understand that she was too old to kindle desire in the loins of men.

The goddess extended a hand to the pelican, and a hand to the woman, and then the woman and the pelican joined hands so that they formed a ring of feminine accord.

"Dear friend," said the goddess, "of course you shall have a turn. There's more joy in the sharing than there is in the keeping."

The goddess then bade them all sit on their blankets, and she rubbed their feet with perfumed oil, and they, in turn, rubbed hers. The dragonfly flew off, intent on its own business. From feet they moved on to hands, the goddess showing them by her unhurried example that they should all take their time, and they did so, touching and being touched. From hands they moved on to backs, joyful moans rising unbidden from them as each was the subject of the others' attentions. The goddess teased them with her wing feathers, and the pelican and the woman teased back with their fain fingertips, their nails tracing lazy lines from nape of neck to base of spine, and then spreading outward until the whole of their backs tingled with pleasure. Now the goddess led them from backs to breasts, surprising her companions with the increasing delight of the moment, and the way their nether lips began to grow moist. Surprising them too, with the adoration shining forth from her eyes, which drew forth that same adoration from their eyes, the delights of the flesh swelling the affection in their hearts.

The goddess bade them lie back, and now her hands wandered from arch of foot to curve of thigh, and from curve of thigh to joy of belly, and from joy of belly to delight of breasts, and from delight of breasts to thrill of lips, hers upon Cariña's, and Cariña's upon hers, while the pelican discovered that the soft skin of her throat pouch wanted nothing so much as to be nuzzled with their lips, and that the hard tip of her long bill was yet another tool to softly tease their skin. The goddess let the bounty of her breasts touch the bounty of theirs, her hardened nipples delicate against the delicacy of their nipples, their skin awakened and alive from tip of toes to crown of head. She spread their legs by slow degrees with gentle touch, and when their legs lay wide and open she pleasured them with her hands and her mouth, their tenderest parts swelling with blood-filled desire, the savory tang of their juices flowing, their hips rising as they pressed forward at long last their eager nubbins to meet her touch in surge upon surge of ecstasy.

All this she gave them, and all this they gave to her in return. Then she straddled herself on the pelican's bill, and rubbed her quim back and forth, showing them how she would ride the crow's beak, polishing her pearl to its utmost brightness, without risking the sharp point entering her tenderest parts.

Thus did she awaken in the woman and the pelican a lust that had lain dormant. And, in satisfying for one another that lust, they formed that day, as the goddess had foreseen, a bond that stood them in good stead as events unfolded.

SO THIS IS HOW IT is, thought the crow. *The goddess is a trickster, and a tart, and she means to make a fool of me.* He was in his crow form, for it was in his crow form that he felt closest to his true nature, and he circled the pyre of smoldering bones in the afternoon sunlight, looking for snacks. He was hungry, as he had not been since the goddess had arrived and stolen his heart. He spied the charred remains of a woman at the bottom of the pyre, a body not yet entirely consumed by the flames. She lay with her back to the pyre, if she'd had a back, for her head and most of her trunk were missing. But her legs were spread, and her nether parts lay between them like a smoked oyster.

"Kiaaw aw aw aw aw aw," said the crow, his voice raspy with anger. He would show that strumpet of a goddess the special purpose of his beak. He bent down and tore the dead woman's oyster from between her legs and gobbled it down. "Aw!" he shouted. Such a tasty treat. If only her nipples were here for dessert. He pulled the rest of the flesh from her thighs. It was crispy on the outside, and not quite as tender within as he might have liked, but it tore away in long strips, revealing the whiteness of her bones. It was as if he were undressing her, and he found that satisfying, aw, yes, in a way he never had before. He moved on, looking for more morsels, his appetite whetted. He had, he found, a particular hankering for the flesh of women, with its distinctly distaff flavor, its hint of the earthy funk of the womb mixed with the silvery scent of the moon.

The goddess was a bawdy, rampallian strumpet, he thought, and she meant to share him around with her covey of cunnies. The thought made his zibik hard. That part of her randy scheme was just fine by him, but he would not be made out a fool. She wants scales carved on her bedposts, does she? Thinks she can have a little fun at my expense, making me wait to sample the fullness of her charms? Naw. Naw, naw, naw, naw, naw.

Never trick a trickster, kiaw, for he who tricks last, tricks best.

It took some hard work on the part of the fisherman, aided by his beloved, and the ever-helpful pelican, who was spending more and more time in her old-woman shape, but together they dug a trench beside the half-built house, and then lined that trench with concrete they made with sand and rocks and Roman cement. The frigate bird assigned the tasks, and the women pitched in, Cariña because the smell of the barley and hops triggered in her a desire to taste the ale that would be made from them, and the pelican because she was caught up in the fisherman's enthusiasm.

"Ale," said the fisherman, with shovel in hand and sweat on his brow, "is the staff of life. It is bread made liquid, and a tankard of ale at the end of a hard day's toil is a balm for the mind and a liniment for the body." And then he broke out in song:

> *Drink, if there's beer in your jar*
> *'Tis far to the sun from the stars*
> *Drink it well, drink it deep*
> *Out of the barrel flows the beer*
> *Semper clara*

"Oh, I like that one," said the pelican, "very classy, with the Latin and all. Sing it again, and I'll sing it with you."

So they sang together while they worked, the woman too, their several hands making the task go faster. The day after the cement was cured, they poured the barley in the trench and sprinkled it with water from the stream.

"Excellent water," said the frigate bird, who seemed to know a great deal about the making of ale. "Crystal clear, with just a hint of flintiness. Perfect for making a pale ale—the minerals will bring out the citrus flavors in the hops."

The fisherman had never thought much about the flavor of ale, but once the frigate bird started talking about it, he realized that every alehouse made its own ale, and each one was a little different. From Anchuria to Zhlatovica he'd drunk ales, some of them divine, most of them good, if uninspired, and a few that were pretty awful.

"Do you know that alehouse in Kumar," said the fisherman," the one just down from the temple of Tammuz?"

"The Three-Legged Pig?" said the frigate bird. "Their sign is a pig whose body is a cask of ale, and one of the legs is broken off? "

"No," said the fisherman, "you're thinking of Cabo Luna, up the coast from Cadiz. Kumar is across the straits. You know it because the legs of an ancient colossus straddle the entrance to the harbor."

"Oh yes," said the frigate bird. "I know the city, if not the alehouse."

"There's a statue of Ninkasi next to the door, sitting on a pig of ale."

"Full of pirates and thieves? They've always got a pig roasting on a spit in the middle of the room?"

"That's the one."

"Ye gods, how I love roast pig."

"Me too. I think the alehouse is called Ninkasi's Pig. Maybe the best ale I've ever drunk. You should try it, next time you're in the area."

"I shall, if the opportunity arises," said the frigate bird, "though I must be careful, walking in to a place like that. Too many of your kind give a six-foot-tall bird, even a talking bird, a lean and hungry look, and think only of their bellies."

They kept the barley moist for several days until it sprouted, and then they built smoldering fires at either end of the trench and roasted the barleycorns, turning them with the shovel, which they had rinsed clean in the waters of the inlet. "That will add just a touch of salt," said the woman, showing her keen interest in the finer points of brewing. They dried the roasted barleycorns for several days, souring them slightly in the process, and then they ground the dried kernels in the mortar and pestle, added more water to make a dough of the mash, and formed loaves. These they baked on the stones around the fire, but not long enough to finish them. They drizzled honey into the cask, "For the yeast more than the sugar," said the frigate bird, as they crumbled the half-baked loaves into pieces. They filled the cask with a mixture of water and the half-baked bread, sealed the bunghole with its bung, and waited a few more days while it fermented.

Meanwhile the walls of the house the fisherman was building went higher and higher, plank by plank. He built himself a ladder, and cut a ridge pole and rafters, and gave the house the simple shape of a pitched roof divided down the middle, with a gable at either end. His beloved helped him set the rafters in place over several days, fitting their notches to notches in the rim joist.

It took them three days to cover the rafters with a raddling of fir boughs and dried sea grass, but when they were done, they had a roof over their heads. They stood under it as the sun filled the room with light and shadows, a room several times bigger than the hut they had occupied in the Spice Islands. This was a proper home, thought the fisherman, with proper windows, two on either side so they could look out, and two up high in each of the gabled ends to let in more light. And to his deep satisfaction, the hinges for the shutters were of brass, brought here by the frigate bird.

The woman was well pleased, and she put her arms round the fisherman and held him close. "Thank you," she whispered. "I am well cared for here, and I owe that to you."

The fisherman wanted to wallow in the warmth of her embrace, and he held her close for a long time, his chin resting on her shoulder and the smell of her filling his nose, until his willy-spigot began to swell the front of his breeches. He let her go, walking out the doorway to hide his condition, for he feared she would turn him away if he tried to press the matter forward. Because he did not turn round he failed to see her empty arms and her crooked smile, a smile he would have remembered as an invitation to a kiss.

On the evening of the day when they finished the roof, the frigate bird returned from the land of the living with a lump of hashish. They celebrated together, the fisherman and his beloved, the frigate bird, the pelican, and the cormorant, all of them laughing and singing and going for a midnight swim beneath the vast roof of the Kiamah's belly. The canoe of the dead paddled swiftly by, and the cormorant and the pelican flew off to meet it. The woman stood next to the fisherman, both of them waist deep in the water, and when their hands brushed against each other, they let them, and did not pull back.

That night, before the fisherman settled into his mossy bed his beloved took his face between her hands and kissed him. "Sleep well," she said. He caught her hands in his and held them, her eyes open to his, his eyes full of memory, and hers full of romance.

"Is it sleep that you desire?" said he. He kissed her in return, their lips lingering and soft as they renewed their old acquaintance, and then hungry, ardent, and fierce. Something long asleep within her was stirring, and the fisherman was only too happy to help her stir it.

"Let me," said she, "be the quiver for your arrow."

And so she was.

THE CROW FLEW HIGH ABOVE the inlet, just below the overarching belly of the Kiamah beast, his spirit in a ruckus. When he thought of the goddess, he wanted to touch her, to rub his beak all over her body, to press his zibik against her loins. What happened after that was not entirely clear to him, but he knew that something urgent inside him would find a release. And yet . . . and yet . . . and yet . . . he wanted something more. Something dark and violent, something just as urgent, just as in need of release. He wanted . . . he wanted . . . yes, this was it. *Kiaw!* He wanted to plunge his beak into her chest and rip out her heart!

He was, after all, a god, and a king, and he was every bit her equal. No, he was better than she, for he was crow, and human, and mole, and dragonfly, and he could take any shape he wanted, if only he practiced a bit whatever the form he chose. She was a gill-flurt, and a whore, and he would slay her and all who loved her. But first he must have her, he must show her what a prize he was, so that she would know her own foolishness as she died on the end of his beak.

What a mountain of dung love was. To feel so hot and so cold all at once. Over the same creature. She was a woman, and a goddess, and how could he kill the only woman he had ever loved? She was a devil. He must avenge her mockery of him—*aw aw aw aw aw.* Love her. Kill her. Love. Kill. *Aw. Kiaw. Aw. Kiaw.*

The crow flew in circles, muttering and considering. Why have a heart if it meant this much sorrow? He was wretched, and his life meant nothing to him anymore. Awww, death would be such sweet sorrow. Death was the answer to his anguish. Hers, his—it made little difference. The crow paused in his flight and passed a wing in front of himself. He would end his suffering in one final gesture of brokenhearted revenge. In his human shape, from high above the inlet, which was the size of a mere puddle below him, he fell from the sky, his arms spread. The wind in his face swept the feathers on his head back. He was a god, but he was not immortal. None of them were. Not Raven, not any of the Old Gods, not Dewi Sri. Wind whistled past. What a splash he would make. She would know then, she had broken his heart. She would die of loneliness, weeping over his broken body, bringing flowers to his grave. With her last breath she would cry out "I have wronged you, O noble crow, forgive me." And he would not. Or he would. Or not.

He fell and fell and fell. Now the inlet rippled with waves. Closer, closer. If he died, he would never have the pleasure. Her radiant skin, the dizzy thrill of her touch. And no vengeance either, its own kind of pleasure. If only she were below, he would fall on her and kill them both.

A quick pass of the arm and now he was crow again, wings spread, still plummeting, but he raised his head and lowered his tail, and he pulled himself out of his deathward plunge, and skimmed across the waves. So close, so close.

To have her he must finish the bedposts, the sooner the better. And for that he needed help.

Love for dinner, and revenge for dessert, kiaw. Let the banquet begin.

THE PELICAN, HER BASKET FILLED with an assortment of eyeballs, lips, scrota, nipples, noses, and conaria, flew higher and higher into the far corner of the sky until she flew into the throat of the beast. His throat was dark, and the air there moist and fetid, as if some foul swamp belched mephitic vapors up ahead, where the back of his tongue grew out of the bottom of his mouth. She landed there, and folded her wings, and crept along the great slab of his tongue, careful not to tickle him, for if she did, he might cough, which would send her tumbling through the air to slam into the back of his teeth. She crept along until his front teeth were just before her, and here, in a hollow of his tongue, she emptied her basket of its treats.

The beast's tongue ran out his mouth in the gap between his fangs, which let in some light. The tip of his tongue rested, as was his custom, on the tip of his long, long tail, which circled round from his hindquarters and lay all along his side until it curled back toward his beastly lips. He was very like, the pelican always thought, a sleeping baby, who sucks his thumb for the comfort to be found there. The pelican crept out between the beast's fangs, and scurried along the tongue until she stood on the tip of the tail.

She turned and faced the Kiamah beast. The Kiamah was never fully asleep, and he lay before her now in a lizardly state of twilight, with his lurid green eyes half-open. She passed a wing in front of her face, and she took on her woman shape. Not the old crone shape that her friends knew her by, with its pendulous breasts hanging low on her jiggly belly, but a more luscious shape, like that of the goddess, and Cariña. For she had taken note of how the fisherman watched her friends, and how there were times when their flesh claimed his eyes, and would not let him look away. And that the women sometimes knew they were being watched in that way, and it made them pull their shoulders back, and sway their hips a little bit more when they walked. She wanted that. She wanted his eyes stuck on her.

And so she practiced, when she came to visit the beast, standing in front of his enormous, drowsy face, drawing her arms up her sides and raising them in the air, swaying her hips side to side and turning a slow circle. Here, in this dance, she shaped herself anew, from the inside out, as a woman who might yet draw forth the attentions of a mate, someone who was hers alone. Perhaps even the Kiamah beast might be swept away with desire for her, although what that might look like she could hardly imagine.

She crept now, as she had done before, up the beast's snout to one of his enormous languid eyes, and stood before it on a fold of his crinkled flesh. The shiny wet surface of the Kiamah's eye was a mirror, and here she could see herself as others might. She passed a hand in front of her face, shifting her shape, and when she looked again her hips were not quite so wide. Again she passed her hand in front of her face, and now the curve of her cheek bones was more comely, and her nose a bit less of a beak. She raised her arms, and swayed her hips, and turned herself round, moving to the rhythm of her own heartbeat. She looked over her shoulder at her backside, reflected in the beast's eye, and she rocked her hips back and forth, ta-tah ta-tah ta-tah ta-tah, and yes, this was very fetching, this mating dance her hips knew all on their own. Ta-tah ta-tah ta-tah ta-tah, and now, all on their own, her nipples grew hard, and her nether parts moist. Her hand wanted to stray toward her loins, although she felt this to be her hand's bidding and not her own.

It was then that the beast blinked. The pelican turned to face him, and she drew her shoulders back, the better to show off her breasts.

"Mmm-hmfff," said the beast. "Is that you, Pelican?"

"Yes, my pet," said the pelican, "and I've brought you your treats. Are you hungry today?"

"I am ever hungry," said the beast. "Are they in their usual spot?"

"They are," said the pelican. She sang the song the crow had taught her to make the treats grow to a size worthy of the Kiamah beast's great maw, and the beast listened, as any creature might listen to a mother's lullaby.

When the pelican finished her song, the Kiamah's tongue pulled in between his lips with a swift, lizardly slurp. His lips closed, and his great jaws began to chew, rising up and down and making the pelican's perch unsteady. The pelican passed a hand in front of her face and took on her pelican shape, and she flew to the tip of the beast's tail. There she stood before him as a woman again, rocking her hips and turning in a slow circle. The beast finished his treat, and his tongue slithered out from between his fangs and licked his lips.

"What news from the Isle of the Dead?" said the Kiamah. "Is that fool crow still besotted with love?"

"He is, lambkin," said the pelican, who had only recently begun asking the newly dead what words they used to talk to their lovers. "Some say there may be a wedding in the offing."

"A wedding, you say? What a thing. Has there ever been a wedding on the Isle of the Dead?"

"Never," said the pelican. She raised her arms, her hands moving as if she were pulling the beast to her with the tethers of love, but the beast was ruminating, and had no eyes for her.

"Tell me, O Pelican, do they sing my praises on the isle? Do they warm themselves with the heat of my sacred pyre? Do they thank me for keeping the spirit world safe within my belly?"

The pelican considered. It would be unkind to answer the Kiamah's questions with too much of the truth. He wanted to be loved, as did all creatures, and so it was with love that she lied to him in answer.

"They do, duckie, they do," said she. "They are grateful for all you do, and have done."

"Good," said the beast, "for I have sacrificed the nimble body with which I was born. When I was newly hatched I was swift, and flew about doing as I pleased. Now my belly is so big, all I can do is lie here."

"Oh, greedy-guts," said the pelican, rather pleased with herself for having invented this new endearment. "What a lot you've given up for the good of all. You miss flying, then?"

"I do," said the beast. "My wings have grown weak, and cannot lift me." The Kiamah tried to raise his wings off his back, but his leathery pinions merely twitched. "Remember me swooping in from the sea, swallowing everything before me? I was feared by all, and respected, and none would stand against me."

The pelican shuddered, and her cheeks flushed with shame, remembering her faintheartedness the night she'd seen the beast devour the moon. She missed the moon, which rose no more because the beast had chewed it to bits. All that was left was the moon's shine, which coated the inside of the Kiamah's belly and gave off a faint glow at night. She had cowered at the bottom of the inlet, and warned no one, and that was the moment when the Old Gods might have banded together and defeated the beast, before he grew too large and powerful. Now it was too late, the Old Gods all devoured, and the blame was hers. She was no longer dancing, and when she spoke again her voice was muted.

"You are still," said the pelican, "feared by all."

The beast ran his long tongue round his lips, and then he snapped his jaws shut. "Of course I am," said he. "I am the greatest beast that has ever lived, and I can swallow anything." His gaze grew fierce, a threat to all that was in the stare of his lurid green eyes, and the pelican fell back, afraid. But then his eyelids lowered slowly, the conaria doing their work, and his perpetual drowsiness overtook him.

"Farewell," said the pelican, who was now more than ready to take her leave. She took on her pelican shape again, and with it her shame, and she flew into the mouth of the beast, and down his throat.

D<small>EEP IN THE FOREST,</small> N<small>EAR</small> the far end of the Isle of the Dead, Dewi Sri sat in lotus position in the hollowed trunk of an ancient cedar tree, the inside lit by a single large candle. The night outside was dark. She followed her breath, only her breath, in, out, in, out, letting her thoughts rise up, letting them go. They were butterflies, her thoughts, delicate, transient things, their lives but a moment in time.

Or so she told herself. In truth, she found no peace in her meditation, and her thoughts stumbled from one worry to the next, not at all like butterflies. Though she had the seduction of the crow well in hand, he was suspicious of her, and possessed of a quicksilver temper. She must handle him with cunning, lest he loose his savagery on her, or the others, whom she now felt to be in her charge. Most especially Cariña, whom she had nursed back to life, and coupled with, and helped to reunite with the lover she could not remember. But they were to be sacrificed, these lovers, a prospect she abhorred. Was she to do this herself? She could not bear the thought, any more than she could give them up to the savagery of the crow.

Surely there must be another way.

This much she understood: to atone for the misdeeds of her family she must mate with the crow, and bear his child. Soon enough she would consummate with him. Yet the way forward beyond that simple act of lust was not at all clear. Somehow, if the Turropsi were to be believed, out of these events the Kiamah beast would be prevented from devouring all that was good.

Thus was her mind filled with the little-death of fear, so that it would not settle.

The crow thought she flew home every night, but it was here she came. She liked this rough camp she had made for herself, such a change from the silk and songket of her palace. The mossy bed she slept on smelled of the earth, and the cedar tree towered above her older and wiser than she was, for the tree, with its perfect stillness, was closer to nirvana. In this she found humility, and in that humility she sought balance, but balance was elusive. More moss hung across the opening into the tree trunk, which faced west, and when the sun rose it filled the hollowed trunk with light. From darkness to light, that was where she was bound.

So much depended on what she did here. On what they all did.

Someone approached. She heard the whispery sound of wings gliding through the air. She opened her eyes. She had known this moment might come, and she welcomed it.

From the dark night a dark, avian shape came gliding in from the west, flapping its wings to slow its flight. Feet on the ground, it walked up and stuck its bill through the curtain of moss.

"So," said Dewi Sri, "you've found me."

"Yes," said the frigate bird. His red throat pouch swelled at the sight of her. A crooked grin spread across the face of the goddess.

"Is that a scarf around your neck?" said she, "or are you just glad to see me?"

The frigate bird thrust his throat pouch at her and shook it from side to side. "Do you have plans?" he said, grinning back at her, "for the rest of the evening?"

"I do now," said the goddess. She unfolded her legs, and she lay back on her bed. "Come," she said, "join me."

The frigate bird nestled in next to her. "Shall I blow out the candle?" he asked.

"Leave it on," said she. "It brings out the sheen in your feathers."

She put her hand on his head and drew him closer. He nuzzled his throat pouch along the curve of her shoulder and neck, and she gave herself up to the shudder of pleasure that came from his caress.

Let the crow wait. And the Kiamah beast, let him wait. She needed this. She needed it now.

SOME FEW NIGHTS LATER, AS the sun set in the east, the frigate bird appeared at the fisherman's house. The fisherman had his arm round Cariña's waist as they sat in front of their fire, their bellies full of roasted fish and vegetables, their heads leaned into each other's so that they had only to turn them to bring their lips together in a kiss.

"It is time," said the frigate bird, "to sample the ale."

"Zounds!" said the fisherman. "It's good to be alive!" His beloved smiled at this, and he sprang up with the vigor of a man a fraction of his age, and offered her his hand, pulling her swiftly to her feet. Now that his beloved was back in his arms he awoke each morning to a world scrubbed fresh, and full of possibility. Everything he needed was here. The work of each day was to make for themselves a better life, and in the evenings they had food in plenty, and well cooked. They had a fine kettle, and salt, harvested from the waters of the inlet. They had friends in the pelican, the cormorant, and the frigate bird, and time to enjoy an idle conversation, to sing songs as the shadows lengthened into night. They had each other's bodies with which to make the pleasures of the flesh.

And now they would have ale. The cask was in a kind of rough cellar they had dug in a back corner of their house to keep it cool, covered by some planks, and beneath those, a thick layer of moss. The fisherman made quick work of uncovering it, and he dropped into the cellar and raised the cask in his burly arms, setting it gently on the dirt floor of their home. He carried it out to the fire, and the three of them stood around it, mugs in hand, or in the frigate bird's case, a hollow reed for a straw at the ready, tucked into his belt.

"There is an ancient incantation," said the frigate bird, "a hymn to Ninkasi, the Sumerian goddess of brewing. Why don't we sing this hymn all together? Then we'll open our cask, and let the ale come." The frigate bird began, in his high raspy tenor, and the other two fell in with him as he went along.

> *You're the one who bakes the steamy bappir*
> *Puts in order the piles of hulled grains*
> *Ninkasi bakes the bappir in the big oven*
> *Puts in order the piles of grain*

You're the one who soaks the malt in the jar
Mixing in a pit the bappir and date honey
Ninkasi soaks the roasted malt in the jar
Mixing in a pit the bappir and date honey

They sang those verses through a few times, and then the frigate bird held up a wing. "I'll teach you the whole thing later," he said. "The hymn has the whole recipe in it, a very useful thing. But for now, let us pull the bung and pour our first taste."

The fisherman tapped on the sides of the bung with a wooden mallet, loosening it until he could pull it out of the bunghole. A heavenly fragrance rose from the cask, a smell at once lemony and honeyed, bitter and ambrosiac, earthy and divine. The frigate bird took the reed from his belt and stuck it through the bunghole, sucked some ale up through it, closed his eyes, swished the ale around on his palate, frowned, and swallowed. The fisherman and his beloved waited, their breath held, their chests trembling.

The frigate bird opened his eyes slowly, and a long grin spread from one side of his bill to the other. "This ale," he said, "is fit for the gods."

"Huzzah!" said the fisherman. He snatched up the cask and poured his beloved's mug full. The head was pure velvet and an inch thick. His beloved tipped her mug into her mouth and took a long slow drink, giving herself a foamy mustache.

"Oh, oh, oh," she said. "This is the best!"

The fisherman took the mug from her and drank his own first taste. The hops were agreeably bitter, and the ale creamy and smooth. The yeasty bubbles sparkled in his mouth and danced their way down his throat. He leaned in and licked the foam off his beloved's lip, and then they gave each other a hoppy kiss while the frigate bird looked on.

"To die for," said the fisherman, smiling at his beloved.

"As some of us have," said the frigate bird, and they all laughed, and poured themselves another. They were soon merry, these three friends, these brewers, sitting around the fire that night, drinking the fruit of their own labor. The fisherman and his beloved had drunk nothing but the water from the stream for as long as they both had been on the Isle of the Dead, and while that water was sweet and clear and pure, there was something heavenly about the ale in their mugs, for it made them feel that all the toil of their days was for something more than mere living.

"Heavenly indeed," said the frigate bird. He spread his wings and looked up at the sky, and he said, "This is proof that Ninkasi loves us and wants us to be happy."

They all drank a toast to that sentiment, ignoring the fact that above them were no stars, and no moon, and no sky at all but the belly of the Kiamah beast, whose heartbeat was ever-present in the night, a low rhythm, and a constant reminder that the spirit world had been swallowed. It was possible, perhaps even necessary, to live like that, paying as little heed as they could to the unpleasant facts of their existence. And to brew ale, to embrace the joy that ale brought them, was as much an act of resistance as any they could muster at the moment.

To share that ale with others was more than an act of kindness. The canoe of the dead entered the inlet, and the dead and the fish eagles sang their song to the drumbeat of the Kiamah beast's heart. The fisherman, the woman, and the frigate bird all stood as the canoe went by, and after a quick meeting of the eyes they refilled their mugs and set off down the beach.

The cormorant and the pelican were there, ready as ever to greet the newly dead. The crow strutted about in his human shape, a bedpost in his hand, which he carried on his shoulder like a cudgel. He was in a foul mood, and full of savage desires, and when he saw the frigate bird he called him over. "Kiaaw! You weasel-faced whip-jack," said he, "you whore's bird, how dare you show your face here?" The crow brandished his bedpost in the frigate bird's face, and the frigate bird was eyeball to eyeball with the two serpents carved there.

"Whoa," said the frigate bird. He took a step back, and raised his wings in mock surrender. "Be of good cheer, Cousin, I mean you no offense."

"Your very presence on this isle is an aw-aw-offense to Us," said the crow. "Be gone, and never shall you return, for We banish you and your tickle-tail from Our kingdom."

The fisherman and his beloved joined them, and the fisherman, who was the happiest he had been in as long as he could remember, and who wanted no discord to spoil the mood of the evening, held up his mug and bowed his head.

"King Crow," he said, "we have made in your honor a special libation, a drink fit for the gods, such as yourself, and we beg of you the favor of tasting our offering."

"What's this?" said the crow. "What have you done?"

"'Tis an ale," said the woman, and she took the opportunity of the fisherman's bowed head to brazenly look the crow up and down. The crow, for his part, stood straighter, his shoulders back to show off his handsome chest.

"Do tell," said the crow. "An ale? I've never heard of such a thing."

The woman smiled at him, taking note of his broad shoulders and his well-formed thighs and the curve of his shiny black beak. He had an air of power about him that she found quite beguiling. "Then let me offer you a nipperkin, for it is a knock-down nappy ale, and you have no acquaintance with strong drink." The woman took the reed from the frigate bird's belt and offered the crow a sip from her mug.

The crow opened his beak, and drew in some ale. "Uff," he said, "it's bitter."

"Have another," said the frigate bird, "and let it linger on your tongue. It has a way of growing on you."

The crow drew in another taste, and he worked it around his tongue. "We like the bubbles," he said. He drew in another taste, and another, until the mug was empty. "Not entirely unpleasant," said he. "It has a warming effect on Us. Is there more?"

"There is," said the fisherman. "But you are busy now." He gestured at the newly dead, some of whom were crowding around.

"Is there an alehouse here?" said a young man, a natty lad by the look of him, no doubt fresh from the gallows, sent there for picking one too many pockets.

"No," said the fisherman, but at the same moment both the woman and the frigate bird said, "Yes."

And so it was that the whole crowd of them followed the fisherman and his beloved along the shore. The evening was fair, and so they gathered around the fire, and though they had but the two mugs, and the one cask of ale, they shared it all out amongst the newly dead and the gods assembled there. The ale grew thick and muddy as the cask grew emptier, but one of the dead, a weaver from Gaza, produced from one of her pockets a piece of gauze, and they filtered the ale as they poured it.

The cormorant, in particular, was an enthusiast. As a scholar he had come across numerous references to ale, but as he told a burly blacksmith after his second mug, "The reality of it far exceeds my greatest expectorations." The crowd was jolly around them, chatting away in a polyglot of pidgin and slang, and their laughter filled the dark night within the belly of the beast. A bout of singing broke out, reels and jigs and sea chanties, and some amongst them danced while others clapped their hands in time. The fire burned bright, and sent showers of sparks aloft when the fisherman threw on more fuel.

The woman stood next to the fisherman as he tended the fire, surveying the crowd of revelers. She put her arm through his, and then spoke of something that had long been on her mind. "I cannot help but notice," said she, "that you alone have blue skin. Has it always been so?"

"Only since I have arrived here," said the fisherman. "And the longer I am here, the bluer I get." His tattoos had faded into his blue skin, and she could barely make out her own likeness on his chest. Her skin had slowly tanned since she had emerged from her clamshell and was now a deeper shade of bronze. "Does it trouble you?" said he.

"'Tis a lovely shade of blue," said she, "and whatever the color, 'tis your touch that matters most." She caressed his arm with her fingers. "This too have I seen, that you've no hair on your person. Is that also a part of the enchantment of this place?"

The fisherman put his arm round his beloved, and drew her close. She lay her head on his shoulder, and he brought her hand to his face. "No more do my whiskers grow since I've come here, nor the stubble on my head. All of it was burned off in the belly of the whale, and has not returned."

"Smooth as a china cup," said the woman. She traced the arch above his eye where his eyebrow ought to've been, and then the creases in his forehead. For all the life he had lived, his hairless head made him seem untouched by it.

'Twas good to be in his arms, blue though they might be. She closed her eyes, and nestled there, quite content. But when she opened her eyes again, there was the crow, across the fire from her, talking to the cormorant. He was tall and his bearing regal, his oiled skin gleaming in the firelight, and something stirred in her belly, a longing to feel those arms around her as well. *I am brought back from the dead,* thought she, *and if this be the afterlife, why should I not have everything I desire?*

The frigate bird took the opportunity of this gathering to speak to the crow, drawing him aside, and telling him that he wished to make peace with him.

"The goddess and I," said the frigate bird, "have come to an understanding."

The crow, suspicious, said, "An understanding? Of what sort?"

"I have no claim on her," said the frigate bird, fresh from yet another liaison with her the night before, "and thus, I leave the two of you to whatever fate has in store."

The crow, who in his position as King of the Dead had asserted his entitlement to more ale than anyone else, tottered back and forth as he considered what the frigate bird said. He knew the frigate bird to be a thief, and the goddess a temptress, and a liar, yet deep in his beating heart he wanted more than anything to believe that he was the goddess's chosen one.

"You've spoken to her of this?" he said.

"I have knelt before her as she extolled your virtues," said the frigate bird. And knelt he had, the better to nuzzle his bill in her cauliflower. "She looks forward to the day, may it come soon, when you have finished the bed you are building."

Awww, the bed. She wanted to school him in the arts of love on it, and he would let her. He would become the greatest lover the world had ever known, the better to make her suffer when he withdrew that love. And in her suffering she would repent. She would renounce her machinations, and fall truly in love with him, and forsake all others. And after he had her truest affections, he would slay this brigand who stood before him now, this beetle-headed codpiece, and roast, O sweet revenge, his plucked body on the pyre.

The pyre. It was time to lead the dead to their proper resting place.

"More ale?" the frigate bird said. "'Tis the last of what we have." He held forth the mug, and the crow put the reed straw in his mouth and sucked it dry.

"You'll make more of this divine libation?" said the crow.

"We shall," said the frigate bird.

"I should like my own cask the next time," said the crow.

"We would be honored to provide you one," said the frigate bird.

"I must take my leave," said the crow. "I have my duties to perform."

"Your Omnipotence," said the frigate bird, bowing, and sweeping a wing in a courtly gesture toward the crowd around the fire.

The crow hopped up on a driftwood log and let loose a "Kiaw!" that cut through the jolly chatter like a whipsaw. Silenced, the crowd raised their fuzzled eyes and looked up at the crow, who grew himself taller by a cubit while they watched. A long, low "ohhhh" moaned its way through the crowd, followed by a burble of comments at this display of divine power.

"Listen up, you band of giglets and applejohns," said the crow. "There's a bigger, better fire awaiting you, down the beach. Follow me there, and I promise you a song the likes of which you've never heard before."

"Will there be more ale?" said a dapper old man with a whispery halo of silvery hair.

"Naw aw aw aw aw," laughed the crow, "I've something far better than ale down there. Follow me and see."

"Must be whiskey," shouted the dapper old man. Hoots of laughter rose from the crowd, and they followed the crow down the beach. So enthused were they that many ran ahead, and the crow, too sozzled to run, let alone take on his crow form and fly, tottered along with the stragglers. When they caught up, there was already a crowd standing around the glowing embers of the pyre. "Form a line, you gleeking sots," said the crow. And form a line they did, eager as they were to keep the merry mood of the night alive.

That was easy, thought the crow. *Dangle the prospect of a drink in front of these swag-bellied soaks and they'd line up to be hung from the gibbet and sawn in half.*

"Where's the whiskey?" shouted a toothless woman, her face cheery in the red glow.

"In just a moment," said the crow, "but first, listen to my song. You have something within you that wants out, and it's of no further use to you. Let it go, and there'll be whiskey for all."

"Huzzah!" they shouted, and then they fell under the spell of the crow's song, and they coughed up their souls.

This whiskey must be powerful good stuff, thought the crow. *I must get me some.*

THE NEXT MORNING DAWNED BLEARY and drear. The crow sat upon the cormorant's shoulders, and the cormorant on the pelican's, and as the light of the sun fell upon them through the haze of clouds above, it was clear that they had been too drunk the night before to assume their brightly painted colors as they fell asleep. Now they all three awoke dry-mouthed, thirsty, and achy of head, none more so than the crow. He spread his wings to flap his way to the ground, but the effort made his head throb, and his sense of balance wobble. He began to climb down, his talons digging in to the cormorant's breast.

"Auk!" said the cormorant. "Watch it, you clumsy corvid."

The crow wrapped his wings tight round the cormorant's head as his foot reached for the pelican's shoulder, and the cormorant worked his bill free and nipped the crow, hard, in his wingpit. The crow shrieked a kiaw and fell to the ground. He lay there moaning, and the pelican stood, throwing the cormorant backward off her shoulders.

"You poor fellow," said the pelican to the crow, and she shifted into her old woman shape and bent over him, parting his feathers with her fingers to see the wound. But the crow shoved her hands away. "Leave me alone," he said, "I think I'm going to up my chuck."

The cormorant stood, his head reeling, the contents of his belly gathering themselves for a tactical retreat. "That makes two of us," he said, and he fergled, and the crow fergled, and the pelican, her sense of smell overwhelmed with the foul stench, backed away, lest she also fergle.

Up the beach, at the fisherman's camp, the frigate bird, who had slept on his perch in the snag above the fisherman's home, was in much better shape than were the crow, the cormorant, and the pelican. Like the fisherman, he knew well the aftereffects of too much ale, and they had paced themselves accordingly. The woman, too, had kept the better part of her wits about her. Although she had no memory of the many years she'd spent as a barmaid, she knew in her bones that ale was a double-edged blade, with one side made for cutting away one's troubles, while the other side sliced off one's common sense.

The three of them ate breakfast together, pleased with themselves for all the jolly good feeling they had spread, and they talked of what they might do next.

"We need more casks," said the frigate bird, "and more grain, and hops."

"More mugs," agreed the fisherman. "Bigger batches of ale."

"A proper privy," said the woman, eyeing several round spots of damp sand too near the fire pit.

"It will take a couple of weeks to brew more," said the fisherman. "What do we do in the meantime?"

"I have an idea," said the frigate bird. "Let us seek out the pelican."

THE CROW, FULL OF SUBTERFUGE in the evening dusk, flew out to sea. As the sky darkened and he was sure he would not be seen, he circled back to the canyon, flying in from the upstream side of the waterfall. He landed on the beach in the rocky bowl, and made his way behind the waterfall, where he took on his mole shape.

Love's distractions had kept him from his tunnel for long enough. He padded along on his mole feet to the end of his burrow, his nose filled with the earthy smell. That smell calmed him, for here in the tunnel his task was simple and clear, and his body was built for no other thing than to dig. He had dug and dug, the earthy smell giving way finally to something fleshy and fetid, and now, as he padded along his burrow, he knew he was passing through the very belly of the Kiamah beast. Beyond that the smell turned woody, and now he was in that lower region of his burrow, where he had dug nearly all the way through the hollow driftwood log that contained the material world. He dug his foreclaws into the fragrant wood, which was many fathoms thick, and rotted to the consistency of the human tongue, which is to say it was firm but yielding. He pulled the rotted wood away, shoving it behind himself and to the sides, packing it tight to the walls and floor with his hind feet, digging ever onward and downward.

The digging was just the thing to clear the last of his headache away. In the burrow, in his mole shape, he knew the world by touch, and as he clawed his way forward his thoughts drifted back to the woman he both loved and despised. The goddess had come to him that morning as he lay on the sand next to the stink of his own bile, heaved up by a belly that clenched itself so tight the crow thought he might just as well die.

"You poor dear," said Dewi Sri. She stroked the feathers on the back of his head ever so lightly, humming a comforting melody as she did so, and the crow's aching head ached a little less.

"Awww," he said, grateful for her soothing touch in spite of the ire he felt toward her.

"What is it that has laid you so low?" she asked.

"Ale," croaked the crow. "Marvelous stuff as you drink it, but it has a nasty sting in the morning's light."

"So I've heard," said the goddess. "I do not take strong drink myself."

"Nor ever again shall I," said the crow.

So do they all say, thought the goddess, but she smiled at the crow, and asked him if he were thirsty. She helped him to his feet, and together they walked to the stream, and drank their fill.

"How goes the carving?"

The crow, his powers renewed by the sweet clarity of the water in the stream, passed a wing in front of himself, and took on his man shape.

"It goes," he said. His hand trembled when he held it out, and he could not will it to stop. The goddess took his hand in hers and faced him. Her dark eyes and her carmine lips seemed to glow. *If only she were less comely*, thought the crow, *she would be easier to hate*.

"I am eager for you to finish," she said, stepping close to him. She put her arms round him and held him close, nuzzling his neck just below where his feathers ended.

How could treachery and betrayal feel so good? She was leading him on, he knew this, but it only made him want her more.

He was far below the surface now, his sinewy shoulders relishing the work, his tunnel sloping down and down and down, when he smelled something new. A zephyrous freshening, as if he neared the cave in Thrace where the west wind dwelt. The ground in front of him gave way, and he pulled back, inching up the slope of his tunnel backward. Just in time, for a hole appeared where he had just been, and there was the sky.

He stuck his snout over the edge. The material world lay below him, just as the cormorant had told him, the world of humans, and it was a riot of smells. Piney forests, and briny sea. So many creatures, and all their breath. So much sweat and manure, smoke and pollen, mold and rot. There was a hint of something sweet and festive in the air, as if a rainbow were nearby, although he could not see it. Far, far below was the material world, a vast, hazy spread of land, with rivers and lakes shining in the sun. Too bright, too bright. His mole eyes squinted, weak as they were, and he passed a paw in front of his face and became a crow again. Now the world was sharp, and he saw trees and fields, hamlets and towns, trails and roads. Tiny, ant-like creatures moved about, and these were people.

All of this would soon be his. The Kiamah beast would swallow it all, and he would rule it as the Kiamah's regent, and when he did, he would be feared by all and loved by whomever he chose.

Off in the distance was the dark gray of a storm, with trails of rain falling from it. Birds flew through the air below him, motes in motion. "Ko! Ko! Ko!" the crow thundered, his voice shaking the very air, "Ko! Ko! Ko!" Hawks and eagles fled that sound, but from far below came a "Kiaw?" in reply. How sweet a sound was that? His own kind were answering his call.

"Awww," the crow called, "aw-awww." And "aw-aw," they answered, "aw-aw!" His people, his tribe, from whom he had been separated his entire life. He called out to them again, and a flock of his fellows rose up from the forest, following the sound of his voice. Higher and higher they flew, closer and closer, heading for a hole in the sky that had never been there before. They were curious, and bold, and they heard the crow calling them, urging them upward.

The crow took on his mole shape again, and while the flock of crows circled beneath him, he widened the end of his tunnel, making a space for them to land. Once more he took on his crow shape. "Come!" he called, "come-come-come-come-come."

Into the hole they flew, some dozen of them, and there they gath-

ered, twittering amongst themselves as they beheld the king of the
crows, who was black and beauteous and many times their size. "Fly,"
he told them, "fly to the end of the tunnel, and await me there." They
did as they were told, and waited while their god sealed up the hole in
the sky, and made his way back to the cave behind the waterfall. They
watched as he emerged in his mole shape, and then passed a paw in
front of his face, and became a crow again, and they knew him to be
their true leader.

"I have work for you," said the crow. "Follow me."

His congress of crows had arrived.

THE FISHERMAN THREW ANOTHER LOG on the fire, and sparks
burst forth and rose into the night sky. He sat down on the driftwood
log and put his arm round his beloved. The frigate bird, the pelican,
and the cormorant were across the fire from him, a curious company,
but his companions nonetheless. It had been a long, long time since
he'd felt the fellowship of friends, and his mind was more at ease
than it had been in many a day.

"Oh, yes," the pelican was saying, "'tis a marvelous notion, to have
a chance to get to know the dead before they cough up their souls.
We've never done that here before."

"As it happens," the frigate bird said, "there's a company of brewers arriving on the canoe tonight, three stout fellows, who perished
when the fire they were roasting barleycorns with got out of hand, and
burned down their entire alehouse."

"How tragic," said the pelican. "They must have suffered a great
deal."

"Not as much as you might think," said the frigate bird, "for they
were parlatic with their own ale."

"Let that be a lesson to us all," said the woman, "not to be plotzed
while we go about our business."

"Too true," said the frigate bird. "But as to the matter at hand,
they will have with them a cask of ale saved from the fire."

"How fortuitous," said the cormorant. "I look forward to furthering
my study of the matter."

"Diligence is the mother of the fortuitous," said the frigate bird. "I simply made sure I was in the right place at the right time."

"One cask?" said the woman. "We'll want more than one cask. What about the next night, and the next?"

"For that we shall need the good offices of the pelican," said the frigate bird.

"The pelican?" said the woman, "how so?" She smiled at her friend and went on. "The pelican is many things, but she is no brewer."

"I see it," said the cormorant, peering over the tops of his spectacles. "She shall vuln herself, and a drop of her blood will make the ale in the cask last all night."

"Oh," said the pelican, "will that work?"

"*Sit non dubium*," said the cormorant. "You're a goddess. Do you know, I spoke to a woman one night, a priestess in one of those obscure messiah cults that keep springing up in the material world? She said that a messiah turned water into wine at a wedding when they ran out."

"In Cana?" said the fisherman. "I've been there. You can't swing a dead cat without hitting a messiah in Cana."

"I'm happy to try," said the pelican. "I hope I don't disappoint you all."

"Perish the thought," said the frigate bird. "I'm sure this will work."

"What is it about the desert and messiahs?" said the fisherman.

"It's the heat," said the frigate bird. "It toasts the conarium like a bagel."

"Bagel?" said the woman.

"A kind of heavy bun," said the frigate bird, "with a hole in the middle."

"Conarium?" said the fisherman.

"Third eye," said the frigate bird, pointing to his brow.

"The source of visions, in some philosophies," said the cormorant. "The Cartesians think it's where the soul resides."

"Did you hear the one about Descartes?" said the frigate bird.

"Descartes?" said the cormorant. "*Cogito, ergo sum*—that Descartes?"

"Just so," said the frigate bird. "Seems Descartes walks into an inn, and he sits down and asks for a meal. The innkeeper asks him if he'd like wine with his meal. 'I think not,' says Descartes. And then poof, he disappears."

The cormorant chuckled, although the rest of the company, having never heard of Descartes, were left scratching their heads. The fisherman asked his beloved if she wouldn't like to go down to the water, and so they left the three birds at the fire. Hand in hand they walked, each enjoying the touch of the other. The low steady cadence of the Kiamah's heart throbbed above them.

"What is this beast they speak of?" said the woman.

"The Kiamah? He is, they tell me, the devourer of all things. They suspect the crow is in league with him."

"The sound of his heart is ever in my dreams," said the woman, and she shuddered. "And some nights the beast pursues me, a great serpent with a fearsome, slavering mouth."

The fisherman put his arms round her, and they held each other close. He stroked her hair, as one comforts a child whose sleep is troubled, and the woman, though she was comforted, shivered in his arms.

"Be not afraid, my beloved," said the fisherman. "I will let no harm come to you." He meant what he said, although he knew that there were forces at play here far more powerful than his own weedy strength. All his life he had kept steely-eyed death at bay with his wits, a stout heart, and luck. He still had his wits, and his heart was as stout as ever, but there was no way to foresee when luck might betray them.

There were clouds building out to sea, and the fisherman smelled rain coming on the freshening breeze. "We have shelter from the storm," said he, "and the company of friends, and whatever fate brings us, we shall face it together."

"So we shall," said the woman. "So we shall."

They walked on down the beach. There was something low to the ground moving about in the orange glow cast by the mound of embers that was the pyre. "That's strange," said the fisherman. He took note once again of the boon of being able to see so well in the dark. "Do you see that?" he said, pointing.

"There, by the pyre?"

"Those are birds," said the fisherman. "Crows, if I'm not mistaken."

"If they are crows," said the woman, "they are uncommonly small."

"Yes, crows," said the fisherman. "That is their customary size in the land of the living."

There were a dozen or so of them, and they were pecking away at a length of stick that lay on the sand. They stood and watched, the fisherman and his beloved, and took note of how purposeful the crows were. They pecked not at random, but as if they had a task to perform. Bits of wood lay scattered about them, and there was a pattern of scales carved down one face of the stick. As if on a signal that only birds can see, the crows lined up on one side, and they turned the stick with their beaks.

"That's one of the bedposts," said the woman. The crows resumed their pecking, muttering "kwurk, kwurk, kwurk" to one another as they worked.

The crow landed in front of them, having flown down from his perch above the pyre. "Good evening," he said, and he passed a wing in front of himself and took on his man shape. "A lovely evening for a stroll." He stalked back and forth in front of them as he spoke. "We see you've met Our band of helpmates. We have summoned them here to speed on the task of carving Our marriage bed."

"Marriage?" said the woman. "You have made a proposal to the goddess?"

"A figure of speech," said the crow. "Although, now that you mention it, a king such as Ourself is in need of a proper queen."

The woman could not help but notice the shine and the shape of the crow's beak. He was indeed a handsome fellow, broad in the shoulders and well muscled in the arms and legs. Though she was growing fond of the fisherman, there were other, darker urges within her, urges the goddess had awakened, urges that she had not the will to put back to sleep. The crow was the King of the Dead, and powerful in ways the fisherman was not. A king might have both a queen and a consort, and she rather fancied the idea of being his fancy.

The fisherman, wary as he always was in the presence of the crow, bowed before him. "By your leave," he said, "we shall continue our stroll."

"Stroll on," said the crow, who, as the fisherman's head was bowed, took the opportunity to wink at the woman, who lowered her eyes, but allowed him the slightest of smiles. "By all means, continue."

The crow watched them as they walked on toward the stream at the back of the inlet. He took note of the woman's backside, which was shapely beneath her sarong, and of the saucy way her haunches swung from side to side. Part of her mating dance, no doubt, and he put his hands on his hips and bumped his loins at her in reply.

"Kiaww!" said the crow. "I can hardly wait."

THE GODDESS FLEW IN, AS she did most mornings, from the eastward sky, and she landed on the beach in front of the crow, who had his congress of crows assembled before him. The crows startled, flapping their black wings and uttering a chorus of caws, and then settled themselves again on the ground. There was a drizzle of rain falling, something between a mist and a shower, and droplets were sprinkled on her coif like jewels.

"Darling," said she, offering her cheek for a nuzzle, "I see we have company."

The crow, who had been telling himself he would remain aloof from the goddess this morning, found his resolve melting like guano in the rain when she stood close to him. He nuzzled his beak alongside her cheek, and the teasing touch of her hands on his back made him flush with desire. Her bare breasts were full against his chest. This was maddening, this push and pull of love, this turning and twisting of his soul, this doubling back of his will. She was a sorceress, and a tease, yet still she owned his heart. But he was King Crow, and he had a few tricks of his own.

"Yes, my lotus blossom," said the crow, "Let me continue, and by nightfall, they will have finished all four of the bedposts."

"Oh, happy day," said the goddess. The congress of crows was arranged in a semicircle around them, and they beheld their master with an attention so fierce as to border on rapture. "Wherever did you find them?"

"Aw," said the crow, "I have my ways."

"Clever fellow." She took his hands in hers, and caressed them, pleased that the crow was proving himself a worthy adversary, for his cleverness made her loins warm. But alarmed as well, for these crows were evidence that he had breached the boundary between the material world and the spirit. It was one thing for the frigate bird to send things across on the canoe of the dead, and something else again for the crow, who was in league with the Kiamah, to have ruptured the barrier.

"Your own kind," said the goddess. "They are, no doubt, a great comfort."

"You know me well," said the crow.

She must hasten the course of events, but in a way that did not arouse the crow's suspicions. She let go his hands, and stepped back. "Please," she said, "do go on."

King Crow twittered and rattled at his fellow crows, urging them to complete the task of carving the scales on the remaining bedposts before the day was out. He bade them to carve well and truly the scales of the snakes, with the same care with which they would build a nest for their own young. For what they were building for their king, he told them, was also a nest, a nest for love.

"Kwurk," said he. "Kwurk, kwurk, kwurk," a magical word in the speech of King Crow, a word that made artisans of the crows, artisans who worked together. Then he knelt, and he took a pair of chisels from his tool belt and held them in his palms. With his upturned palms before his face he blew a breath of air across them at the assembled crows, passing, as he had done the day before, the skill of a master carver from his hands to their beaks. Thus did he spread the boon the goddess had given him, and turn it to his own purpose.

The goddess waited for him to finish, and watched as the crows hopped along the sand to the nearest bedpost, and set themselves to the task at hand. *Or perhaps*, thought the goddess, smiling, *we should call it the task at beak.* They pecked away, slicing off slivers of wood and tossing them over their shoulders, rattling and cawing in low throaty voices to one another as they worked, *Aww, aw-aw, kaw-ka-kaw-kaw-aww.*

The goddess stood behind the crow, looking over his shoulder and nuzzling his neck feathers with her chin. "Clever, clever crow," she whispered, her breath hot. The crow shivered, and goose bumps rose all along his well-muscled arms. She ran her fingertips lightly across his shoulder blades, her wing feathers teasing him with the barest touch, and again he shivered, and moaned a low "awwwww" of delight. The bedposts would be done by sunset, and she would be his tonight.

Now the goddess wrapped her wings round the crow and caressed his chest, her breasts pressing up against his back. She took note of his q'hram, growing stiff beneath his loincloth, and she said, "You have pleased me well, my lord. Soon shall we enjoy the fruits of your labors."

The crow, overcome with the thrill of her touch, could only moan "awwww" in reply.

"No doubt you've already milled the rails and slats," she cooed.

"Awww?" said the crow. He had done no such thing, nor, having never built a bed before, had he given any thought to what else, beyond bedposts, the building of a bed might require.

"Yes, darling, a bed requires a frame," she said, her voice full of the promise of delights to come once the bed was built. "But, silly me, you know that, of course."

"Awww, yes," said the crow. "Of course."

"The fisherman," said the goddess, "is quite the carpenter, I've noticed."

"Yes," said the crow. "So have I noticed as well."

"No doubt you have enlisted his aid in this endeavor," said the goddess.

"Yes, my sweeting," said the crow, "I have."

"Then I will leave you to it," said the goddess. "Adieu, my lord," she said, stepping back.

"Awww," said the crow, forlorn in the absence of her touch. He turned, hoping to embrace her, but her wings were already raised, and she flapped them and rose, pausing only to smile at him and blow him a kiss.

The crow watched her fly away, his beak wet with drizzled rain, his back now cold where she had been pressed up against him. She grew smaller and smaller, and he grew angry and angrier in her sudden absence. He undid the tool belt that was slung across his hips, wrenching the belt free from its buckle, and he threw it at her diminishing form, though it fell well short of hitting her, and dropped into the waters of the inlet. "Wench," he said, spitting the word out like contagion-fouled sputum. "Fobbing, tickle-brained tart." The feathers on the back of his head raised themselves in revolt against the fickle cruelty of love. "Oh brazen-faced, ruttish, wanton harlot," said he, "you plague me."

His congress of crows was at his feet, whittling away, and he took some solace in this. They were his loyal vassals, and they would help him no matter what he asked of them. He got down on his hands and knees, and he joined in the comfort of their crow conversation. The crows chuttered and cawed with him while they carved the scales into the bedpost with their beaks, and he chuttered back, growing calmer, and the feathers on the back of his head lay flat again.

"That goddess is no match for me," he told the crows. "I will eat her love for dinner. And for dessert, kiaww, I will avenge my honor."

They cawed their accord with him, and the crow stood. He'd best go see that whore's turd of a fisherman, and see if he couldn't trick him into helping with the bed.

DEWI SRI FOUND THE FRIGATE bird some several farsakhs out to sea, returning from Isla del Ombiglio, one of his haunts. She told him the news, that crows had arrived from the material world.

"They do his bidding, these crows?" said the frigate bird.

"They do," said the goddess.

"Troubling news," said the frigate bird, "given what the Turropsi have told me."

"You have seen them," said the goddess. "And what do they tell you?"

"War is coming. We are to prepare ourselves," said the frigate bird.

"War with whom?" said the goddess. "The Kiamah beast? The crow?"

"The crow, methinks, though they were miserly with details, as is their custom," said the frigate bird. "If the crow has breached the barrier between here and there, there's no telling what trouble he might brew."

They flew in tandem, through the misty tops of rain clouds, both of them aware of the delicate threads of fate being woven around them.

"Events are overtaking us," said the frigate bird. "We must act swiftly. The crow remains intent on finishing the bed?"

"He does," said the goddess.

"What would you have me do?"

"The crow will soon approach the fisherman, seeking his aid in finishing the bed frame. See to the negotiations, lest their mutual enmity erupt in violence."

"You may rely on me, my love."

The serenity of the goddess's smile gave way, for just a moment, to something more akin to affection. He was only one of many admirers, but he was intrepid, and had a brave heart. She brushed his wingtip with hers, that feathery touch some small token of her esteem. The frigate bird's throat pouch swelled red in return.

"And something else," the goddess said. "I have bed linens, and a mattress, in my palace. I need them brought to the Isle of the Dead. The crow is suspicious of me, but if I produce these things, I will gain back a portion of his trust, and that will serve our plot."

"Leave it to me," said the frigate bird. "I know just the thing."

Fate was leading her she knew not where. She must be willing, lest she be hauled into an uncertain future like so much drayage. There would be pleasure, and there would be pain. She must not cling, and neither should she flee, but death awaited them all if she failed.

IT WAS THE FISHERMAN AND the woman's habit to retire to their bed once the newly dead had made their way to the pyre. Some nights they made love before they slept, and some nights they simply spooned each other as they passed into slumber. Their days fell into a new rhythm, a few hours sleep until dawn, gardening and brewing and carpentering in the mornings, a siesta in the afternoon, a few chores and a meal as the sun set, and then a nap after supper. For an hour or so before midnight they readied the alehouse, and then they welcomed the newly dead, and served them all a mug of ale, and the evening's revels would begin.

The sun was nearing its zenith on one such day, with a light rain falling, and the fisherman watched as his beloved and the pelican headed down the beach to the stream, buckets in hand, to fetch water. A batch of barleycorns had been in their cement trench for three days, and they were on the verge of sprouting, and so must be kept moist.

His task for the rest of the day was to smooth planks for shelves to accommodate the mugs that kept arriving on the canoe of the dead. His sawhorses were set up beneath the eave that ran the length of the house, where he had rigged a tarp to provide some extra shade while he worked. He was just beginning to plane the first plank when he heard a thump from above, as if something had landed on the roof.

"Hallo," said a familiar voice, and when he stepped back a few paces, he saw the frigate bird perched on the ridge of the roof, with his spyglass and his pistola stuck into his belt.

"Hallo, Frigate Bird," said the fisherman. Rain fell lightly on his upturned face, and he shaded his eyes from it with his hand. "What news? Have you come from the sea?"

They talked of the winds and the weather, ever a subject of interest to both fisherman and bird, and he was pleased to learn that fair skies approached from the west. The fisherman lodged his latest complaint about the crow, who, just the night past, in the early hours before the sun rose and the crow settled on the cormorant's shoulders to sleep, had dropped another gobbet of guano on their fire, very nearly putting it out. He had awoken to this mess, and he was vexed by it. He had shoveled the guano onto their guano pile so that his beloved would not be vexed by it as well, though he spoke to her when she awoke of his ire for the crow.

The frigate bird flew down from the roof and landed on the twisted roots at the end of a driftwood log. The fisherman went back to planing his cedar plank, curls of fragrant wood falling to the sand at his feet, and he thanked the frigate bird once again for the fine tool he held in his hands. The blade was of a very fine grade of steel, and it held its edge well.

"That reminds me," said the frigate bird, "I have something for you. It's tucked into my belt at the back." He turned, and the fisherman saw a leather sheath there, just the size and shape to accommodate his knife. He pulled it free of the frigate bird's belt. It was deftly stitched and made from a sturdy leather by someone who knew well the leatherworker's art.

"Thank you," the fisherman said. His knife was near his sawhorses, stuck in the sand there. He fetched it, and the blade fit perfectly into the sheath. "I am in your debt," the fisherman said.

"You may repay me in ale," the frigate bird said, and at this, the fisherman smiled.

"Prepare yourself," said the frigate bird, and when the fisherman looked up, the frigate bird pointed with his bill at the crow, who was walking up the beach toward them.

"By Pluto's stinking arse," said the fisherman, "here comes the ruination of a perfectly good day."

"Patience," said the frigate bird, "lest the heat of the moment boil away our wits. And follow my lead, for there are things at play here beyond your ken."

The fisherman nodded, though he reminded himself that, in the end, his only allegiance was to himself, and his beloved.

The crow sauntered along, the very picture of a regent out for a stroll, his bearing regal and upright. He was in no great hurry, but neither did he tarry. He raised a hand at the fisherman and the frigate bird and waved it, the gesture midway between indolent and dismissive. The fisherman nodded, and went back to his cedar plank. Let the crow understand that the task at hand was more important than anything he might have to say.

"Loyal subjects," said the crow, "and valiant vassals, a fine day to you both."

The frigate bird bowed his head. "Your crow-ness," he said. "We are honored."

The crow regarded him with a baleful eye. "We should prefer a form of address with a bit more regality to it."

"What could be more regal than a crow?" said the frigate bird. "I have racked my brain for the answer to this question. Your black-ness? Your king-ness? Your shifty-ness? No, none of these, for it is ever your essence as crow that defines you, not the dark sheen of your feathers, which are beyond fuliginous, nor the eminence of your office, prestigious though it may be, nor the perspicacious prowess with which you change shape. And so it is 'your crow-ness' that suits you best. In my humble opinion."

The crow, his vanity feasting on this banquet of polysyllabic morsels of encomium, stood taller, despite the fact that he knew not the meaning of several of the words. "Very well," said he, "since you've given it so much thought."

"Thank you, your crow-ness. May we inquire what brings you to grace our humble camp with your presence?"

"You may. You, sir," said the crow, directing his remark to the fisherman, "might We have a word with you?"

The fisherman finished the stroke he was in the midst of, brushed away a bit of shaved wood, blew gently on the plank, scattering a few tiny motes of wood to the air, and laid his plane down.

"Sir," he said, bowing his head. How he hated speaking to this whipjack as if he truly deserved to be flattered so. "How may I be of service?"

The crow ambled his way to the corner of the house, and he stood there with his back to the fisherman while he watched the waves on the inlet. He clasped his hands behind himself, a study in nonchalance. He must want something very badly, thought the fisherman, to put on such a false guise.

"As you know," said the crow, "We are carving bedposts for a bed in which the goddess, Dewi Sri, will repose in a manner suited to her divinity."

"Yes," said the fisherman. "So I've been told." Repose was hardly the word, but he'd best not quibble with it now. The gods were a lusty lot, and if they wanted to couple with one another, it was no affair of his.

The crow waved a lazy hand at the house. "This is a fine building. The planks are smooth, and well fitted." He turned, facing the fisherman, and he offered him his grinning beak. "It occurs to Us that we are fellow woodworkers, We and thee, members of the same guild, as it were."

"I suppose," said the fisherman, "if it pleases you to think so."

"Yes, it does," said the crow. "We have come to the point where We shall require the proper pieces of wood to form the frame."

"Ah," said the fisherman. "You want the side boards."

"Just so," said the crow. "What We require are the side boards."

"Rails, they are called," said the fisherman.

"Rails, yes," said the crow, "to connect the bedposts."

"And slats?" said the fisherman.

"Slats?" said the crow.

"Yes, slats," said the fisherman, "to support the mattress."

"Just so," said the crow, "rails and slats, with which to connect Our bedposts, and support Our mattress."

It was at this moment that Cariña and the pelican returned with their buckets of water. Cariña raised an eyebrow as she came close, and the fisherman gave her the barest shake of his head to signal that he did not wish to be interrupted, and so they walked on by and busied themselves with sprinkling the nearly sprouted barleycorns in their cement trench.

The frigate bird, who had positioned himself behind the crow so that he could signal the fisherman without the crow seeing, mouthed the word *bargain*. Given the length and shape of his bill, he had to mouth the word several times before the fisherman caught his drift.

"Aha," said the fisherman. "And should I take on this task, what might I ask in compensation?"

"Aww," said the crow. "We haven't given that much thought." He turned and gazed across the inlet, as if his thoughts had perhaps taken up residence there. "What would please you?"

The fisherman regarded the crow as he might regard a mountebank offering a potion for eternal life. There was no trusting this shapeshifter, this peddler's dog, barking his wares here on the sand. What would please him most was safe passage back to the land of the living for himself and Cariña.

"I wish to go home," he said, "with my beloved."

"Home?" said the crow. His hands were again clasped behind his back as he gazed across the inlet, the fingers of one hand grasping the fingers of the other. "A simple request," he said. "Very well. Let it be so. But only after you have lived here for the year and a day that was our original bargain."

"Too long," said the fisherman. The crow was in need, and now was the chance to press home his advantage.

The crow faced him, scratching at the ground with his feet, as if he wore his crow shape. "You drive a hard bargain, sir," said he. "Throw in a cask of this fabled whiskey I've heard about, and I may meet your terms."

The fisherman and the frigate bird held a meeting of the eyes, and when the frigate bird nodded, the fisherman said, "Yes, your crowness, we can do this for you."

"A month and a day then," said the crow. "We may have further need of your skills." *We may, for example,* thought the crow, *want to have you build Us a gibbet.* A gibbet would be a fine thing indeed. Perhaps he would hang the goddess from it, once he was finished with her.

The fisherman nodded his assent. "A month and a day, from this very day, and we shall go home."

"Kiaw," said the crow. "Let it be so."

"The two of us," said the fisherman, for he was wary of the crow and his tricks. "Cariña is to go home with me."

"Home, the two of you," said the crow. "Let it be so."

Now Cariña joined the fisherman, taking his arm with her hand, and stood shoulder to shoulder with him. "Thank you, Lord Crow," she said, and she bowed her head. She gave the fisherman's arm a sharp squeeze, and he bowed his head as well.

The frigate bird pointed with his beak at the fire, and again at the mound of guano at the far corner of the garden. Back and forth he pointed, again mouthing the word *bargain.* It was Cariña who seized the opportunity.

"Lord Crow," said Cariña. "We have one more favor to beg of you."

"Yes?" the crow said. He spread his arms in a courtly manner, and he said, "How may I be of further service to milady?"

Ye gods, thought the fisherman, *such airs did this lowly, carrion-eating demigod put on.*

"It concerns your guano, Lord Crow. May I speak freely?"

"Of course," said the crow.

Cariña stepped forward and bowed again to the crow. "We have discovered your guano to be most useful in the garden. No doubt you are aware of its beneficial qualities as a plant food?"

"Why, yes," said the crow, "now that you mention it." Not that he had considered the matter before, but of course his guano would have beneficial qualities, for he was a god, was he not? Yes, he was.

"If we could just trouble you to drop it over there," Cariña said, pointing at the spot where the pelican was even now mixing a drop of her blood into their fertilizer, "rather than here," she said, pointing at the fire.

"The guano over there," said the crow, pointing with his beak, "and not over here."

"Yes," said the fisherman, "that spot, and no other."

"Fair enough," said the crow. "We can do this."

"Thank you, Lord Crow," said Cariña. She bowed again, and stepped back to stand beside the fisherman.

"You are most welcome, milady," said the crow, his voice as kindly as a mother crow cooing her simps to sleep. "Now," he said, his voice a shade raspier as he spoke to the fisherman, "When might I have my rails and slats?"

The fisherman considered. Shaping the boards the crow wanted was a day's work for him, if he did nothing else. But he was ever a rebel in the face of authority, and he could not pass up the chance to work a trick on this tricksiest of tricksy varlets.

"In three days' time," said the fisherman.

"So long?" said the crow. "Am I asking for so much? The bedposts will be done by the end of the day."

What did he care if the crow had to wait to enjoy the favors of Dewi Sri? Let this bastardly god, this scabrous sauce box, this cullionly shabbaroon, let him suffer. He should have said it would take a fortnight to shape the boards. A fortnight and a day.

"Lord Crow, to make boards fit for the bed of a goddess will take at least three days' time," said the fisherman. "Maybe four."

"Make it three," said the frigate bird. It would take him that long to arrange for the goddess's bedding to arrive. Best to keep things moving along without unnecessary delay.

The fisherman again nodded his assent. "I'll be needing those bedposts," said he, "as soon as they are finished."

"Of course," said the crow. "Do we have an accord?"

The fisherman offered the crow a curt bow of his head. "Your crowness," said he. "Yes, we have an accord."

The crow departed, and our little band of friends gathered around the fisherman's fire.

"Well done," said the frigate bird. "You shall have your freedom in a month and a day."

The fisherman was not so sure, but he kept his doubts to himself.

"And," said Cariña, "the crow will drop his guano where we want it. We shall have to eat for a month and a day, and this will be a great help." She leaned her head against his, and spoke so that only he could hear. "I know you think the crow difficult, but do you see what a little flattery gets us? He can be handled, as anyone can, with some kindness and some respect."

The fisherman nodded his assent, but what he was thinking was that the best crow would be a dead crow, for the dead could be trusted to keep their word like no others.

On the morning of the third day hence, beneath the waves, a great shadow approached the mouth of the inlet from the seaward side. It was the pelican who saw it first, for she was soaring on the onshore breeze between the twin pinnacles of rock that framed the mouth. She squawked at the sight of it, this shadow from the deeps, looming long and broad, gliding silently toward her home. Her first thought was that the serpentine line of muck from which the Kiamah beast had formed itself so long ago had produced another monster, and her very heart trembled from the fear that all she knew and loved was about to be devoured. But as the shadow neared the mouth of the inlet, it breached the surface in order to swim over the sandbar there, and she saw that it was a great whale.

"Awwwwk!" the pelican cried. "Awk-awk-awk-awk-awk!"

The whale swam between the rock pinnacles and on into the inlet, its flukes rising and falling in the shallow waters. The pelican's cries drew the cormorant and the crow, and their cries drew the fisherman and the woman, and they all stood along the shore and watched as the great whale swam past, and then turned and beached itself with a great lunge.

"Ye gods, what a ziphius," said the fisherman. He shuddered to think that this might be the self-same beast that had brought him here. His beloved leaned against him, her hands soothing his shiver.

"You have survived the whale before," said she. "Let us keep our distance."

Now from the sea came the frigate bird, who had followed the whale across the sea from the island where the goddess reigned. The frigate bird landed on the sand next to his old friend, the whale, and he reached out a wing and touched the creature, and he could be heard clucking and rattling, murmuring sounds of encouragement. The whale opened its mouth, and from it, bit by bit, came a green, squarish shape, as the whale worked its tongue to disgorge the cargo it had carried some considerable distance.

Dewi Sri flew out of the sun now, her wings spread as she soared down to a landing on the beach. She stood next to the crow, who was cawing and krucking fiercely.

"He had better not put out the sacred fire," said the crow, "or I'll peck his eyes out and feed them to the Kiamah."

"Have no fear," said the goddess. "He is only here to deliver my mattress."

"Mattress!" said the crow, and he passed a wing in front of himself and took on his man shape.

"Yes, my love," said Dewi Sri, "and the bedding to go with it. See that bundle sitting atop it? We shall have a proper bed as soon as you finish the frame."

The crow, overjoyed, hopped and hopped, circling the goddess, his tongue waggling inside his open beak. At last the day was come. The bedposts were done, slats and rails had been promised him for this very day, and now, this enormity of a whale had brought them the bedding.

The goddess watched him, a bemused smile on her lips, this god jigging before her like a boy given the day off to go to the fair. Such ardor. Such zeal. It was catching, and she felt her divine womanly juices begin to moisten the furrow in her garden of delight.

The fisherman and his beloved walked up to the green bundle that was the mattress, keeping a wary eye on the whale, who startled everyone with a great exhalation from its blowhole. They were joined by the cormorant, who studied the leaves in which the mattress was wrapped.

"Arum leaves, if I'm not mistaken," said the cormorant. "Large enough to be bedsheets."

"Yes," said the fisherman. "I've seen arum flowers bigger than I am. Corpse flowers, they are called."

"How fitting," said the woman, "that the leaves of such a plant have been brought to the Isle of the Dead."

"*Amorphophallus titanum*," said the cormorant, "the titan arum."

The fisherman untied the knots that held the bundle of bedding together, and out spilled yards and yards of the finest silk, woven in bright colors. The patterns were of gods and goddesses and men and women cavorting with one another in a veritable bounty of poses, pleasuring their partners in myriad ways. The pelican, who had joined them, passed a wing in front of herself and took on her old-woman shape, and she regarded the pictures with the greatest of interest, stopping, occasionally, to examine her own cat's heads and cauliflower, and casting sidelong glances at the fisherman's loins.

"So this is how it's done," said she. "I had no idea there were so many ways."

The crow and the goddess strolled up arm in arm, and the pelican said, "This bedding would make a gill-flurt blush."

At this the goddess grinned at the crow, the bow of her mouth stretched wide, and a lusty, come-hither look in her eyes. The pictures, she thought, would be invaluable when it came time to instruct the crow in the art of love. "Well," she replied, "I am, after all, a fertility goddess."

"Friends," called out the frigate bird, "lend us a hand. We must help the whale unbeach himself."

The whale was indeed struggling with his flukes to drag himself back into the water, and they all joined in, pushing on him, putting their shoulders into it, even the fisherman, who stayed well clear of the beast's mouth, the lot of them heaving and ho-ing and generally getting nowhere with all that effort until Dewi Sri bade them all stop.

"Allow me," said she, and she put her palms together and closed her eyes. A low hum came from deep within her, a sound that trembled inside all their chests, man, god, and whale alike, tuning the very air between them, so that they were all of them enveloped in a sacred chord that swelled louder and louder, and grew ever more forceful as their own voices joined in. The goddess held her palms up and pushed steadily into the air, and they all held their palms up and pushed, and the great whale began to slide bit by bit backward, and together they all hummed and pushed the leviathan into the water.

The whale turned and faced the mouth of the inlet, and rolled itself completely over, washing the sand off its skin. It raised a flipper in a salute of gratitude, and then, with an undulate wave of its tail, pushed off to sea, pausing only to scoop up from the bottom of

the inlet, as the Turropsi had instructed, the crow's tool belt, and
with it the magician's glass that the fisherman had once claimed as
his own. The last they saw of it were its flukes disappearing into the
surf beyond the sandbar.

"Do you not see," said the goddess, "what miracles we can bring off
when we work together?"

There were murmurs of assent all around, although the crow was
so besotted by the thought that he would enjoy the goddess's favors
before the day was out that he wasn't listening. He leaned in to kiss
her, forgetting that he had a beak rather than lips, and he poked her
face so that she cried out in pain.

"Restrain yourself, my love," said the goddess, "the moment is not
yet come."

The crow, though the goddess had spoken gently to him, felt
rebuked, and grew angry. "Kiaww-aw-aw," he said. "Where are my
slats and rails?" he said, his crowish voice raspy and gruff. He strutted over to the fisherman and eyed him with one menacing black eye,
as if he might peck his nose off if he didn't like the answer to his
question.

"Are they done?" he said, "and if they are not done, why are you
idling about here instead of working on them?"

The fisherman, his hands forming fists, gave back to the crow his
most baleful look, his eyes fierce, his teeth bared, and a low growl
coming from his throat. The crow clack-clack-clacked his beak right in
the fisherman's face, so close the fisherman saw that the fine grooves
along its length were marked with traces of blood. They were ready to
have at it, the both of them, but the woman stepped in between.

"Lord Crow," she began, in her most soothing tone, and she curt-
sied before the King of the Dead, who turned away from the fisherman
with one last clack.

"My lord," said she, "the slats and rails are indeed done. We were
just about to bring them to you." She bent her head down, humble
servant to the crow, and bade the fisherman to fall back a step with a
gentle wave of her hand.

"Finished, you say?" said the crow. His gaze settled on the woman's
comely figure, and his ire cooled. "Well, that's quite another shade of
black."

"Yes, my lord," said the woman. "May I take you to them, Lord Crow?"

"Why, yes," said the crow. "We should be delighted."

The woman offered the crow her arm as if she were a lady of the court, and the crow took it, each enjoying the other's touch, although the woman was careful not to reveal her pleasure to the assembly about her, and most especially not to the fisherman. The crow, however, as they walked up the beach toward the house, cast a glance back at the fisherman, his beak parted in a sly grin. The fisherman was not amused. But the frigate bird put a wing on his arm and said, "Patience, friend, let the moment unfold." The fisherman scowled, but he let the crow and his beloved go.

The woman and the crow spoke of nothing but the bed as they walked up the beach. How beautifully carved were the bedposts, how striking were the linens. Where did milady think he should place the bed? Well back from the waters of the inlet, beyond the sacred fire, at the edge of the forest. He should consider the need for some privacy. Of course, of course, the goddess would want that. Perhaps he would banish everyone from the beach for the rest of the day.

They arrived at the house, and stood in the open doorway. "You built this yourselves?" said the crow. He ran his hand along one of the planks that formed the walls.

"Yes, my lord," said the woman. "As you know, the fisherman is a carpenter of some considerable skill. He fashioned all of this."

They stepped inside. Light from the windows cast crisp shadows on the floor. The crow pointed at the mound of moss in the back of the room. "That is your nest?" said he.

"Nest?" said the woman.

"Yes," said the crow. "The place where you sleep."

"Ah," said the woman, "so it is."

"The two of you together," said the crow.

"Yes," said the woman. "Together." His round eyes were black on deeper black, and rimmed with delicate white dots, and in them she saw the glitter of his want for her. Her chest flushed, the heat rising from the tops of her breasts and spreading up her neck. Even in the shadowed space of the house he must be able to see it, for he touched her neck just where she felt the edge of the heat. His fingertips were teasing and feathery as they traced the line of her jaw. His breath smelled pleasantly of cloves. She closed her eyes, the better to feel his touch.

There came a thump from above. The crow's hand fell away from her, and she stifled a moan. She fetched the rails and slats from where they were leaned up against the wall, moving quickly, and she turned to the doorway, and beckoned the crow to follow.

The fisherman called out a "Hallo," and from the roof the frigate bird did the same. The woman and the crow stepped into daylight as the fisherman rounded the corner of the house, ready to brandish the hoe in his hand. One glimpse of the crow and his beloved together drew a foul look to his face. The woman gave him a quick rise of her eyebrows, and the slightest shake of her head. *No*, she was telling him, *the crow has taken no unwanted advantage of me.* She gave him her broadest smile, and she went to him, and held out the boards. She put her cheek to his, the better to quietly instruct him. "Keep the peace," she said, her voice not so much a sound as it was the shape of the words on her lips. "Give him the boards."

The fisherman took a breath, and, taking his time, let out the wind in his chest through pursed lips. This was no time to let himself be carried away with his hatred. He leaned his hoe against the house, and he took the boards from her. The frigate bird, perched above them at the end of the ridgeline, croaked his encouragement.

"Your crow-ness," said the fisherman, bowing his head. "Here are the boards I have promised you."

"We are grateful," said the crow. "Will you be so kind as to carry them down the beach? We shall require some assistance in fitting the pieces together. Milady here has graciously offered to help me pick the site. Please follow us."

And so this small procession headed down the beach to the pyre, the crow and the woman in front, arm in arm, and the fisherman behind them in the catch-fart's position, his arms full of boards. What kept the fisherman's temper in check was the promise of their release, in less than a month's time, from their sojourn here. He was ever a patient man, and he understood his beloved's attention to the crow to be mere flattery, and nothing more, although he wished her to be a little less convincing.

While the crow watched, the fisherman fit the tenons on the ends of the rails into the mortises he'd cut in the bedposts. The fit was tight, as it should be, and he bade the woman fetch his wooden beetle, which she did, and with it he tapped the pieces together until the whole frame was as stout and steady as a Portuguee caravel. They dropped the slats into place. They fetched the mattress from its wrapping of arum leaves, and set it on the slats.

Now the goddess joined them, accompanied by the woman, the two of them carrying the bed linens up from the shore. They sent the crow and the fisherman away, the goddess explaining that it was bad luck for the crow to be present while the connubial bed was prepared. The woman helped the goddess make up the bed, and together they draped the whole thing in the ribald silks from the goddess's own boudoir. The goddess produced perfumes and scented oils from a silk purse that had been sent along with the linens, and with these they anointed first themselves, and then the pillows. They scattered lotus blossoms and jasmine flowers on the bedding, and when all was ready, Dewi Sri and the woman took a moment to lie on the bed.

"'Tis a canopy suited for the bawdiest of revels," said the woman, looking up through the cornucopia of couplings woven into the silk.

"So it is," said the goddess. "A woman needs a touch of the harlot in her, or else she's a dry stick. We are here to bring as much joy as we can into the world."

The woman pointed at one of the couples above her head. "I've never thought of sitting on the Man Thomas in quite that way."

"Oh, that one's lusty good fun," said the goddess. "'Tis called Virsha, the Bull, and it makes you the queen of both your pleasures. Your man will see your lovely backside in all its glory, and he will want you all the more for the lusty motion of your hips."

"So have I seen," said the woman. "The fisherman is most attentive when I am most lewd."

"Go to him," said the goddess, "perfumed and oiled as you are, and show him this new way of coupling. It will make you happy, and when the queen's happy, everybody's happy."

"I am no queen," said the woman, though she smiled at this bit of flattery from the goddess.

"Of course you are," said the goddess. "Every woman is the queen of her own home. Go on, go to him, and lead him to your shared throne. I have a pupil who awaits his lesson."

The crow was indeed pacing back and forth on the sand, muttering to himself, and casting glances full of desperate yearning at the canopied bed. The two women he fancied were dallying there, making him wait. When the woman parted the silks and looked out, he took the opportunity to go to her, offering his hand to help her step down.

"Thank you, my lord," she said. His hand was feverishly warm, and she let his touch linger before she strolled away, the sashay of her hips rolling side to side beneath her sarong.

"Uff," the crow said, his chest so full of heat and ardor that he thought he might explode. He passed a hand in front of his face and grew taller by a cubit, and in his thunderous voice he said "Ko ko ko! This beach is closed to all my subjects until further notice. Be gone from here, at once!"

From down the beach the cormorant and the pelican were seen rising into the air and flying out to sea, while the frigate bird circled high overhead, riding the current of air above the inlet. The crow returned to his normal size, his blood thumping through his veins.

"Lord Crow," said the goddess, "present thyself."

The crow parted the silks with his neb and looked in. There she was, reclining on one elbow, her sarong tied low round her hips, the bounty of her breasts there for him to feast his eyes upon. Her coif was partly undone, and a coil of her shiny black hair draped fetchingly down the front of her shoulder. Her smoldering gaze was full of smoke and mystery, her lips were voluptuous and painted hibiscus red, her smile was slight and bespoke an inward amusement.

The goddess took a long, slow breath, drawing in the scent of her inamorato, a scent of wind and sea, of smoke and roasted meat. "Enter, my darling, this chamber of passion," said she, and she bade him enter with her finger, crooked and beckoning.

And enter he did, crawling awkwardly across the bedding on his knees, his black eyes glistering with lust, his chest wide, his greedy hands at the ready, his loincloth tented ludicrously. The goddess rose to her knees and met him, clasping his hands with hers and thus corralling his grasping ardor.

"Patience, Lord Crow," said Dewi Sri, "for as long as we have waited for this moment, let us make the most of it."

The crow's breath was ragged, as if his throat were sticky, and the air he pulled into his lungs caught on every fold and turn. The goddess brought the palms of his hands together in prayer position in front of his magnificent chest.

"Close your eyes," said she, and when he had done so, she untied the leather cord that held his loincloth on his hips and let it fall. There it was, his q'hram, rigid with blood and throbbing, and of a size befitting a god. The goddess smiled broadly in approval. She leaned down and blew her own hot breath on it, which made the crow moan and shudder, and then she put her hands on the crow's chest. "Lie back," she said, pushing him gently. His back was arched, and the goddess helped him free his legs one by one on either side of her, stretching them past her hips.

The goddess then anointed the crow with scented oils, sandal wood, lavender, and anise, rubbing them into his temples, his third eye, his navel, and then reaching beneath him to anoint the top of his spine where it disappeared beneath his neck feathers, and his sacrum. Through all of this her bare breasts touched his bare skin, and Lord Crow trembled, his blood hot and churning.

The goddess undid her sarong from her hips and tossed it aside. Her own ardor overtook her, and she straddled the crow's hips, and she took his q'hram in her hands and stroked it.

"Aw!" gasped the crow. "Aw aw aw aw aw!"

"Oh yes," said the goddess, "we are too, too ready."

There was no further room for delay, and the goddess guided Lord Crow's arrow to her quiver. The crow babbled, "Humma-humma-kuruk-ma-ha-ha-ha-ka-kaw-kaw-kaw." The string of his bow had been pulled taut for so long that the moment the head of his arrow touched her opening his shot was spent.

"Aww!" said he, "Aw! Aw-Aw! Awwwwwwwww."

The goddess rolled her eyes and hid her smile. Her nether lips were slick with white ribbons of seed. A very great deal of seed, by the feel of it, and no surprise, given that he had waited a thousand times a thousand years for this moment. "There, there, my darling," she cooed, "it is done. Thou art a man now."

"Humma-kuruk-ma-ha-ha-ha," said the crow. His tongue lolled out the side of his beak, and he gazed up at her, muzzy eyed and depleted.

Such a man-child he was, but if he was quick to release, he would be quick to recover. And with his first time out of the way, she could begin his schooling in earnest. She cleaned his spewery from her loins with a bit of cloth she'd laid by for that very purpose. She knelt beside him, and she traced the trailing edge of her flight feathers down his chest, eliciting a low moan. She tizzled his whirligigs with her finger-nails, and his moan grew louder. His q'hram, O happy day, began to stiffen. She anointed his root chakra with jasmine to give the crow greater longevity in the second act.

"Pay heed," said she, "to the way I touch thee, for it is just so that I wish to be touched."

The crow did pay heed, for her touch was not a thing to ignore, and set him aquivering with pleasure. "Touch," said she, "is how the flesh knows the divine. When we touch each other so, we bring earth and heaven together."

"Aww," said the crow.

"Your turn," said the goddess, "touch me."

"Where?" said the crow.

"Wherever your hands are drawn," said the goddess. His hand, as it happened, was drawn to the bounty of her breasts, and now it was her turn to moan.

"Like this?" said the crow.

"Just so," said the goddess, "but keep your hand moving."

"Like so?" said the crow.

"Oh, yes," said the goddess, returning his caress with one of her own, "like that."

Then the goddess placed a pillow beneath his head, the better to arrange his beak to her purpose. His beak lay on his chest, perfectly shaped for her to polish her pearl along its hard and gleaming length. She crouched over his head facing his feet, and she took the lusty ride she had long been promising herself. His beak was well-formed for the task, as she knew it would be, and she slid herself back and forth on a slick of her own divine juices. Yes, here was a rare pleasure, a new and exotic way to bring forth the oldest of raptures. She spread her wings and threw her shoulders back, grinding her loins into the hard curve beneath her. "Krmfh," croaked the crow, his beak held shut by her exertions. She grabbed the crow's q'hram, churning his butter, like this, and this, and this, drawing the moment out, urging them both forward, her second chakra swelling, her loins rutting, just so, and so, and so, her hands urgent on the crow's q'hram, all else falling away, like this, and so, and this, and so, and with her thousands of years of experience, she saw to it that they erupted together, the crow gibbering and thrusting, the goddess's eyes rolled back, her breasts bouncing, her juices flowing, their raptured cries loud and long, her loins grinding, her loins, her loins, her loins.

Thus spent, the both of them collapsed, side by side and head to toe. Slowly they came back to the world of sense, god and goddess, the canopied bed, the sound of the sea. The goddess nuzzled the soles of the crow's feet, and the crow nibbled at her toes with his neb, and then they both fell to giggling.

"I had no idea," said the crow.

"I know," said the goddess.

The crow, looking up at the bawdy canopy, said "There is more to learn, yes?"

"Oh, yes," said the goddess, "much more."

"Teach me," said the crow.

"'Twill be my pleasure," said the goddess. She was flushed, and deliciously sweaty, and she breathed in the sweet-and-sour funk of their coupling. She gave the crow her broadest smile.

"I am to pleasure you as you pleasure me," said the crow. "That is how it's done?"

"That is the first rule," said the goddess. "To give as good as one gets, and then to give even better."

"And so we feed on each other's delight."

"Just so." The goddess sat up, her entire body humming with joy. "Remember this, Lord Crow," said she. "When the goddess is happy, everyone is happy."

And so it was that the goddess schooled the crow in the art of love. They spent the rest of the day beneath the canopy, and the evening as well. Their cries of passion carried all the way to the fisherman's home, where he and his beloved answered them, for they too were at school, the woman imparting to the fisherman some several new ways of coupling that she had learned from the goddess's silks.

When the canoe of the dead arrived at midnight, only the cormorant and the pelican were there to greet them, for the others were all fast asleep. They had to drag the crow out of bed to get him to sing his song, which he sang with little enthusiasm, although with just enough vigor to accomplish its task. Then he hurried off to the canopied bed, and while the dead piled onto the sacred fire, new cries of rapture came from within its covering. But the dead did not hear them, for without their souls, they had no ears for such bliss.

EARLY THE NEXT MORNING, BEFORE the sun's rays cleared the twin pinnacles of rock at the mouth of the inlet, the fisherman and his beloved awoke on their bed of moss. They were spooned together, he to she, their loins fully sated, the fisherman's hand cupping the woman's breast. They murmured sleepy greetings to each other, and lay there luxuriant in the warmth of their own bodies. Their thighs were weak from the exertions of the day before, though they would not know this until later, when they each rose in turn to get on with the day. They smelled of their own spent juices, and that smell, still fresh enough to be earthy and pleasant, sent each of them into reveries of passion fulfilled, their most favored moments returning to them in the form of happy sighs.

"By Ashtart," said the fisherman, "never have I had such pleasure before."

"No?" said the woman. She rolled over and faced her lover, taking his Man Thomas in her hand to warm it. "Be truthful," said she, "for I know you have lain with others before me." There was no jealousy in her, and the coupling they had done the day before had stripped away any shyness she harbored.

"Not even with her temple whores," said the fisherman, "who are skilled, but too well-used to perform their task with such honest enthusiasm."

"Ah," said she, "so that is how it is? The goddess Ashtart maintains temples full of whores?"

"Yes," said the fisherman. "It is so. Though they call themselves priestess, and insist that the payment they ask is a gift to the temple."

"And for the women," said his beloved, "is there a temple where they might enjoy such sport?"

"None that I know of," said the fisherman.

The woman turned this thought over in her mind, looking beneath it, behind it, and beyond it. "That hardly seems fair," said she. She withdrew her hand from his Man Thomas, and rolled onto her back, and now the two of them stared up into the dark space above the rafters.

"You are right," said the fisherman. "It is not fair. There is much in the world that is not fair, in fact, I would say that fairness is the exception rather than the rule."

Some light began to seep into the room through the window set high in the gable. Another dawn, thought the fisherman, another mark on the wall. Soon they would be going back to the world, with all its inequity.

The woman turned on her side again, and raised herself up on an elbow. She put her hand on the fisherman's chest, bluer in the blue light of morning. She had seen her own face in the still waters of the pool below the waterfall, but she could not find it here, on her lover's chest for the ink in his skin was now the same blue as the blue of his skin.

Let it fade. Her face on his chest did not make her his property.

"We were not the only ones in love's temple yesterday," said the woman. "By the sound of it, Dewi and the crow made quite the lusty pair."

The fisherman nodded. "I heard them too. There were times when their cries spurred me to greater heights."

"Yes," said the woman, "it is catching." The crow, she was thinking, would be his own delicious frolic. "The goddess," said she, "is taming the crow."

Perhaps, thought the fisherman, *and perhaps not.*

"You give him too much regard," said he. "I am not so sure he can be tamed."

Do not underestimate me, thought the woman, for she had just spent the night showing the fisherman that she was every bit the woman that the goddess was, and the fisherman had howled out his pleasure for all to hear. When her chance came, she would show the crow such skill and ardor as to make a supremely happy god of him. They would all be the better for it, and even the fisherman would have to admit she was a woman to be reckoned with.

She frowned. "Why do you hate him so?"

"Because," said the fisherman, his ire at the crow, and the woman's regard for him, rising in him like some vile sputum he must spit out into the world, "he is a charlatan, and a scoundrel, and a foul scavenger. Because he lied to me about his capacity to restore you to me as you once were. Because he is a savage tyrant, who tortures the dead for his own sport, and picks at their corpses like a vulture."

"He has never been anything but a gentleman in my presence."

"Yes," said the fisherman, "and that proves the point. He is tricksy, and not to be trusted."

"So you say," said the woman.

"So have I seen," said the fisherman. Somehow, his finger was now pointed at the woman's face. She pushed it aside.

"You hate him because you fear him," said she.

"Just so," said the fisherman. "I hate him as I hate all tyrants."

And rivals, thought the woman. *You fear he will take me away from you.*

"The goddess will make a new man of him," said she. "He is already changed. You saw it yourself, when he agreed to drop his guano where we want it. And again, as he worked with you on the bed yesterday, and without rancor. If we treat him with respect and kindness, he will become respectable and kind."

"No," said the fisherman, "he has tricked you into thinking this, and we shall both pay a heavy price if you do not see through him."

"If all you look for is the worst in him, then that is all you will see." The woman sat up and threw aside their blankets.

This, thought the fisherman, *is the way it always goes.* "You are a fool," he said, "and the crow will make of you a bigger fool."

"He likes me," said the woman. She slapped her hands on the moss beneath her, and she stood up. "He will not treat me so."

The fisherman looked up at her, at the flush in her face, now just visible in the dawning light, which spread down to the tops of her breasts.

"You want him," he said. "Don't you?"

The woman huffed out a harsh breath of air. "You're jealous," said she. "Over nothing. Nothing at all. I barely know him." Her voice rose now, until she was shouting at him. "And I am no fool. It is you who are the fool, and it is you who has a withered heart, and you who cannot see anything but evil around you. I will leave you," said she, her voice raw and raspy, "to your despicable thoughts." She turned then, and walked out of their house naked, and left her man there, shaking his head.

If we were the last man and woman in the world, thought he, *which we are, we would still find something to fight about.*

The sooner they left here, the better.

THE CROW SLEPT SOUNDLY AFTER his revels with the goddess, her front to his back, her wings covering them both. He awoke in darkness, before the first glimmering of dawn, the piquant tang of the smoke from the pyre savory in his nostrils.

Meat, he thought, *there's nothing better.*

He pulled the goddess's arm more tightly round him, soaking up the warmth of her. Perhaps there was something better than meat. This coupling, this pleasuring of the flesh, it was truly divine. He wanted more. His zibik began to stiffen. Would she welcome him again between her legs? Of course she would. She had tutored him on how to touch her there, and told him he was a gifted pupil.

But he was forgetting something. She was out to betray him. She had already given herself to who knows how many others.

He was a god. He was the King of the Dead. No one had the right to treat him so. She was his now, and if she would not be his, and his alone, he would kill her.

He rolled onto his back. That smell, that wasn't just the pyre, that was her. Her nether juices were all over his beak. Her hand drifted down to his zibik. "Mmmm," she murmured, "Lord Crow."

"Humuh," he said. "Kurawk."

"You want me," she said.

"Ummuh," he said, "uh-huh."

"And you shall have me," she said, "but first, we must speak."

"Awww," he said. "Couple now, talk later."

She pulled her hand back from his q'hram. It was time to set the hook. "You are suspicious of me," she said.

"What?" he said.

"You are jealous, and want me all to yourself." She stroked the feathers above his brow. "You think I will make a cuckold of you."

The crow began to sweat despite the soothing of her hand. She had the power to read his thoughts. He should kill her now. He put his hand on her chest, above her breast, close to her throat.

"How do you know this?" he said.

"You spied on us," she said, "at the waterfall. You came in the shape of a dragonfly."

"You knew that was me?"

"Yes, my darling, I knew. And you heard me say that I would have the fisherman, and that his woman could have you. You have been cold and aloof with me since then. For this I do not blame you."

"I am forgiven?"

"Yes, forgiven. Any man would be angry. But know this: I am a changed woman now."

"Changed? How so?"

"Because of you, my darling. Because no one has ever taken me to the heights as you have. Never have I schooled a pupil so apt."

Well, yes, thought the crow. *I am, after all, King Crow*. His hand slid away from her throat, and drifted down to her breast.

"I forsake all others," said the goddess. "I am yours, and yours alone, from this moment forward."

"Truly?" said the crow.

"Truly," said the goddess.

The crow, never having been in love before, was unprepared for the deluge of feelings that rose within him. She loved him, and he her, and nothing else mattered. Her nipple hardened between his fingers.

The goddess put her hand on his q'hram again. The handle by which a man is best led, it swelled to her touch. Poor fellow, he was no match for her. She nuzzled him where his neck feathers gave way to his skin, that soft hollow above his collarbone that, she had discovered, made his moan quaver. She could play him like a gamelan gong. The crow closed his eyes, giving himself over to the pleasure of her hand.

"I am yours," said the crow, "forever."

Yes you are. She was only leading him on, and certainly not forever, but for now, she would give him plenty of honest pleasure. And take her own full measure of delight along the way.

"Let us seal our covenant," said she, "thusly," and she lowered herself upon him.

Done.

DEWI SRI, THE PELICAN, AND Cariña—goddess, demigoddess, and mortal—having bathed in the pool just below the waterfall, sat one behind the other on a flat rock, their legs splayed. The pelican was in her old woman shape, her heavy breasts slumped over her round belly. The goddess's hair was down, and the pelican was preening it with her bill, while the goddess combed the woman's hair with a wooden comb. Their freshly washed sarongs lay on the rocks around them, drying in the sun, and next to them were their vials and kohl pots, and a mirror the frigate bird had brought them. Their loins were sated with Sapphic delights. Their skin was oiled and perfumed, and shiny in the light of the sun.

"Is he dangerous?" said the woman. "The fisherman says the crow is a savage."

"Oh, he is," said the pelican. "He is easily provoked, and violent."

"He can be cruel," said the goddess. "Make no mistake about that. But he is easily flattered, and a slave to the pleasures of his own q'hram, and therefore easy to rule."

"This is the way it's done?" said the pelican. "It's all about their zibiks?"

The goddess and the woman both grinned. "That is the biggest part of it," said the goddess. "Handle the q'hram the way they like, and you can lead them wherever you care." The woman made a circle of thumb and forefinger, and thrust the first finger of her other hand through the ring she'd made, and she held her hands over her head so the pelican could see. They all three of them fell to giggling, and when their laughter had subsided, they fell silent.

"The flattery is important as well," said the goddess. "You must tell them they are good at pleasing you, and more than that, you must teach them how you most wish it to be done. In a true love match, the pleasure the woman gives the man is fed by the pleasure the man gives the woman, just as it is with the three of us."

"And are they all willing to be trained?" asked the woman.

"Some more than others," said the goddess, "and some not at all. With those, it is best to move on, after one has given one's best effort, for if they will not play the game of love as your equal, they are best left to their own devices."

"How is the fisherman?" asked the pelican. "Is he well trained in the arts of love?"

The woman considered for a moment. "I believe so," she said, "though I have no one to whom I might compare him."

"He is a good man," the goddess said. "One senses these things. He is tender and patient with you, and it would surprise me if he were not equally so in bed."

"He has lain with many others in the land of the living," said the woman, "and he was quick to show me what pleased him."

"His experience in these matters is a boon to you both," said the goddess.

"I heard you arguing with the fisherman," said the pelican, "early this morning."

"He thinks I hold the crow in too much esteem," said the woman.

"And do you?" said the pelican.

"Who is to say what is too much?" said the woman. "The fisherman is jealous, although I've given him no cause to be."

"Yet you wish to," said the goddess, for she had taken note of how the woman looked at the crow, secretly and with lust, "and you have let slip your hidden feelings."

"All I said was that the crow liked me, and would do me no harm."

The comb the goddess was using found a tangle in the woman's hair. She set it aside, and deftly plucked the tangle apart with her fingers.

"Perhaps he has guessed what is in your heart," said the pelican.

She had finished her preening, and was now coiling the goddess's hair on top of her head.

"And more," said the goddess. "He has seen the yen in your loins for the crow."

"What am I to do, then?" said the woman. "The more I deny it, the less he shall believe me."

"Truly," said the goddess. "Men may be foolish, but when it comes to spying a rival, they are not fools." The tangle in the woman's hair now unraveled, the goddess resumed combing her hair. *There was a great deal at stake here*, thought she. *They must be careful.*

"I have heard the two of you," said the woman. "The crow must be very skilled."

"Yes," said the pelican. "I had no idea that coupling was such a loud affair."

Again they all laughed, for they had rent the air, both the goddess and the woman, with their lusty cries, and they had been shameless about it.

"He is an apt pupil," said the goddess, "and full of pent-up spunk." *And enthusiasm*, thought she, *and stamina.* Her nether lips were rubbed raw.

They might as well take what pleasure they could while there was still time. War's havoc would render all these carnal intrigues trivial, and who knew if any of them would survive? Perhaps she should send them away, and face what was coming by herself. But there was too much at stake, and she would need her friends at her side.

She found the gold hibiscus flower she wore on the front of her coif and handed it to the pelican, who slid it into its place.

"You may have the crow if you must," said the goddess, "and I will teach you what he favors best."

"I haven't asked for the crow," the woman protested.

"Yet he is what you desire," said the goddess, "and we shall arrange things so that the fisherman does not know." He would be easy to distract, she thought, though there was risk in that. She must not lose the crow's trust, fragile as it was.

The woman leaned back, resting her head on the goddess, her eyes lit with the heat she felt for the crow. "Thank you, my queen. I am in your debt."

"And something else," said the goddess. "You may have him only the one time. The delicate threads of fate are being woven here, and the crow is at the center of them. We dare not disturb them too much."

The woman bowed her head. "It shall be as you wish. You have my word."

"What about me?" said the pelican. "You promised I would have my chance as well."

Frogs and princesses, thought the goddess, *what to do about the pelican?* She swung round on the flat rock, and the woman too, and they looked at the pelican, the sag of her breasts, the rumpled flesh of her round belly, the folds of skin at her neck, her puckered thighs, the wrinkles and crinkles at her knees and elbows and on the backs of her hands. The woman caught the eye of the goddess, and she shook her head.

"The fisherman will not take you," said the woman. "Forgive me, but you are too old, and too unshapely."

"'Tis true," said the goddess, "that a man is best aroused by a woman of child-bearing years."

"I've thought of that," said the pelican. "I have something to show you."

She turned away from her friends, showing them her back. She passed a hand in front of herself, and when she turned round again, she appeared as Cariña did, with her face, and her body. Only her eyes were different, as they kept their yellow color. That, and the silver necklace the woman wore round her neck.

"Swive me," said the woman. "You're me."

The goddess laughed. "Stand next to each other. Let me look at the pair of you."

They were as two rosebuds on the same stem, the one a mirror for the other. A handsome woman, mature and comely, her body edging toward old age but not yet arrived there, and now doubled. A good match for the fisherman, who, unlike some old men, did not require a youthful partner to feel desire.

"Is this likeness enough?" said the woman. She put her hand to the pelican's face, and gently traced the curve of her cheekbone, her own best feature.

"It is more than enough," said the goddess. "Well done."

"I've been practicing," said the pelican. She took a few steps in front of them, swaying her womanly hips back and forth. She had indeed been practicing, for her sashay was saucy, like the woman's, and would be the more so when she wore a sarong.

So there was the way. It was risky, for the pelican was a novice, but with the woman distracting the crow, and some guidance from herself for the pelican, it just might work. She might even find time for another tryst with the frigate bird, a pleasure she'd thought she must deny herself. Or the cormorant, if the frigate bird was off on one of his many errands. There would be sport for all, and the men none the wiser.

"What about her eyes?" said the woman.

The pelican blushed. "The eyes," said she, "They're the hardest part." She closed them, and her brow furrowed, and when she opened her eyes again, they were blue.

"Perfect," said the woman.

Yes, perfect. The woman would have her chance with the crow, and the pelican her chance with the fisherman. They would be bound to her, and when the time came to call in the debts, they would not refuse.

"You must do exactly as I say," said the goddess.

And so they put their heads together, and they laid their plans.

THE FISHERMAN DID NOT WAKE when his beloved rose from their bed for her nightly trip to the privy, though he came close enough to wakefulness to think, *Tomorrow I must finish the privy door, and hang it*. He was already fully asleep when she returned, and slipped beneath their coverlet of silk to spoon her body against his back. The coverlet had been a gift from the goddess, out of the store of bed linens the whale had brought, and beneath its warmth the fisherman felt the soft skin of his beloved. She moaned, her breath hot on his neck, and her hand groped its way to his cods. His Man Thomas was not rampant, and the woman pulled at it, her fingers eager and somewhat clumsy. He rolled onto his back, and her mouth was upon his in a trice, her kisses fervent, urgent, almost desperate. She kissed him everywhere at once, his lips, his cheeks, his neck, his brow, and all the while she gripped his Man Thomas as if it were the tiller of a skiff she steered larboard and starboard.

"Gently," he whispered. In her hunger for him she seemed to have forgotten the way to tease forth the spine of his Thomas, and he put his hand on hers to show her. "A tizzle for the pizzle," said he, a phrase from their own private dictionary of love, and to which his beloved always replied, "A shiver for the quiver," and so might they commence a rainbow kiss. But in the moment she did not reply in her usual way, nor swing her nether lips round to his, nor swallow the head of his Man. No, she only loosened her grip on the tiller, following the lead of his hand on hers, and kissed him the more ardently, and now his own desire caught fire from the sparks of hers. After some fumbling about she managed to place the tip of his arrow in the opening of her quiver, although not at all with the sureness of touch to which he was accustomed, and she lowered herself upon him, and sighed.

The woman bounced and jiggled on him so eagerly that she fell off several times. She had ever been an ardent lover, but this night the fisherman found her so eager as to be almost clumsy in her enthusiasm, as if she had forgotten, with all else she had forgotten, the rhythm and the form of their coupling dance. Her lovemaking was fervent, her kisses earnest, but she was awkward and graceless at times, and in the end he found it best to roll her over and take the high ground. Thus positioned, he rode her home, spending himself within her. He withdrew himself, gave her an affectionate and leisurely kiss, and then lay on his side, his back to her front, a return to his slumbers fast approaching.

To his surprise she reached for him again, and the fisherman groaned. He had labored the day long as a carpenter, shaping the boards for the privy door, and his ardor was sapped. He let her hand play for a while, but it was to no effect, and he said, finally, that he was tired, and must sleep.

"That's it?" she said. "That's all you have for me?"

"The spirit is willing," said he, "but the flesh is spent."

"But I am ready now for more," said she.

"Yes, my beloved," said he. "Perhaps in the morning."

"The morning will be too late," said she. She tugged harder on his

Thomas, but the poor fellow remained tepid, and soft. The fisherman placed his hand over hers, and pulled it away.

"I need sleep," said he, "and the Man Thomas will be of no use to you until I do sleep." He turned over and faced her, and he traced his finger along the links of the silver chain round her neck. Her gaze was full of ardor, and his finger stopped, arrested by the color of her eyes.

"Your eyes," said he.

"What about them?" said she.

"They're yellow," said he.

Her lips rounded themselves into a circle, and she closed her eyes, her brow furrowed between them, and when she opened them again, they were blue.

"Are you sure?" said she. "It's dark in here."

"I can see well in the dark, as you know."

His woman licked her lips, as if they were suddenly dry. "Then you can surely see that they are blue," said she.

"They are now," said he, "but a moment ago, they were yellow."

"A trick of the light," said she. She traced his lips with a fingertip while she looked steadily into his eyes, her gaze randy and wanton.

There is no light in here to trick, thought he, but her touch was teasing, and arousingly so, and led him toward the pleasures of the flesh. He kissed the tips of her fingers.

"The light of love burns hot in you tonight," said he, "but strangely so."

"Lover," said she, "I am no stranger to thee." She pulled his face to hers with her hand on the back of his head, her mouth like the sucker of an octopus so hungry she was. The fisherman was far from recovered, but her eagerness for him would not be denied, and he put his hand between her legs, stroking her quim, and this, by the sound of her moans, she found most pleasurable. 'Twas a skill he had long since perfected, and he brought her swiftly to the top of the great wave, whereupon she cried out lustily, and then coasted down the other side.

Again the fisherman kissed her, and rolled on his side, ready to slip back into the slumber of depletion. Again the woman put her hand on him, and begged for more, and would not let him be. Although his wrist ached, again he used his practiced hand to fetch her what she wanted. But when she wanted still more, he feigned sleep, and would not be roused, though she pleaded with words and lips and hands.

At last she gave up, and sat next to him in the darkness, and felt the sweat cooling all over her skin. Her flesh tingled from within, as if every jot and tittle of her being trembled each against the other. She had never given herself over so completely to pleasure. All her worries were pounded into dust, and scattered on the merest puff of air. She felt wondrously emptied, and yet filled with desire.

The fisherman was now well and truly asleep, and so did not hear the footfalls that approached the door, nor see the head of the goddess peer in, nor her hand beckoning the woman to come out. She left the bed, and found both her own twin and the goddess outside. Her twin embraced her, her smile broad, and the one woman took off the silver necklace and gave it to the other. One twin entered the house, and lay next to the fisherman, and the other walked off into the night with the goddess.

"How was it?" said the goddess.

"'Twas good while it lasted," said the pelican, "But I could've done with more."

"Such is the nature of desire," said the goddess. "The more we get what we want, the more we want what we have not yet got."

When he woke again in the light of dawn, the fisherman gazed upon his beloved, who lay sleeping next to him. He touched the silver necklace round her neck, tracing its path across her collar bone.

"Cariña," he said. Her sleepy eyes opened into his, and they were blue, as ever had they been.

"Hold me," said his beloved. "But let me sleep."

The fisherman wrapped his arms round her, her back to his front, and with the rise and fall of her breath, he let himself fall back to sleep.

THE FRIGATE BIRD PERCHED ONE-FOOTED on the roof of the world, his position precarious, his spyglass to his eye, held there by his other foot. What he had first seen, mere weeks ago, as a single distant point far out in the Fetch, was now an enormous dark mass in the middle distance. He watched there a swarm of the Turropsi, hovering in front of it, dwarfed by its gargantuan size. The Turropsi had forbidden him to approach it, but they had told him that it was not so much a thing they could touch as it was a blind spot, an abyss beyond which they could see no future. Not for the spirit world, nor the material world, nor even for themselves. They told him that as they approached it seemed that they never met its surface, yet when they turned to look back, they found themselves already enveloped by darkness. Many Turropsi had flown into it. Only a very few had ever returned.

Now swarms of the Turropsi labored at the edges of this vast blind spot, trying to move past it, but whenever they did so, it simply expanded, blocking them so that they could not move over it, nor under it, nor around it. Other swarms of the Turropsi used their paddle arms to move aside the mists at the edges of the blind spot, trying to change its course, to turn it away from the great standing wave of the present. He had never seen the Turropsi so urgent in their churning of the mists, and yet the dark mass grew ever closer, and ever larger. Their failed efforts gave him, beneath his breastbone, a desperate chill that shriveled his red throat pouch.

The frigate bird flipped his spyglass round in the manner of a knife handler showing off his skills, a piratical sort of trick that he had often used to impress any buccaneer who might question his authority, though he did it now simply to calm his own rattled nerves. Just behind the great standing wave, he found the tale of his own band of heroes on the Isle of the Dead, writ there as if in a tapestry whose leading edge was constantly woven anew. There his compatriots were busy with the brewing of ale, and Dewi kept the crow sozzled with desire, and the pelican waddled about being helpful and compassionate to everyone in her path. There the Kiamah dozed, his eyes ever half-open, waiting to devour the world should his supply of conaria falter.

The frigate bird flipped his spyglass round again, and looked into the mists being sucked into the present, where countless Turropsi used their many arms to sort through all that was possible, narrowing the choices. The mists were too thick to see much beyond a turbulence full of dark shapes, but there, in the middle distance, and closer than the vast blind spot, he was able to make out a thick, fractious horde, milling and tumbling about. A horde of marauders so large as to be beyond numbering.

This was the army waiting its moment to do battle on the Isle of the Dead. The Turropsi paid it no mind, and this army would soon enough arrive on their shore. War was coming, and beyond that was the obliteration of all good things. The frigate bird shivered.

Ye gods, he thought. *What have I gotten myself into?*

EVERY MORNING WHEN HE AROSE, the fisherman took a piece of charcoal from the fire and added a mark to his tally of days on the side of the house. He worked side by side with his beloved, hauling water from the stream, making ale, gardening. Every night they met the canoe, and led the newly dead to their home, where they shared the bounty of their lives, eating and drinking, singing and dancing, giving everyone one last chance to make merry, and forget that their lives were over. The cormorant expounded on the history of ale, and settled bar bets on any subject with genial authority. The pelican gave succor to the high-strung and the fearful, assuring them that they had nothing to fear. The frigate bird came and went as his duties required, but he joined them often, mingling with the newly arrived, offering his pipe to those who partook, and collecting the objects he had placed in their hands or their pockets before they found themselves on the far shore. Even the fish eagles joined in from time to time, for they, too, had discovered the beneficent, generous, public-spirited virtues of ale, and they were fond of sipping this divine beverage through hollow reeds, which they then kept in their mouths like materials for a nest as they flew back to the canoe of the dead. The crow and the goddess made their entrance when the festivities were in full swing, a royal couple now, king and queen of the dead, the crow charming and personable, the goddess gracious and serene, and after a time they led the dead to the sacred fire, where they coughed up their souls and surrendered their bodies to the flames.

Every morning the crow held court, but later than had been his custom before he began trysting with Dewi Sri. He sat on his throne, which the fisherman had built, however begrudgingly, according to his instructions. Cariña had urged him to do so in an effort to stay in the crow's good graces, though the fisherman only pretended that the crow's good graces mattered one whit to him. The cormorant and the pelican were there always, their shoulders a little less burdened than before because they no longer slept with the weight of the crow atop them. The crow, for his part, held forth on whatever subject caught his fancy, and his congress of crows stood at his feet, thoroughly entranced by his crowish speech, their dark eyes staring up at him, fierce, proud, and loyal.

The days passed in relative calm for a week, and then another, the quiet of the days broken only by the cries of passion from within the canopied bed, where the goddess taught her lover the four and sixty positions of their bawdy silk canopy, and by the calls of the congress of crows, who found perches in the trees, and spent their days scavenging the pyre for tasty bits of roast flesh.

It was on one such morning that the fisherman approached the King of the Dead, his tally of days till it was time to return home now a week short of fulfillment. His friends the cormorant and the pelican stood behind the crow's throne, both of them sober of face, although a sly smile briefly curved the pelican's bill.

The fisherman bowed low, then stood up straight and looked the crow directly in his shining black eyes. "Oh, great and magnificent King of the Dead," he began, but the crow interrupted him. "How is your handsome woman friend this morning?" said the crow.

"She is well," said the fisherman, a note of puzzlement in his voice. "I thank you for asking after her." Since when did the crow care about anyone but himself?

"Excellent," said the crow. "Please do Us the favor of sending her Our compliments."

Perhaps the goddess was teaching this arrogant bird some manners, thought the fisherman. *A man would do a lot to please the object of his affections.* "I shall," said he. "Allow me to extend her compliments to you."

"Aw," said the crow, "did she instruct you to do so?"

"Not in so many words," said the fisherman, "but I know her mind well, and I know that she holds you in the highest esteem." No harm in flattering the king, especially now that he was about to let them go. Behind the crow the pelican fidgeted, bored no doubt, shifting her weight from foot to foot.

"Kiaw aw aw aw aw aw," laughed the crow. "We are certain that she does."

Ye gods, this sack of turds is full of himself. Best to get down to the matter at hand, or we will waste the whole morning blandishing and truckling.

"Lord Crow," said the fisherman, "I come before you seeking to know the hour and the manner of our return to the land of the living."

"Return to the material world?" said the crow. "We are puzzled. To what do you refer?"

This reply from the crow sent a trickle of sweat swiveting down the fisherman's side, although he kept his composure, and resisted the urge to draw his knife. The crow was not a foe to be taken lightly, and it was better to argue his way through if he could.

"You will recall," said the fisherman, "that in exchange for my services as the carpenter of your rails and slats, you promised me that I should return to the land of the living."

"Oh, that," said the crow. "We do recall the conversation, and We daresay We recall it more accurately than do you." The crow had his hands on the arms of his throne, and he leaned forward now, as if to share a royal confidence with his subject. His black beak was gleaming and sharp. "We believe that what We promised you was that you would return home."

"Yes, Lord Crow. That was the promise."

"Excellent, Sir Dungpile," said the crow. "We are glad you agree. We are happy to comply, and that is something that it is well within Our power to do."

Good, thought the fisherman, *we are one step closer to settling the matter.* "Yes, Lord Crow," said he, "your powers have long been evident to me. I am wondering when and how this shall take place. By what means are we to return home? Will the journey be long? Shall I provision myself?"

"So many questions for so simple a matter," said the crow. *What a dotard this fop-doodle is.* "But first, let Us clear up any confusion about the precise meaning of Our promise. We made no mention of the material world. Nor of the land of the living, as you prefer to call it."

Now the fisherman's hand went to the hilt of his knife. Let the crow understand, if this vile poltroon meant to betray him again, it would be the last trick of his wretched life. But the crow did not flinch, nor shrink back in any way, and so the fisherman pressed his case forward, his voice calm, but steeled.

"Surely the meaning was clear," said the fisherman. "My home is in the land of the living."

"We beg to differ," said the crow. He sat back in his throne, and his head lolled to the side, as though the matter at hand were of no consequence. "Your home is here, in that house you built yourself. You are free to return there at any time you wish, and if you need assistance, We are at your service."

Betrumped again? A rage of heat rose in the fisherman's face. His hand fairly ached to draw his blade. *Swive me*, thought he, *I'll kill this man-harpy. I was not born to be his fool.*

"You would do well to remember," said the crow, "the fate of the last man who drew that blade against Our person." He opened his beak wide, and snapped it closed several times, *clack clack clack clack clack*. There was murder in his black-on-black eyes. The crows at his feet were all staring at the fisherman, ready to pluck his bones clean.

The fisherman clasped his hands behind his back. He was outmatched. He'd best be tricksy himself if he wanted to slaughter this tricksy varlet. He would bide his time, and slay this whore-pipe of a god when he could take him unawares. He lowered his eyes and took in a long slow breath. "I hear the wisdom in your words," said he.

"Do you?" said the crow. "Clever fellow. Do you require Our assistance in returning to your home?"

"I think not, Lord Crow."

"Then you are dismissed," said the crow, "and our bargain is fulfilled. Is it not?"

The fisherman was already walking away. He raised his hand, waving it without turning round to look.

"Let the record show," said the crow to the cormorant, "that the supplicant agreed." And then the crow laughed his awful laugh—*aw aw aw aw aw*.

"Yes, my lord," said the cormorant, and when the crow looked away, he allowed himself the barest shake of his head, but he produced his book of records, and made note of what had just happened.

"A cheeky lad," said the crow to his congress. "Someone should teach him some manners."

"Cheek-cheek-cheek-cheek-cheek," said the congress of crows.

THE PELICAN STOOD AT THE edge of the crowd, on the far side of the fire from the fisherman. She was in her crone shape, an old woman with her bill nestled between her sagging breasts, her skin wrinkled, her round belly hanging over the top of her sarong, and her bottom flat. This was what the fisherman saw, and though he was friendly enough, there was no hint of desire in his eyes when he looked at her, any more than there was when she was in her pelican shape. She was ugly in this shape, she knew this now. She wanted him to look at her the way he had when she was bouncing and jiggling herself atop his q'hram. What a night of coupling they'd had, though too short, too short. It was all she could do not to pass her hand in front of her face and take on the shape of his beloved. She would walk over to him and offer herself, this very moment, in front of all of them. His hands held a mug of ale, those powerful hands of his, hands that could smooth boards until they felt like silk. The tips of his fingers were tender and fierce at the same time, and how they made her quim sing.

"Stop staring at him." It was the woman, who had sidled up behind her while she was lost in her reverie. Her whisper was harsh. "He will guess the truth if you do not watch yourself."

"I want him again," said the pelican.

"If it were up to me you could have him again," said the woman. "I would love to have another romp with the crow." She put her arm round the pelican and turned her away from the firelight, and together they walked a few steps into the night. "But the goddess said we could only do this once, and we dare not go against her wishes."

"Why not?" said the pelican. "Why does she decide what is right for me and thee?"

"Because she's the goddess," said the woman. "There are things afoot here beyond our knowledge."

"I am a goddess too," said the pelican. She passed her hand in front of her face, and took on her pelican shape. "Can Dewi Sri do this?" She passed her wing in front of her face, and took on the shape of the woman. "Or this?"

Cariña grabbed her hand and pinched her, hard. "Stop that. Change yourself back before someone sees us."

The pelican tugged at her sarong, smoothing it round her hips, and shifting it down a bit to reveal the tops of her cat's heads. What lovely curves she had in this shape. "Dewi Sri need not know. We shall bide our time until she is busy with other things."

"It is too risky," said the woman.

"One time in a thousand times a thousand years. Is that all I am to have? You have the fisherman every night."

"Change yourself," said the woman, "or we shall both suffer." Her eyes were fierce, and her hands, hanging at her sides, were fists. "We cannot do this," said she. Her fists trembled. She looked back at the fire, where the fisherman was talking to the frigate bird. He knocked back his mug of ale and looked around for the cask.

"We can, and we shall," said the pelican. She stepped back, away from the firelight and farther into the darkness, drawing Cariña with her. "If you do not aid me, then I will show the fisherman your shape, and tell him that I have lain with him, and I will tell him you were with the crow that night."

The woman's mouth gaped. "You would not." She folded her arms in front of her, as if that settled the matter.

"I would. What have I to lose? And you, you have another night with the crow to gain, and all we need do is wait and watch for the moment."

"It will never happen," said the woman. But already within her desire stirred, and she fought to keep her lips from taking on a saucy smile.

"Patience," said the pelican. "We bide our time, and then we seize the moment, just like skimming a fish out of the water."

The woman's head fell forward, and she let out a puff of air. The crow had been courtly with her in speech. "Enter, milady," he had said, holding back the ribald silk for her with his beak. The canopied bed was lit with candles, and his skin was the color of copper. He touched her face, tracing the line of her jaw, and then her lips, and she stroked the length of his neb, black and shiny in the candlelight. Then his hands were on her everywhere at once, and hers on him, fondling, feverish, ravishing, frenzied, his need feeding hers, her need feeding his. She brought his zibik to her quim and gave him entry while he nibbled her nipples with the tip of his big, black beak.

Swive me, she thought, *the thrill of it!* The fisherman was ardent enough, and well-practiced, but, for all his skill, her body knew his every move, and there were no surprises. Where he was patient with her, the crow was desperate.

She trembled within, remembering the urgent glitter of his black eyes in the candlelight. Where the fisherman asked, the crow took, as a king takes whatever he wants. And with that taking, she gave, with all her body, willingly, over and over, and again and again.

When she looked again at the pelican, there was the trace of a smile on her lips, and the barest rise of one eyebrow. The crow made a woman of her in ways the fisherman did not. He made of her a goddess.

"You want this as much as I do," said the pelican.

"No promises," said the woman. "And we must not be caught. Do you understand? I will not give the fisherman reason to suspect me. Now change yourself, or we shall never have our chance."

"We shall be as foxy as pickpockets," said the pelican. She took on her crone shape again, and she put her arm round the woman's shoulders and gave her a wink. The woman leaned into her, and gave her belly an affectionate rub.

"As sly as sleuth hounds," said the woman.

"And as bold as bobcats," said the pelican. "I'll not spend the next thousand years wishing I had been brave enough to get what I want."

THE CROW, IN HIS MAN shape, lay on a driftwood log near the pyre. He was stretched out on his side as if the log were a roman lectus, with his arm bent and his head propped up on his hand. This was a manner of repose the goddess favored, and the crow found it befitting to his station in life. It was late in the afternoon, the sun nearing the eastern horizon, the hour of the beast fast approaching. His zibik lay fat and sassy beneath his loincloth, having been well-used that morning by the goddess, and again in the middle of the day. His congress of crows cawed sociably from their perches in the nearby trees, and one or another of them hopped about on the pile of bodies slowly roasting atop the embers of last night's pyre.

Never in all his days had his life been so good. When he was not belly-to-belly with the goddess, he was drinking ale with the newly dead, or sitting atop his throne with his subjects admiring his every word. And kiawwww, now he had coupled with the fisherman's woman. He had given her the ride of a lifetime on his beak, and she had pleasured his zibik with hands, mouth, and quim. "Swive me," she had said, "it's so big!"

Of course it was big. He was King Crow, was he not? The woman had covered him in kisses, and teased his nipples with her teeth. She had bathed his feet, and rubbed them with fragrant oil, and sucked on his toes, a delight not even the goddess had shown him. Now their eyes shared the secret of their lusty swivance whenever they met. And that was part of the fun, wasn't it, to share the secret with the woman, and not the cuckold.

Such a crowish word, *cuckold*. He liked it. He liked it a lot.

Yes, his zibik was large. The goddess had told him so, she of a thousand times a thousand lovers, so adept in the arts of love. But she was his now, and only his, and she had taught him how to pleasure her for hours on end, and she had given him the woman so that he might practice his carnal arts on someone new. "You are the lover of whom women dream," she said, "and it is time you know this."

Yes, it was good to be the King.

From the direction of the alehouse came the frigate bird and that sailor fellow, the sailor wheeling a wheelbarrow in front. They were headed his way. His personal cask of ale, no doubt, though they'd just brought him one a day or two before. It was beneath his bed, still more than half full, in the cellar the fisherman had dug for him as a token of his fealty to his kingly self. But a King could never have too much of anything, and so he beckoned them forward.

"Greetings, O magnificently beaked one," said the frigate bird.

"Ho, cousin," said the crow. "And ho, featherless one."

"Lord Crow," said the sailor fellow. His voice was quiet, and he kept his eyes on the cask in the wheelbarrow, a befitting posture for one so lowly. This mephitic whale dropping had been a lot less insolent since he'd been made to understand his foolish bargain for the rails and slats.

"Another cask of ale?" said the crow. "For Us?"

"Something much better, Cousin," said the frigate bird. "'Tis a cask of aged whiskey, brought from the Isle of Fogg, in accordance with your bargain with my friend here."

The fisherman scowled at this, but the frigate bird ignored him. "Would you care to try some?"

"Awww!" said the crow. "The fabled whiskey, of which We have heard so much acclaim. Yes, We think We would like to try some."

How delicious this was, to watch this cuckold of a sailor tap so daintily at the bung with a wooden mallet, knocking it loose. His loyal vassal, come to serve him. The sailor poured whiskey into a mug, filling it full, and careful not to spill a drop. He tucked the mallet into the waist of his breeches, and came forth, his watchful eyes on the whiskey brimming the mug.

"Your whiskey, Lord Crow."

The crow sat up, and took the mug from him, and their eyes met, and in the sailor's eyes the crow found no fear. He should seek an opportunity to remind this rank petard of his power, as he had by plucking his eye out when this walking, talking manure stack first arrived. He took the hollow reed the turd ball offered him, and he took a sip of the whiskey. It was warm on his tongue. He swallowed.

"Ka-kawww," he yelled. His throat was afire. But only for a moment, and then he felt the heat spreading in his belly. A most pleasant feeling, this warming from the inside. He took another sip, and this time the burning in his throat was less, and the warming in his belly more. Another sip, and another, and soon the mug was empty.

"I trust this is to your liking," said the frigate bird. "'Tis strong drink, much stronger than ale."

"Kiaww!" said the crow. "It is indeed. And We like it very much."

"A mere mortal could not swig it down so deftly," said the frigate bird.

"Of course not," said the crow, "but then, We are no mere mortal. Pour Us another mug."

"As you wish, Lord Crow," said the sailor fellow. He and the frigate bird traded glances, no doubt impressed with his prowess. They were weaklings, and he was all powerful, and of course they were impressed. There was a word the cormorant used. Ompimpitence? Impompousness? Pontificence? Something like that, and in any case, whatever the word, he was all of those things, and more.

He sipped more whiskey, and bade the sailor fellow to wheel the wheelbarrow to his canopied bed and to set the cask of whiskey there. The frigate bird left with him, and the crow stretched himself out again, whiskey mug in hand. The sun was beginning to set behind the peaks at the center of the isle. Soon his congress of crows would retire for the night. He called them down, and they gathered at his feet. He was feeling exceptionally good, and he began to sing, "Kaw-aw-aw-aw awww," his fellow crows joining in. "Kiaw-aw-aw, ka-kaw, ka-kaw, kulkui ka-kaw," he sang, making the words up as he went along. He had never been in better voice. The light of the setting sun was golden, and his belly was warm. He would put that sailor fellow in his proper place, and soon enough. He stood, and raised his mug of whiskey, and he began to sway back and forth as he sang. His congress of crows swayed with him.

"Ku-kaw, ku-kuld," sang the crow. "Ku-kaw, ku-kuld."

"Ku-kaw, ku-kuld," answered the congress of crows. "Ku-kaw, ku-kuld."

LATER THAT EVENING DEWI SRI and the frigate bird stood in the darkness, watching the nightly revel at the alehouse. There were minstrels playing and singing, the frigate bird having seen to it that rebecs and viols, flutes and crumhorns, cymbals and tambours had all found their way to the Isle of the Dead. Before them a crowd of the newly dead danced and sang and drank the latest batch of the fisherman's ale, flavored with hops from Hallertau. The frigate bird offered the goddess a sip, telling her that these hops gave the ale a spicy tang, but she declined.

"Never do I take strong drink," said she. "I prefer a cup of tea."

"And our cousin, the crow, have you introduced him to the delights of tea?"

The goddess's smile allowed a bit of levity to show through the usually serene curve of her lips. "I daresay that tea would not have gotten us the results we desire."

"The king is in his cups, then?" said the frigate bird.

"Quite in his cups, and beyond," said the goddess. "He lays snoring on a driftwood log by the pyre."

"Too drunk to perform his office this evening?"

"We shall have to rouse him," said Dewi. "Only he can sing forth their souls."

"More whiskey will bring him around," said the frigate bird. "You see to it that the dead find their way to the pyre, and I shall have him roused enough to sing his wretched song."

The goddess put her hand on the frigate bird's shoulder. "Do not despise him. It is not for us to know why the Turropsi have chosen him for this office. 'Twas you who taught me this."

"He is a scoundrel," said the frigate bird. "He is a liar and a cheat."

"I have heard the same said of you," said the goddess. "You are widely known as a thief."

"I steal only what is needed for our enterprise."

"So you say now, when you are well-fed and prosperous. But in other circumstances you have stolen the unhatched eggs of your cousins and eaten them without the slightest regret."

"I was meant to survive," said the frigate bird.

"Perhaps," said the goddess, "although the Turropsi may have other instruments at their disposal, and care little about which of them performs the task."

"You think so little of me?" said the frigate bird. "You think anyone could do what I have done, and will do?"

The goddess embraced her friend, and wrapped her wings round them both. "I think a great deal of you," she said. "You cannot doubt this. All I am saying is that the crow is not so different from you, or any of us. He merely plays the role into which he has been cast."

"You have a weakness for him," said the frigate bird.

"I have a weakness for scoundrels," said the goddess. "And you of all persons should be grateful for that." She nuzzled his cheek from within her feathery embrace, and then stepped back from him. "And you are jealous, and that is something I find most unattractive."

"Jealous? Of that spleeny, rough-hewn simp? Perish the thought."

"May it be so," said the goddess. "To rise above jealousy is to find the truly divine within." The goddess put her palms together, and touched her own forehead, and then her friend's. "You miss me, don't you?"

"I do."

"Give the crow plenty of whiskey when you rouse him, and he will sleep the rest of the night away. Once he is beyond wakefulness, come to me, and we shall once again renew our friendship."

The frigate bird's red throat pouch swelled. "I shall do as you say." The goddess nodded, and looked then across the crowd of revelers, her forehead, so unfailingly serene, now creased with worry. "The crow's drunkenness may be the least of our troubles," said she. "You've seen no sign that the coming war may be turned aside?"

"None, milady."

"And the devouring beast will awaken in its aftermath?"

"Yes, milady, so it would seem," said the frigate bird. "There is no way out but through, and naught we can do to change that." The musicians started a lively reel then, and the frigate bird began to bob his head from side to side. "In the meantime," said he, "will you not dance with me?"

The goddess fluttered her wings coquettishly. "'Twill be my pleasure," said she. And so goddess and frigate bird began to dance, circling each other, their wings spread wide as they moved in time with the music. The frigate bird's gaze was bold, and proprietary, and the firelight brought out the green iridescence of his flight feathers. The goddess kept her eyes lowered, only looking up to meet his gaze momentarily, the beat of her wings like the throb of a lover's heart. The frigate bird stepped closer, and with his raised wings beating in time with hers, he shielded her eyes from all others. The swell of his throat pouch was taut.

The goddess leaned into the frigate bird, her lovely neck nestled next to his. "I shall miss all this," she whispered, "when it comes to its end."

"As shall I," said the frigate bird. "As shall I."

THE CROW FOUND WHISKEY VERY much to his liking. A mug of whiskey in the morning made of him a brilliant orator, one who could speak for hours on any subject that drifted through his mind.

He held forth from his throne on topics as diverse as why crows were superior to all other birds, and why whiskey was superior to ale, and why he was superior to everyone and everything. The pelican and the cormorant learned that they could stand behind the throne, out of the crow's line of sight, and occasionally shout huzzah, the cormorant all the while reading his books, and the pelican preening herself, rooting around in her feathers for feather mites.

A mug of whiskey for lunch made of the crow a brilliant napper, one who could sleep the afternoon away in the comfort of his canopied bed. Dewi Sri joined him there, making sure his mug was full, massaging his shoulders as he mumbled on about dictating his memoirs to the cormorant, and assuring him when he woke at sunset that they had indeed enjoyed a stellar romp through the gardens of carnal delight. The crow could never remember these delights, but another mug of whiskey as the sun went down banished any worries he might have about his powers of recall.

The goddess was never there when he awoke again in the evening. This was when he wanted her most, and he would lie in bed, remembering her cries of pleasure as her haunches clasped themselves on his beak and rode him. His zibik stirred. He filled his mug with more whiskey. He ached for her touch, and he called out to her, "Dewi, kiaww, come to me." When she did not, he called out again, "Ko, ko, ko," his voice as loud as thunder now, "Goddess, come!" And still she did not come, and the crow drank whiskey to dull the ache in his loins. The sun would set, and the thump of the Kiamah beast's heart filled the dark night, and every now and again the crow shouted, "Dewi, Dewi, your love lies waiting, Dewi."

Anon and anon the goddess did indeed appear at the canopied bed, but not until the crow was well into his cups. If he was curt with her, she flew off. If he was maudlin and tearful, she climbed in beside him and soothed him with her wings, trailing her feathers up and down his form. She plied him with more whiskey, and when he was too drunk for his zibik to rise, she clucked her tongue, and told him to go back to sleep.

After many such evenings the goddess came to him and said, "It is whiskey that is your lover now."

The crow belched. His breath was sour as a bale of sorrel, and the goddess wrinkled her nose at its foul stench. "I have other lovers," said the crow, "and what is wrong with that?"

"Nothing," said the goddess. "I am happy for your many loves. Only, I am no longer amongst them. We have come to the end of our liaison."

"End?" said the crow. "What do you mean, end?"

The goddess backed away from him, and swung her legs round to meet the sand. "The word needs no explanation, my sweet. End, as in end, as in we shall no longer make of ourselves the beast with two backs. I wish you only the best."

"You're leaving me?" the crow said. He hiccupped, and through his hiccup he said "Wh-why?"

"Because, my darling," said the goddess, "it seems you have found your true love in your cask of whiskey. Do not trouble yourself over the matter. It is the way of these things, that sooner or later lovers part. We are both now free to pursue whomever we please."

"But it pleases me to be with you," said the crow.

"'Tis sweet of you to say so," said the goddess. "But as you say, you have other lovers. I will not stand in your way."

"Kiaww," said the crow, "don't do this. I need you."

Only the goddess's head poked through the silk canopy as she spoke her last words to the crow. "I am off to my home across the sea," she said. "Drink some more whiskey, and you won't even miss me."

And with that, the goddess flew off. The fisherman and his beloved were reunited, and just this morning Dewi Sri had felt the first faint stirrings of the crow's child in her belly. Now it was time to see if the Turropsi still meant her to sacrifice Cariña and the fisherman on the pyre. She must persuade them otherwise, if only she could, lest the birth of this love-child be darkened by the blackest deed she had ever done.

THE CROW, FOR HIS PART, filled the hole in his heart with whiskey. His raspy calls filled the canopied bed as he sang a song he made up.[††]

[††] To the tune of "Evil," by Muddy Waters.

The goddess done left me
Don't even know why
She says it's the whiskey
I say that's a lie

I feel so lonely
I feel so mad
But she wasn't my only
So life ain't so bad

'Cause I'm evil
What a bad, bad, bad, bad bird I am
You know I'll swallow your soul, baby
'Cause I'm the hoochie coochie man

Get over here, dolly
Get hold of my zibik
You know that you want me

And here the crow always stopped to drink more whiskey, because he could not think of a rhyme for zibik.

Somewhere in the drunken depths of his night he heard the canoe land on the beach, and the newly dead making their way to the fisherman's camp. He poured more whiskey into his mug, the cask now nearly empty, and he staggered up to the revels. He had souls to harvest, and he was hungry for man-flesh.

FIRELIGHT FROLICKED ACROSS THE FACES of the revelers, and sweet music from the minstrels amongst them filled the air as the newly dead drank their ale. A warm stew of barley and vegetables steamed from a large kettle on the fire, the stew never giving out, for, like the ale, it contained a drop of the pelican's blood, and so there would always be enough.

In a moment between songs, the fisherman raised his mug and shouted for silence. "Welcome to the Isle of the Dead," said he. "It's time to eat, drink, and be merry, for yesterday you died, and tomorrow never knows. Huzzah!"

"Huzzah!" they all shouted, and together they drank. The music started up again, and the revel went on its merry course. But beneath the music, always, was the steady throb of the Kiamah's heart, a rhythm as dark and dire as the drums of war.

The fisherman stood next to his beloved, and the frigate bird. The wind off the sea was stiffening, and the frigate bird said, "There's another storm out there, and this one is worse than the last." He was just back from another trip to the material world.

"It seems they are getting stronger," said the fisherman.

The frigate bird nodded. "They have never reached here before, but I fear this one may."

"What is the cause?" said the woman.

"It's the beast," said the frigate bird. "The foul humors of his belly grow worse from all he has swallowed."

The fisherman took his beloved's hand. "Fear not," said he, "for we have a stout home, and we will not suffer."

It was at this moment that the crow appeared. The feathers on his head were askew from lolling all day in bed, and his eyes were lit with the fire of whiskey. There was a rakish slouch to his bearing, as if he were too sure of himself to bother standing up straight.

"Ho, cousin," said the crow to the frigate bird.

"Your crow-ness," said the frigate bird, bowing his head ever so slightly.

"I need more whiskey," said the crow. His voice rasped like a whip-saw with a dull blade. "My cask is nearly spent."

"Do tell," said the frigate bird. "You have quite the appetite for the stuff."

"I am the King of Whiskey," said the crow. "When can you bring me more?"

"Oh, a day or two," said the frigate bird.

"I do not wish to wait," said the crow.

"These things take a little time," said the frigate bird. "I'll make the necessary arrangements."

"See that you do," said the crow. He drained his mug, and then looked around, the mug raised as if trying to decide where to throw it.

The woman took the mug from his hand, stealing a moment to admire his regal nonchalance, and she asked, "Where is the goddess?"

The crow kicked at the sand, sending a small flurry into the shins of the fisherman, who scowled. "Gone," said the crow, taking no heed of the fisherman. "Home," said the crow.

"Gone?" said the woman. "For how long? She said nothing to me about leaving."

"Oh, she'll be back soon enough," said the crow, "when she's ready for more of this," and he put his hands on his hips and thrust his loincloth forward.

The frigate bird ruffled the feathers below his throat pouch, a sure sign that he was angry, although the crow took no notice. "Excuse me," said he. "If I am to procure more whiskey, I shall be off." He tilted his head toward the beach. "Mind giving me a boost?" he said to the fisherman.

When they had gone the woman said, "So you shall be alone tonight?"

"I shall," said the crow.

"It need not be so," said the woman.

"Awww," said the crow, his black eyes glittering in the firelight. "You wish another frolic with me."

"I do," said the woman. Her eyes were lowered, the better to gaze at his loincloth.

"As do I," said the crow. "I'll be waiting."

"Until then," said the woman. She traced her fingertips ever so lightly down the soft underside of his forearm and across his upturned palm. There was lust for her in his gaze, and lust for him in hers.

She cast her eyes across the crowd and found the pelican.

THE GODDESS DEWI SRI FLEW from her palace high atop Mount Agung to the roof of the world, and from there she made her way to the realm of the Turropsi. *They must know*, she thought as she approached, *that I am coming. Were they ever surprised?* Life could be dreary with no surprises in it, something she knew full well from her long, peaceful reign over Bali Dwipa. Often had she found relief from that dreariness in coupling with a new lover, or in fomenting some romantic intrigue amongst her courtiers. But if war were truly coming, there was no more time for such pursuits.

She was soon surrounded by a swarm of the Turropsi, who gathered around her like a bloom of jellyfish, though legions more continued their labors ahead of the great wave. She heard them murmuring in her mind, and then their voices joined together. Welcome back, they said.

I have done as you asked, Dewi told them. The fisherman's beloved is revived—

Yes, they said, we know this.

Then you must know that she has no memory of their life together, she told them.

No matter, they said. She loves him now, does she not?

She is fond of him, Dewi said, but she is drawn to the crow.

Yes, they said, we know this also, and then their voices separated, and she heard amongst them the mutterings of what sounded like a wager, or many wagers, as if they were betting on whom Cariña would cleave to more.

Must the lovers die? The goddess said. You said their bodies must burn upon the pyre.

The needs of the many, they told her, outweigh the needs of the few. But beneath that dictum their mutterings grew louder and more contentious, and many of the Turropsi fingered the gold beads on their abaci.‡‡ Dewi caught bits and pieces of it, some saying lovers always made the best sacrificial victims, and an answering voice calling that idea deterministic heresy, and others saying the woman's desire for the crow was what mattered, and if she carried the crow's daughter things would be different, and still others saying we told you so, but too late for that now, and through it all their gold beads made a sound like the clink of coins.

How can you wager amongst yourselves, she asked, with so much at stake?

---

‡‡*Abaci*, dear reader, is the plural of *abacus*, just as *cacti* is for *cactus*, and *radii* for *radius*, though some, whose ears are less sensitive than ours, prefer to say *abacuses*, and *octopuses*, and *hippopotamuses*, ignoring the inelegance of all those unnecessarily sibilant extra syllables.

Her question silenced them, though she felt their consternation. They had let slip their own discord. That great dark mass out in the Fetch grew ever closer, and still the Turropsi had no way around it, nor over or under it, and no way to push it aside.

We do not gamble, they told her, we only keep score.

The goddess considered. They were lying about their wagering, she was sure of that, and they did not wish to speak of it, for it made them appear frivolous, and not at all the invincible beings she had once believed them to be.

Do you not determine what happens, she asked, out of all that is possible?

We narrow the choices, they told her, and then let the choices made determine the pattern that is woven. She heard them muttering again, about the eternal play of free will and destiny, and about the likelihood that they themselves would survive. She heard the clinking of yet more wagers being laid, their gambling rising to its peak.

They were gambling on their own deaths. An absurdity, the goddess thought, for who would be left to collect on their wagers if their whole race were devoured by the Kiamah? She felt then the Turropsi within her mind, and knew that they knew what she was thinking. All wagering stopped, and the Turropsi pointed an arm, each and all of them, at the great wave of the present below them, and speaking with one voice they said, The choices you make down there—and now they pointed a second arm at the great dark mass out in The Fetch—will determine what happens when that arrives here.

The future is uncertain, then, Dewi said. You do not know the outcome.

What we know, said the Turropsi, is that you carry the daughter of the crow. She is the future, but she will be of no use to us if you perish in the coming war. What we know is that now you must make haste. The crow grows more savage, even as we speak. He will come for you, with murder in his heart.

I am no warrior, Dewi told them. What would you have me do?

You are the daughter of a warrior, they told her, and you will rise to the occasion, or we shall all perish. More than that we cannot say.

The crow might kill me? she asked, but even as the question formed in her mind, the Turropsi withdrew.

Go back to the Isle of the Dead, they told her. Your destiny awaits.

GUSTS OF WIND RIPPED THROUGH the treetops, and carried flurries of sand along the beach. The crow strutted back and forth before the crowd of the newly dead, a hungry look in his eye. "Behold Lord Crow," said he, "King of the Dead, and Regent of this Isle. Bow down before Us. We suffer your presence here even though you are not worthy of being Our subjects."

They all looked at one another, glassy eyed and tipsy, wondering where the jolly mood of the alehouse had gone, and who did this crow-headed fellow think he was, anyway? He'd promised them whiskey and led them off into the dark, sending away those other two birds, the cormorant, so trepidatious about the storm that he'd drunk too much, and the pelican, who seemed only too happy to leave.

"It's just a mask," someone muttered, "like a hood over his head." A woman put the back of her hand to her mouth and blew a loud petard at the crow. The crowd erupted in giggles, and a man's voice called out, "Where's the whiskey you promised?"

"Who said that?" thundered the crow, and he grew himself taller by a cubit. The crowd was cowed into silence by this show of divine power, and when no one answered, the crow spoke, his voice as loud as thunder.

"I said"—the very air shaking with his every word—"Who. Said. That?"

A meek voice rose from the back. "'Twas me sir."

The crow strode forward, the crowd parting before him, yielding a path to a man in a leather apron with the stains of a tanner on his hands.

"Kiaw," thundered the crow. "You?"

"Yes, my lord."

The crow grabbed the man round his middle with his beak and tossed him high into the air. He landed with a thump on the sand, and everyone heard the crack and crunch of a bone breaking. The man screamed, and the crow laughed his terrible laugh—*aw aw aw aw aw.*

"Kneel before your King," said the crow.

The tanner gasped with pain. "I cannot, my lord," he said, "for my leg is broken."

"You can," said the crow, and again he picked the man up with his beak, squeezing him hard. The man's eyes bulged, and his breath was naught but a wheeze as he struggled to take in air. The crow brought him down hard on the sand, his knees bent, and again he screamed in pain as he landed.

"Bow down!" the crow thundered. "All of you!"

Men shivered, and women wept, and all the newly dead did bow down.

"Listen to Our song," the crow said. "You have something inside you that wants out. Let it go now, for it belongs to Us." And this night he sang louder and more fiercely than ever he had before, twittering and clicking, cawing and kiawing, rattling and rasping. The newly dead coughed up their souls, and the crow gobbled them up faster than they could burrow into the sand. He would turn these souls into guano, never to be reborn again.

"Tasty," said the crow when he was finished. He belched. Rain began to fall, pelting down from storm clouds that hung heavy over the Isle of the Dead. The steady throb of the Kiamah's heart grew faster, as if the beast were waking up. The crow took on his crow shape, and he spread his wings and herded the bodies of the newly dead to the pyre. The heat of their bodies burning would calm the beast.

His work for the night done, the crow flew to the canopied bed. He passed a wing in front of his face, and became his man shape again, and he climbed in. He feared no storm. His belly was full. He had whiskey to drink, and a woman to bed. And if the goddess returned, he would rip open her belly, and feast on her guts.

THE WOMAN LAY IN BED, listening to the storm outside, waiting for the fisherman's breath to slow into the steady rhythm of sleep. The crow's voice from the pyre had rumbled out of the wind. He was powerful in ways the fisherman was not, and that thought made her heart flutter.

Soon enough the fisherman was asleep, and the woman waited for the pelican to arrive. Soon enough she heard a scratching at the door, and she rose from the bed. The fisherman did not stir, and she crept to the door and stepped out. She put a finger to her lips, pointed at the bed with her eyes, and was off, eager to begin her tryst with the crow.

"Wait!" the pelican said.

"Shh!" the woman said.

"Your chain," the pelican whispered.

"Here," the woman whispered. And then they were off, each to her loins' desire.

The pelican crawled in beside the fisherman, and she closed her eyes, and furrowed her brow, making sure her eyes were now blue. And once again she gave herself over to the pleasures of the flesh.

The woman ran through the rain to the canopied bed. The wind had died down somewhat, and she could make out the dark shape of the crow inside the silk coverings. The coverings parted, and the whiskey cask came sailing out, splintering from the kick the crow had given it.

He needs a woman's touch, she thought. *He is distraught by Dewi's leaving. I shall tame him, and we will have a night together we shall never forget.*

THE FISHERMAN AWOKE IN THE light of the risen sun, his beloved beside him. His loins were spent, and deliciously empty. What a bobtail his beloved had become of late. He turned to her, and drew her into his arms, her back nestled against his front. For all the ordeals and tribulations of his life here under the rule of the accursèd crow, he was happy as he had never been. His beloved sighed, and reached her hand round his buttocks and drew him even closer.

His lips were bruised. Cariña had ground her cauliflower against his mouth and brought herself to the pinnacle of passion over and over until his tongue could lap no more. She must, at long last, be in love with him, to cleave to him so. Her breast was warm in his hand, and he nuzzled his cheek to her shoulder, glad for the boon that the whale's belly had given him of never having a whisker.

She sat up, wide awake and sudden. Her hand went to the silver chain round her neck. She looked at the fisherman, her lips moving but her voice silent, her eyes blinking as if she had been torn from a dream and could not yet see.

"G'mornin', my darlin'," said he.

"It's dawn," said she.

"It's dawn and past, but only by a bit," said he.

"I must be off to the privy," said she.

She rose, and snatched her sarong off the floor where it lay, wrapping it about herself as she walked out the door. She went round the corner of the house and looked down the beach toward the pyre, which was smoking in the distance. She could not see the canopied bed, for it was hidden by the curve of the beach.

She hurried to the privy, following the path into the woods behind the house. She must let loose her water and find her twin before the fisherman rose, or else they would be found out. She opened the door to the privy, and there was Cariña, on the bench, slumped against the corner.

"Oh," said the pelican, "there you are. I was worried." The door closed behind her, and the two women were alone in the dark. She took the silver chain off her neck and held it out to the woman, who looked up at her in the dim light. Her shoulders began to shake, she was crying, and even in the shadows of the privy the pelican could see that her face was swollen, her eyes blackened.

"He beat me," the woman said. From her trembling lips came a keening, high and quavering, the inarticulate speech of the broken heart. Her lips were puffy. Three lines of dried blood marked them, a tally of cruel blows.

The pelican sat next to her. What had they done? For the pleasures of the flesh, what had they done? She put the silver chain round Cariña's neck, her touch gentle and soothing.

"The crow did this to you?" she said.

The woman nodded. "He was drunk, and his zibik was slack. I tried. I tried everything, but I couldn't. It wouldn't. And when it wouldn't—" And here the keening broke from her again, piercing the pelican's heart until she thought she would die from the sorrow of it. Tears ran down her friend's cheeks and fell to her chest. She sobbed, once, twice, thrice. She pulled her sarong tighter round her shoulders, her knuckles white. Her trembling abated.

"When it wouldn't," said she, "he beat me. And then he threw me out." Her voice was flat. "Like a common gill-flurt."

The pelican stroked her shoulders and cooed, soothing her as best she could. What a fool she had been. Dewi had told them, only the one time. She should have listened. These bruises, she had put them on her friend.

They heard the fisherman outside, singing a sailor's song of fair winds on a bright morn. He was already in the woods, coming their way. The path to the privy was short.

The woman looked at the pelican, her face full of fear. "He'll know," said she.

"Oh, my beloved," the fisherman sang, "my bladder is full, and I must make water."

"Not if we're quick," said the pelican. She raised her hand to pass it in front of her face. The door swung open, and there he was, with the grin of a fool in love on his face.

"Not quick enough," said the woman.

THE FISHERMAN HONED HIS KNIFE with the sure strokes of a man who knew how to go about his business. The blade was half the length of his forearm, and as wide as his two thumbs together, the steel well-hammered, the handle, made of ironwood, unadorned, heavy enough to balance the sturdy blade. It was a knife built for work, whether that work be cutting, carving, shaving, slicing, or the thrust and parry of a close battle.

The woman was in the house. He would deal with her later.

When the edge of the blade was sharp enough to shave with ease a thin slice from the driftwood log on which he sat, the fisherman stood. The sun was risen above the twin pinnacles at the mouth of the inlet. It was a fair day, last night's storm having passed, the breeze light and fresh. His hands were steady, his mind clear. He walked along the beach toward the pyre. The congress of crows called out a warning from the trees as he passed their perches.

The cormorant was in his customary spot, his spectacles glinting in the sunlight, reading Ovid's *The Art of Love*.

"Ho, fisherman," said the cormorant. "A good morning to you on this fine day." The fisherman strode on by without a reply.

"Have you seen the pelican this morning?" said the cormorant.

The fisherman did not pause nor turn his head. He raised his arm and pointed behind himself in the direction of his house. The canopied bed was ahead of him, its gaudy silks ruffling in the breeze. The whiskey cask lay on the sand, a hole kicked in its side.

The fisherman parted the silks and looked in. The crow, in his man shape, lay on the bed face up. He was snoring. An empty cask of ale sat next to him, listing to one side in the bedding. The fisherman leaned over the bed, his knife at the ready. The crow's loincloth was askew, his miserable pizzle exposed, the loincloth piss-stained and stinking.

The fisherman knelt on the crow's chest, pinning his arms with his knees. The crow did not stir. His breath reeked of ale. He pushed his beak back, revealing the crow's throat. He was feathered to the base of his neck. The fisherman used the edge of his hand to lift the feathers along their bottom edge, exposing a band of skin the width of a finger. Beneath the skin, on either side of the neck, were the thick arteries that fed blood to the crow's head.

The fisherman drew his knife in one swift motion across the crow's neck. The skin parted. His blade was in a thumb's width. This was no different than slaughtering a pig. He sliced right through both arteries. Blood spurted with the pulse of the crow's beating heart, once, twice, then stopped.

The wound was a red line, already closed. "Shite!" the fisherman yelled. "Smegma! Putino!" He sliced the crow's neck open again, and again blood spurted, then stopped.

The crow's eyes opened. His beak parted, his tongue black and dry within.

"Awww?"

The fisherman shifted his weight and reared back. He plunged the knife into the crow's chest, sinking the blade deep into his heart with both hands.

"Aww!" said the crow. Again there was blood, but only for a moment. The wound was sealing itself around the blade, and the fisherman pulled his knife out. The crow struggled against his knees, trying to free his hands. The fisherman stabbed him again, hitting bone this time as the crow struggled. He was knocked off balance. The crow freed a hand and slapped at him. The fisherman slashed at his wrist. Again the crow squawked. Again the fisherman stabbed him in the heart, but the first wounds were already healed, as if they had never been. The new wound sealed itself as soon as he pulled the knife out.

"Die, you miserable poltroon, die!"

The crow freed his other hand, and he grabbed the fisherman's arm. His terrible beak closed round it, clamping down so hard the fisherman feared his bones would be crushed. The crow jerked his head back and forth, wrenching at him, his hands trying to free the knife. The fisherman grabbed the knife with his left hand and plunged it into the crow's eye. The crow threw him off, his hands going to his eye, and rolled to his side. The fisherman stabbed him in the back, and this time he left the knife in. He rolled off the bed. He rubbed his forearm where the crow's beak had squeezed him. The crow's blood was hot and sticky on his hands.

The cormorant's head poked through the silks. He said, "You cannot kill him."

The crow sat up, his eye already healed. He reached both hands behind his back, trying to grasp the knife.

"Why not?" said the fisherman.

"Only a deity can kill a deity," said the cormorant.

"Then kill him," said the fisherman. He was shouting, his face red with rage. "Kill him." His hands shook. His fingers were bent to wrap around a throat and crush it. "Do it."

"He cannot," said the crow. The rasp of his voice was oily and gloating. He had a hand on the knife in his back, but he could not draw it forth. "He has not the power to kill me."

"Justice!" the fisherman screamed. "He has made a cuckold of me, and beaten my woman." He gave the cormorant a sharp cuff to the side of his head. "You said only a god can kill a god." The cormorant only looked at him, his spectacles askew. The fisherman raged on. "Are you a false god? Be not false in my hour of need."

"I am not false," said the cormorant. "I am a lesser deity." There was a deep sadness in his eyes, and he shook his head back and forth. "I said only a deity could kill a deity. I did not say any deity could kill any other."

"So now you split hairs with me?" The fisherman turned and leapt up on the bed. He dropped to his knees behind the crow and grabbed his beak in both hands. He wrenched his head sideways. The crow's neck snapped. He went limp. The fisherman stood and let the crow fall back.

"Yes!" the fisherman screamed. "I've done it."

The cormorant leaned in from the side of the bed. He straightened his spectacles and studied the crow, who lay still, his back bent, propped up on the knife in his back.

The fisherman leapt down. "You see?" he said. "He's dead."

The cormorant put his head to the crow's chest, over his heart, and he listened. The fisherman too leaned in, but the cormorant held him back with an outstretched wing.

"Is he dead?" the fisherman said. "He's dead. Tell me he's dead."

"Be still," said the cormorant. "I'm listening."

The fisherman held his tongue. He raised his head to the heavens, his arms wide, his palms up, his lips moving in a silent prayer. By all the gods held holy, let this nithering foul tyrant, this piss-reeking chancre of a king, this whoreson, this pustulent, cullionly canker-blossom of a crow, let him never draw breath again. Let maggots eat his brains, let flies lay eggs in his rotting cods, let worms crawl up his dungbie and devour his stinking guts.

"I thought it was not possible," said the cormorant, "but I detect no signs of life."

The fisherman tore the silks aside, letting light into the sordid bedchamber. He clapped his hands, and he danced a quick jig, whistling the tune, turning in place, hopping from one foot to the other, and slapping the soles of his feet.

"We shall have to revise our theories of deicide," said the cormorant, "to reflect what has just happened here."

The fisherman leaned over the crow, whose beak was open and slack, his black tongue hanging to the side. He sang a sailor's jolly verse to the crow's corpse:

I snapped his neck with my bare hands,
How sweet the sound of death,
I stilled the villain's beating heart,
He drew his final breath.

And he put his hands under his ribs to roll him over so he could pull his knife out of the crow's back.

The crow's eyes opened. He winked at the fisherman, and he laughed, "Aw aw aw aw aw."

"Swive me!" the fisherman screamed. His face went purple. He pounded on the crow's chest with his fists, but the crow pecked him, hard, and he had to stop. There were tears of rage at the corners of his eyes. He looked the crow in the eye, and he spat a gobbet of spit at him. He spat so hard he missed.

The crow cupped his zibik in his hand, his black eyes glinting with malice. "Aw aw aw aw aw," he laughed. "Aw aw aw aw aw."

The fisherman's head drooped at that raspy sound, and the cormorant put a wing round his shoulders. He turned him, and they stepped away together. "You'd best leave if you value your life," the cormorant said.

"Help me," croaked the crow. "Pull out the knife."

"Leave," said the cormorant.

"We are not done," said the fisherman. He stared at his bloodied hands. What good were they if they could not kill the crow?

"Kiaw," cried the crow. "Too true. Too true."

THE FISHERMAN WALKED DOWN TO the water. He stripped off his breeches and waded in. He was spent, his battle lust burnt away. The water was cool, the waves calm, endless, soothing. He had failed, and put his life at risk in the bargain. They must flee. Or find a way to kill the crow. Neither the pelican nor the cormorant possessed the power, but the frigate bird was endlessly resourceful. Perhaps he could do the deed.

He swam to the other side of the inlet, and stepped out on the beach there. He had never been on this side before. He turned and looked, and there was his house. A thin trail of smoke rose from the fire pit.

They must flee. He would take his woman and find a way off this cursèd isle.

His woman. His betrayer. He had forgiven her much, and she him, but this? She had bedded his sworn enemy. He did not know if he could forgive this.

Ye gods, what a hellish morning this had been. The sight of those two women in the privy, his beloved and her double, his beloved's face swollen and bruised. He'd gone dizzy. And then the pelican passed her hand in front of her face and became herself, and they all started talking at once, answers and questions jumbled back to front. His whole world was shattered to bits and tossed into the air, and came crashing back down in shards and shreds. He beat her. Who? The crow. Why? Forgive me.

He sat on the sand with his head between his knees. That night when he'd glimpsed the pelican's eyes for a moment, was that the first time? She'd been so impatient, and so clumsy. Last night she was just as demanding, waking him from deepest sleep with her kisses and her eager hands. He'd felt old in the face of her need. So urgent, she was. Like a young maiden, and he an old goat past his prime. But that was not his beloved. No, she had been with the crow. And of her own will, for it was clear that they had plotted together to make this happen.

He could kill her. She was a mortal. He could kill her, and himself. They would become clams, sleeping in their shells, waiting for the next life.

But the crow would know who they were. He would find a way to torture them again. There was no escape from the crow, not if they stayed here. And killing his woman would bring him no satisfaction. It would only put her blood on his hands.

Across the inlet, the cormorant came out of the canopied bed and walked down to the water. He drew forth the fisherman's knife from where he had it tucked under his wing, and he held it in his bill, and he washed it in the lapping waves. The congress of crows plucked at the pyre, gobbling bits of charred flesh. Their thorny squawking prickled the fisherman's ears.

The sooner he was quit of this place the better. He swam back across the inlet to where the cormorant stood in the shallow water. The cormorant gave him his knife.

"How much time do I have before he comes for me?"

The cormorant considered. "His wounds are healed," he said. "But he cannot walk. He is still drunk from last night. He says the cask of ale was half full when he started, and it is empty now."

"So he must climb the rope back up the well before he can toddle after me. Is he out for my blood?"

The cormorant sighed. His turquoise eyes blinked from the bottom up, once, twice. "He will kill you at his leisure," he said. "You cannot escape him."

"So you all say," said the fisherman. "I say we gather ourselves together and find a way to kill him."

In reply, the cormorant only gazed at the gentle waves around his legs. His spectacles glinted in the sunlight. The crows at the pyre croaked and cawed. The wretched sound of the crow fergling up his guts came from the canopied bed. The fisherman stood with his hands at his sides, naked before the world, and he smiled.

"At least he is sick as a sailor's dog for the nonce."

The cormorant nodded. "I'm sorry," said he. "I am a scholar, not a fighter."

"Then study your scrolls and your books," said the fisherman, "and find a way to kill him."

He gathered up his breeches and slung them over his shoulders, and he walked up the beach toward his house.

THEY WERE THERE WHEN HE opened the door to his house, the pelican in her old woman shape, and his beloved. They sat on a low bench, the pelican with her arms round Cariña, cradling her like a mother soothing a troubled child. Her long bill lay on top of his beloved's head. His beloved's face was no longer swollen, her eyes were no longer blackened. No doubt the pelican had vulned herself and healed her. A useful skill for a lesser god to possess, and they had made ample use of it in providing food and drink for the nightly revels. But the pelican, whom he had taken at her word in every way, was a tricksy varlet like the crow.

Never trust a shapeshifter. Or a god. They had too much power, and like a tyrant, they were bound to put that power to ill use sooner or later.

The pelican looked up, and said "Ho." His beloved's eyes opened, and met his, and looked away.

She had lain with the crow, that was the gorbellied bur in this. She had betrayed him with his enemy, this tyrant, may he be gutted and choked to death on his own entrails. And she had done so while he was here, not away on a voyage. She had never done that before.

But this was not the same woman. If there had been any doubt of this before, it was gone now.

"Ho," said the fisherman. There was nothing else to say.

She had the face of his beloved, and her eyes, so full of the beauty and sadness of the troubled world. But she knew nothing of their past.

"Thank you," said the fisherman to the pelican, whose yellow eyes had remained on him.

"For what?"

"For healing her." The pelican opened her bill wide, and the old woman inside nodded in reply.

"Come," said the pelican. She invited him in with her beckoning hand, and when he got to the bench, she stood.

"She needs you." The pelican walked to the door and left.

He took his breeches from his shoulders and hung them on a peg. He sat on the bench and wrapped his arms round her. It was what a man did if he were not bent out of shape by his own spite. She was stiff for a moment, and then let him pull her in, and he rocked her in his arms. Tears flowed down her cheeks.

"I didn't know," she said.

"You didn't know what?" said he.

She began to sob, and between sobs, she spoke. "You warned me," she said. "I didn't believe you," she said. "I thought there was only pleasure," she said. She sobbed harder, her whole broken world gasping out of her chest. She said, "I didn't know there was pain."

So much had he endured to find her. He could not forsake her now.

"I tried to kill him," said the fisherman. "He would not die."

"I wish I were dead," she said. "Death was easier than this."

She would know which was easier, the fisherman thought. *But life was never meant to be easy. If it were, there would be no need of it. We could spend all our time inside a clamshell, dreaming.*

"Let us leave this place," said he.

"How?" said she.

"I know a way," said he.

A shadow crossed the open doorway, and there was the goddess, Dewi Sri.

"It has come to my ears," said she, "that you are in need of some aid."

The crow's consort. The fisherman regarded her with baleful eyes. "Thank you, but I have the situation in hand."

"Yes," said the goddess, "for the moment. But the pelican tells me you sharpened your blade and went after the crow."

"It's true."

"And yet you could not slay him."

"No."

"'Twas a noble effort on your part," said the goddess. "I commend you for that. But you are both in danger now, danger that I have brought upon you. The crow will come for you, and you are no match for him."

"Why should I trust you?" said the fisherman. "Are you not his lover?"

"I was," said the goddess. "It was my fate to be so."

"Fate? You blame this on fate?"

"Dear fisherman," said the goddess, "I understand your suspicion of me. But we have no time to waste. There are forces at play here beyond your ken. We are all of us in danger. And fate has everything to do with it."

The goddess stepped into the room, and the pelican followed her. "By your leave," said the goddess, her gaze resting on the fisherman, "I would speak with you alone. Will you not grant me this favor?"

The fisherman held his beloved tighter in his arms. "She needs me now more than you ever could," he said.

"In any other moment I would agree," said the goddess, "but not now. And our friend the pelican will stay with Cariña."

The pelican came over to the bench. "We meant you no harm," she whispered. Her eyes were wet with tears. The fisherman unwound his arms from his beloved, and he went out with the goddess.

Together they walked toward the Sea of Bones. They were silent for a time, gaining some distance from the fisherman's camp, the sound of the sea growing closer as they neared the mouth of the inlet. And then the goddess spoke.

"I know that I must seem a villain to you, for my liaison with the crow. But I am here on this isle as a thread woven by the hands of fate. I will not lie to you. I went willingly to the crow, and I made the most of every moment with him. It is my nature to couple, to bring forth abundance."

"He is a foul tyrant," said the fisherman. His voice was rough with ire. "You gave him your love. And so you are his accomplice in all the foul things he does."

The goddess nodded, her dark eyes taking in his wrath, and not refusing it. They stood now in the shadow of one of the rock pinnacles at the mouth of the inlet. The goddess took the fisherman's hands in hers.

"It was I who put the pelican and Cariña in mind of trading places," said she. "If you blame someone, it must be me you blame."

There was something oiled and queasy roiling around in the fisherman's guts, as if fingers pierced his flesh, and toyed with his liver. "Did you force her into the arms of the crow?"

The goddess shook her head. "She was willing. As you have been, given the opportunity, to take the pleasure of the moment. As all of us are, no matter how much we may love our mates, for we crave in our loins the touch of someone new. Listen, my friend." Her face was serene, the face of the wisdom of the ages, and her eyes looked into his without calculation.

"Long ago, before there were rice paddies and gardens and orchards, before there were cities, this was how we all lived. We shared our stored food, and the warmth of our bodies at night, each of us cleaving to many others, as the opportunity arose. We reared our children as if all children were our own blood. We did this without rancor, or jealousy, or complaint." The gold hibiscus flower at the front of Dewi's coif was shiny against the black coil of her hair. "And why?" she asked. "Because we were bound together by the pleasure we shared, and so when trouble came, we willingly shared the danger."

The fisherman picked up a stone from the sand and threw it into the water. "What has any of that to do with my beloved's betrayal of me?"

"Only this," said the goddess. Again she took his hands in hers. "That her willingness to lie with the crow is not cause for you to love her less. That there was no malice in what we did. That she loves you no less for her tryst with the crow. That she meant you no harm. It was I who counseled secrecy, and that was to keep you from pain. And it was I who saw to it that the pelican came to you in Cariña's place, and that was to give you pleasure."

The fisherman scowled. The goddess smiled at him in return, as if she liked him the more for scowling.

"You did enjoy the pelican, did you not?" she said.

The pelican had worn him out, that was the truth of it. She had swived him raw. But she was lusty, and easy to please, and quick to return the favor.

"You were her first, you know," said the goddess. "She is wild for you, even now. She thinks you are my gift to women."

The fisherman could not help but smile at this. "I am that," said he. Confound this goddess, she was flattering him, and twisting everything around.

"She could learn a great deal from you, should the occasion arise," said the goddess, "about love, and loyalty, and about setting jealousy aside."

"A pox on all that," said the fisherman. "The crow has made a cuckold of me. I want revenge."

"And you shall have it," said the goddess. "You shall live to see the crow's demise. But only if we all work together against him. I need your help. For once the crow is dead, we shall all of us have to slay the greater beast. The Kiamah will awake."

First the crow, and then the Kiamah. He had no desire to be drawn further into the affairs of the gods. The price of his vengeance might well be his own life. "These are deeper waters than I care to sail," said the fisherman.

The goddess squeezed his hands, imploring him. "We must all of us put our heads together," said she, "for separately, we shall surely lose them."

Here he stood, naked as the day he was born, a winged goddess holding his hands and asking for his help. He had no friends here, save the frigate bird, and he'd best take care of himself. But her gaze was steady, and would not leave his alone.

"All right," he said. Let her hear what she wanted to hear. He would gather up his beloved and flee. They had come too far and endured too much. He could not leave her behind.

Dewi's red lips smiled wide, and then wider. There was an abundance of gratitude in her kohl-rimmed eyes, and then something more. A sparkle of mischief, a glimmer of glee, the glint of lust.

He looked at the bounty of her breasts. They were magnificent. She drew his hands to them. And let her own hand fall to his Man Thomas, O sweet caress, how deep the thrill. Her nipples hardened between his fingers, and she uttered a low moan.

She said, "Let me show you how the goddess thanks her friends."

THAT EVENING, BEFORE THE CANOE of the dead arrived, they gathered around the fire pit at the fisherman's camp. "His bowels are loose," said the cormorant. He was speaking of the crow. "His head aches, and he can barely keep down a draught of water. He was asleep when I left him, though fitfully so. But he is in no shape to do us any harm for the moment."

"By morning," said the frigate bird, "that advantage will be lost."

"We must take him unawares, the sooner the better," said the fisherman.

"And do what?" said the cormorant. "You have already tried to slay him and failed."

The fisherman sighed. "Surely there is a way." Cariña sat next to him on the driftwood log, and she drew him closer with both arms. He looked at the frigate bird, who shook his head, and at Dewi Sri.

"It is not in my nature to kill him," said the goddess, "nor any creature by my own hand."

"Perhaps the old nimpsy will drink himself to death," said the frigate bird.

"He could kill us all in the meantime," said the fisherman. There was fear in the pelican's eyes, and the cormorant's, but the goddess's countenance was calm and unreadable. Full of surprises, that one. "We must act, and act swiftly." The pelican nodded in agreement. She was in her pelican shape, sitting in a shallow scrape in the sand.

"Better to be cunning and alive," said the frigate bird, "than to be bold and dead."

"His mind is troubled," said the cormorant. "And has been ever since the goddess took him into her arms. I watched him, some several fortnights ago, as he fell from the sky. He was in his man shape, and I think he meant to do himself in."

"What happened?" said the goddess.

"At the last moment he took on his crow shape," said the cormorant, "and saved himself."

"You see?" said the fisherman. "His mind may be troubled, but not troubled enough. And we are undefended."

"Amare et sapere vix deo conceditur," said the cormorant. "Even a god finds it hard to love and be wise at the same time."

Around and around they went, the fisherman arguing for immediate action, the goddess and the frigate bird counseling patience, and some form of guile rather than another assault. Just before midnight the crow surprised them all by walking into the firelight. His black eyes were watery, his neb was dingy and drab, his shoulders slumped, and he had nothing of the regal and manly bearing that had turned so many heads at the nightly revels.

"Ho," said the crow. His eyes went round the circle, taking them all in, but offering no one of them any more regard than another. No one returned his greeting until the goddess spoke.

"Ho, Lord Crow." Her face was as serene as ever. "We are honored by your presence."

The crow nodded. "As are We by yours," he said. "Let us dispense with the formalities, for We have a royal headache." He closed his eyes and put his hands on either side of his head and pressed the heels of his hands against his skull. "We have come here to say"—and here he dropped his hands and opened his watery eyes—"that we have all been through a great deal of late. Much drinking, and much sporting about in beds. We fear that, under the influence of strong drink, We

have given aw-aw-offense to one or another of you." Here the crow
looked at the woman most particularly, and he wiped a tear from
his eye. "If that be the case, We inform all present that We are most
sincerely sorry. We think it best not to dwell on the details of any such
offense, for by all appearances no permanent harm has been done.
Nor do We hold anyone here," and here he looked most particularly
at the fisherman, "accountable for any attempts to commit murder on
Our person. It is possible that We may have provoked such an attempt
by Our own deeds."

All now looked at the fisherman, who held the crow's gaze with
his. The woman nudged the fisherman with her foot. He nodded at
the crow.

"Thank you, Lord Crow," said he. "We are all of us grateful for
your beneficence."

"You are welcome," said the crow. "And so, from this moment
forward, We say let the past be forgotten by all, and we shall renew
our friendships, as of old."

The crow bowed, and then he turned and walked away.

No one spoke until they were sure he was out of earshot, and even
then, they kept their voices low.

"It's a trick," said the fisherman. "He means to lull our defenses."

"That may be so," said the goddess, "but it gives us some time."

"Only until he catches us unawares," said the fisherman. "He will
slit our throats while we sleep."

"I'll stand watch," said the frigate bird. "We cannot all be asleep
at once."

"A sensible precaution," said the goddess. "But I do not think he
will come tonight. He has something else in mind."

"What?" said the pelican. "Do you know something the rest of us
do not?"

"No," said the goddess, "'tis only the inkling of my intuition."

The canoe of the dead entered the inlet then, the fish eagles keening, the dead singing, their paddles dipping into the water as one.
They went down to the water to meet the canoe, all of them together,
for they felt that if nothing else, there was some safety in numbers.
They fell to the task at hand, leading the newly dead to the fisherman's

camp, filling their mugs with ale, and offering them what comforts they had. It was what they could do, and it was far better to do it than it was to give themselves up to worry.

THE CROW, HIS MIND CLEAR for the first time in days, did not sleep after he led the newly dead to the pyre. The cormorant climbed atop the pelican's shoulders, a good deal farther from the pyre than their customary spot. They did not trust his peace offering, that much was clear, but it was of no matter to him. Apologies and contrition were for mortals, and though he had indulged himself with such feelings, most particularly toward the woman, he was past all that now.

He waited while the pelican and the cormorant settled and became still, pretending to fall asleep himself. Then he flew to the waterfall, and in his mole shape, padded down his tunnel to the hole in the sky of the material world. He uncovered the hole, and peered down upon forest and plain, taking in all the rich smells, of plowed earth, of smoke from hearth fires, of mounds of rubbish and the wriggling worms and busy beetles crawling within. So much to eat down there, and soon enough, he would rule it all, and have his fill of whatever he desired.

He passed a paw in front of his face, and he took on his crow shape. He stuck his head down through the hole, looking about for his fellow crows. It was near sunset, the sun low above the horizon. "Ko, ko, ko," he thundered, and in their roosts and on the wing they heard him, crow upon crow upon crow. They came to his call in their thousands, rising to the sky in great flocks, whirling and wheeling, spinning in gyres and spirals, turning and circling. "Ko, ko, ko," they called to one another, the racket of them screeching and squawking, drowning all other sound from below, their flocks joining together and rising ever upward, following, in their multitudes, the cry of King Crow. A thousand times a thousand of them rose, turning the sky black, a great long line of crows rising above that black mass and flying ever upward.

They rose like a great tornado turned upside down, and disappeared, through the hole in the sky.

THE FISHERMAN DID NOT SLEEP that night after the revels but lay awake, thinking. His beloved lay next to him, and for her the blessing of sleep came, for she was tired beyond the troubles of the night before, and this long day of grief just passed.

The fisherman was calculating the odds, and he did not like them. He had no faith in the goddess, who had all but led his woman to the crow's bed. And the crow was too powerful for these lesser gods, none of whom had the will nor the wherewithal to slay him. His performance at the fire was nothing but a ruse. He would seek vengeance for what they had done to him, and his vengeance would be cruel.

He must flee. To stay was to die, and he had no wish to die for this motley crew of bird-gods.

Cariña stirred in her sleep and put her arm around him. The warmth of her body was welcome, as ever. Perhaps she loved him, but it was not the love they'd had before.

If he left her behind, she would surely die. And she would die alone, without the companionship of her own kind. Who would dig his beloved's grave, if not him? They would throw her body on the pyre without ceremony. He would have to live with that for the rest of his days, if he survived the journey home.

Home. If he'd stayed home, none of this would have happened.

He shook her gently. "Cariña," he whispered. She huffed in her sleep. "Cariña," he said, "wake up." Her eyes opened.

"We're leaving."

"What?"

"We're leaving. We'll die if we stay here. Let these gods handle their own affairs. We must leave, and now."

"How?"

"I know a way," said the fisherman. "Bring some water, and some dried fish. We have little time."

They rose in the darkness, and gathered their few things together. The fisherman rolled up the tarp he'd been using for shade when he worked. His compass and his whetstone were in the pouch that hung from his belt, and his knife was sheathed and slung round his shoulder on a cord. His woman carried a skin full of water and a leather bolsa of dried fish slung round hers.

The frigate bird, standing watch in the snag where he customarily perched, pretended to doze. The Turropsi relied on him to use his best judgment, and in this matter he judged it best to let their fate play out.

The fisherman led her down the beach, their footfalls silent in the sand, their bodies leaning forward in the nighttime glow of the belly of the beast. They strode past the pelican and cormorant sleeping in their brightly painted colors. Past the throne of King Crow, where the congress of crows stirred in their sleep and began muttering, in crowish voices the fisherman refused to hear, kukuld, krook, kukuld, krook, kreep, kreep, krawl, krawl, kukuld. *Mammering, clay-brained harpies*, he thought, but he held his silence and walked on. Past the canopied bed, where the cursèd crow no doubt lay sleeping. He led her all the way to the foot of the inlet, where the clear waters of the stream from the canyon flowed. They waded across the stream and started up the sand on the other side. The canoe was ahead of them, beached. The fish eagles were busy gathering clams, which they put into baskets, ready to be put on board. The fisherman and his beloved waited in the darkness until the fish eagles worked their way round to the far side of the canoe, and then they scurried forward. In a trice they were aboard, and they crept silently into the prow, where the fisherman pulled the tarp over them.

They laid themselves together, settling in by jot and tittle with great care, for their silence and their stillness were all that would keep them from being discovered. Cariña found a hollow reed beneath her, and then another, digging into her hip, and these she tucked into the top of her sarong, for they vexed her, and she could not risk tossing them aside. Soon enough they heard the thumps of the baskets of clams dropping into the bottom of the canoe. The fish eagles climbed aboard and walked the gunwales, the canoe rocking a bit as they made their way, one to the stern, the other to the prow. There was a thwart over their heads, and it was here that the he-eagle perched, so close they might have reached up and grabbed his foot. The fish eagles began beating their wings, and in the silence of the night the fisherman could hear the air against their feathers. They sang in their high-pitched, keening voices, and the canoe, quickened into motion by their song, slid into the water bow first, and made the turn to the mouth of the inlet.

The fisherman wrapped his arms tighter round his beloved, and she her arms round him. They cleared the mouth of the inlet, the canoe riding high as it cut through the waves of the sea. The seas were stiff, a remnant of the storm that had come through, and the prow rose and fell on each successive wave.

They were on their way to the far shore. *'Tis good to be on the sea again*, the fisherman thought, with the briny tang of the salt air sharp in his nose.

Now King Crow flew out of the cave behind the waterfall, and behind him came a thousand times a thousand crows. He led them through the canyon, and then they burst forth from the canyon's mouth and filled the dark night over the inlet. King Crow bade them be silent so that he might exult in the sound of all those wings beating the air. He led them in a great circle aloft, the air riven with their thrumming wings, such a throng of followers as would cow any enemy into submission. At dawn he would surprise the other gods with his host of followers, and none would dare oppose him.

His congress of crows rose from where they slept by his throne, and they came to him. "Kukuld, kukuld," they said, "kreepy kreepy kukuld, krawly krawly aw-aw-away," they said, and they pointed far out to sea. There, in the darkness before first light, the crow with his keen eyesight saw the canoe of the dead, making its way to the far shore, he now knew, with that pustulant gob of walking guano, the fisherman, on board. Was his simpering coquette with him?

"And the woman?" the crow asked.

"Kaw, kaw, Kariña," they said, "kreepy krawly away."

So they thought they could simply steal away, did they? No one was allowed to leave the Isle of the Dead save by the King's leave, and he had given them no such leave.

"Follow me," King Crow cried, and the great horde of crows did follow, his congress of crows now beyond numbering. Over the open sea they flew, and King Crow cried "Ka-kill, ka-kill."

"Ka-kill, ka-kill," the great horde did answer, "ka-kill, ka-kill."

"Vengeance," crowed King Crow, "is Mine."

THEY HAD FALLEN ASLEEP, CARIÑA and the fisherman, beneath their tarp, but as the western sky lightened toward dawn, Cariña roused herself, careful to keep as still as she could. The canoe of the dead sliced through the swells on its way to the far shore, and for that she was glad, but somewhere in the distance, a croaky, grating sound approached.

She put her hand over the fisherman's mouth and brought her lips to his ear. "Listen," she whispered. "Please, just listen." Her lover's eyes opened, and he gave her the barest of nods.

Gulls? he wondered. *But there were no gulls here.*

"Crows," he mouthed, and Cariña nodded.

Crows it was, a great ruckus of them, and they were coming fast.

Kaw, kaw, ka-kaw, *kiaw,* *ka-kaw,* *kaw,* *ka-kaw,*

kiaw, *ka-kaw,* *kaw,* *kaw,*

kiaw! Louder and louder they came,

until the air was thick with the chuttering cacophony of their cries, the canoe of the dead surrounded with a whirling maelstrom of crow upon crow upon crow. The fish eagles, alarmed, gave up their singing and ceased the beating of their wings, and the canoe slowed to a stop.

Then Cariña and the fisherman heard the thump of King Crow landing. "Ho there, cousin fish eagles," he said, his voice thunderous loud, and all the other crows shushed their calls as if on a signal only birds could hear. Cariña trembled, and the fisherman wrapped his arms round her more tightly.

"Ho there, cousin crow," said the fish eagles. "What brings you here?"

"You've something on board that doesn't belong," said King Crow.

The canoe was beginning to broach, and the fish eagles flapped their wings to keep the prow headed into the swells. "Clams on board," said the she-eagle, "nothing more."

King Crow reached into a basket of clams with his crow foot and tossed a foot-full of them overboard. The fish eagles shrieked at this blasphemy, but King Crow paid them no mind. "I beg to differ," he said, so beside himself with anger that he forgot, for a moment, to use the royal We. He crow-hopped to the prow of the canoe, where he grabbed the tarp with his crow foot and pulled it aside. "Stowaways!" he cried, and now Cariña and the fisherman could see King Crow standing over them, and the mob of crows perched all along the gunwales, and the greater murder of them swarming in the air above.

"Swive me," muttered the fisherman. "We're caught."

King Crow brought his fearsome beak down close enough to pluck their eyes out. "I've got you, my pretties," he said. "Now stand up, and face your fate."

They stood together, hand in hand, and face to face with the crow. "You," said King Crow, fixing an eye on the fisherman, "shall burn on the pyre, though first I'll have the pleasure of ripping your still-beating heart from your miserable chest. And you, you ripe little skainsmate," he said, fixing an eye on the woman, "shall return to the Isle of the Dead, where you may yet win back your once favored position"—and here the crow bent forward and rubbed his lascivious beak between Cariña's legs—"in my bed." He straightened himself and winked his crowish eye at her.

"And if I refuse you?" the woman said.

"Refuse Me?" said King Crow. "Refuse King Crow?" He sent a snort of air through his nostrils, lifting the fine feathers there. "Refuse Us and die," said he, "in the selfsame manner as your scurrilous consort here. We shall dine on both your hearts, and We shall gobble down your puny little souls, and that will put an end to your line, the both of you. We shall throw your lifeless bodies on the sacred fire and roast your flesh," he said, "and We shall eat your nipples, and your lips both hither and nether," he said, his carrion breath now hot in the woman's face, "and We shall dine on your pitiful willy-spigot," he said, the sharp point of his beak a finger's width from the fisherman's eye, "and We shall eat your danglers like oysters roasted in their own shell."

The crow glared at them both, and then, crow-hopping a step away, showed them his back, raising his tail as if he were about to drop a gobbet of guano in front of them, though he did not. Cariña put her lips to the fisherman's ear. "Forgive me my trespasses," she said, "and follow my lead."

The fisherman squeezed her hand. All the sorrow that had passed between them mattered not a whit to him in the face of their imminent deaths.

"I do," said he. "I will."

King Crow turned, ready to berate them yet again, but to King Crow the woman said, "Kiss my bleeding arse, you poxy pumpion," and with that she leapt overboard, her body knifing into the water and disappearing. King Crow's beak fell open in astonishment as he reached a wing after her in vain. The fisherman, only slightly less astonished, leapt overboard on the other side of the canoe.

"After them!" King Crow thundered. His rabble of crows flew to answer his call, wheeling and turning in the air, skimming the surface of the sea, screeching and squawking, swooping in mobs and gangs, King Crow himself taking to the air to lead them. A thousand times a thousand crows watched the sea, waiting for the lovers' breath to run out. But they could not swim, these crows, not a one of them, and Cariña and the fisherman did not surface.

"Let us be on our way," the she-eagle said, as King Crow flew by. "They are drowned." He wheeled round the stern of the canoe and found a perch on the gunwale.

"Drowned, yes," said the crow, "but where are the bodies?"

"Drowned bodies sink," said the he-eagle.

They do? thought the crow. But then he realized that if bodies floated, they would not drown, so of course they sank. Still, he wanted the bodies to burn on the pyre, and so they lingered on, he and his army of crows, hoping to find them. Though soon enough it came to him that he had no way to raise the dead bodies from the water to the canoe.

And so the fish eagles were allowed to continue their journey to the far shore, and King Crow led his army of crows back to the Isle of the Dead.

THE PELICAN, ASLEEP BENEATH THE cormorant, dreamt that her head was so weighty that she could not wake herself. Her bill lay heavy on her breast, as if it were made of ironwood. Try as she might, she could not lift it. The crow was laughing at her—*aw aw aw aw aw*—the sound so loud it seemed to come from inside her own head. Something wet and sticky dripped down the back of her neck. Wakefulness was a slippery silver fish swimming around the tip of her bill, but she could not open her neb to swallow it.

At last she managed to open an eye. She saw a crow's foot gripping her bill. She opened her other eye, and yes, it was true, a crow perched on her bill. She was awake, the cormorant's feet gripping her shoulders, and there was the inlet in front of her. The calls of crows came from everywhere. There were crows on the beach, hundreds and hundreds of them. She croaked from deep within her throat and shook her bill from side to side, and the crow there cawed and flew off.

From above her head came another caw—*ka-kaw aw aw aw aw*—and she stretched out her neck and looked up. Another crow sat atop the cormorant's head, and the cormorant raised a wing and swatted at it. The crow flew off with an angry *kiaww*, but not before dropping another gobbet of crow guano right on her bill.

"How rude," said the pelican. The cormorant hopped down from her shoulders, and they both looked about. Thousands upon thousands of crows filled the air above the inlet, flying in great flocks, the ruction of their caws and cries drowning out the sound of wind and sea. Thousands more strutted around the pyre, the boldest amongst them braving the heat to dash forward and tear bits of flesh from the bones. The sand was littered with their guano.

"We've been invaded," said the cormorant. He had to shout to be heard. He pointed with a wing at the trees, where every branch had crows perched on it.

The shadow of King Crow passed over them, and in a trice, he was there, strutting back and forth on the sand.

"Kiaww!" he shouted. "This is the best day of my life!" He passed a wing in front of his face, and made himself a cubit taller. He spread his wings and turned in a circle, taking in the great multitude of his fellows. "Ko, ko, ko," he thundered, and they gathered around him in a great horde. They covered the sand and turned the beach black.

King Crow folded his wings and stood tall. He hopped forward until he was beak to bill with the pelican and the cormorant, his sharp neb close enough to pluck out their eyes.

"Either you are with me," said the crow, "or, kiaww, you are against me. Which is it?"

The pelican and the cormorant looked at each other, and they looked at the mob of crows, their beady eyes upon them, and they trembled.

"We shall stand behind you, as is our custom," said the cormorant.

"Good," said King Crow. He turned his back on them, and he began to speak in the language of crows, rattling and croaking, rasping and cawing, screeching and squawking. Their time had come, he told them. They were his army, and he would lead them to victory. Soon he would rule the material world and the spirit world both, and all things crow would be paramount. Never again would he wear the shape of man, for that was a shape inferior to the shape of crows. This was his true nature, to be black and feathered, to be sharp of beak and loud of call, to be King of the Dead and the Living alike.

"The Great Age of the Crow is dawning," King Crow cawed. Their enemies were falling before them—look at what had just happened to that hairless blue turd the fisherman, and his featherless hag of a woman, drowned at sea. There remained only the last of the lesser gods. "Find them," he cawed. "Find that salt whore of a goddess, that three-penny upright, may she choke on her own quail-pipe. Find that frigging frigate bird, her whore's bird of a consort, may he smother himself with his own throat pouch. Find them and peck the feathers off their wings. Find them and peck out one of their eyes."

"Bring them to me, alive," cawed King Crow, "and I will gobble down their nether parts while they watch with their one remaining eye. And then I will crack open their skulls and feast on their brains."

The congress of crows kiawed their approval, *King Crow, ka-kill, King Crow, ka-kill.* They rose up, thousands upon thousands of them turning the sky black with the enormity of their flock, and as they did so, the pelican and the cormorant stepped back, and back, and back. King Crow spread his wings, exulting in the power of his flock. "The congress of crows," he cawed, "is invincible. Nothing can stop Us now." Back and back and back stepped the two bird-gods while crows flew all about them, the flapping of their wings like wind blowing in all directions at once. Back and back and back they stepped, until they turned and flew off toward the middle of the island, where they found a quiet bit of shade beneath a giant of a fir tree.

"What do we do now?" said the pelican.

"We must warn the others," said the cormorant.

"There are too many crows," said the pelican. "Not even the goddess can resist this many crows."

"It's true," said the cormorant. He stared over the tops of his spectacles into the place where he would have a thought if he had a thought, and he considered. The pelican was silent while he thought, but in the distance she heard the raucous cries of the invaders, and she was afraid. The cormorant, too, trembled, but at length he gathered himself together, and stilled his shaking body. He must rise to the occasion, lest they all die.

"Perhaps," said he, "there is a way."

THEY PULLED THEMSELVES ASHORE ON their hands and knees, the fisherman and Cariña, coughing and retching up sea water, so tired they collapsed on the sand where the last of the waves still washed over their legs. They lay there a long time, letting the fact of their survival sink in.

"How far?" Cariña asked.

"A league?" the fisherman said. "Two? Farther than I've ever swum before."

They had found each other beneath the canoe of the dead, and they swam along the keel until it rose to the prow, and their heads broke water. They could hear the crows above them, the racket of them harsh, and they saw them flying by just above the water, and they sank their heads beneath the surface. The fisherman stuck his knife into the keel, so that they would have a purchase on the boat. And Cariña pulled the hollow reeds from the top of her sarong so that they were able to draw air into their lungs. So did they survive until King Crow left.

When the canoe of the dead began again to make headway toward the far shore, Cariña and the fisherman swam off in the opposite direction. The fish eagles whistled at them, urging them shoreward. At the top of the swells they could just see the central mountain of the isle, which gave them hope, though the distance was great. They swam for their very lives, steady and strong, for as long as they could, and when their arms leadened with fatigue, and their legs could scarcely kick another kick, the shore was yet so far away that they would surely drown. The fisherman looked at his beloved then, and she at him, the two of them treading water, and they each thought of the love they still felt for the other, in spite of all their trespasses, and the fisherman took his beloved's hand in his.

"Are you ready to die?" he asked. They were face to face, rising and falling on the swells.

"No," Cariña said. "I want to go home."

"To the isle, then?" said the fisherman.

"No," said his beloved. "To the land of the living."

The fisherman nodded. "Then we must live," said he, and they swam on.

Now on the shore Cariña raised herself to her knees and coughed up seawater. The fisherman, too, rose and coughed, and they both sat, with the waves lapping at their feet.

"Thank the gods for your knife," Cariña said.

"And for your hollow reeds," the fisherman said. "We were not meant to die out there, for the gods gave us what we needed."

They had beached themselves not far from where the twin pinnacles of rock marked the opening to the inlet, and now they heard, on the wind, the cries of thousands of crows.

"Where did all those crows come from?" said the fisherman.

"They were many, out there on the water," said Cariña. "We were lucky not to be seen."

Slowly, slowly, they stood. "We cannot be seen now," the fisherman said. "We must find a place to hide." Their one advantage was that King Crow thought them drowned.

"Where?" said Cariña. The shoreline offered them little protection, and the cliffs were too sheer to climb.

"The tide is changing," said the fisherman. "We'll have to steal our way to the forest. We can ride the incoming tide through the mouth of the inlet."

To go back into the water, to go toward King Crow, thought Cariña, was more than she could bear. But there was no other place to go.

"You saved us out there," said the fisherman, "leaping overboard. You were quick of thought, and quick to act. I am in your debt."

Cariña considered this, and then she said, "No, for you brought me back to life. If I saved your life out there, then we are merely even."

What a woman Cariña is, the fisherman thought, *even if she does not remember our shared past, for she has been my best companion in one life, and now another.* He put his arms round her, and held her close, and though he could feel his rage at how she had wronged him with the crow like a dark heat beneath his breastbone, he chose to ignore it. He could do that, at least for now.

"Come," he said. "We're not safe here."

"Lead on," she said, and they walked hand in hand toward the twin pinnacles of rock.

THE PELICAN AND THE CORMORANT, having slipped deeper into the forest, sat beneath the carcass of a great cedar tree that lay on its side. The rotting wood was a deep orange color, and they were nestled beneath an overhang at one end. From time to time they heard crows overhead, flying in ever greater circles, searching the island for their quarries.

"What do we do when the canoe arrives?" said the pelican.

The cormorant looked at her over the tops of his spectacles. "We've fled. Surely we are persona non grata by now."

"I've never missed the arrival of the canoe. Not once."

"The dead will find their way without us. It is the crow's problem now."

"And the Kiamah. He will expect me to arrive with his basket of treats this evening. I took him no conaria yesterday, I was so distraught, and now I should bring him a double dose, lest he awake."

"That is a more pressing problem," said the cormorant. "Let me give it some thought."

The cormorant thought for a long time, rooting around in his feathers for feather mites as he did so. When at last he spoke again he said, "It will be disadvantageous when the Kiamah awakes."

"Yes?" said the pelican. "That much I knew."

"I've given this a lot of thought," said the cormorant.

"Go on," said the pelican.

"My thought is this," said the cormorant. "I have no solution to the problem."

The pelican sighed and shook her head. The cormorant might be a scholar, but there were times when he was all foam and no ale.

"Perhaps I should simply return to the pyre and go about my business," said the pelican. "As if nothing has happened."

"I fear for your life if you do so," said the cormorant. "The crow is mad. He may well set his flock upon you, and you will be pecked to death."

"The crows cannot kill me," said the pelican. "Can they?"

"Perhaps not," said the cormorant, "but the crow surely can."

They heard crows approaching, their raucous cries rasping through the forest air. They drew farther back beneath the overhang of the cedar tree and became still as stones. The crows flew from treetop to treetop, from branch to branch, their search slower and lower this time. It took them some time to work their way past, but at last they were gone.

"Sooner or later they will find us," said the cormorant. He peered out from beneath the overhang, searching the canopy above. A flash of color caught his attention, but when he turned his head to look, it was gone.

"Did you see that?" he whispered.

"Did I see what?" the pelican said. Her head turned in all directions, as did the cormorant's, their long necks stretched out and twined round each other's. Seeing nothing, they untwined their necks and pulled back beneath the cedar tree.

"There's something out there," said the cormorant. They felt then the barest breath of air moving, the beating of wings, and a pair of shapely feet descended in front of them, with a bracelet round the ankle of one, and then the hem of a sarong.

"Dewi!" shouted the pelican.

"Shush," said the cormorant.

"Hello," said the goddess, who stood on terra firma in front of them now. "We'd best keep our voices down," said she. "There's a butchery of crows about, and they mean us no good."

"They were just here, searching," said the cormorant.

"And they'll be back," said the goddess. "Have you seen the fisherman and Cariña?"

"Not since last night," said the pelican.

"They must be hiding somewhere," said the goddess. She put her palms together, and touched her forehead with her fingertips in a moment of silent prayer. "At least I've found you."

She beckoned them to follow her, and together they flitted through the shadows, listening for the caws of crows, working their way deeper into the forest, until they came to Dewi's nest in the hollow of an ancient cedar. She parted the curtain of moss that hid the entrance, and inside, they found the frigate bird.

"Well met, good friend," said Dewi, her smile broad at the sight of her sometime lover.

"Indeed," said the frigate bird, whose throat pouch swelled red in answer to the goddess's smile. "I feared for your lives with that rabble of crows about."

"They are many," said the goddess, "but we have evaded them thus far by flying where they are not."

The frigate bird lifted a duffel at his side, full of large pointy shapes that clanked. "I have brought some things we may need from the material world."

"Excellent," said the goddess. "But 'twill do no us good if we do not gather everyone together. Have you seen the fisherman and Cariña?"

"No," said the frigate bird, "but I have news." He told them of seeing the fisherman and his beloved leave in the middle of the night. When the multitude of crows arrived, he had himself left for the material world, to fetch what weaponry he could. He had met the fish eagles upon his return as he approached the Isle of the Dead, and heard their report of the stowaways, and the crow's discovery of them.

"The crow thinks they are drowned," said the frigate bird, "but the fish eagles saw them swim for the isle. They think they survived."

"We must find them," said the goddess. She rose, as if to go immediately, but the frigate bird rose as well, and put a restraining wing on her arm. They heard, just then, the squawking and krucking of crows in the distance.

"It's too dangerous," he said. "Wait for the cover of darkness."

THE FISHERMAN AND CARIÑA LAY hidden beneath a blanket of moss, deep in the forest, while above them mobs of crows flew hither and yon, searching for the last of the demigods. The incoming tide had brought them into the inlet, where they'd made their way to shore and into the woods without being seen. But they had seen thousands upon thousands of crows down the beach, and they had heard the crow speechifying to them in his creaky, screechy voice, and so they knew that King Crow was on the rise. They knew their lives were forfeit if they were found. They wanted to find their friends, but they had no idea where to look.

They lay with Cariña's body spooned against the fisherman's, each of them lost in their separate thoughts. Thoughts they left unspoken, for their hearts were bruised, and they dared not risk further injury. It had been one thing for Cariña to ask for the fisherman's forgiveness with death so close at hand, and for the fisherman to give it. Now, in the silence of hiding, other feelings roiled within them. Had they dared to speak, they would have learned that each of them doubted love, for love had betrayed them. Love had led the fisherman to the

Isle of the Dead only to find his beloved's body alive, but her memories gone. And love had led the woman away from the man who loved her, had led her to the crow, who loved only himself.

Yet the fisherman still desired Cariña. Perhaps she would have him now, and in their lovemaking they would find their way back to love. He pressed himself against her, remembering her ardor the last time they had made love. He moved his hand to her breast and ground his tiller into her backside. But she moved away from him, pulling his hand from her breast, and it was only then that the fisherman realized that the lovemaking he was remembering was that of the pelican, shapeshifted into Cariña's form.

I have been spurned by the crow, thought Cariña, *and now in my turn I am spurning the fisherman.*

She has made of me a cuckold, thought the fisherman, *and forgiveness eludes me.*

The only way he will ever forgive me, thought the woman, *is to slay the crow, and that he cannot do.*

Perhaps we can go on as friends, thought the fisherman, *and perhaps as friends we might still give each other the comfort of our bodies.*

Curse men and their need for revenge, thought the woman, *and curse my own fate for marooning me here, where the one man who might be loved is the one man I cannot love.*

Love's fire has burned down to mere coals, thought the fisherman, *and yet rage lies hot within me.*

I must find my way back to the land of the living, thought the woman, *and get on with my life.*

I must find my way back to the land of the living, thought the fisherman, *and get on with my life.*

Weariness overtook them, and with it came sleep.

KING CROW PERCHED ON HIS throne in his crow shape, the strand around him black with his congress of crows. They were so many, this great flock of his fellows, that the sand could not hold them all, and they gathered in their multitudes on every branch of every tree on either side of the inlet. Their raucous cries filled the air, *kaw, kakaw, ka-kaw-kaw-kaw*. King Crow spread his wings for silence, turning about on his throne until he had the attention of every crow in the flock. His fierce eyes bored into them, and they looked down rather than meet his fearsome gaze.

"They are here," thundered King Crow, "yet you cannot find them. They are here, and yet you let them mock me by remaining hidden. Are you a flock of simps? No, you are not. There is not a fledgling amongst you. We are crows, brethren, and we are not to be trifled with. We shall be masters of this world and the other, for that is our destiny. But first, kiaw, we must find our enemies and destroy them." King Crow flapped his wings, and rose above his fellows, and they all looked up at him.

"Find the lesser gods," he cried, "find that wagtail goddess, and that blackguard the frigate bird. Find those traitors, the pelican and the cormorant, for I shall have my revenge on all who have opposed me! Ko, ko, ko," he thundered, "are you with me?"

"Kiaw!" the multitude cried.

"Follow me!" King Crow thundered. "We shall start on the eastern tip of the isle, and we shall form a line, and search from one end to the other. They cannot escape us."

And so the great congress of crows followed King Crow to the beach, the Sea of Bones at their backs, and they formed a great line, and they moved forward on King Crow's command. They searched the sandy beach, with its rack and ruin of broken bones, but they found no one. They scaled the cliffs, hopping their way upward from clawhold to clawhold, flapping their wings to keep their balance, but they found no one. Over the top of the cliffs they went, the sun now starting to set in the east, but they found no one. With King Crow's counselors gone, and fled from his wrath, there was no one to point out to the crow that it was late in the day to start such a painstaking search.

Kwurk, kwurk, kwurk, they muttered, *ka-kill, ka-kill, ka-kill*. They left in their wake no unturned stick nor stone. They left only their guano behind them, in sticky gobbets, the white daubs of it bright in the fading light. When night was completely fallen, and the beast's heart beat above them, the line of crows had barely made it down the back side of the sea cliffs. Nearly the whole of the Isle of the Dead lay before them, waiting to be searched, but it was too dark to see. And so, at King Crow's command, they left off their search, and they slept where they stood.

THE FISHERMAN AND CARIÑA MADE their way deeper into the forest under the cover of darkness. They had heard the line of crows coming down the back side of the shore cliffs as the sun set, and they were far too close for comfort. They took care to not make any noise, and yet they moved with the urgency of those who flee a certain death. They were nearing the crow's mound of shiny things when a fluttering sound above them stilled their steps.

The crow? mouthed Cariña. The fisherman shrugged, but there was fear in his eyes.

A moment later the goddess descended and stood before them. Cariña greeted her with great relief in her heart, for surely the goddess would lead them to safety. The fisherman's feelings were roiled. On the one hand, he was still trying to escape the machinations of these infernal gods, for he wanted no part of the troubles they were brewing. On the other hand, this selfsame goddess had knelt before him but a day before and made, with more prowess than he had ever known, his Man Thomas stand tall. Yet that was a poor reason to follow her into an uncertain and deadly future. Though what alternative he might have was unknown—there seemed to be no way off this cursèd isle, and the crow would kill them if he found them.

"The crow," whispered Dewi Sri, "has brought forth a great army of crows from the land of the living. You've seen them?"

Yes, they nodded.

"They sleep now, but at first light they will continue their search," the goddess whispered. "Let me take you to a place deep in the forest where we shall be safe a while."

Yes, they nodded, Cariña with trust in her heart, and the fisherman with resignation.

The goddess bade Cariña climb upon her back. "I'll be back for you," she whispered to the fisherman. "Stay here. The others are out searching for you as well. If you see any of them, tell them to go back to my nest."

They flew through the dark forest, dodging tree limbs, the night air cool upon their brows, until at last they came to the hollow cedar tree where Dewi had built her nest. She parted the curtain of moss and ushered Cariña in, and there was the frigate bird, his black feathers shiny in the candlelight.

"You'll be safe here," Dewi said, "and you'll find the frigate bird is good company." With that she flew off to fetch the fisherman.

"We feared you were captured," the frigate bird said, "or worse. The crow has declared us all his prey, and now he hunts us."

"We escaped," Cariña said, "or nearly so." She settled herself on the bed of moss that filled the hollowed cedar, and she told the frigate bird the story of their adventure on the canoe of the dead, and how they came to be back on the isle.

"Where were you headed?" said the frigate bird.

"To the far shore, to return to the land of the living."

"The far shore? You cannot return to the material world from there."

"Why not?" Cariña asked.

"There is no connecting passage from the material world to the far shore," the frigate bird said. "Trust me, I would know if there were."

"There must be," Cariña said, "or else how do the dead arrive there?"

"Through a kind of alchemical migration of their souls," the frigate bird said. "More than that I do not know."

She looked at the frigate bird, with his pirate's pistola and his spyglass stuck into his belt. Next to him was a large duffel that bulged from within as if it held things bulky and sharp.

"Yet you come and go from here to the land of the living," said she. "How is that so?"

"There are passageways," said the frigate bird, "known only to a few. The nearest one is on an isle to the west, just beyond the horizon. Isla del Ombiglio it is called. It is the navel of the spirit world, and it connects to the land of the living through a kind of umbilicus. There's a cave there, with a ladder that goes a very long way down, through a dry well."

"So it is possible for us to return home? We sail to this island, and find the cave, and climb down a ladder?"

"Well, yes," said the frigate bird. "That is, you could go to the material world, but you wouldn't likely arrive at your home. The other end of the well shifts about. Sometimes you end up one place, and sometimes another, and then again a dozen more. One never knows."

"But it is the world we lived in before we came here?"

"Oh yes, it is the same."

"And so, it is beneath us? The spirit world is hollow?"

"It is this way," said the frigate bird. "The material world is inside a hollow log of great immensity, and this log has drifted through the ocean of time for a thousand times a thousand years. The spirit world was on the outside of the log, only now it is swallowed up inside the belly of the Kiamah, and us with it. And the Kiamah sits atop that hollow log like a lizard basking in the sun."

"And this umbilicus, it passes through the belly of the beast, and through the log to the world below?"

"It does," said the frigate bird.

"And by this means you travel back and forth from the one world to the other?"

"By this means and others. There are passageways that bring one to the roof of the world, and from there one can see all that is, laid out below. And from my perches in the roof of the world I see what was and what will be through my spyglass."

"You see the future with that?" She pointed at the spyglass tucked into his belt.

"In a manner of speaking. The future is not a thing to be seen, because it does not yet exist. What can be seen are the swirling mists of possibility. Oft times I fly into those mists. They have no more substance than a cloud, but there are visions floating in them, of things that might be, of wonders not yet dreamt of, and of horrors that may yet happen. One hears things that might be said, and the noise of battles that might be fought, and songs that have not yet been written."

The woman pondered all this. Just beyond the edge of the present, it seemed, the land of the living was becoming what it was. The spirit world was all she knew, but the land of the living called to her. She wanted to go home, even though home was not a place she could remember.

"So," the woman said, "if we survive the crow and his army of crows, you could take us to this Isla del Ombiglio, and we could go home?"

"It is possible," said the frigate bird. "I cannot promise. All I know is that our destiny, for the moment, lies here, on the Isle of the Dead."

There is no way out but through, thought the woman. Just then they heard the goddess return, her wings fluttering, and the sound of the fisherman's feet hitting the ground as he slid off her back.

"May the gods preserve us," said Cariña to the frigate bird.

Dewi Sri poked her head through the curtain of moss.

"We'll do our best," said she. She stepped in, and the fisherman behind her. And behind them, arriving as if by a signal that only birds can see, came the pelican and the cormorant. Our little band of heroes nestled together in the mossy confines of Dewi's nest, their faces lit by candlelight.

"Now," said the goddess, "let us put our heads together, and plot our way forward."

DEWI SRI STOOD, HIDDEN, IN the shallow cave just below the peak of the highest mountain of the Isle of the Dead. The congress of crows was behind her, finishing their search of the forest. Luck was with her, for though the crows had found her nest in the hollow cedar tree, Lord Crow flew up and down their line, hectoring them to find, kiaw, find, kiaw, find their quarry, and so they were too rushed to dig through the many layers of moss beneath which she had hidden with her companions.

'Twas the frigate bird who had a pirate's knowledge of how to spring a surprise attack upon their foe. At Dewi's side was a linen bag full of soot that he had brought from the material world. Below her was the inlet, and at the twin pinnacles at the mouth were the pelican, the fisherman, and his beloved, hard at work on the task they had been given.

Would the fisherman and Cariña stay when the battle began? She had done what she could to gain their loyalty. Perhaps their failed escape had been useful, showing them that they had no real choice but to stay and help defeat the crow.

They were so outnumbered. The crow was mad with power, and she needed everyone working together if they were to prevail.

She was an unlikely general, with nothing in the way of battle experience of her own. All she had ever done was to bring forth abundance into the world. She patted her belly, which was starting to swell with the child she carried. They must drive the crow off his throne, so that his offspring might rule in his place. It was her own story reprised, only now it was she who was cast in the role of the father-killer, and it was not a role she relished.

The cormorant was working his way up to her, flying from branch to branch, staying hidden. Dewi Sri stepped out of the shallow cave and climbed to the mountain peak above it so she might peer eastward at the other end of the island. The crows in their multitudes were a dark line slowly sweeping forward. They would be done before the sun set in the east. Lord Crow would gather them at the inlet to harangue them again, of that she was certain, so fond he was of the sound of his own voice. The hour of battle was drawing nigh. Death, she reminded herself, was a necessary part of the cycle, and many would die before the night was through.

Now the cormorant flew to her side from a treetop below.

"I have been practicing," said he. He passed a wing in front of himself and stood before her.

She looked him up and down. He was every inch the warrior she had hoped for. His fierce gaze was unnerving, even though she knew him to be an ally. Yet he trembled, and she put her hands together in prayer and hummed, that his fears might be stilled.

"It is not courage that makes a hero," said she. "It is his service to a cause greater than himself." The trembling in his body calmed.

"You can do this at any size you choose?" she asked.

"I can be very, very large," he said.

"Excellent," she said. "You are formidable beyond measure." She led the cormorant back to the cave, and there she picked up the linen bag. "Help me get ready," she said. "We'll hide here until the sun is low enough for our purpose."

Though his trembling had stilled, the cormorant was still unsettled, for no matter what his size, he was still only a gentle scholar within.

THE CONGRESS OF CROWS WAS gathered on either side of the inlet enduring yet another berating from King Crow, who was perched on his throne. Their enemies were here, yet they had searched the Isle of the Dead from west to east, and found no one. They were bungling blunderers, they were bumptious fools, they must be blind, deaf, and stupid to have missed their quarry.

Against the sun setting to the east, from the top of the highest mountain on the Isle of the Dead, came a great horned owl, an owl of immense stature, gliding on his silent wings.

"Hoo, hoo, hoo," he called, and this was a sound that sent terror into the hearts of all crows. Back in the land of the living, owls snatched them out of the air in midflight, or plucked them still sleeping from their roosts. Owls drove them from their nests and stole their eggs, only to drop them to the ground so they could eat the tender unborn simps inside. Their taloned claws were formidable, their hooked beaks were cruel.

Far back in the throng of crows, a ruckus broke out. A chorus of crows cawed a warning, *ka-woo-oo, ka-woo-oo, ka-woo-oo*. They were no longer paying any heed to their king, for the great horned owl was their mortal enemy. The ruckus spread, wings flapping, crows rising to the air, fleeing the flying menace. The great horned owl grew ever larger as he approached, and the congress of crows was sore afraid. He was as big as a wolf, then as big as a tiger, then as big as a sphinx.

"Ko! Ko! Ko!" thundered King Crow, rallying his troops. "Mob him! Peck him! Drive him away!"

Crows rose by the thousands in a great flock, their ear-piercing clamor of kiaws deafening. They flew at the owl, cawing, beating their wings at him. Onward the owl came on his silent wings, flying straight at the center of the mob. "Hoo-hooo," he called, "hoo-hooo," his feathered feet with their terrible hooked talons spread and slicing a swath through the mass of black bodies, severing wings from shoulders and heads from necks, snatching dozens of crows from the air and crushing them. The center of the mob gave way, and when they tried to close around him from the flanks, nipping and pecking, the owl flapped his wings and rose, swatting them aside, and though hundreds of crows pursued him, he circled around and flew into the mob again. They swarmed around him like hornets bent on stinging him to death, and they drew some blood, but the owl gave them no quarter. His amber eyes with their huge black pupils were savage, and his cruel curved beak ripped crows from the sky and tore them asunder. Loose black feathers and sudden mists of blood filled the air. The falling dead bodies pelted the waters below like giant black hailstones.

From his hiding place atop one of the pinnacles, the fisherman waited until all eyes were on the great horned owl, and then he shot a bolt from a crossbow to the other pinnacle. His beloved sprang from her hiding place on the other pinnacle as soon as she heard the bolt clatter to a landing. The bolt trailed a line, and she grabbed the line and began pulling. The pelican joined her, wearing her old woman shape, and together they pulled, while the fisherman, on his side, played out a net. The women hauled hard on the line, and the net stretched from one pinnacle to the other, and from the tops of the rocks all the way to the water below. They clambered down, and tied off the net at the bottom corners with rope. Then the fisherman and the woman climbed back up, and the pelican flew off to join Dewi.

"Hoo-hooo," the owl cried again, and now the crows, the sand and water below strewn with their fellows, began to fall back, their crow hearts filled with fear. One by one, and then many by many, the crows turned away and fled. King Crow called to them, commanding them to stay and face the enemy. They did not. Thousands upon thousands took flight, all of them crying their fear cry, "Kulp, kulp, kulp."

"Ko! Ko! Ko!" thundered King Crow, slowing the mob in its flight, rallying them for one last attack. Thus encouraged, the crows turned and faced the great horned owl. But from a hiding place in the forest came the frigate bird and his dark companion, the two of them black and blacker, flying on silent wings, the goddess covered in soot and wearing a crow mask. Behind them was the pelican, a length of cord in her bill. They swooped in from behind King Crow, unnoticed in the confusion of the great horned owl's attack, and the frigate bird crashed into the crow and beat at him with his wings. Just behind the frigate bird, the goddess flew in with the sooty linen bag the frigate bird had brought her. She dropped the bag over King Crow's head and held it there like a hangman's hood, her feet planted in the sand, the frigate bird thrashing at the crow's legs, trying to bring him down, the crow twisting and flapping to break himself free, unable to rise with the goddess holding him by the hood. Now the pelican landed and swiftly passed a wing in front of herself, and in her Cariña shape she wrapped the cord round the bag, binding it to the crow. Thus blinded, King Crow cried out to his fellows, his voice muffled by the bag, but his frightened fellows, fleeing the owl, were deaf to his cries.

King Crow tried to reach the cord with his claws, and when he could not do so he passed his wingtip in front of his face to take on his man shape. But with his head hooded, his magic did not work. The goddess and the pelican wrapped his wings tight to his body with more cord, and thus was the crow subdued.

Now, as the sun was just setting, the goddess flew swiftly upward, until she was above the pandemonium of crows. They wheeled and turned in every direction, leaderless and confused. "Ko, ko, ko," the goddess thundered, "follow me." Crows by tens of thousands answered her call, breaking off from their attack on the owl. She flew westward, low over the inlet, leading them straight for the gap between the twin pinnacles of rock. The sun was at her back, and ahead of her, atop the twin pinnacles, the fisherman and the woman lay in wait. They held warrior's shields in front of themselves, the shields polished to the brightest of shines. Beams of light from the setting sun hit their shields and bounced back, blinding the crows in flight. Their mob split in two, some flying above the blinding beams, and some below. At the last moment the goddess rose enough to skim herself over the top of the net. The crows behind her followed, and while many skimmed over the top of the net with her, thousands more flew straight into it.

The net turned black with their bodies and bulged seaward as more and more crows piled in behind their fellows, a great flapping mass of crows trapped together. The fisherman and Cariña waited atop the pinnacles until the net could hold no more, and then they cut the line at either end. The net collapsed, dragging the multitude to the water, where they sank, and drowned.

DEWI SRI FLEW OUT OVER the Sea of Bones, and all the remaining congress of crows, chased by the great horned owl, followed the goddess, whom they took to be their king. She cawed and cawed, urging them forward, until her throat was raw with the rasp of speaking the crowish tongue. Onward they flew as night fell, and the thump of the Kiamah's heart filled their ears. They flew, and flew, and flew out to sea for many farsakhs, the goddess leading them away from any landfall on any island, the great horned owl ever behind them, harrying stragglers, and snatching the weak out of the air with his claws. And in that darkest hour before the dawn, exhausted crows began to fall into the sea.

By the thousands they fell, their black bodies landing on the waves, their wings too tired to flap, their feet thrashing but gaining no purchase in the water. And so they sank beneath the surface, their necks stretched long and their black beaks gasping for air but filling with lethal water, as one by one and many by many the multitude of crows drowned. The goddess watched this great slaughter, finding some small comfort in the fact that she had done nothing violent to bring it about, save bag the head of the crow, yet even so her heart was heavy with her part in it. The drowned crows floated to the surface like a great slick of death, their lifeless bodies jostling and clumping together on the swells, and though they had been out to kill her, she still pitied them as she flew over their countless corpses. And so she did not see the great horned owl pass his own exhausted wing in front of his face, and become the cormorant again. She did not see the cormorant's wings give up their struggle for flight, nor his senseless body falling into the sea.

Dewi Sri threw off her crow mask and let it fall from her hands. She circled back to meet her friend, but she could not find him. She flew and flew, back and forth above the empty sea, searching dark sky and darker waves for her companion, but she found him not. She called for him, her voice hoarse and her throat sore, but no answer came. Her eyes were filled with tears as the sun began to rise in the west, and it was through those tears that she saw, at long last, the cormorant, that gentle scholar, his pelagic body floating flat on the waves.

She scooped his dead body from the sea, and slung it as tenderly as she could over her shoulder, and she flew back with it to the Isle of the Dead.

Book Three

THE KIAMAH AWAKES

THE KIAMAH BEAST RAISED UP his head. It had been a long time since he had been this wakeful. There were strange stirrings within him, tiny tremblings and queasy little hiccups, as if the flora and fauna he had swallowed were in revolt, and bent on puking themselves free. His belly was bilious and sour and full of the colic. His bowels were costive, his sphincter obstipated. There was a ringing in his ears. His throat was thick with phlegm.

He hacked and hawked, trying to clear his throat. He could not.

His sphincter was at the base of his tail, many farzhooms§§ away from his head, and he struggled to open it so that his foul winds might escape. It was more work than he cared for. His fetid bowels had been bellybound ever since he swallowed the Isle of the Dead. He pushed

---

§§ A farzhoom, dear reader, is an ancient Persian measure of distance equal to one hundred forty-four farsakhs. The material world is thought by some to be 28 farzhooms around, and by others to be forty-four farzhooms around, and the Kiamah beast is big enough to swallow the material world. All of which is to say that his sphincter is a long, long way from his mouth. How far exactly? Opinions vary, and try as he might, the author of this chronicle is unable to say exactly how far, except to remind readers that the Kiamah swallowed the moon, and had plenty of room left over.

and pushed, and when he was not pushing, he barked and coughed, but nothing within him fell loose. He gave up.

Tired of the struggle, the Kiamah brought his tail round, running it up the length of his body to his face. The beast had never known a mother, and the only comfort he knew was that of his own touch. He licked the end of his tail with his tongue, and found that pacifying, so he drew the tip into his mouth and sucked on it, something he had never thought to do before. Thus soothed, he managed a belch, and his queasy guts settled themselves.

After a time a whiff of something crept up his throat, drawn there by the restive winds eddying within him, all the way from the crow's tunnel behind the waterfall. A fresh smell, a smell of rainbows and wind, of plowed earth and hearth fires, of brine and manure. It made him hungry, and for more than a mere basket of treats.

For a hundred times a hundred years he had lain here, riding a hollow log drifting through the Sea of Time, his belly full, his mind drowsy, so drowsy. No more. He was awake now. He was made to swallow all in his path. He must grow larger. He opened his great jaws. He turned his head sideways, and he took a bite. His teeth could find little purchase on the smooth surface of the log, and they slid along until they caught on an old knot. He bit down, hard. His mouth filled with wood, cracking and splintering between his teeth. He chewed and chewed, his molars grinding, the power of his jaws unstoppable.

He swallowed. He knew the log to be hollow. He knew the material world was inside it, waiting to fill his belly. He had only to eat his way through the surface, and then he would swallow the entire world.

The Kiamah was awake.

DEWI SRI SAT ON ONE end of the log in front of the fisherman's fire, the cormorant cradled in her arms, not sobbing, not wailing nor gnashing her teeth, but weeping silently in the morning light. She had led the brave cormorant to his last breath, but not before he turned the tide of battle in their favor. Behind her the beach was strewn with dead crows, and beyond the sand dead crows floated on the waters of the inlet.

All of this death was her inheritance, and she had little to show for it. The great devourer was all around her, and she, for all her wisdom, could think of no way to slay him. She let her tears flow, and she looked at the sky above, where in the night his great heart would beat, and she considered. There would be more blood shed, of that much she was sure.

While the goddess brooded, and found no peace, the others argued over the fate of the crow. They had him tethered to a tree at the edge of the forest, the hood still over his head, his wings bound to his body, far enough away that they spoke as if he were not there. The frigate bird stalked back and forth, his pistola and his spyglass tucked into his belt, his bearing piratical and full of menace. The fisherman sat on the driftwood log away from the goddess, honing his knife, with naught but butchery in his heart for the crow. They were spoiling for an execution. It was justice they wanted, and that meant punishment, and there was no other punishment for a rogue such as this crow than the punishment of death. The pelican argued for mercy, clucking and cooing about the redemptive power of forgiveness, and the woman agreed: they should all forgive the crow, as she had, although the truth was she was struggling to forgive him far more than she let on, and she did so more because she thought that was what the goddess wanted than she did of her own volition.

The goddess's silence, at length, became its own voice in the argument. Cariña stood next to her and wiped the tears from Dewi's cheeks with her hand.

"What is your thought?" Cariña asked. "What shall we do with the crow?"

In answer the goddess stood, holding the cormorant close. The frigate bird pointed at their dead comrade, and said, "His death alone is enough to call for the execution of the crow."

He would have gone on, but the goddess silenced him with a fierce look, though one softened somewhat by the tears brimming her eyes. "Consider the gravity of what we must do next," said she, "and tell me how, if you can, we are to deal with the Kiamah. For that is our greatest concern now. The fate of the crow can wait."

To the others she said, "I would speak with you all, but first, let me lay my burden down." They followed Dewi Sri as she bore the cormorant's body into the fisherman's house, and laid it to rest on a bed of moss. The fisherman brought more moss from the forest, and they bid the cormorant farewell, and then covered his body with it. There was a great outpouring of grief from all of them, and Dewi Sri wept with them, and then they returned to the fisherman's fire.

"All of you fought bravely last night, and we have won a great victory," said she, "but it will mean nothing if we do not slay the beast. The Kiamah is dull of wit, but he is large almost beyond measure, and he is powerful."

She stood before them, her eyes cast down while she considered what to say next. It was one thing, and a terrible thing at that, to go into battle and to cause the deaths of thousands of crows. It was yet a more terrible thing to have led the cormorant to his own demise while in her service. And to kill the crow herself, that was the most terrible thing yet. She had been belly to belly with him, and together they had climbed to the heights of pleasure. Could she slay him now, while he was captive? Could she slit his throat as if he were no more than a boar slaughtered for a feast, and would that even work? Truth be told, she had not the stomach for it. But she must lead them forward, and it was best to do so without them having any doubts about her. She spread her wings, making herself larger, and, she hoped, more the leader this small band of heroes needed.

"Even now the crow feeds off the Kiamah's power, though my own power is the greater for our defeat of him. The crow is subdued by his defeat, but he is still a god." She paused for a moment, and in the silence the beat of the Kiamah's heart drew her attention skyward. *His life's blood passes through there*, thought she. "The cormorant taught us," and here the voice of the goddess trembled with grief for a moment, "that only a god can kill a god, and this is so, but it might be better said that only a greater god can kill a lesser god."

She moved amongst them as she spoke, letting the serenity of her face shine forth, and using the most dulcet tones of her voice to persuade them. "None of you has the power to kill him," she went on, and she stopped to speak directly to the fisherman, saying "The crow is still a god, and cannot be killed by a mortal man." She moved on to the frigate bird, the serenity of her gaze more than her paramour could meet. "His death is beyond your means as well," said she, "for he is still the Kiamah's favored one, and diminished though he is, he will not succumb to any injury you might deliver to him." At this the frigate bird clawed at the sand, muttering his discontent, until the goddess spoke again.

"I do have the means," said she, though she only guessed this to be so, and would not know if it were true until she put it to the test, "but the need of the moment is to slay the Kiamah beast. The Kiamah threatens all that is, and if he devours the land of the living, as is his intent, we shall all perish. The life or death of the crow will not matter then, and nothing will exist save the beast and his great belly."

All the while the goddess spoke, the crow had been edging his way forward, the better to hear. He was at the end of his tether now, and though he had been silent since his capture, he was no longer subdued in his thoughts. Yes, they had won a great victory over him, and his congress of crows was defeated, their bodies awash on the beach. But he still had all his guile, and he knew that if he could but speak to the Kiamah, he would have his way with the great beast. For the beast was more than a devourer, capable of gnashing to bits all that was with his great teeth, and his great jaws. He was capable of swallowing the material world whole, of this the crow was certain. Had he not already swallowed the spirit world, and all that was within it? Yes he had, *kiaw aw aw*, and what these fools did not realize was the difference between devouring and swallowing. The beast could be led, and when the material world was in his belly alongside the spirit world, the crow would rule all of it as his regent. He would keep the beast sedated, and flatter him as needed, and everyone, man and beast, god and goddess, would bow down to the crow.

"Aw aw aw aw aw," said the crow, and they all turned and looked at him.

"Sorry," he muttered, "I was just clearing my throat." He retreated then, going back to the tree to which he was tethered.

The frigate bird put his mouth to the goddess's ear and said, "I still think we should kill him now. I don't trust him any farther than a mouse can hurl one of its own turds."

The goddess nodded. "First the beast," she whispered back. She bade the frigate bird pull back with the rise of one of her lovely eyebrows, and he did so. Again she looked skyward, where the Kiamah's heart beat on.

"I have a notion as to how to slay the beast," said she. She gathered them all in closer with her wings. "'Twill be best if the crow does not hear what I am about to say . . ."

THEY HAD ALL OF THEM spent the middle part of the day gathering the bodies of the dead crows in their thousands and dumping them on the pyre to burn. It was sobering work, and they spoke little amongst themselves, but at length the sacred fire, which had been smoking and sputtering, burst into flames, and the carnage of the night before was sent the way of all flesh. All the while there were strange rumblings in the air, and ominous clouds gathering in the sky. The pelican reminded them that she had not fed the Kiamah for three days, and he had therefore had no conaria to keep him drowsy.

"If we are successful this evening," the goddess said, "that will not matter."

The crow, for his part, stood muttering and krucking as the day wore on, pecking with his hooded head now and again, as if he sought a meaty morsel to eat, and the frigate bird in particular kept an eye on him. He was planning something, the frigate bird was sure, and he said as much to the fisherman.

"So have I seen," said the fisherman. "If I were he, I would be planning my escape."

By mid-afternoon the beach was nearly clear of dead crows, though more washed ashore on the waves. A storm was gathering to the west, dark-headed clouds piling themselves taller and taller against a sky the color of tarnished pewter. The frigate bird took up a perch where he could keep an eye on the crow, and the fisherman and the pelican, who was in her old woman shape, went off to sleep in the fisherman's house. They were both weary in body and spirit, and they lay down together. The fisherman was mindful of whom he held in his arms, this ancient bird who held within herself the shape of his own beloved. They had been lovers, and each was aware that they might be lovers again with the mere passing of the pelican's wing in front of herself. But for now what they desired was the warmth of each other's embrace, and nothing more.

"What if Cariña comes upon us like this?" said the pelican. "She will be jealous, will she not?"

The fisherman let out a long slow breath. "I am too weary to care," said he, "and we are giving her no cause. Let her join us here, that we might all give ourselves what comfort we can." He held the pelican more tightly in his arms, her capacious bill resting on his cheek. "Or not, if she so chooses." And with that, he let himself drift into sleep, and the pelican followed.

Meanwhile, the goddess and Cariña sat on the driftwood log, the two of them also weary, but each of them too disquieted to sleep. They, too, took note of the gathering storm, glancing up when the distant flash of lightning caught their eyes, and they edged closer together until Cariña laid her head on the shoulder of the goddess. The goddess wrapped her winged arm round the woman, and stroked her hair with her other hand.

"May I speak with you?" Cariña said.

"Of course," said the goddess. She stood now, and put out her hand. "Let us walk together along the shore."

They set off hand in hand, the waters of the inlet calm beside them. "What troubles you, my friend?" the goddess said.

Cariña trembled, holding back tears. Her roiled heart carried her this way and that. When she was near the fisherman she wanted his sheltering arms around her, and yet she had done him such wrong she was not worthy of his touch. Whenever she looked at the crow, hooded and bound, tethered to a tree, she wanted to pound her fists on him one moment, and bed him again the next. At length she spoke. "Was I wrong to love the crow?" she said.

"Oh, Cariña, my friend," the goddess said, "I have forgotten how new you are to all this." Now she faced the woman, and put her hands on Cariña's shoulders. "My dear, dear friend. Understand this: love and desire are two different things. They often travel together, and either one can lead to the other. You desired him, as did I, for he is well-formed, and powerful, and yet so much in need of a woman's tutelage, in so many ways. It is no surprise that we both desired him, and there is no shame in that. But desire will burn itself out over time, and love is what remains, glowing in the embers. And when we truly love someone, then we can bring forth desire from those embers whene'er we want it."

"Is it always so?" the woman asked.

"It is not. It is often the case that desire exhausts itself, and we move on. And when we look back on the object of our desire we can scarcely fathom what it was that overtook us so heartily for a time."

The woman considered this for a moment, turning the thought over in her mind, and looking beneath it, behind it, and beyond it.

"I fear the crow still," she said, "for the beating he gave me. And fear also that I have lost him, and that I shall never win him back. I want him still, and I want the chance to tame him, for I am sure that I could."

The goddess took her friend's hands in hers and said, "You might, if given the proper circumstance. But the time for that is past, and the crow's fate is sealed. Let go of your affections as best you can, and you will suffer less."

The woman's eyes brimmed with tears. She wiped them away, and together they walked on. So much had gone awry, and yet, when she looked back on what she had done, there was little she would change, save the crow delivering his blows to her. And the fisherman—she would never have made him suffer.

"This is the fisherman's tale," she said, "that he loves me still, and has always loved me, and so he desires me still?"

"Just so," said the goddess.

"And yet I have caused him pain," she said, "because I desired the crow more than him."

Now the goddess put an arm round Cariña's shoulders, her wing feathers trailing down her side.

"We want what we want," said she, "and we love whom we love. But we should never let desire rule us."

"And yet it does," said the woman.

"If you let it," said the goddess. "To rise above desire takes discipline, and practice. We must learn to let go of what we want, and at the same time to accept what comes our way."

"I made him suffer," the woman said, "the fisherman, I mean."

"Yes," said the goddess. "'Tis so. But not because you meant him to. And his suffering was not without compensation. The pelican was there to balance the scales."

They walked on farther, the goddess still with her arm across the woman's shoulders, who was comforted enough to follow where her thoughts led.

"Did you love the crow?" said the woman.

"I loved the pleasure we gave each other," said the goddess, "but not the one who gave it to me. And there is nothing wrong in that, to love pleasure for its own sake."

"Why?" said the woman. "Why did you send me to him?"

A bilious wind blew past them, ripe with a smell of rot and putrefaction. The woman wrinkled her nose and covered her mouth with her hand, but then it was gone. The goddess was unperturbed.

"What is that horrid smell?" the woman said.

"The beast awakes, and his foul humors awake with him," said the goddess. The goddess knelt, and she picked up a dead crow, one they had missed earlier. She cradled it in her hands, and she stroked the feathers on the back of its neck with her thumb, smoothing them. "Why did I send you to the crow? Because there was a chance that your desire would have bloomed into love, and your love might have redeemed him," said she, "and if that had happened, we could have spared ourselves a great deal of killing." *And I,* thought the goddess, *could have held on to the creed by which I have lived for a hundred times a hundred years, and saved myself from the grief I feel now.* "But he would not have it so," said she. "He was overcome by his own ambition."

"And by whiskey," said the woman. "'Twas whiskey that made him beat me."

"And for that, I am truly sorry," said the goddess. She gave the dead crow to the woman, who held it as tenderly as the goddess had. Then Dewi Sri stood, wrapping her wings round the woman, and she held her, and hummed a sound that was a balm to the woman's troubled mind.

"I disobeyed you," the woman said, "and for that I am truly sorry."

The goddess gave her the serenity of her smile. "Let us forgive each other our trespasses. I should not have left you here alone."

The goddess put a hand on her belly then, the hope of the future warm beneath her touch. She had sacrificed much for this. She had let evil come to the woman who stood before her.

"The whiskey was the frigate bird's doing," said the goddess. "He never believed that love would redeem the crow, and he sought to finish him more quickly with the poison of strong drink. Though, truth be told, I furthered his plot willingly, and did not foresee the harm that came your way because of it."

They walked now to the sacred fire, and Cariña laid the dead crow to rest on the embers. She thought of how the fisherman had been patient with her in the beginning, yet she had not understood the gift of his patience till now. The dead crow's feathers caught fire, and in the flames she saw the fisherman's anger, and she understood that in his heart he had moved on, and he no longer sought the path that led back to their love. If they were to rekindle that flame, it must be by her desire for him. The dead crow's feathers burned away, and now its flesh began to cook, and she turned from the pyre so as to see it no more. Then the woman and the goddess walked along the shore of the inlet together, holding hands now, and it came to her that the goddess, who had nursed her into being, and taught her how to give pleasure to both a woman and a man, was as true a friend as she might ever hope to have.

"I wanted to prove," Cariña said, "that I . . ." Tears filled her eyes, and her throat grew tight around her voice. "That I was . . . as good a lover as you." Now her tears flowed down her cheeks. "I wanted to tame the crow with my love. And thereby save us all."

The goddess nodded, and she gave her friend's hand a reassuring squeeze. "That was a noble effort, even though it failed. I bear you no ill will because of it."

A distant rumbling came to their ears, and they felt a sudden tremor, a shuddering of the very ground beneath their feet.

"The beast stirs," said the woman. The hairs on her arms prickled, and she held the goddess's arm for comfort.

"We are in danger," said the goddess, "and we shall all of us have to work together to overcome it."

The woman looked about, at the waters of the inlet, where she had gone bathing with the fisherman, at the green forest surrounding them, at the wisp of smoke rising from the fire pit next to the house the fisherman had built. His friendship had also been true. She was in his debt, though she doubted he meant to collect on it. This was the only home she knew, the one he had built for her, and yet she longed to be away from here, to seek her destiny elsewhere.

"What would you have me do?"

"Whatever is asked of you," said the goddess, "but know this: I am old, and my time is near spent. This is the end of an age, and sacrifices will be asked of us. I shall need your aid."

"I am frightened," said the woman.

"With good cause," said the goddess. "But we must do what we are called to do, or many more than ourselves will suffer."

There came then a sound that traveled through the sand, a shattering, cracking, splintering sound that again shook the Isle of the Dead.

"The beast is restless," said the goddess, "and hungry. The moment is coming when we shall have to rise to our best selves."

Swive me, thought the woman. *I fear I left my best self behind when I had my tryst with the crow.*

THE FISHERMAN'S NAP WAS BRIEF, cut short by a tremor that shook the bed beneath him. He rose, and found a spade with which to dig. The goddess and his beloved were nowhere in sight, and the pelican slept on. The cormorant's body was where Dewi had left it, in a corner of his house, beneath a covering of moss. He knelt and pulled the moss back, and there was the cormorant's corpse. His wings were spread. His eyes were closed and sunken in death, and his spectacles, which had never left his bill in life, were there still, but askew.

The fisherman ran his hand along the long graceful curve of his friend's neck. He had watched the battle the night before from one of the pinnacles at the mouth of the inlet. The battle was fought aloft, out of the reach of his blade, and so he'd had naught to do, once he'd dropped the net and captured what crows he could, but bear witness to the cormorant's ferocious attack. In his guise as the greatest of great horned owls, an owl as big as a barn, he had shown the courage of a seasoned soldier. "I shall never forget you," said the fisherman, wishing that his friend's corpse still had the capacity to hear him. "I underestimated you, and for that, I offer my regrets." He did not wipe away the tears that fell from his cheeks, and he let them drip as an offering onto the cormorant's feathers. He covered his friend again with moss, and then he stood, and took up his spade again.

He went to the edge of the forest, and he chose a spot beneath the shade of an old grandfather of a cedar tree. He slipped the sharp edge of his spade into the dirt, and he began to dig a proper hole. He took his time, cutting the sides in plumb and true, doing the last good thing a man could do for a fallen comrade.

By the time he was finished, the others had joined him, the frigate bird leaving his watchful perch above the crow, the pelican, in her old-woman shape, carrying a bundle of moss, and the goddess and the woman bearing the body of the cormorant on their shoulders. His spectacles were still perched on his bill, and before they lowered him into the grave, the goddess gently took them from the place they had occupied for a hundred times a hundred years. They wrapped him with moss, and set him in his final resting place, and they stood around his grave.

"He was the least likely of heroes," said the frigate bird, "yet he saved us all."

The goddess hummed a mournful tune, and they all joined in, and then one by one they each threw a handful of dirt atop his corpse.

"Good-bye, friend cormorant," said the fisherman. "You shall be sorely missed."

They all murmured their assent. The goddess handed the cormorant's spectacles to the fisherman. "It comes to me now," said she, "that these should be in your hands." The fisherman took them, and like the others, he wept.

THE CROW HEARD THE WHISPER of the frigate bird's wings when he flew off his perch, and at this, his spirits rose. While his captors busied themselves with burying the cormorant, the crow, though he could not see them, listened to the sound of their conversation, which was too far away for him to hear what was said, yet close enough that he might divine where their attention lay. Most times he stood still, but when he heard the sobs of the pelican, he clawed at the rope that tethered him. Strand by strand he worried it, pulling it apart and sawing his way through with a claw, until he heard them heading for their fire.

Now he stood still. The frigate bird had not returned to his perch, and the crow kicked sand over his tether where he had compromised it. He flexed his wings against the rope that bound them to his body, as he had been doing all day long, loosening his bonds. Better to flee blind than to remain here. He would run, he would fly, and when he was out of their reach he would work the hood off his head. Too long had he plotted with the Kiamah to be defeated now.

He would have his revenge on all of them, that dung fly the fisherman, that dastardly frigate bird, that traitorous pelican, and that watercolor wife, Cariña. Let the beast devour them between his gnashing teeth, after he swallowed the material world.

And for Dewi Sri, that tickle-tail strumpet, he reserved a special fate. He would break her wings so that she could not fly. He would tie her to a gibbet, and tear her eyelids from her eyes, and force her to watch the Kiamah swallow the world. Her bleeding, bald eyes would be unwilling witnesses to the deaths of her friends. He would rip her still beating heart from her chest, and the last thing she would ever see would be King Crow gobbling it down before her very eyes.

He must remember, before he killed the fisherman, to have him build the gibbet.

NOW THEY ALL, SAVE THE frigate bird, stood around the fisherman's fire. It was late in the day, the sun almost disappeared in the eastern sky. The strange rumblings in the air and beneath their feet had gone on all afternoon, leaving them pensive and troubled. The sky to the west was blacker than a tyrant's heart and split with lightning, though the air on the Isle of the Dead was eerily still.

No one had spoken for a long time. A sudden gust of wind made the fire burn bright, and then the air stilled again and grew heavy. The frigate bird, wings wide, swooped in from a scouting flight over the Sea of Bones, and joined them in their silence. A few wayward drops of rain, harbingers of the storm to come, fell on their heads, and stirred them from their brooding.

"The seas must be rough out there," the fisherman said. "Will the canoe survive the crossing this eve?"

"Let the canoe see to itself," the goddess said. "We must slay the beast as soon as the sun sets."

"Rough seas and more," said the frigate bird. "There are splinters of wood flying about like daggers in the winds aloft, more proof that the beast is awake."

"Splinters of wood?" the fisherman said.

"He is chewing his way through the log upon which he sits," said the goddess. "And what he swallows enters his belly through the far corner of the sky."

"Perhaps," the pelican said, and then paused to make the sound of a fart, "some roughage will do his digestion good." She offered them all her skew-whiff smile, and they returned it with a brief chortle of glee.

Away from them, at the edge of the forest, the crow continued his krucking and muttering. The frigate bird returned to him, accompanied by the fisherman, and they looked him up and down. He held his wings flexed so as to hide any slack he had made in his bonds, and he stood atop the spot in the sand where he had covered his tether.

"Am I to starve to death?" said the crow, "or might I have some morsel to eat?"

The fisherman looked down the beach toward the pyre. "There's nothing cooked but crow," said he, a cruel smile forming on his lips. "A proper feast for the likes of you. Shall I fetch you some?"

The crow stood silent at this, not deigning to take the bait the fisherman put before him. Then he bowed his head ever so slightly, as if he were humbled. "I deserve that riposte, I suppose," said the crow. "Might I have some water, at the least?"

"Clever crow," said the frigate bird. "You want us to remove your hood, so that you might work your magic upon us. But we are not fools." He turned to the fisherman and said, "Give me your shoulders to stand on, and I will fly to yonder perch, and watch this foul bird from there."

The fisherman did as he was bade, and then returned to his

fire. The crow listened to his footsteps until they could not be heard. "When aw-aw-all is said and done," he muttered, "we shall see who's the bigger fool."

THE SUN WAS SET, AND as the night grew dark, the thump of the Kiamah's heart grew louder. It emerged in the gloom above them like a dark star, a throbbing bit of darkness even darker than the night. The fisherman gazed up at it, as if it were the pole star, and he must navigate a great tempest by it. The others, too, Dewi Sri, Cariña, and the pelican, wearing her old woman shape, looked up, their fears writ deep on all their furrowed brows.

"The hour has come," said Dewi Sri. She hummed a low tone, as much to calm herself as the others, and she formed the abhaya mudra to ward off fear, her hand open, her fingers pointed upward at the night.

The frigate bird swooped in then, wings wide, and settled himself on the driftwood log. "Fate is upon us," he said. "The only way out is through." He put his wing across the fisherman's shoulders. "Had the gods given me hands," said he, "I would go in your place."

The fisherman smiled ruefully at his friend. "If the gods had given you hands," he said, "you would be an even greater pirate than you are. There wouldn't be enough booty in all the world for you."

The frigate bird's throat pouch swelled at these words, for he loved his friend the fisherman, and he knew the peril before him was great. If things went badly, they might never speak again.

"Are you ready?" said the goddess.

"I am," said the fisherman. He checked the blade of his knife with his thumb, for he had been honing it while the sun set. He tucked the knife back into its sheath, and slung it round his neck on its cord. His gaze fell upon Cariña, who looked back at him with such sorrow in her eyes that he went to her and took her in his arms. She held him then with more love than she had felt since she first emerged from her clamshell. "Tell me," she whispered, "that our story is not yet over."

The fisherman was taken aback by her request, which belied feelings he thought she did not hold. "Of course our story goes on," he whispered. 'Twas a reassurance he offered more to meet her need than because he knew it to be true. Would the gods be so cruel as to rekindle her love for him now? For there, a mere arm's length away, stood the pelican, with longing in her eyes. He scarcely knew what his own feelings were. He had a monster to slay.

The goddess bent forward and braced her hands on her knees. The fisherman climbed onto her back, wrapping his arms round her shoulders, and clasping them below her neck. Then Dewi Sri beat her wings and rose, circling the inlet, flying ever upward in a spiral.

The rest of them watched from the fisherman's fire. The fate of the world was in the hands of their two companions now.

And as they watched, the crow, ever stealthy, clawed at the rope that tethered him to the tree. There was but a strand left to cut. His freedom was nigh.

THEY FLEW ACROSS THE INLET, the goddess and the fisherman, over the chop of wind-frothed waves, rising higher and higher, the fire below them shrinking to a spark. In the gathered darkness the pyre was now the greater light, its mound of embers, the last remains of the congress of crows, glowing red.

The fisherman's arms were wrapped round the shoulders of the goddess, and he felt the great strength of her wing muscles beating against his chest. She had shown herself to be formidable during the battle, and she was formidable now.

"You've no doubt been high in the riggings during a storm," said the goddess.

"Of course."

"That will serve you well," she said, "in what we are about to do."

The beating of the Kiamah's heart grew louder and louder as they rose, until there was no other sound. The goddess flew higher still, and now above them the fisherman saw the Kiamah's heart. It was as big as the house he had built, and it pulsed like a thing alive unto itself only. It was hung from the roof of the belly with a cord as thick as the fisherman's body.

Now the goddess flew round the cord, and they landed atop the beating heart. The heart thumped beneath them as if it were trying to shake them off, and the fisherman slid sideways off Dewi's back as she fell to her knees. They were in a flat spot, the heart itself sloping away on all sides, the Isle of the Dead far, far below them. The cord was a body's length away, and the goddess worked her way forward on her hands and knees, her movements timed for the rest spots between each thump of the beast's heart, the fisherman following her. When the goddess reached the cord, she pulled herself upright.

"You do the cutting," shouted the goddess, "and I shall steady you." She reached a hand out to the fisherman and pulled him to his feet. The fisherman drew his blade, but the next thud of the beast's heart nearly threw him off. Only the goddess's firm grip on his arm saved him.

"Quickly," she cried. She had one arm wrapped as far round the cord as she could reach, the rest of her wing stretching out beyond, the strength of her wing muscles serving her well to keep her purchase. With her other arm she held the fisherman round his waist. "Now," she shouted, "I cannot hold you thus for long."

The cord was tough, but the fisherman's knife was keen. He drew a slice halfway round, the flesh of the cord parting. The slice was a knuckle deep. He cut again, and again, and each time deeper, but it was slow going, and he felt as if he were trying to cut down an oak tree with naught but a penny knife. His other arm was wrapped round Dewi's waist, and they were locked together in a kind of danse macabre, urging the Kiamah on to his death. He had the slice deep enough to bury his hand in it when he hit blood. It spurted up his arm, hot and as black as tar. He nearly dropped his blade in surprise. The goddess tightened her grip on his waist. "Keep going," she shouted. "You must finish."

The fisherman sliced ever deeper with his knife, the blood now a veritable fountain, great gouts of it splashing down at their feet, and pouring off into the night. The smell of it was sour and smoky, and it burned in their nostrils. Together they worked their way round the cord, slicing through its flesh to the hollows of the blood vessels within, but the more he sliced, the more the heart tilted. It hung by less and less, although its relentless beating kept on. Their footing grew ever more treacherous, slickened as it was by the beast's blood. Only the goddess's great strength kept them from falling, but the strain robbed her face of all its serenity, and she grimaced with the effort. Sweat poured down her forehead and stung her eyes, leaving tracks in the sooty gray pallor there. And still the fisherman cut.

BLACK BLOOD FELL OUT OF the night sky and landed close by the glowing pyre.

"It's there the beast's heart will fall," said the frigate bird. "We'd best keep our distance."

Cariña wrinkled her nose. "There's a bitter smell in the wind."

The pelican nodded. "Like the smell of hair burning on the pyre," said she.

It was then that the crow clawed through the last strand of the rope. He sniffed the air, his sense of smell quickened by the many blind hours he had spent with the hood over his head. That way was the fisherman's fire, where his captors were gathered. Over there was the pyre. Behind him, the forest. He could not fly, and to stumble through the forest, blind as he was, promised a quick recapture. He began to edge his way toward the pyre, moving slowly so as not to draw attention to himself, staying close to the edge of the forest so that he might not be seen. Step by slow step he moved, the rope around his leg dragging behind to its frayed end.

The frigate bird looked to where the crow had stood, checking on his captive. He peered into the dark night, and saw nothing.

"Look sharp," he said to his companions. "Methinks the crow has escaped."

They all looked then, and it was Cariña who spotted him. He was some distance down the beach, slinking along, his body bent forward so that it was almost parallel with the ground.

"There," she said, pointing.

"Swiftly, but silently," said the frigate bird, the tip of his wing to his bill. They all three set out, their footfalls silent in the soft sand, but then the frigate bird had a better thought, and he climbed up on Cariña's back and launched himself into the air. He beat his wings once, twice, thrice, and then he was upon the crow, his claws digging into the crow's back, the crow twisting and turning and trying to throw him off. The crow fell to his side and rolled, knocking the frigate bird loose. He rolled to his feet and hopped off in that slow gallop peculiar to crows, two-stepping his way down the beach. The frigate bird lay on the sand, the wind knocked out of him.

Cariña and the pelican had caught up by now, Cariña holding a stout piece of driftwood that she had snatched up as she ran. It was the pelican who saw the rope trailing behind the crow. She grabbed it with both hands and pulled, and the crow, midhop, fell to the ground. He rose again, but now the pelican had him, and she dug her heels into the sand and kept him from fleeing. He was almost to the pyre. Cariña caught up to him, with no thought in her head other than the chase, and with all of her hurt and anger at what the crow had done to her, beating her in his drunken rage, all of her longing for love, and her ire and vexation at not finding it where she sought, all of this in her arms, she swung the club and smote him down.

The crow fell to the sand senseless, but still breathing. The woman sobbed, great shudders of feeling shaking her body. She dropped her club, and the pelican joined her, putting her arms round her friend. But even though the woman was overcome, the pelican's smile was broad, for she found that she loved this feeling that came with running toward danger. Tripping the crow, holding him back, and watching Cariña lay him low, made her feel that she was the most alive she had ever been.

The frigate bird caught up to them. He looked at the crow, and he looked at the pyre, and he looked at the black blood falling out of the sky and marking the sand next to it. He looked up at the night sky, and he saw that the Kiamah's heart was falling.

The frigate bird snatched up the rope with his beak, and tried to drag the crow forward. "Quickly!" he said. He pointed with a wingtip at the falling heart of the beast, and then at the ground next to the pyre, covered with the beast's black blood. "Drag him there!" he shouted. Cariña hesitated, still afflicted, the pelican thought, by her affections for the crow. But the pelican did not hold back, and she grabbed the crow by his feet, and dragged him to where the frigate bird pointed.

"Leave him!" the frigate bird yelled. "Run!"

The pelican looked up and saw the heart bearing down on her, and that glance upward nearly cost her life. She leapt away headlong, and felt the wind of the falling heart on the soles of her feet. So close was it. So near to death.

She felt the thud of the heart's landing in her chest as she lay on the sand. She heard the stomach-churning crunch of the crow's demise. "Huzzah!" she called out, "I'm all right!" She stood, and turned to look.

The heart was enormous. She walked around it to where her companions stood, Cariña with her lips parted, and a face ready to laugh or cry or both at once, the frigate bird with his head cocked to the side, the better to see what lay before him.

"Ye gods," the frigate bird said, "it's as big as a house."

The crow was not to be seen, save for his feet, which stuck out from under the beast's heart on one side, and, less than a fathom away, the tip of his beak. They stared in silence, all of them with breath held, waiting to see if the crow would move, for they knew that the fisherman had tried to kill him, and could not, and that the crow had sprung back to life time and again.

The pelican then spied a bloody bit of gristle on the sand, just beyond the tip of the crow's beak. *His syrinx*! she thought, *the secret to singing forth the souls of the dead*, and so she gobbled it down. Now she would have the power, and she would use it more wisely than he.

"Is he dead?" Cariña asked.

"May it be so," the frigate bird said. "The crow and the Kiamah both."

He bent down and pecked a vicious peck at the crow's feet. They lay there, as still as death, save for the welling up of blood. The frigate bird pecked and pecked again, drawing more blood, and more blood, until the crow's feet were covered in ruby red. Still there was no response.

He stood. "We've killed him," he said. "It must be so." Yet still he stretched his neck out, and turned his head from side to side, looking at the crow's feet with first one eye, and then the other.

"Surely the heart of the Kiamah beast is god enough to kill the crow," the pelican said. They all nodded at one another, hope rising in them. They had done it.

The goddess, with the fisherman on her back, landed next to them, and they were both covered in the beast's black blood. They took note of the crow's feet, and of the others gawking, and of the blood on the crow's feet and the frigate bird's bill. The fisherman slid down and planted his feet on the firm ground again.

"Both of them?" the fisherman said. "We've slain two tyrants with one blow?"

The goddess looked upward into the dark night and felt a great relief. This is what the Turropsi had asked of her, and she had done it. "'Tis a fortune beyond good. We are all of us blessed."

"It took more than fortune to do this," said the pelican. "We all had a hand in it."

"It's true," said the frigate bird, "for we gave the crow some encouragement as to where he might situate himself to best witness the end of the beast." His bloody bill stretched wide in a piratical grin.

Cariña let out a great sigh and turned away, to hide the tumult within her from the fisherman. She had wanted her lover back, but could not have him without his darker side. Her lover, her tormentor. And now he was dead at her hand. She was dizzied, her head spinning, and she sat down hard on the sand.

The fisherman thought to comfort her, but did not, for he knew what she wanted to hide from him, and was wounded still by her desire for the crow. Moreover, the death of the crow made him want to shout *huzzah*, and to hide that feeling from his beloved was a favor he chose not to grant. The pelican, for her part, felt something she had never felt before. She felt triumphant. She had helped to kill the crow, and though killing was a bad thing, the death of the crow was not.

It was at this moment that the Kiamah's heart began to beat again.

"Curse me!" shrieked the goddess. "After all we have done the beast still lives?"

"So it would appear," said the fisherman. He looked at his blood-drenched arms, and he, too, sat himself down on the sand, too weary to shed tears.

"Why does his heart still beat?" the woman asked.

The wings of the goddess drooped, and in the furrows of her worried brow, she showed her great age.

"Because," said Dewi Sri, "I am not a greater god than he."

THEY SAT AROUND THE FISHERMAN'S fire with the beating of the Kiamah's heart louder than ever before, and a constant reminder that they had failed to slay the beast. The crow's death, which might have buoyed their spirits, was as nothing if the Kiamah still lived. From time to time they heard in the far distance a splintering sound, and felt the ground beneath then tremble and shift, and they knew the beast was hungry, and trying to eat his way into the land of the living. To the west they heard the sound of waves pounding on the beach beyond the mouth of the inlet, and they knew the storm would soon arrive.

Their only plan was to wait for the canoe of the dead to arrive, to gather as many conaria as they might, and then to feed them to the Kiamah beast so as to sedate him again. What would happen then they did not know, and it was this that kept them silent, most especially Dewi Sri, who was as forlorn as she had ever been in all her days and nights. She was their leader, and she had failed. She could not fathom what the Turropsi wanted of her, what more she might have done. Did they still want her to kill Cariña and the fisherman? No, their gambling had exposed how hollow their dicta were. She was responsible for her own fate. They all were.

When the pelican asked if she should sing to the dead that night to free their souls, the goddess barely raised her head.

"Yes, I suppose," said she.

The pelican went off by herself to practice. Her song, which she devised in the moment, was made of clownish honks and squawks and high-pitched barks, a song that sounded like laughter, and she imagined that when the dead heard it, they too would fall to laughing, and as they laughed their souls would creep up their throats and spill out onto the sand. The dead would then stare at their souls with foolish grins on their faces, happy as only the half-witted can be happy, and the pelican would ask them to stand in a line and join hands, and when they did, she would lead them to the sacred fire.

There they would form a circle around the red glow of the embers, and the dead, cold as they were, would be drawn to the heat, and one by one and many by many they would lie down in the embers and catch fire. Their souls would by then be burrowed into the sand, soon to be safe inside their newly formed shells, as happy as only clams can be. Their bodies would roast away, and no one would be made to suffer. She had the power now, and this thought made her breast swell with pride, for she would rule the Isle of the Dead with a kindness and a benevolence never before seen, not even when Raven ruled.

She returned to the fisherman's fire after a time, the wind now blowing stiffly, and her head still filled with thoughts of how she would act as ruler. Should she appear in her pelican form, or in her old-woman shape, or might she stand before the dead in the shape of Cariña, who was more comely than the other two? Her thoughts were interrupted by rain, which fell in scattered drops at first. They all looked up, and lightning split the darkness above them, and then came a great clap of thunder. The storm was upon them, and the thunder was so loud it drowned out even the beating of the beast's heart. They all stood, but before they could make their way into the fisherman's house, the fish eagles swooped in out of the darkness and landed before them.

"The canoe," the she-eagle said. "Capsized."

"The dead," the he-eagle said, "gone overboard."

"Failed," the she-eagle said, her eyes sad as she gazed at her husband.

"As never before," the he-eagle said.

They stepped into the light of the fire, and now our small band of heroes saw that their bodies were riddled with splinters of wood.

"Strange times," the she-eagle said.

"End times," the he-eagle said. "The sky rains wood."

They were covered in blood, both of them, and their bodies trembled. The wind drove rain sideways, blowing harder than ever, and all of them leaned into it lest they be knocked over. From out of the storm-dark sky a great splinter slammed into the sand and stuck there, quivering like an arrow. It was taller than any of them. More splinters filled the wind, mixed in with the rain. They covered their faces and ran into the fisherman's house. There the walls and the roof protected them, though the wind was already peeling bits of the roof away.

The storm beat at the house from the outside, while inside they huddled together, the shutters shuttered, seeking what comfort they could from each other's company. None of them knew what would happen, but they all felt that the end of everything was at hand. The fish eagles nestled together in a corner, leaning against each other for support, the she-eagle with her wings round her husband. She rocked him gently, as if he were a nestling still in downy feathers. The rest of them, save the pelican, fell into fits of sleep, for they were all exhausted. The pelican wept silently, for she had been counting on her moment of glory as the ruler of the Isle of the Dead. Now, it seemed, that moment would never come. The canoe was no more.

And all those souls, lost forever. 'Twas almost as much a horror as when the crow ate them. The pelican wept, for the lost souls, for the thousands of crows dead in the battle, for the fisherman's suffering, for all of it, even the crow himself. Her own sorrow was the least of it. And yet she cried for that as well. But at last, hollowed out by the shedding of the great rabble of her tears, she gathered herself and went to the fish eagles, and offered to vuln herself, to heal them with a drop of her own blood.

The she-eagle shook her head. "Too, too late." Her voice was tremulous. Slivers of wood scattered the ground before her.

The pelican stretched her neck out, the better to look at the he-eagle. The she-eagle pointed with her bill at her husband's neck, where a large splinter pierced him. Much blood had flowed from that wound.

"You should have told me," the pelican cried. "I might have saved him."

"He died almost as soon as we nested here," the she-eagle said.

"I have the power to save lives," the pelican said. She was shaking, so bereft did she feel. She lived to serve, and had been denied the chance twice now in a matter of hours. "That fellow over there, the fisherman, he lives because my blood saved him when he washed up on our shore." She shook her head. "I could have saved your husband. I could have."

The she-eagle looked at her with sad, wet eyes. "Thank you," she said. "My husband," she said, rocking him still, "all done with living."

The pelican bent her neck and pushed the tip of her bill into her chest feathers.

"Thank you," the she-eagle said, "but no."

"No?" the pelican said. "You must, or you too will die."

The she-eagle shook her head, her round eyes fierce, and brooking no cajolement from the pelican.

"End times," she said. "No more living." Her hooked beak was built to tear fish apart, for such was the way of things, that the living fed on the living. Now the she-eagle, her beak delicate and precise, pulled a sliver from her flesh with it, and let it fall to the ground.

"Help me join my husband," said she.

The pelican watched her pull more slivers. Fresh blood flowed from the wounds, staining her feathers. The pelican had spent her days healing her friends when the occasion arose, rare though that was on the Isle of the Dead, and the healing of the fisherman had been one of her finest moments. But now this fish eagle wanted not to be healed, but to be helped on to her death.

On the Isle of the Dead the dying of all those people had been a thing that happened elsewhere, and she had been an instrument in the cycle of life. But so much had happened, with the crow, with the goddess, with Cariña. The pelican had been to war, and she had felt a new kind of love when she lay herself down with the fisherman. She was not the same pelican she had been before he arrived. She was the pelican who had snatched up the crow's broken tether and brought him down. Yes, yes she was. She could do this.

She leaned in, her eyes on the she-eagle's, who nodded at her, yes, I really mean it, yes, help me. Such a personal thing it was, to bring about the death of another. The pelican tried to pluck a sliver from the she-eagle's breast with her bill, but she had trouble distinguishing between the she-eagle's feathers and the slivers. She kept trying, anxious to be helpful in any way she could, rooting around as if she were looking for feather mites, but her efforts were so inept as to be clownish. The she-eagle opened her beak and chir-chir-chirupped at her, *chir-chir-chirrup, chirrup-chirrup-chirrup*, and the pelican understood that even in this dire moment, there was room for laughter. She honked her own laughter back at the she-eagle. Then she stepped back, and she waved her wing in front of herself, and took on her old-woman shape. She used her hands to pluck slivers from the she-eagle's flesh, and the she-eagle looked back at her with gratitude in her eyes.

The pelican pulled a particularly stout sliver near the she-eagle's heart, and now her blood began to spurt in time with her heartbeat. The pelican reached her hand out to stop the blood, but then caught herself, and pulled back.

"Yes," the she-eagle said. "Let it flow."

The pelican sat down beside the she-eagle, and put her hand on her head, soothing her, she hoped, as she sped on her way to death. The she-eagle closed her inner eyelids, rendering her eyes cloudy. Her breathing grew rapid, and then slowed. She let her head drop down, overcome now with a great fatigue. The spurts of blood slowed, and then stopped, and the she-eagle's eyes grew dim, and she was gone.

The pelican reached out to her, her hand trembling, until her fingertips touched the delicate skin of her outer eyelids. She closed them, one last good thing to do for a fallen comrade. She took the two bodies, he-eagle and she-eagle, and laid them down together in the corner where they had nestled. She took the moss from the bed where she had slept, and she covered them with it. She bade them a silent farewell, and she wondered where their spirits might be heading, for the way of things that had been the Isle of the Dead was no more.

The rest of her companions slept, but she could not join them. Too many thoughts tumbled through her head. They had no way to sedate the Kiamah beast. The goddess, she was sure, was out of plans. None of them was god enough to slay the beast, but perhaps she could reason with him. She knew him better than any of them.

Outside the storm slowly blew itself out, and the raining down of splinters abated. It would be best, the pelican thought, if she went all on her own to visit the Kiamah. The beast trusted her, and she him, and she must now use that trust to persuade him not to devour the material world. She was certain that he ate things out of habit rather than hunger. She would promise him more sea grass, to soothe his troubled belly. He needed roughage to aid his digestion, but it needn't be from the driftwood log. If his belly were less bilious, his own good nature would emerge.

She would tame the beast with her love, and thereby save them all.

While the others slept in the light of dawn, the pelican flew to the far corner of the sky, and entered the beast's throat. She flew upward through the familiar passage, singing a soft lullaby as she went, and crawled along the slab of meat that was the beast's tongue. He seemed to be at rest. She took note of the splinters of wood stuck between his molars. Perhaps he was like a puppy, chewing on things he should not chew, but out of mere boredom rather than any real malice toward the material world. He was a reasonable fellow, she was sure of that, for in all the times she had been here, he had never once tried to eat her. Now she crawled out between his teeth, and stood on the tip of his tail, and in her Cariña shape she sang a hymn of praise to the beast.

> *O Kiamah, O Kiamah,*
> *you are the beast most beloved!*
> *How often you give us delight,*
> *devouring all within your sight*
> *O Kiamah, O Kiamah,*
> *you are the beast most beloved!*[¶¶]

The beast raised his lazy eyelids, which he never completely closed, and he looked at the pelican with his lurid green eyes, and he felt around with his tongue for the treats the pelican usually brought him.

"How are you this fine day?" said the pelican.

"Mmmfh," said the beast. "Where are my tasty tidbits?"

"Well, my pet," said the pelican, "it seems that there's been a storm, and the canoe of the dead has been capsized."

"Mm-hmmf," said the beast. "Then find me something else to eat."

The pelican took on her pelican shape, and flew to the spot above and behind the beast's eye where his ear hole was.

"Listen, my pet," said the pelican. "I've come to warn you. Bad things will happen if you eat your way into the material world."

"Bad things? What sort of bad things?"

The pelican had no ready answer to the Kiamah's question, and so she decided in this case, it was best to lie to him. A good lie might save his life.

"The earth shakes, and rivers run backward. Kings fall down from their thrones, and—umm, umm—and the temples of the gods are torn asunder!"

"Mmmmfh," said the beast. "You see how powerful I am."

"But people will be hurt!"

"Mm-hmm," said the beast. "Why should I care about that?"

¶¶ To the tune of "O Tannenbaum."

"Oh, greedy-guts," said the pelican. "Of course you care. You have a great big heart."

The Kiamah beast licked the tip of his tail with his tongue to soothe himself. "What I have of late," he said, "is a great big case of heartburn. What is going on down there on the Isle of the Dead? I feel a discombobulation inside of me."

The pelican took on her Cariña shape, and scratched the beast around his ear hole, something that he had enjoyed in the past. She really had not thought this through. They had tried to kill him, cutting his heartstring the way they had, and he felt the injury of that, even though he did not know the cause. She had bought his affection with grisly treats, but without the canoe of the dead, there was nothing to harvest for him. She must find a way to reach him.

The pelican took on her pelican shape and flew to the tip of the beast's tail. There she shifted into her Cariña shape, and she swayed her hips back and forth. The beast took no notice, not that he ever had, but she needed his full attention. She pulled her sarong down, wearing it round her hips as the goddess did, baring her breasts. The fisherman was very fond of her breasts, and she hoped that the Kiamah would like them too.

"Hmmmmf," said the beast, "you look like a tasty morsel." His tongue came out from between his lips, ready to slurp her up, and the pelican ran backward. This was not going at all well.

She made one last attempt to reason with him. "Listen, my pet," she said, "you can't go on the rest of your life eating everything there is. Sooner or later you'll run out of things to eat, and then what will you do?"

The beast opened his jaws wide and yawned. His mouth was gargantuan, and there were scrapes on the inside of it, no doubt from the wood he had been eating. The pelican looked down at the driftwood log, and she could see there was a deep gouge in it, with the beast's toothmarks roughening either side, and the wood within it splintered and torn. At the bottom of the gouge there was a long crack through which she could see the sky of the material world, with clouds passing by, and far, far below them was the world itself, where lived all its countless beings, and all of them at risk. A cloud leaked up through the crack, and with it the earthy smell of rain not yet fallen.

Time was running out, for the beast was about to break through, and when he did, he would swallow it all, just as he had swallowed the spirit world. She had failed to stop him then. She must not fail now.

"What would you have me do?" said he. "I am growing ever more hungry, and it is my nature to eat whatever is before me." The beast licked his lips, and then he bared his fearsome teeth at her. "You, for example, are before me right now."

What could she offer him? She backed away from him, but there was really no escaping his reach. He could eat her up this moment, and then all would be lost.

And then it came to her, that she was thinking like a woman, when she should be thinking like a pelican. She was, after all, a goddess. A lesser goddess than Dewi Sri, but she was goddess enough to have just what the beast needed.

She ran forward to the tip of his tail, toward the very mouth that had swallowed the spirit world. She was done with reason, and she saw only one way to end this. Old greedy-guts, she would trick him. She took on her pelican shape, and she vulned herself, and she let drip a drop of her own blood onto the tip of the beast's tail. She sang the song the crow had taught her, and the drop of her blood became a good-sized puddle. Then she stood back, and called out to the Kiamah beast, telling him to lick his tail, for there was a special treat for him there. His long tongue slithered out from between his fangs, and though the puddle of blood was tiny on the enormity of his tail, his tongue was dexterous, and sensitive. He found her blood, and he slurped it down, and it was good.

"Mmm-hmmm," said the beast, "delicious. Is there any more?"

"Yes, lambkin. Does it calm you, and soothe you, and staunch the hunger in your belly?"

"Mmm, perhaps." The beast ran his tongue round the tip of his tail, licking at the pelican's feet, and she couldn't help herself: she laughed at his tickling touch. "Let me have some more," said the beast, "and I will tell you how much it soothes me."

The pelican vulned herself again, and this time she let more of her blood flow, for the beast was large, and she wished to give him every opportunity to take the bait. Again she sang, and again the beast licked at the blood on his tail, beslobbering himself, and again he slurped it down. "Yes," said he, "it is very soothing. A bit more, and I shall be ever so much better."

The pelican vulned herself yet again. She backed away from his slavering tongue, leaving a trail of blood, singing it larger, and the Kiamah swallowed more of his tail as he licked it clean. *That's it, old greedy-guts,* she thought, *keep going. Keep going, and you'll swallow enough of your own tail to choke yourself to death.* A bad, bad, terrible thing, to kill the Kiamah this way, but his death would be a good thing. She served the greatest good for the greatest number, and that was all that mattered. The beast ran his agile tongue round and round, slurping her blood in, groaning with pleasure all the while. So much pleasure that his lurid green eyes closed all the way.

Ichorous love, that was her weapon. The beast, born from the bloodlust of fallen warriors, had never known a mother's love. His tongue had yet to miss a drop of the pelican's blood. What better way to trick this motherless beast than to bleed for him?

She let a great deal more of her blood drip onto him, smearing it with her breast as she backed along his tail. She was getting just the slightest bit dizzy with the giving of so much of it. She pulled her bill from her chest, and her bleeding stopped. The beast opened his jaws, and he drew more of his long tail into his mouth, the better to suck it clean. She backed away from his sucking lips, and she watched as they came closer and closer to her, following the trail of her blood. Then he coughed a muffled cough, and he began to pull, ever so slowly, his long tail back out of his mouth.

There's no turning back now, she thought. "Oh, greedy-guts," she said, "you are the greatest beast that ever lived. You can do this. Keep going." His lurid green eyes opened, and in them she saw his lust to swallow all in his path.

"Mmmmffh," said the beast, "I eat, therefore I am." Though with his tail so deep in his mouth, this last bit sounded more like "Um-hmmf, furm-furm um-um."

"Oh yes," said the pelican, who had learned, over the course of a thousand times a thousand years, some Latin from the cormorant. *"Ego manducare, ergo sum."*

"Mmm-hmmm," said the beast. The tip of his tail must be at the top of his throat now. Her mind was growing fuzzled, and she could no longer remember the song, but she had to keep the beast swallowing, she knew that much. She lay her breast on his tail, and she plunged her bill into her chest, and she bled for him, dragging herself backward. This time she let the blood flow and flow.

THE SUN WAS AT ITS zenith over the fisherman's house, and sunlight filled the room inside. Dewi Sri, the frigate bird, the fisherman, and Cariña lay where they had slept, in a jumbled row of arms and wings and legs and bodies. The ribald silk coverlet was in disarray, their limbs woven under and over it, and they had all of them been too exhausted to enact any of the many positions of coupling depicted on it. Now their eyes were open, and they lay on their backs staring up at the raddled roof, which was full of holes where the storm had torn away the thatch. The day's task was before them, to slay the Kiamah beast, and the mood was somber, for none of them had the slightest idea how they might accomplish this.

It was the fisherman who rose first. "Let's be off," said he. "The sooner we leave, the sooner we can put this foul task behind us."

"Has anyone seen the pelican?" asked Cariña.

They had not. She was not in the scrape of a nest she had made for herself in the sea grass. She was not floating on the waters of the inlet. And she was not flying above, looking to skim a breakfast fish out of the waves. Those who could fly flew, searching for her, and the fisherman and Cariña went into the forest, calling out for her. They did not find her, but when they came upon the crow's pile of shiny things, the fisherman was reminded of the gold brooch he had taken when he first arrived. Now he took it out of his pouch and showed it to Cariña.

"If we make it back to the land of the living, this may be of some use," he said. Cariña nodded, and put her finger to his lips. He was saying they might yet have a future together, and she was glad to hear it.

"When we make it back," said she. "Not if." He tucked the brooch back into the pouch, and they headed back to the inlet, where their companions waited. No one had seen any sign of the pelican.

"Where could she be?" asked Cariña.

The goddess and the frigate bird looked at each other, and they looked at the far corner of the sky.

"She's gone on ahead," said the frigate bird.

The goddess nodded. "I fear for her life," said she.

Icy tendrils of fear slithered round each other inside the fisherman's belly when he heard this. "Then we must make haste," said he. He had buried his friend the cormorant only the day before, and he had no wish to bury another friend so soon. Especially not the pelican, who had loved him so ardently in her guise as his beloved.

"Let's be off," the fisherman said again, and then, "Wait." Something told him he might not be returning here. He ran into the house and found the cormorant's spectacles where he had left them on a windowsill. He looked around for something to wrap them in, and spied the ribald silk coverlet. He cut a square from the cloth with his knife, and wrapped the spectacles into a small bindle, and he tied the bindle to his belt. He ran back out and said, "I'm ready."

The goddess bade Cariña to climb aboard her back, and the frigate bird and the fisherman climbed a tree, for the extra loft it would give the frigate bird, and there the fisherman mounted the frigate bird's back. Together they soared off, joining the goddess and Cariña. They flew to the far corner of the sky, where they entered the Kiamah's throat, and made their way up the long neck of the beast until they stood in the cavern that was the back of the beast's mouth. Above them, and behind them, was the beast's blowhole, a passageway that led to a spot at the back of the beast's head. This was to be their escape route, but first they hoped to find the pelican.

"What's that?" said the fisherman.

Something blunt and bulbous was in the Kiamah's mouth, something very large, the tip of which was moving about, touching the beast's molars here and there as if searching for something.

"Mmmffh," the beast said, and then his jaws opened, and they saw that the beast had his own tail in his mouth, and the pelican stood atop it, just beyond his lips. And as they watched she plunged her bill into her bloodied breast and her blood flowed red, and she leaned forward, the better to let it drip onto the beast's tail. The beast closed his lips round his tail then, and the last they saw of the pelican was her feet backing away.

The beast drew more of his tail into his mouth, and its waving, searching tip threatened to beslobber them. They backed away from it, but the tongue sought them out, as if to squash them against the walls of the cavernous mouth. The fisherman stuck his knife into it, and the beast coughed. The tip of his tail receded from them a bit, but then it came toward them again.

"This way," the frigate bird cried, pointing upward, "through the blowhole," he shouted, for the beast's mouth was full of slurping noises, and they could barely hear each other. "Launch me down the beast's throat," he cried, "and then be ready."

"Ready for what?" said the fisherman, but the frigate bird had already sailed away from him, and did not reply.

"Climb on my back," the goddess said to Cariña, and the woman did so. The goddess fluttered her wings, and rose with Cariña, and together they disappeared up the beast's blowhole.

"Ready for this," shouted the frigate bird, who was now gliding back up the throat of the beast, his legs and talons extended, and he snatched the fisherman with those talons, and then flapped his wings mightily, and they too rose through the beast's blowhole.

Now they stood atop the beast's head, and they had a clear view of the pelican. She was backing away from the Kiamah's lips, which swallowed ever more of his own tail, greedy as he was to taste her blood.

The pelican saw them, and she waved, but her wings moved languidly, as if she had all the time in the world. She vulned herself, and her blood flowed, and she pressed her breast against the beast's tail and backed away. The beast's lips followed her.

"We have to save her," the fisherman shouted. He stepped forward, ready to climb down the beast's snout. His shoulders were bloodied from the grip of the frigate bird's talons, but he paid that no mind.

"No," the goddess said. She put her hand on the fisherman's arm. He glared at her, but she answered him with the serenity of her smile, and drew him back. "No," she said again, "we must let the pelican do what she will. Perhaps she has a plan."

"That's it, greedy-guts," they heard the pelican say, "keep going."

Shiny spots flashed in front of the pelican's eyes, and her head began to spin, but she opened her chest, and she let her blood flow. The beast was spinning around her, and her tired, tired head found its way to a resting spot on the Kiamah's tail. She was dying, she knew that, but she thought of the she-eagle, who loved her husband so much she died so that she might join him—what a shiny, shiny thought that was—and she thought of the fisherman, and the love they had shared, and how some day he would join her, though she knew not where.

"Hmmmfh," said the beast, and in a trice the beast drew more of his tail into his mouth, and his fearsome teeth bit down and crushed the pelican. Her head was smashed flat, and ground into the beast's tail. The tip of his tongue found the smudge of feathers and bones and blood that was all that was left of her, and all this he slurped into his mouth.

"Swive me!" the fisherman shouted. "She's gone!"

And still the beast lives, thought the goddess. Was there no killing him, no matter how many might sacrifice their lives?

"Mm-mmffh," said the beast, "delicious," but with his tail in his mouth "delicious" sounded like "mm-mptious."

"I'll kill him!" screamed the fisherman. He drew his knife, and he made to stab at the beast's head, but the frigate bird wrapped his wings round his friend. "You cannot," he said, "so do not draw his attention here."

Cariña wailed, and the fisherman sobbed. The goddess, who felt the need to grieve as keenly as anyone, nonetheless kept her wits about her, and took note of the fact that the beast seemed to be swallowing more and more of himself. She peered down his blowhole, and saw that his tail blocked the bottom of the passage like some enormous earthworm. Perhaps this, she thought, is what the Turropsi have led us to.

Once he had started, the Kiamah could not stop himself, for he was entirely a creature made to swallow whatever went into his mouth. The fisherman mounted the frigate bird, and Cariña mounted the goddess, and they flew circles above the beast, watching and wondering, crying and mourning and marveling all at the same time. Never, in all the days of all their years in the spirit world or the material, were they more alive than they were at that moment, nor ever were they closer to the great mystery of life and death, of destruction and renewal. And so they were filled with awe as well as grief. The great beast swallowed his long tail bit by bit, pulling his hindquarters toward his jaws, his neck turning sideways, his body forming a loop. His hindquarters followed his tail, disappearing between his jaws, his hind legs waggling until they too were swallowed. Then his jaws unhinged themselves and he began to pull his belly down his throat, the loop of his body tightening. The belly, as wide and full as it was, took some considerable time to swallow, but his unhinged jaws gaped, his lips slavered, and his mouth gobbled and gobbled, squeezing the broad girth of his belly tighter and tighter with each ingurgitation, until the beast had swallowed his belly right up to his foreleg pits. His forequarters came next, and with them his leathery wings, long since atrophied, his spine bent double now, his long neck stretched and straining, but with the bulk of his belly now swallowed, the rest came faster, just as a baby is birthed the more quickly once the head has squeezed through, and his neck vanished down his throat, the back of his head inhaled as if it were naught but a bit of popped corn, and the serpentine slither of his tongue with it, then his jaws breaking loose and gobbling themselves up, until his lips turned themselves inside out and swallowed themselves, and there was nothing left of the Kiamah beast, nothing at all.

*And so, dear reader, we have come to the end of our tale. The tyrant has been overthrown, the beast slain,*** the material world saved. The Turropsi have survived and will go on weaving the present from all that is possible. On the barren plain where once lay the Kiamah, the goddess Dewi Sri will bring forth the egg she carries, and that egg will hatch, and that hatchling shall be Queen of the Dead. And the goddess Dewi Sri will scatter the broken shards of the eggshell across the plain, and from those shards will grow a new spirit world. The Queue of the Dead will rule there with her father's sense of mischief, and his sly cunning, but not his cruelty, for her nature will be tempered by a kindness and a wisdom borne of her mother's love. And the dead shall not suffer.†††*

Some say Cariña went with the fisherman and the frigate bird to the material world, and that the moment she arrived, she turned to ash and was blown away by the wind. They say the fisherman put his arms round her to save her, but that all he could save was the silver chain round her neck. They say he grieved her loss for forty days and forty nights, weeping and wailing and howling at the moon, and that on the morning of the forty-first day he rose and wept no more.

Some say Cariña became a goddess, the goddess of the forgiven, and stayed behind with Dewi Sri, and that they live together in the Spirit World. They say the daughter of the crow and the goddess is the Crow of Many Colors long foretold by oracles and seers. They say Dewi Sri became the Gray Goddess, who accepts love in all its forms, and judges not. They

*** Of the many sorrows that come from the untimely passing of the cormorant is the following: were he still with us, he would surely have said, in regard to the death of the Kiamah, "Edo, non ero."[1]

1. "I ate, therefore I am not."

††† Until, dear reader, a stranger comes to town. As one always does.

say that Cariña, the Gray Goddess, and the Crow of
Many Colors are the three bright stars that, together
with Gienah, the Raven's wing, form the constellation
Corvus, which hangs in the southern sky between
Virgo and Hydra. They say that a tryst carried out
in the open beneath the constellation Corvus will be
blessed by them, and that the earthly lovers beneath
will never know the sorrow of love lost.

They say the fisherman's body remained hairless,
and his skin blue, and that he lived for a thousand
times a thousand days. They say the only sign of his
aging was the pair of spectacles he took to wearing
perched on his nose, and that with them he could
translate any scroll that was brought to him, no matter
how ancient the language. They say he traded a gold
brooch covered in rubies for an alehouse, some say in
Hav, and some say in Cex, but most say in Cerdes, the
City of Marvels, beneath the shadow of the two-pronged
unicorn that guards the gate to the city. They say he
lived out his days there. And whether the alehouse was
in Hav or Cex or Cerdes, they all say that he brewed
the best ale the city had ever drunk. He called his
establishment the Alehouse at the End of the World.
They say that late at night, when the fire burns low
and the candles gutter, a piratical frigate bird emerges
from the shadows and tells stories about a great beast
who swallowed the spirit world, and a tyrant crow on
the Isle of the Dead.

All the tales agree that the fisherman happened
upon a comely woman in a slave market, a woman
neither young nor old, but with a look of wisdom in
her face, and of kindness in her heart. They say he
paid for her with a silver chain, very finely made, and
that she knew a great deal about the brewing of ale.
They say he freed her, and they soon fell in love, and
that he made her his wife.

They say she had yellow eyes.

ABOUT THE ILLUSTRATOR

REID PSALTIS IS AN ILLUSTRATOR from the Pacific Northwest. Always interested in expressing an interest in animals through art, he majored in oil painting at Western Washington University, completed the science illustration graduate program at California State University Monterey Bay, and interned in the exhibitions department at the American Museum of Natural History in New York. Recent achievements include the publication of *The Order of Things: A Bestiary* by Secret Acres Books and being awarded a grant from the Regional Arts and Culture Council. Reid currently lives in Portland, Oregon, where he works as a freelancer and manages a shared studio space called Magnetic North.

ABOUT THE AUTHOR

STEVAN ALLRED LIVES IN PORTLAND, OREGON, halfway between Hav and the Isle of the Dead, which is to say he spends as much time burrowed into his imagination as he possibly can. He is the author of *A Simplified Map of the Real World: The Renata Stories*, and a contributor to *City of Weird: 30 Otherwordly Portland Tales*.

ACKNOWLEDGMENTS

IT TOOK A COMMUNITY TO raise this book. My deepest gratitude to
everyone who helped:

Nikki Schulak, you listened to every single word of this novel
multiple times, and never failed to give me heartfelt encouragement
and intelligent critique.

The Dream Team—Joanna Rose, Kate Gray, Cecily Patterson,
Mary Milstead, Jackie Shannon Hollis: you workshopped an early
draft with me, and gave me your collective wisdom.

The Quartet—Michelle Fredette, Tanya Jarvik, Cris Colburn,
Steve Denniston: you read a middle draft, and let me interview you
for hours about what was working and what was not.

The Salon at the Edge of the World: you gathered for sixteen
Sundays in a row, and you listened to me read a late draft of the whole
novel aloud, laughing at all the right places, gasping deliciously at plot
twists, and hanging around afterwards to provide fellowship and to
share delicious food. I list here everyone who attended, starting with
the most stalwart attendees: Calvin T. Wonderdog, Steve Barber,
Nikki Schulak, Cheryl Lynn, Dina Rozelle Renée, Shannon Brazil,
Katy Murphy, Martta Karol, Suzanne Sigafoos, Helen Sinoradzki,
Byron Palmer, Jan Baross, Mohamed Asem, Irene Parikal, Eric Lee,
Michelle Fredette, Betsy Porter, Pierre Provost, Celeste Hamilton
Dennis, Yuvi Zalkow, Edee Lemonier, Golda Dwass, Stephen Mickey,
Steve Arndt, Janell Lee, Chad Burge, Catherine Kumlin Gamblin,
Harold Johnson, Leah Baer, Desiree Wright, Donna, Barbara, Janie
Cohen, Greg "Woody" Nyeholt, Nicole Rosevear, Sherri Hoffman,
Susan Brazil, Eva Gibeau, Ry Allred, Ben Poliakoff, Cris Colburn,
and Joanna Rose.

Tom "it-is-this-way" Spanbauer, you taught me a most excellent
set of writing chops. Without the foundation you gave me I would not
be the writer I am today.

Dan Rhiger: half a century we've known each other, and every one
of those years mattered when you opened up your Medicine Whistle
Studio to me for making the audiobook. You gave an inexperienced

voice actor—me—the creative space to develop the voices for my crazy bird gods in a first-rate recording studio. Zounds!

Gigi Little, you designed the cover, and oh my god, what a sweet piece of eye candy you have designed. Delicious!

Reid Psaltis, you did the ravishingly beautiful illustrations, huzzah!

Dr. Bruce D. Dugger of Oregon State University, you gave me a crucial anatomical fact about the frigate bird when I needed it most.

Throughout my years of work on *Alehouse*, I got by with a little help from my friends and family:

Shannon Brazil, you sang the praises of this novel loudly to anyone who would listen, and you wrapped your arms around it with so much love; all of the Polymamas: you cheered me on and had my back whenever I needed it; Jan Baross, you have been unstinting in your praise, and generous with your time and your camera; Cado Allred, you covered my day job so I could write (with help from Taryn Winterholler); Ry Allred, you listened to my kvetches and nodded your head wisely at all the right moments; Wiley Allred, at seven years old you listened to the first thirty pages as a bedtime story, and gave me a crucial thumbs up: "almost as good as Harry Potter, Grandpa"; JoAnn Allred, you teach me compassion and humility every time I see you; Ben Poliakoff, you fed me such good dinners, followed by feasts of leftovers, and you listened sympathetically to my worries, and you celebrated with me when things went well; Haru Schulak Poliakoff, you made lovely posters, one with the crow, and one with the frigate bird, for The Salon at the End of the World; Leo Schulak Poliakoff, you helped me find the hero's journey in my own life.

And you, Laura Stanfill, most especially you: you are friend and publisher, editor and publicist, advocate and promoter, visionary and literary savant; you are fierce and brilliant and indefatigable; and you have made me part of the family at Forest Avenue Press. My gratitude to you knows no bounds.

The Alehouse at the End of the World

Readers' Guide

Reading Group Questions

1. What does the author gain or lose by making several of his characters shapeshifters and demigods?

2. The fisherman does not think of himself as a hero. Would you agree? Who are the true heroes of this novel? If we are the heroes of our own lives, what does that imply about how we should approach each day?

3. This novel has an unusual sound built into its sentence construction and vocabulary. Some words are made up. Others are intentionally antiquated. How does the language serve the story? Did you spot any of the made-up words?

4. Are some mythologies sacred? Or are all mythologies invented? Can a mythology be both?

5. What is the central myth of our times? Is there more than one? Can we change ourselves by changing the myths by which we live, and the stories we hold in common?

6. There are more than fifty references to pop culture in this novel. What are some of your favorites? What purpose, other than the author's delight, do they serve?

7. Do you believe in fate? What does fate mean to you?

8. The Kiamah beast swallows all in his path. Is he merely a character in this tale? What might he represent? Does he frighten you?

9. How does *The Alehouse at the End of the World* examine the relationship of the body to the mind?

10. Do you believe in an afterlife? If yes, then how do you imagine it to be? Will your personality persist after death?

11. Are there political leaders who remind you of the crow? How about the goddess? Who are they? What are the similarities?

Some Notes from the Author

IN JULY OF 1891 THE story of James Bartley, a man who claimed to have been swallowed by a whale, began circulating in American newspapers. Bartley said he was a crewmember on the whaling ship *Star of the East* when a wounded sperm whale surfaced beneath his longboat, tossing him into the sea near the Falkland Islands, where the whale swallowed him. When the now-dead whale was recovered by the crew of the *Star of the East*, Bartley was discovered in the stomach, hairless, bleached white, babbling incoherently, but alive. Or such was his account.

Historians have not been kind to Bartley's tale, but for me, it opened the door into *The Alehouse at the End of the World*.

I WROTE THIS NOVEL BY candlelight and the glow of my laptop, starting before the sun rose each morning, and working into the daylight. Candlelight carried me backwards in time, and the computer gave me access to the eternal now of the internet, where I found many odd bits of language that suited this tale.

I HAVE OVER TWENTY T-SHIRTS with crows on them, and a few with frigate birds and pelicans, and one with a goddess and a pelican. The daily ritual of putting on a crow shirt before setting out to write reminded me that I do not own the story. I serve it.

ALEHOUSE DRAWS ON HISTORICAL AND analytical sources as well as mythological ones. The work of Joseph Campbell is an obvious influence. I found *Watunna: An Orinoco Creation Cycle*, by Marc de Civrieux, to be a fascinating case of a living mythology that has incorporated into itself the story of first contact with the outside world.

Barbara Tuchman's *A Distant Mirror: The Calamitous 14th Century*, with its narrative clarity, sent me time-traveling into a world view centuries earlier than my own. For readers interested in the sixteenth & seventeenth century spice trade, which forms the backdrop of the fisherman's story, I recommend *The Scents of Eden: A History of the Spice Trade*, by Charles Corn. I also drew upon Charles C. Mann's two exemplary history volumes, *1491* and *1493*, for a sense of the world as it might have been during the fisherman's lifetime.

Readers interested in the sexual mores of Dewi Sri, the pelican, the fisherman, and Cariña may find *Sex at Dawn: How We Mate, Why We Stray, and What It Means for Modern Relationships*, by Christopher Ryan and Cacilda Jethá, as engrossing as I do.

ALEHOUSE IS STREWN WITH PARAPHRASES of classic rock lyrics, Victorian slang, bits of my own Mormon roots, and references to Mae West, the Bible, Natalie Goldberg, John Keats, Mel Brooks, and Adelaide Crapsey, to name but a few. There are traces of books I have loved my whole life through. Some of them are well known (*The Left Hand of Darkness, The Lord of the Rings, One Hundred Years of Solitude*) but I would like to call out Jan Morris' novel *Letters from Hav* for special mention.

I HAVE LONG HAD A fascination with fiction that creates a strongly imagined sense of place. In my short-story collection *A Simplified Map of the Real World* I built a town called Renata. For "Notes from the Underground City," my story in *City of Weird,* I built a city called Melquiopolis. Here, in *The Alehouse at the End of the World* I have created the Isle of the Dead, with an afterlife as strange as any I have ever heard tell of, and one suited to the world of this novel, a world in which the Abrahamic religions have never taken root.

CROWS, CORMORANTS, PELICANS, FRIGATE BIRDS, and fish eagles (osprey) are all beings I admire. Crows because they are smart, and socially sophisticated, and because I love watching them in the evenings when they gather to roost in the neighborhood trees. Cormorants because I have watched them dive for fish from the surface of the Willamette River, and then pop up as much as twenty yards away from where they started, with fish in bill. Pelicans because they fly in stately formation, like the Canada goose, and because their capacious bills are magnificent adaptations. Frigate birds because I have watched them in the skies of Manzanillo, Mexico, spending all day spiraling upward on a thermal. Osprey because they build their huge, cartoonish nests in the tallest trees along the water's edge in the Pacific Northwest.

I am not a traditional birder (long may they prosper) nor any sort of expert. What I love is watching the birds that are right there in front of me.

THE STORIES WE TELL HAVE the power to change who we are. *The Alehouse at the End of the World* gives us a vision of a world in which a small band of heroes take on a tyrant. I can think of no better story to tell in these troubled times.

Also by Stevan Allred

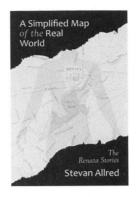

A Simplified Map of the Real World

"Stevan Allred's stories strike to the very heart—the pathos, the humor, the hope—of the American frontier. He is OUT there. Raymond Carver would love this book."

—Robin Cody, author of *Ricochet River*

FIFTEEN LINKED STORIES CHART A true course through the lives of families, farmers, loggers, former classmates, and the occasional stripper. In the richly imagined town of Renata, Oregon, a man watches his neighbor's big-screen TV through binoculars. An errant son paints himself silver. Mysterious electrical humming emanates from an enormous barn. A secret abortion from three decades ago gets a public airing. In *A Simplified Map of the Real World*, intimate boundaries are loosened by divorce and death in a rural community where even an old pickle crock has an unsettling history—and high above the strife and the hope and the often hilarious, geese seek the perfect tailwind. Stevan Allred's stunning debut deftly navigates the stubborn geography of the human heart.

Blackstone Publishing released the audiobook edition of *A Simplified Map of the Real World*, narrated by the author, in February 2018. It's available wherever audiobooks are sold. Allred's debut collection, which launched Forest Avenue Press's fiction catalog, was named a top title of 2013 in the Powell's Staff Top 5s and a 2014 Multnomah County Library PageTurners Book Club Pick.

City of Weird:
30 Otherworldly Portland Tales
Edited by Gigi Little

CITY OF WEIRD CONJURES WHAT we fear: death, darkness, ghosts. Hungry sea monsters and alien slime molds. Blood drinkers and game show hosts. Set in Portland, Oregon, these thirty original stories blend imagination, literary writing, and pop culture into a cohesive weirdness that honors the city's personality, its bookstores and bridges and solo volcano, as well as the tradition of sci-fi pulp magazines. Editor Gigi Little has curated a collection that is quirky, often chilling, at times surprisingly profound—and always perfectly weird.

Contributors include: Stevan Allred, Jonah Barrett, Doug Chase, Sean Davis, Susan DeFreitas, Rene Denfeld, Dan DeWeese, Art Edwards, Stefanie Freele, Jonathan Hill, Justin Hocking, Jeff Johnson, Leigh Anne Kranz, Kirsten Larson, B. Frayn Masters, Kevin Meyer, Karen Munro, Linda Rand, Brian Reid, Bradley K. Rosen, Nicole Rosevear, Mark Russell, Kevin Sampsell, Jason Squamata, Andrew Stark, Adam Strong, Suzy Vitello, Leslie What, Brigitte Winter, and Leni Zumas.

Pacific Northwest Independent Bookseller bestseller
#1 Powell's Books bestseller
#1 Powell's Books holiday bestseller, 2016
Powell's Pick of the Month and Pick of the Season
#1 Annie Bloom's Bestseller
Adapted for live radio by The Willamette Radio Workshop
Now in its fourth printing

More Fiction Titles from Forest Avenue Press

Parts per Million
Julia Stoops

WHEN JOHN NELSON ABANDONED HIS government job to join a scrappy band of activists, he didn't realize trying to save the world would be so hard. His ideals remain strong, but his optimism is wearing thin. His fellow activists—computer hacker Jen Owens and Vietnam vet Irving Fetzer—still think he's a square. And their radio show can't compete with the corporate media. *Parts per Million,* Julia Stoops's socially conscious, fast-paced debut novel, is set in Portland, Oregon, in 2002. As the trio dives into anti-war protests and investigates fraud at an elite university, Nelson falls in love with an unlikely houseguest, Deirdre, a photographer from Ireland—and a recovering addict. Fetzer recognizes her condition but keeps it secret, setting off a page-turning chain of events that threatens to destroy the activists' friendship even as they're trying to hold the world together, one radio show at a time.

Queen of Spades
Michael Shou-Yung Shum

QUEEN OF SPADES REVAMPS THE classic Pushkin fable of the same name, transplanted to a mysterious Seattle-area casino populated by a pit boss with six months to live, a dealer obsessing over the mysterious methods of an elderly customer known as the Countess, and a recovering gambler who finds herself trapped in a cultish twelve-step program. With a breathtaking climax that rivals the best Hong Kong gambling movies, Michael Shou-Yung Shum's debut novel delivers the thrilling highs and lows that come when we cede control of our futures to the roll of the dice and the turn of a card.

The Hour of Daydreams
Renee Macalino Rutledge

MANOLO LUALHATI, A RESPECTED DOCTOR in the Philippine countryside, believes his wife hides a secret. Prior to their marriage, he spied her wearing wings and flying to the stars with her sisters each evening. As Tala tries to keep her dangerous past from her new husband, Manolo begins questioning the gaps in her stories—and his suspicions push him even further from the truth. *The Hour of Daydreams,* a contemporary reimagining of a Filipino folktale, weaves in the perspectives of Tala's siblings, her new in-laws, and the all-seeing housekeeper while exploring trust, identity, and how myths can take root from the seeds of our most difficult truths.

Froelich's Ladder
Jamie Yourdon

FROELICH NURSES A DECADES-OLD FAMILY grudge from his permanent perch atop a giant ladder in this nineteenth century madcap adventure novel. When he disappears suddenly, his nephew embarks on a rain-soaked adventure across the Pacific Northwest landscape to find him, accompanied by an ornery girl with a most unfortunate name. In their encounters with Confederate assassins, European expatriates, and a general store magnate, this fairytale twist on the American dream explores the conflicts between loyalty and ambition and our need for human connection, even at the highest rungs.

The Remnants
Robert Hill

THE TOWN OF NEW EDEN, peopled with hereditary oddities, has arrived at its last days. As two near-centenarian citizens prepare for their annual birthday tea, a third vows to interrupt the proceedings with a bold declaration. *The Remnants* cartwheels through the lives of wood-splitters, garment-menders, and chervil farmers, while exposing an electrical undercurrent of secrets, taboos, and unfulfilled longings. With his signature wit and wordplay, Robert Hill delivers a bittersweet gut-buster of an elegy to the collective memory of a community.

Founded in 2012, Forest Avenue Press
publishes literary fiction on a joyride
from its Portland, Oregon, headquarters.

forestavenuepress.com
stevanallred.com
#alehousenovel